To My Friend Jim

Thank you so very much!

Jim West
1-19-10

DNAlien II

DNAlien II

THE HUNT FOR GENE

A Novel
By
Jim West

Library of Congress Control Number: 2008905860
ISBN: Hardcover   978-1-4363-5457-8
                 Softcover   978-1-4363-5456-1

To order additional copies of this book, contact:
Xlibris Corporation
1-888-795-4274
www.Xlibris.com
Orders@Xlibris.com
40060

Foreword

                    Although this book is not really about alien events, its premise is based on the possibilities of past reported occurrences. It is based on what the government might do if such a program was real and the evidence was subsequently released to the public. How to regain something that they can not admit exists? That is the crux of the story.

The issues of extraterrestrial travel, unidentified flying objects (UFOs), alien life-forms, abductions, and crashes have been around for ages. Some say evidence is found in biblical documents, Aztec paintings, and others that prove there have been visits to our small planet for centuries. For over one hundred years, newspaper articles have reported sightings. As far back as 1897 in Aurora, Texas—and of course the grandfather of them all, Roswell, New Mexico, in 1947—people have been seeing UFOs. Recent sightings in such places as Stephenville, Texas, continue the belief that we are not alone.

According to the May 14, 2008, issue of the Vatican newspaper L'Osservatore Romano, the Roman Catholic Church has finally said that it is now alright to believe in aliens. Does the Pope know something we don't?

Those that truly believe in the UFO phenomenon point to the mountain of evidence and accuse the government of a massive cover-up. Granted, there are many reasons that our government keeps information from the public. It may be due to political reasons, security issues, or it might just mean they don't want to deal with the ramifications of disclosure. This doesn't prove nor disprove the existence of life outside our small planet.

The advances in medical science have produced many hybrids, some in plants and others in animals. While many are public knowledge, others are not. Just as cloning became a viable method of reproducing, genetic manipulation has provided us with the means to alter the basic foundation of every form of life on earth.

It is entirely possible now to design your next child. You can pick the color of its eyes, the color of its hair, choose from a wide variety of body types, and some say you can influence athletic abilities or intelligence. The advances in genetic engineering have accelerated geometrically over the last few years. The mapping of the human genome has opened the doors to every conceivable alteration of plant or animal life.

While we might like to think we are the only intelligent form of life in the vast complex of the universe, I believe it is one of the most arrogant things a person can think. Billions and billions of stars and galaxies, and we are at the top of the ladder? The advances we have made in travel and science had expanded exponentially over the last hundred years. If this rate of advancement were to be extended even another hundred years, where will we be?

Now, what if there exists another intelligent life-form somewhere far beyond our meager view that has been there just three or four hundred years before us. If they attained the same rate of advancement that we have made over the last couple of centuries, what do they know that we may not discover for the next few hundreds of years?

Next, as to our government's capabilities to monitor our every move, listen to every conversation, follow any subject, view your computer usage, is it possible? We have seen how they can ferret out any specific word or phrase and evaluate the need to monitor specific phone calls. Airport screening is advancing with face recognition capabilities far beyond the wanted posters hanging on the post office walls of mere years ago. Are they doing this? Some would say yes, and that our civil liberties are in danger.

What about tracking chips? They are already in use with dogs, horses, and other high value animals. Are we next? Even just to protect our children, wouldn't it be good to know where they are if ever lost? What if you were lost on a ski trip, or hiking in the woods? It would sure be nice to have a satellite find you and relay your exact position to the rescue teams. Can we do this now? Are we doing it? Wouldn't it be great to locate your lost dog (or husband) by a simple click on your computer?

Is any of this possible? I certainly don't know, but it makes a great story. Maybe someday in our future, there will be proof that others have been here. If that day were to come, would we be ready to accept that everything we've been taught in religious doctrine (up until the latest Catholic decree) has been wrong? I'll leave it to people a lot smarter than I am to determine what should be done with any of the "evidence" of extraterrestrial visits.

I'll just be happy with visits from my friends and family. Besides, what would I serve these little green men? I hope they don't like Jack Daniels, Dr Pepper, or Butterfingers. I can hardly keep them away from my current visitors.

Acknowledgments

First, I would like to thank my very good friend, John Fleenor. He painstakingly read every word and quickly let me know that I would never be an English professor. Without his invaluable assistance, this book would probably be indecipherable (see, John, I do know big words). As he said on several occasions, I have the slipperiest grasp of the language of any single person he has ever known. He did his best to correct that. Thanks, John.

Next, I would like to acknowledge all those unsuspecting people whose names appear throughout this book. From friends and family, I stole their names and bandied them about with careless abandonment. Some of them are somewhat related to their characters in this book. Some of them are just my way of letting them know I remember them, usually fondly.

Finally, I would like to thank my children, Renee and Vicki. They quietly sat by and let me misrepresent them throughout the entire process. They aren't nearly as bad as I portray them, although they do tend to drink all of my Jack Daniels, Dr Pepper, and eat my Butterfingers when they visit. I guess I'm stuck with the minor flaws. I still love you both.

To everyone that has had to suffer through our acquaintance, thanks.

Disclaimer

It should go without saying, this is *FICTION!* The characters aren't real, the events did not happen, and I did none of the amazing things written within this book. Even Butch North is a figment of my imagination, although some of his friends are roughly based on people I know.

One of the very few things I have written that bears any resemblance to actuality is Butch's philosophy of life. You must determine for yourself who he truly is. Of course, some people may believe they know who I refer to in this book. They may be wrong, but then again.

Most of the places described are real. I have tried to be as accurate as possible with the geography, restaurants, bars, stores, etc. as possible. If I misspelled, mislocated, or misrepresented your business, my sincere apologies. Also, I do not mean to say that these are the only businesses in the area, nor do I mean to say that I don't support those not mentioned.

So with that in mind, I will leave it to the publisher to add the "legal" disclaimer. I just wanted to tell you one thing, *I made it all up!*

Prologue

In the years following the UFO crash in Roswell on July 7, 1947, and the clandestine cover-up that almost immediately followed, the US government began to systematically remove all traces of alien visitation and develop stories to disavow any knowledge of their activities. President Harry Truman established a group of well-respected scientists and high-ranking military officers to take charge of each event as it occurred and to develop installations to research and reverse engineer any and all material recovered. This group came to be known as the Majestic 12, or MJ 12.

As part of their directives, MJ 12 constructed several facilities within existing sites, such as the previously known Fort Worth Army Airfield, or Carswell AFB as it was designated following World War II. Later, renamed the Naval Air Station/Joint Reserve Base (NAS/JRB), it was the site of one of MJ 12's most secretive projects, combining alien DNA with a human embryo. Additional facilities were used for storing and analyzing the mechanical material that had been recovered, such as the now known Area 51 in the Nevada desert.

As part of the mission of the NAS/JRB facility, located deep underground beneath one of the numerous hangars on the base, all alien organic material was stored and analyzed. The primary focus of this effort was experimentation with genetic manipulation. The goal, simply put, was to create a species combining human traits with the intelligence and, hopefully, the memories or intuitions of the alien donor.

These efforts, as well as concurrent activities across the nation using civilian scientists, produced extraordinary results. Information and techniques developed by the facility were fed to outside agencies under the guise of genetic research for eradication of birth defects or disease. Their results, decades ahead of their civilian counterparts, finally produced the first viable "product." He became known as Gene, standing for Genetic Embryonic Nucleus Enhancement. The entire project was considered a "black" program, meaning that only a handful of people would ever know of its existence. This included hiding funding, personnel assignment, and facility purpose.

Even the current president, as had all others, did not know the depth of the program. MJ 12 had unfettered reign regarding anything having to do with everything "alien." This included misdirection of information and cover stories for any civilian interest. MJ 12 was so cloaked in secrecy that very few ever heard of them; and no one, outside the US president, ever knew the membership. Any member replaced was recommended by other members, appointed by them, with cursory approval from the president.

As part of their directive, any previous report of UFO activity was re-examined, and any physical evidence confiscated. This included a little-known event that occurred in Aurora, Texas, in 1897. There, an alien ship had crashed and the local community buried the alien body in the local cemetery and disposed of the wreckage in the water well located on Judge Proctor's farm. Coverage of the event was reported in the newspapers at the time, and the incident continued to garner sporadic activity from UFO researchers within the civilian community for years to come.

The final product, Gene, was successfully brought into existence in the late months of 1979. The infant was such a success that the billions of experiments and failures were almost forgotten. Further experiments continued with the same technologies and techniques, and limited success continued. But most of the effort of the team at the NAS/JRB facility was directed to raising and exploiting the "star" of the program.

An ex-air force nurse named Vicki Grubbs was assigned to watch over the growing "child" and to assume responsibility for its education and every aspect of its welfare. Vicki became essentially Gene's mother. Under her watchful eyes, the entire project continued to produce amazing results. Any residual memories of an alien past had failed to surface, but hopes remained high that some knowledge of his heritage would produce information regarding life outside the known world or provide insight to the mechanical aspects of recovered material.

After over twenty years of nurturing Gene, Vicki had predictably become as attached to him as any mother to her offspring. After being diagnosed with breast cancer and learning that no cure was available, she resolved to set Gene free of the facility and permit him to escape the future she believed in store for him at the hands of MJ 12.

In the very early morning of September 11, 2001, Vicki smuggled Gene from the facility at the NAS/JRB and set him free on the north side of Fort Worth, Texas. Here, Gene was ultimately picked up by Ray Downey at an all-night convenience store well-known as a pickup point for illegal day laborers. The only other person who knew of Gene's escape was a very old friend of Vicki and her deceased husband, Lieutenant Colonel Don Pratka. With his help, she was able to bypass the elaborate security systems and drive Gene off the base.

Mr. Ray Downey took Gene to a small ranch just north of Azle, Texas, and Gene had his first brush with civilian life. It was while there that the traumatic events of the day exploded across the face of America. The cowardly attacks of the Islamic radicals on the World Trade Center towers ultimately provided Gene with both a chance of escape, and ultimately provided the cover story the government needed to mount a nationwide hunt to recover the item they could not admit they had.

This is the continuation of the story that began with *DNAlien*.

Characters

Military

1. General Mike Nelson—Project Revive commander, facility commander, and member of Majestic 12 (MJ 12)
2. General Gary Brown—Naval Air Station/Joint Reserve Base (NAS/JRB) Fort Worth, Texas commander
3. General Paul Modelle—White House/presidential staff adviser and a senior member of MJ 12
4. Colonel Rick Erickson—facility deputy commander and operations officer for Project Revive
5. Colonel Karyn Lynch—communications officer for Project Revive and the facility
6. Colonel Amy Moore—facility laboratory commander
7. Lieutenant Colonel Mark Mallory—facility security commander
8. Major Jerry Fleenor—White House liaison
9. Major Cory Romine—facility engineering
10. Kathy Blevins—General Nelson's secretary

Civilian

1. Butch North—owner of the Equestrian Center of Aurora Vista
2. Mischelle and Jeannie North—Butch's daughters
3. Kevin Knox—friend of Butch from Vashti, Texas, and former marine
4. Mikey Carmichael—owner of the KC Ranch
5. Nannette Bost—owner of Southern Delight Restaurant in Boyd
6. Levi Wilson—owner of Southwest Hay Exchange in Boyd
7. Tammy Terbush—romantically linked with Butch
8. Leslie Barber and Stacy Hyden—two ladies that met Gene at Red's
9. Gay Lynn Buck—owner of Red's Take 5 Sports Bar

TM

Chapter 1

Butch North had just returned from being interviewed by a group of air force personnel regarding a supposedly terrorist who had evaded capture following the tragic events of September 11, 2001. He and his two daughters, Mischelle and Jeannie, had been taken from his house on the morning of September 13, driven to his stables, and then flown to the Naval Air Station Joint Reserve Base (NAS/JRB) in Fort Worth, Texas.

During the interview conducted by a single man wearing a dark suit, two air force officers stood silently behind the man. Both of the officers wore dress blue uniforms with an impressive array of ribbons beneath their silver pilot wings. Butch noticed that along with the Vietnam Service ribbon, both were command pilots. Two stars shone brightly on one officer's shoulders while silver eagles adorned the other.

The interview concerned Butch having hired what he assumed was an illegal Mexican to work at his stables, the Equestrian Center of Aurora Vista, while his main hand took off for a couple of days to visit his family out of the area. During the interview, he began to question in his mind the veracity of why he was being questioned. The story of a terrorist that had been denied boarding at the Dallas-Fort Worth (DFW) airport and was on the loose in the area had been on the news, but Butch had just seen it that same morning when the black Suburbans and the black-suited men arrived at his door.

He and his daughters had first been taken to the stables after he acknowledged having Gene, the name he had been told, to pick him up. He had thought it strange that the only uniformed officer with them at the time wore the badge of an air force nurse, not security, if they were truly looking for a known terrorist. That was just the first of the soon-to-come numerous questionable occurrences. The fact that there were no armed officers—whether from the county, the state, or federal—did not jive with what he considered would be normal procedures to take a known terrorist into custody.

After a quick search of the stables and his hand's house, where Gene was supposed to be staying, the helicopter with Butch, his girls, the air force nurse, and one dark suited man flew directly to the NAS/JRB where they were taken to a conference room. Even the story they told him did not fit what little he knew of Gene. During his career with the US Air Force, Butch had taught student pilots from numerous Middle Eastern countries, had worked with others while involved with the F-5 program, and was certain that Gene was not the crazy rag-head as they tried to portray him. Not much of their story rang true to him. Even after returning him and his daughters to his house in Aurora, he doubted almost every word of the story they had tried to sell him.

Now, having left his daughters at the house and driven to the stables to care for the horses boarded there, he could not come up with a plausible explanation for the morning's strange events. The picture of Gene dressed as a Middle Easterner, with their typical attire and a beard he had seen briefly on the TV and had been shown during his interview, did nothing to make him believe their intent. Now thinking about it, he had not seen even the slightest amount of stubble on Gene's face. Nor was there any accent of any kind, not even Mexican.

No, something wasn't right. He didn't know just what it was, but the entire production didn't fit what he knew. He had spent a career in the air force, flown fighters, trained pilots, and had worked with all levels of security while in the Naval Intelligence during Vietnam. Even the local law enforcement put on a greater show of force when stopping a suspected drunk driver than he had seen in this manhunt for someone who was supposed to hijacked an airliner and then fly it into God knows what as the other cowardly bastards had done only two days ago.

As he walked into the main barn and turned the lights on, it was obvious that the horses had not been fed. The racket they made stomping and neighing was evident of them missing their eight o'clock feeding. Butch quickly filled a wheelbarrow with pellets and began putting a scoop into each feed bucket hanging in their stalls. Several had special feeding requirements and had their own feed in barrels just outside their stalls.

Once each horse had their feed, he quickly pulled the hose down the aisle to fill each one's water bucket hanging just inside the stall doors. As he opened each stall and began refilling the buckets, he tried to figure out what the people back at the NAS/JRB had been after. Once completing the stalls on one side of the aisle, he began to fill the buckets along the other side. Having fed and watered each horse, he refilled the wheelbarrow and started to push it out to feed the horses in the outside areas.

As he was passing the locked cage where the hay was stored, he heard a noise coming from the stacks of coastal Bermuda and alfalfa. Stopping, he glanced into the cage thinking it was probably one of the barn cats that kept the mice and snakes away. "Hey, cat, you trapped in there, or are you in there having another litter of those kittens you keep having?" he called.

Looking closer, he noticed that the lock was on the inside of the steel mesh that covered the two sliding doors that comprised the front of the cage. "What the hell?" he said as he walked to the cage and tried to pull the chain that held the doors together through the mesh. "How did this get twisted around like this?"

As he was reaching for the key he kept in his jeans, he heard another sound. This time it was definitely coming from the top of the stacked bales of hay. "All right, who's in there?" he asked.

"You better come on down. There's no way out except through these doors, and unless you show yourself right now, I'll have the cops here before you can get this lock open," Butch said as he stepped back from the cage and picked up one of the pitchforks sitting against the side of the barn. "I mean it. You better show you ass or I'll break my key off in the lock, and you'll be stuck until the cops get here and I have to use bolt cutters to open this up."

"Please don't," came a voice from behind one of the bales on top of the stack. "Please don't call anyone. It's me, Gene."

As he stuck his head above the bale, Gene looked at Butch and asked again, "Please, Butch. I'm scared, and I don't want to go back there."

"Get your ass on down here," Butch said. "I've got some questions for you, and you're not doing anything until I get a good answer. And you better not try to blow smoke up my shorts either. I've just gone through a couple of hours of someone trying to persuade me that you're some shithead radical Muslim that was going to hijack an airplane and crash it like those other chicken-shit rag-heads did."

"OK, I'm coming down. But please listen to me. I'm not sure what you were told. Honestly. Just listen to me for a minute," Gene said as he looked pleadingly down at Butch.

"If your story isn't good, and I mean really good, I will turn you over to the first cop I can find. And you don't have long to tell it. Now, get down here where I can see you, and don't try to open those doors or you'll have this pitchfork shoved through you quicker than a fat lady can eat a doughnut," Butch said as he stepped back, slightly holding the pitchfork pointing toward the mesh doors.

Gene climbed down the stack of bales, still wearing the clothes he had on when Butch last saw him at Red's Take 5 Sports Bar last night. Holding his hat in one hand and finally standing just inside the cage doors, Gene said, "I won't try to run. I don't have any place to run to. I just can't go back there."

"Back where?" Butch asked.

"Back to the laboratory where I came from before you picked me up," Gene said.

"What lab? What are you talking about? You told me you were working in a stable, not a laboratory," Butch asked.

"I didn't work there," Gene replied. "I lived there, for as long as I can remember. I had never been out until my friend, Vicki, took me out three days ago. I had been taken to a couple of places with some of the people that worked there to see some wrecked things, but I had never been on my own outside of the place where the laboratory was."

"What do you mean, you lived there? Is this lab you're talking about like a prison or insane institution? Were you a prisoner or an inmate of some sort?"

"No, nothing like that. I'm not completely sure what I actually was, but Vicki told me that if I didn't get away from the 'facility,' as she called it, I would never be free, and they would probably dispose of me when I became no longer useful to them," Gene said as tears began to run down his cheeks.

"What the hell are you talking about? Where is this 'facility' you are talking about?"

"I'm not sure," Gene answered. "All I know is that I have been there my entire life until Vicki took me out and told me to never mention it to anyone. And to never try to get in touch with her. She was like my mother, but I know she wasn't. There were only a few people that ever came around me, and they were just asking questions or giving me tests."

"All right, this Vicki, where did she take you?"

"After we drove through some gate and some man in a uniform told her that her base sticker was about to expire, she drove me up to a gas station where they sold food and drinks, and a lot of guys were waiting for someone to take them to a job.

"Then, I got in a pickup with this guy who only needed one helper for part of a day, and he took me close to where you picked me up."

"Wait a minute. Let's go back a little. Did you say a 'base sticker'? What else did you see when you were going to where the man in uniform stopped you?" Butch asked as he began to lower the pitchfork.

"Not much," Gene answered. "It was pretty dark, but I could see a few lights. There was this one tower I could see. It had these flashing lights on it, and it was taller than anything else around."

"Flashing lights? What color were these lights?" Butch asked.

"Green and white."

"How did they flash? Did they flash together, separately, and what order did they flash?"

"I think they flashed separately, and I'm pretty sure it was green and two real quick white flashes," Gene replied, looking at Butch. "Does that mean something?"

"Sure as hell does. Were there any airplanes there?"

"I didn't see any, but when they took me places, there was always an airplane in the hangar by the laboratory."

"Well, I'll be damned," Butch said as he put the pitchfork back against the wall. "I'm not sure what this means, but it's starting to make more sense than that fairy tale I heard this morning."

"Does this mean that you aren't going to call anyone to come get me?" Gene asked hopefully.

"Not yet, but I still have a few questions before I let you out. Just sit back down. I need to think a little, and you can throw that key to the lock out to me. I don't believe that you're what they told me you were, but I haven't made up my mind what you are just yet. Until I figure out what I'm going to do with you, you're stuck right where you are. Now, get that key and toss it out to me. And that knife I gave you too. Pitch them both out."

Gene pulled the key from his pocket and tossed it through the mesh door, and it landed in the loose hay and dirt just outside the door. Pulling the knife from his pocket, he looked at it for a couple of seconds and tossed it out.

"I'll be back in a few minutes. I've got to get these horses fed and turned loose. While I'm doing that, you better get ready to answer any questions I have when I get back. You ain't out of the woods yet, shorty. Not by a long shot."

Chapter 2

              Back at the base, General Mike Nelson and Colonel Rick Erickson sat with General Paul Modelle, discussing the ramifications of Gene's disappearance and the repercussions they knew would follow. General Nelson—commander of the facility and ultimately responsible for each aspect of the program, which included the escape of Gene—suspected that his days with this project were shortly numbered.

Colonel Erickson, deputy commander and operations officer for the project, held no illusions as to his future either. Failure of this magnitude would surely mean the end of his career, if not his life. Very few, if any, people survived any breach of security involving this project.

General Modelle, as a current member of MJ 12, knew what the reaction of his organization would entail. As close as he had been to both Mike and Rick, he would bear the responsibility to carry out the directions of both MJ 12 and any orders from the president. This was not a position he relished holding right now.

"All right, Rick," General Nelson said, "we need to immediately put taps on every phone belonging to Mr. North or his two daughters. I want to tape every conversation any of them have with anyone, even orders for pizza. I don't think he knows what he had, or don't know if he even knows where Gene is. But I know he did not believe for a second the story we told him, and that man could either provide assistance or, more likely, be instrumental in losing Gene for good."

"Yes, sir," Rick answered. "I'll ensure every known phone number is linked to a recorder and get any calls placed or received. I'm also placing several agents in the local area to monitor his movements. I've already asked our White House liaison, Major Jerry Fleenor to scour every database known for either Stacy Hyden or Leslie Barber. If Mr. North's story is true, one of those ladies may provide the best information as to Gene's whereabouts."

"Gentlemen," General Modelle told them as he stood, "I have a couple of very important calls to make right now. I suggest we meet with the rest of the staff within the hour to organize our efforts and ensure any further breaches of security do not occur."

"Yes, sir," both men answered as they stood.

"I'll have everyone concerned in the briefing room ready for you at your convenience," Mike said as he and Rick stood at attention. "We'll all be in the briefing room when you're ready."

Mike and Rick remained standing, and it was several seconds before either of them took their eyes from the closing door. The tension in the room remained palpable as each knew what they thought was their careers, or worse, leaving the room. Failure was not necessarily new to either, but this one weighed heavily on both. Not just failure, but the possibility of being responsible for public knowledge of this project sobered both, and the possible results each may suffer remained at the forefront of their minds.

"Sorry, Rick," Mike said as he slowly relaxed and walked back behind his desk. "I'm not sure how this is going to play out, but since we can't control that aspect of our future, I suggest we get on with developing a plan to retrieve our boy Gene. Regardless of our futures, we need to get going on protecting this program. The civilian world is not ready for what they might find if either we or our replacements don't get a handle on this immediately."

"I understand, sir," Rick told him. "I accept full responsibility for this problem. I'll make sure General Modelle understands that I'm the one that had operational control and that I alone bear the blame."

"No, you won't," Mike told him as he stood from behind his desk. "You work for me. I'm the commander, and I'll take the hit. You're not to even think about discussing this any further with General Modelle."

"Do you hear me?" he told him as he pointed his finger directly at his face.

"Yes, sir, I hear you," Rick responded. "I know you want to protect me, and I certainly do appreciate your loyalty. But I know I let you down, and there is absolutely no reason for anyone, including General Modelle, to blame you for my failures."

"These are not *your* failures," Mike almost shouted. "These are mine. I alone decided to leave Vicki in charge of Gene. I alone knew she was getting too close and that their relationship posed a threat. I alone knew about her ties with Don Pratka and the potential for her to take advantage of their friendship. I could have changed any one of these situations, and I should have. They are not your responsibility. They are mine.

"Now that we have that straight, and I'm sure we do, I want you to get Colonel Lynch, Colonel Moore, and Major Fleenor into the conference room immediately. Are we clear on this, Colonel?"

"Perfectly, sir," Rick said as he snapped to attention and saluted his boss, "I'll have them ready for you as soon as I leave."

Mike relaxed a little as he stared into Rick's eyes. "All right, tell Kathy as you leave to arrange for Major Romine to pick up something for all of us to eat. This is going to be a long morning," Mike told him as he returned the salute.

General Modelle was in his assigned room using a secure satellite communications link with the already-convened MJ 12 group in their Washington DC, office. He dreaded this call as much as he could remember having to make any other time. He vowed to do everything within his power to divert the ire of the president and his other MJ 12 members. It certainly was not going to be easy.

"Gentlemen," he spoke upon hearing the phone answered. "I have some extremely disappointing information to report."

He paused while he waited for the chairman to ask the question he knew was coming. That question was not long in coming, and there was no doubt that his answer would not be welcome.

"Sir, the project has avoided our attempts at recovery. I will be meeting with the staff here shortly and will have an answer to your questions following that. First and foremost, I strongly recommend that no personnel changes be discussed at this point. I still have the utmost confidence in General Nelson and Colonel Erickson. I will review every aspect of this operation and will make my recommendations some time later today. But for now, we need these people to remain in charge. It would not be in our best interest to try to import anyone new and attempt to bring them up to date on the situation. With your permission, I'll assume command of the project and will report back as soon as we have developed our plans."

Paul remained listening quietly for several minutes while the other members of MJ 12 discussed the situation. He knew that none of them wanted to place the blame yet, but he also knew that unless he could convince them that his was the best option at this point, two of his closest friends and longtime colleagues would be facing dire consequences.

"Absolutely," he said once again talking to his group. "I'll report back within the day. General Nelson and Colonel Erickson have already started on the basics of relocating our project, and I'm to meet with the entire staff as soon as we finish our discussion. I am certain that whatever can be accomplished, these officers are the ones that can provide our best hope."

Seconds later, Paul replaced the phone into the briefcase and disconnected the satellite. As he stared at the now passive receiver, he couldn't help but think that he had just held in his hand a weapon more destructive that any pistol. That phone and the call it made could result in the termination of his friends, and even himself if positive results were not soon in coming.

Leaving his room, he slowly made his way to the conference room where he knew several people waited for what they assumed would be the end of their careers. Very seldom do people get a second chance in a game with the stakes as high as this one. At least he could hold out some encouragement for them. He also knew the enormous strain that was weighing on each and every one of them. He knew that he had linked his fate to theirs, just as if he had been the one in charge of the disaster that could possibly change the future of the world. Success was the only way of avoiding their doom, as well as the ramifications of the world learning that every scientific fact, every religious belief, and every single acknowledgement of human existence could come tumbling down in an unpredictable way.

TM

Chapter 3

Butch pushed the wheelbarrow out of the barn and toward the outside stalls. Seeing Gene had been a shock, but having heard the beginning of his explanation started him wondering exactly what sort of mess he had gotten into this time.

First, the "interview" at the NAS/JRB had certainly not been what they had wanted him to think, of that he was sure. Exactly what they were trying to determine was unclear at this time, but it definitely had nothing to do with any terrorist activity. That there had been an attack by the gutless Muslim shitheads, he had no doubt. But his years spent working with Middle Easterners made him sure that Gene had no ties to anything related to that part of the world.

He continued down the sandy aisle between the stalls and gave each horse a scoop of pellets as he racked his brain to come up with a logical explanation. As he opened each stall door, he would ask each horse just what the hell was going on. He knew their only response was to watch him pour the feed into the troughs; the only thought in their walnut-sized brain was when they would be allowed to step forward and get their breakfast. But it helped to vocalize the questions.

As he fed each horse, he checked each water system to ensure a clean supply of water was available and none of the exposed pipes were damaged and leaking. The questions kept coming as he completed each of the seventeen outside stalls.

Returning to the barn, Butch parked the wheelbarrow back in its usual location and turned to the still-locked hay cage. Seeing Gene sitting on the stack of bales, looking forlorn and helpless, further strengthened his belief that the group of individuals at the NAS/JRB had been pissing on his boots and trying to make him believe that it was raining. If there was one thing he did not accept in his life or that of others, it was dishonesty.

"All right, Gene," Butch said as he took his keys from his pocket, "I'm going to unlock the gates, but I want you to stay sitting right where you are. I need to get a couple of bales out to finish feeding, and if you try anything, and I mean *anything*, you won't have to ever worry about tomorrow again. Do I make myself clear? I don't want to see a single muscle move."

"Yes, sir," Gene answered, "I'll sit right here. I promise, I don't intend to do anything to make you worry. I just need to talk to you and try to make you understand. I'm not sure what you think, I'm not even sure what I think at this point. I just know that I can't return. I'll do anything you ask."

"That's good," Butch said as he unlocked the gates and pushed one side open. "I'll be glad to listen to you when I'm done here."

Taking two of the 125-pound bales from the stack and sitting them outside the gates, he slid the gate back and relocked it. After loading one of the bales on a wheelbarrow, he turned his back on Gene and walked back into the main barn. Cutting the three strands of cord that held the bale intact, he realized that he had used the very same knife that he had given Gene.

Kind of makes you think, here I present a fellow with his first knife, and I have to worry about what sort of man he is. I still remember the first knife my dad gave me and how I thought that I had finally earned his respect. Now, I'm having to rethink my ability to read a man's worth, Butch thought as he broke a four-inch flake off the bale and placed it in the hay racks bolted to the sides of each stall.

Finishing the inside, he returned to reload the other bale before continuing outside to finish feeding the remaining horses. Again giving each horse a flake and checking on how they were eating, he shut each stall door before pushing the wheelbarrow back into the barn.

"All right, Gene," he said as he walked back to the locked cage where Gene sat. "Let's start from the beginning. First, you lied to me about where you were from and about having worked around a stable. I don't like that. Lying is way up there on things I just don't tolerate. So bear that in mind when you start telling me anything else. I'm going to give you the benefit of the doubt, but you better make sure that anything you say is the no-shit truth."

"I understand," Gene answered. "I didn't mean to lie to you, and it was partly true. What I mean to say is that the only job I've ever had was helping clean horse stalls. I've never done anything besides live in the facility. I certainly couldn't tell you about that. Vicki made me promise to never speak of it. Since she was the only mother I've ever known, I had to try to keep that promise. And I didn't know what to expect from you or anybody else."

"OK, that's fine," Butch replied. "I'll accept the fact that you had a past that you weren't supposed to discuss, but that's all changed now. Whether or not you know it, I've been placed in a situation that I don't quite know what to think of. Right now, I just want straight answers. And I expect to get them from you."

"Yes, sir," Gene said. "I guess the best way to go about this is to tell you what I know and maybe what I think about what I've heard over the years I spent in the facility. First, Vicki, the lady that took care of me for as long as I can remember, never really told me anything about my real parents. She sometimes said that they had died right after I was born, but she wouldn't talk about it any more than that.

"I only know that for some reason, I was never allowed outside the one area within the facility where my room was. Except, sometimes they would take me to an airplane in the hangar that must have been right over the facility, and we would fly somewhere during the night. After two and a half or three hours, we would land in some isolated place where there were several hangars, and they would take me to look at some strange machines or pieces of something. I never knew what they wanted me to do or say, they just kept asking me if I knew what I was looking at or if I knew what something was or how it worked.

"That seemed to happen a couple of times a year, but I do remember that it seemed to happen more frequently during the last four or five years. Even after I returned to the facility, they would show me pictures or ask me questions. I never knew what they were after, but they seemed disappointed when I couldn't answer their questions."

"When you say they took you somewhere in an airplane, what did the country look like?" Butch asked.

"Well, it was very hard to see much. We would go into a hangar before they let me off the airplane and get into a big bus with really dark windows. Then they would drive out to where we would pull into some place that looked like a hangar or huge cave before they would let me out. Since it was always during the night, I never got a good look around. But I do remember that it looked kind of like a desert and seemed to have a lot of hills all around. Sometimes when the moon was full and I could see out the front of the bus, I only got a glimpse of it, but there were lots of buildings and lots of fences.

"We had to stop lots of times and wait for some gates to open. Some of the places seemed to be a long way from where we landed and seemed to be dug into the hills."

"All right," Butch said, "did you ever hear these people talk about extraterrestrial or alien material?"

"Not really," Gene replied. "Most of the time, Vicki and the other doctors and lab workers seemed to say something about DNA or genetic strands or something. I know I had to go through a lot of tests, especially when I was much younger. They kept saying that they were looking for something to do with some abnormality that I may have."

"Abnormality?" Butch asked. "Just what do you mean? Are you supposed to have some rare disease or condition that you got from your parents?"

"I don't really know. I just know that they kept taking samples of my blood, sometimes they scrapped the inside of my mouth. A few times, they took some fluid from my spine. Most of that happened when I was younger, and the older I got, the more they just gave me tests to take."

"What do you mean *tests*?" Butch asked.

"Oh, I'm not sure exactly, but they seemed to be like, can I tell what someone is holding or what is written on a card or what number someone is thinking of. I guess they were trying to tell how smart I was or if I could see things that weren't right there."

"What about *mental telepathy*? Did they ever use that term?"

"Maybe, I'm not sure. The people never really talked much to me, just to each other, except for Vicki. She would always tell me that I had done just fine and that it was normal testing that everyone took," Gene said as tears began to form in his eyes. "She was always so kind and interested in how I felt or what bothered me."

Butch waited as Gene put his head between his hands and shook slowly side to side. He could see the tears falling on Gene's pants and hear the quiet sobbing. *This isn't some radical jihadist,* Butch thought. *He's just some poor, scared little boy lost and alone in a strange world.*

"All right, Gene," Butch finally told him. "Here's what I want you to do for now. There's some Dr Pepper and a couple of hot dogs in the refrigerator in the kitchen. I'm going to get them and bring them back here. After that, I need to go home and take care of my kids.

"While I'm gone, these gates stay locked. It's not that I'm worried about you leaving, but anyone coming in today would expect them to be locked. Also, as long as you stay back behind the hay and out of sight, maybe nobody will see you. And make sure you don't make any noise or leave anything out for someone to see, such as a can or one of the hot dog wrappers.

"I'm probably going to be gone most of the day, but you've got to trust me. I'm not going to turn you in or let them get to you. At least not right now. I just need to make a few arrangements that will give me, and you, a little time to sort this mess out. For right now, let's just say I believe you. I know that I believe more of your story than I do of that batch of *authority* people I dealt with this morning."

"I understand," Gene replied as he wiped the tears from his cheeks. "I don't know much more about this than you do. But Vicki was so afraid that the people at the facility would never let me go. I think that she was more afraid for me than for herself."

"OK, let's not worry about that for now. The main thing to do now is to avoid any detection and get you some place where we can figure out what was going on and what needs to be done. I'll be right back, and I'll help you stack some of the back bales toward the front so you have a cozy little hiding place."

Butch left the gates locked as he walked back into the main area of the barn. Reaching the kitchen, he opened the refrigerator and took out a six-pack of Dr Pepper. Sitting it on the counter, he looked on the shelf behind where he kept several bottles of antibiotics for the horses and found an unopened package of hot dogs. Pulling several sheets of paper towels from the holder, he walked back down the aisle toward the hay storage area.

As he walked past the office, he noticed the time and realized that he would have to turn all the horses out into the pasture before he left. He was surprised that no one had arrived by now. Usually, several of his clients would have been here to ride or groom their horses.

Reaching the locked gates, he sat the Dr Pepper and hot dogs down in front of them. Using the key he had taken from Gene, he unlocked and slid one side open.

"Here," he told Gene as he picked the food back up. "Take this and sit it behind you on the bales against the wall."

As he handed him the six-pack, Butch climbed up on the lowest row of bales. After moving a couple of other bales to make it easier to climb to the top, he began taking bales from the middle and stacking them on the front and sides to build a hiding place for Gene.

"OK, little fellow," he told him. "This is going to be home for the next few hours, and maybe longer. I'll bring something else for you to eat when I get back, but don't expect much. If I was one of the people I spoke to earlier, I'd be watching me real close right now. That means that I've got to be very careful to make sure I don't do anything out of the ordinary and that everything seems normal to everybody that I run into."

"I understand," Gene told him. "And, sir, I really do mean this. I promise to tell you anything I know. And I'm so very sorry I lied to you before, and it will never happen again."

"That's forgotten. You just keep your ass hidden until I can figure out a way to get you somewhere safe for now. Here, take back your key. Just in case. But remember, if you leave here without me, I'll toss your ass under the bus faster than my ex-wife could unzip another man's pants. And she could sure enough find one of those, bless her poor little ol' cheating heart. Just remember, there are lots of folks still looking for you, and I wouldn't doubt for a minute that they are watching this place real close."

TM

Chapter 4

When General Modelle walked into the conference room, everyone stood to attention. He slowly walked to the head of the table and looked around the room, making sure he made eye contact with each person standing.

"Folks, I'm positive that each and every one of you knows exactly what kind of trouble we are in right now," he said. "But before we get too caught up in past mistakes, let's sit down and see what we can do to get our little 'Gene' back. Regardless of what has happened, we still have a job to do, and it doesn't help to worry about what went wrong, just what we can do to resolve the problem. As of right now, no one is to blame. I've assumed full responsibility, and we'll do everything possible to contain the situation and rectify the problem. Please have a seat, and let's get started."

Everyone waited until Paul had taken his seat before they slowly looked at each other and sat. Still half holding their breath, they busied themselves pulling stacks of papers from their briefcases and tried to get comfortable in their chairs. The tension remained within their bodies as evidenced by the way they sat.

"General," Mike said as he placed his elbows on the table and clasped his hands. "I want you to understand that I still place all the blame on the original escape upon me alone. Having said that, I agree that what is done is done. Our mission remains the same as it did the day that Vicki Grubbs took Gene out of our facility, mainly to recover him and prevent civilian knowledge of his existence and that of our projects here."

"Exactly," Paul replied. "Nothing more and nothing less. We'll start with his last known location and work from there."

"As of right now," Mike said as he nodded his head, "we have phone taps on every number belonging to Butch North, both of his daughters, and the Equestrian Center. That includes all the known cell phones and the home phones of Mischelle and Jeannie."

Turning to Rick, he asked, "Where do we stand on getting a dedicated satellite to monitor the stables and Mr. North?"

"We'll have one in geosynchronous orbit within the hour," Rick said as he took several sheets from his briefcase. "It will be able to provide real-time video of up to twelve separate sites. The enhanced images will be of sufficient quality to read the keypad of their cell phones if they are using them or to read anything they are writing. The material I'm handing out will show the coverage area and there are examples of the quality of the photo capabilities. The satellite is currently being repositioned and will be linked directly to our communications room, as I said, within the hour. We will be able to direct any of the sensors remotely and have zoom control as well."

Everyone scanned each of the pages and looked at the examples of the photos. The clarity was unbelievable. Almost studio-quality portraits of people's faces and newspapers that could be read as if you were holding the paper mere inches from your face. All this from a satellite orbiting over a hundred miles above the ground.

"In addition to the standard video," Rick continued, "we can have infrared and lock onto the subject. That way, if any of the people we are tracking happen to be mobile, we can keep up. Also, we can keep several locations under surveillance to monitor any movement there. As you can see, our coverage extends from Mr. North's house at the center, out to roughly one hundred miles. However, anything over twenty-five miles starts becoming oblique, and the data lose some of its clarity."

"Who authorized the satellite dedication?" Paul asked. "And is there any chance of losing control in the event of other more pressing situations?"

"I can answer that one," Major Jerry Fleenor answered. "I went through Communications Satellite Command, or ComSatCom, using our unit from the Jet Propulsion Lab at Kirkland AFB. This particular satellite was being held in reserve and mainly used to track illegals crossing along the Texas and New Mexico border. Additionally, it was also the test bed for infrared imaging and lock to track technology. This satellite is not slated for any other service unless one of the Middle East birds goes down or implementation of major hostilities in any other part of the world."

"Good," Paul answered. "I damn sure don't want to be relying on a system that could be jerked out of our control just when we may need it to monitor the ongoing program. Where do we stand regarding the two ladies that were involved with Gene at that place in Bridgeport?"

"General," Karyn Lynch answered, "I have submitted the names of both into our computers using any variety of combinations. I started with Stacy Hyden and Leslie Barber, but it will search for any variation of those names or spellings. Additionally, it will cross-reference with the Internal Revenue Service, the Texas Department of Motor Vehicles, and every major credit card company in the United States. I expect information from all these entities to be available later today. I will then concentrate on any matches with a residence in either Arlington or Bowie, Texas."

"Good," Paul said. "What about the fifth hijacker program we were running in the initial search?"

"We plan to continue the same coverage that resulted in the Downey's report. Since we have 'captured' the other four and Gene has never been officially captured, we needed to continue the program anyway. We can now narrow the search to Wise, Dallas, Tarrant, and Montague Counties unless we get a spotting from another location," Mike answered.

"Next," Paul said, "we need to go over every aspect of the facility security measures, including a system of tracking everyone assigned to work here. What do you suggest?"

Lieutenant Colonel Mark Mallory answered, "Sir, I have reviewed every facet of the security operation and have a list of recommendations. The major one, and the one that may cause the biggest problem, involves the tracking of personnel."

"Exactly what problem are you having?" Mike asked.

"Well, sir," Mark said as he turned to look at Mike, "mainly the issue of implanting tracking chips in each individual. I see no

problem with inserting a chip in our test subjects, but I'm not sure
about the legality of implanting civilian or military members."

"Do you have the personnel releases available?" Paul asked.

"Yes, sir," Mark answered. "They are all on file in my office, but I'm
pretty sure there was no mention of invasive procedures mentioned
in the security portions of the documents."

"Get me one, please. We'll see if there are any open clauses that
we can use to interpret for this problem," Mike told him. "As far as
the military personnel are concerned, I'm sure we have everyone in
this room's assurance that there will be no problem. The remainder
will be told that it is part of a new program being tested for battlefield
locators and that while participation is strictly voluntary, it is
considered essential to continued assignment at this location."

"Mike," Paul asked, "just what do you plan to do with anyone that
refuses to allow you to implant a tracking device in them? Not only do
they have the right to refuse, that may lead to more questions than
we can answer right now. Maybe you better think this through a little
more and come up with another solution. I don't have a problem with
the tracking chips, just in how you intend to implement the insertion."

"Certainly, sir," Mike answered. "We'll start procurement of the
devices for now, and I'll get with Rick and Jerry to see if we can come
up with another reason for their insertion."

Colonel Amy Moore raised her hand for recognition and asked,
"General Nelson, I may have an answer."

As everyone turned to her, Mike asked, "What do you have in
mind, Amy?"

"Well, we have been working on a device within the lab to monitor
any hazardous material, either bacterial or otherwise, that remains
in contact with the personnel," she answered. "Up until now, we
have been using disposable clip-on monitors that change color upon
detecting excessive levels of various substances, including radiological
material. We have been experimenting with subcutaneous systems,
and everyone within the labs has volunteered to participate."

"Do you have signed releases for this program?" Paul asked.

"No, sir," Amy said, "but I'm sure that would be no problem.
Especially since the people involved are as interested in detection of
bacterial or radiation material infecting them as we are. It may take
a day or two to get the releases, but as long as they are unaware of
the tracking capabilities of the chip, I don't see a problem."

"That sounds workable," Paul told her. "Mike, even though I'm officially in charge of the operation, I want you to follow each of these programs and make your recommendations later today. Security of this facility is of vital importance of course, but we need to put our main effort into the recovery portion of the project. Does anyone believe that it would do any good to reinterview either Mr. North, his daughters, or any of the other people that had contact with Gene? I know we need the two ladies, but I mean anyone else?"

"Sir, I don't believe that we need to directly contact any of the North family. I'm sure Butch would become even more suspicious, if that's possible. However, I do think it would be prudent to send someone out to Red's in Bridgeport to interview anyone that was there that night to see if we can get a better fix on the two ladies," Rick told him.

"That's a good idea," Paul acknowledged. "Who should we send out there, and how do we keep this as low-key as possible?"

"Personally, I would like to involve one of the members of the Wise County Sheriff's office," Rick answered. "Since Red's is somewhat of a country bar, any strange face would arouse suspicions. By using a local man, we could be more certain of getting the patrons to talk. I propose we take a look at the deputies that live around that area and concentrate on anyone of them that frequent either Red's or any other of the local bars."

"Good idea," Mike responded. "Mark, why don't you take this project and give us a list of deputies that might fit our need? We can review the list and pick a couple to interview, off the record. Then, we can take one of our own men and make contact at one of the local saloons. We just can't have any suspicions that this is anything other than the initial reported search for a terrorist."

"Yes, sir," Mark replied. "I'll take care of it. If I may suggest, what about one of the initial search teams? There is one that I have in mind, and he is certainly aware of our situation."

"That's probably a good idea," Paul said. "The initial cadre of personnel was briefed and knows the consequences of any breach of security. Just which one of them do you have in mind?"

"Bob Wilson," Mark answered. "I had a chance to talk to him for a little while when we were setting up the motel accommodations. He grew up down around San Antonio and has some experience in cattle and roping. He might even get close to Mr. North, if he returns to Red's. I know Butch has an arena at his house and practices roping there. We may be able to get Bob involved that way and have a close contact with Butch."

"Sounds good, but let's concentrate on getting the deputy first. It could take several days to manage a 'chance' encounter with Mr. North," Paul told them. "Having someone close to Butch would certainly be an asset, but he might be a little harder to get to know than you think. Especially since he seems to be wary of the terrorist story. We have to take that very slow."

"Certainly, sir," Mark acknowledged, nodding his head.

"All right then," Paul said as he stood. "Let's take a break for lunch and reconvene in an hour. Mike, let's go over to Dos Gringos for lunch. We need to have a little discussion anyway."

"Yes, sir," Mike replied as he stood. "Rick, I want you to stay here and help Karyn sort through the names to find those two phantom ladies. I still think they may be the clue to solving this puzzle. I've asked Kathy to have something brought in for lunch. You guys stay here and enjoy it. We'll talk again when General Modelle and I return."

"Yes, sir," Rick said as he stood at attention while the two generals left the room.

TM

Chapter 5

Butch walked out of the stables and looked up at the morning sky. *Almost noon,* he thought, *and I haven't got much done. Just listening to some bullshit story at the base, finding Gene hiding here, and feeding a bunch of hungry horses. Bet my two darling daughters are gnawing on everything I have in the refrigerator.* He continued toward his truck, carefully looking around as he went. He was sure he would be watched.

Starting the diesel engine, he backed away from the hitching post in front of the barn and turned to drive out to Old Base Road. As he started forward, he caught a glimpse of a helicopter passing just to the north, over the Aurora Vista addition. He wasn't sure whose it was, but he had to be very watchful from now on. And he had to get his girls home as soon as possible. He didn't want them involved with whatever was going on than had already happened. If the military wanted to play games with him, that was one thing. But he didn't want his kids involved any further.

The short drive up Old Base Road and down Highway 114 proved uneventful. The normal stream of rock trucks and tanker trucks hauling water to the ever-increasing gas wells being drilled was normal, and he saw no suspicious vehicles as he turned onto Farm Road 718. As he passed Tater Junction Restaurant, he noticed a familiar pickup parked in the gravel parking lot.

Turning into the drive leading to his house, an idea began to form as to how to get Gene out of the stables and maybe to a safe area while he further investigated the mystery surrounding his appearance and the interrogation he and his girls had been given.

Parking under the carport, he went through the back door and called to Mischelle and Jeannie. As he hung his hat on the rack made from old horseshoes, he heard them talking in the living room. Entering, he told them to get ready to go for lunch.

"Come on, you little credit-card abusers, I know you've been sitting here wondering when I'd take you to eat. I imagine you've gone through my refrigerator and eaten anything that didn't have a little harmless mold on it," he told them. "How about a good ol' chicken fried steak?"

"Sounds good to me," Mischelle said as she got up from the couch where she had been watching television. "You haven't fed us since last night. I may report you to the child abuse people."

"How about you, Jeannie? I know you'll have to give up my recliner, but I'm sure you'll try to take it away from me when we get back. How's lunch at Tater Junction sound?" Butch said as he glanced at the news program still showing pictures of the "known terrorist" he now knew to be Gene.

"Yep, I'll take anything right now. How are things at the stables?" Jeannie asked as she lowered the footrest and sat up.

"Just fine," Butch said as he continued to watch the television. "I finally got all the horses fed and turned out. Y'all see anything new on TV or just the same stuff we saw this morning?"

"Not much new," Mischelle told him. "Do you really think Gene was a terrorist as they are saying? I just can't believe that he would be. He's way too quiet and nice."

"No, I don't think so. But that's not our problem now. We told them everything we knew, so let's forget about it and go get something to eat. It's just not right, me having to feed horses before I get to eat. That's just not right," Butch told them as he turned the TV off and started back down the hall.

"I don't care about you," Mischelle said. "Why do you think more about those horses than you do your own children?"

"It's not that I care more about them, you little poopy butt. They can't get into the refrigerator like you do. And I'm more concerned about the ASPCA and PETA than I am about child services. If child services were to come and see you kids, they would probably throw y'all in jail for mistreating your poor ol' poppy," Butch remarked as he took his hat and settled it firmly on his head.

Locking the door behind Jeannie as they headed toward the truck, Butch placed a single blade of grass against the bottom of the door. Using the remote to unlock the truck, he cautiously glanced around and watched the sky to see if the helicopter was still in the area. Seeing nothing, he opened his door and started the truck.

As he backed from under the carport, he stopped and said, "Girls, I don't want to seem unnecessarily suspicious, but I don't think this thing is over yet. I don't want to talk about it in the house or anywhere else public. And I want to get you kids back home as soon as possible."

Waiting for their response, Butch looked at both girls' faces. He could tell from their expressions that they weren't entirely comfortable either. This morning's "interview" had shaken both of them and left them wondering what was going to happen.

"Daddy," Jeannie started, "I don't think Gene was a terrorist, for sure. But I don't know what's going on, and I don't think you should get involved any more than you already are. I know how you are. You'll start digging around and wind up in more trouble than you want. I just want you to promise me that you'll let it drop unless they come to see you."

Mischelle nodded her head and chimed in, "Me too, Daddy. Just because you've seen and done a lot of stuff in the past that makes you think you know more than anyone else, you need to stay out of this, whatever it is."

"Don't worry, girls," Butch told them as he started out of the driveway, "I'll be my normal, quiet little self and just go on with my life. I just wanted to make sure you know that I don't think it's over yet, and I don't want you two involved any more that you already are. If they have more questions or anything, I'll answer. But I do want to get you back home and away from any more problems. To make sure nobody gets any strange desire to talk to you again, I don't want any further mention made, especially where we might be overheard. Do you understand?"

"Sure thing, Poopy Poppy," Mischelle said from the backseat. "Can we just go eat now?"

As they pulled into the parking lot, Butch saw the truck he was interested in still parked in front. As they exited the truck and walked to the door leading into the restaurant, Butch told them to go get a table while he washed his hands.

Both girls headed into the back of the restaurant while Butch looked around for the man he knew had driven in ahead of them. Spotting Mikey Carmichael sitting off to the side of another room, he walked over and sat down across the table from him.

"What's up, Butch?" Mikey asked him. "Didn't I just see those two sweet daughters of yours come in with you?"

"Yeah, daughters for sure. Sweet? I'm not so sure. How you doing? I guess you got nothing to do except sit around swilling coffee and spending all that money you make from selling your 'beef for the elite'," Butch asked him as he reached across the table to shake his hand.

"You know me," Mikey answered as he shook Butch's hand. "I got nothing but money and fine clothes. At least until my wife decides to take them away from me like my last ex did."

"Guess you've become an expert at poor choices in women," Butch acknowledged as he smiled. "I need a favor from you."

"What's that?" he asked as he sat his coffee cup down. "You know I'll do anything I can for you, within reason."

"I just need to borrow your phone for a second," Butch told him. "I need to make a quick call and mine doesn't get a good signal in here."

"No problem," Mikey told him as he pulled his phone from its tooled case on his belt. "Just don't make any of those 900 calls I know you use when you're sitting home all alone and in the mood for love."

Butch took the phone and told him, "Not today. But I'm going to start my own '900' system for lonely housewives. Then maybe I could afford to sit around drinking coffee like you and the other rich ranchers do."

"Let me know how that works," Mikey laughed. "I swear the only way to get rich in the cattle business is to start with a couple of millions and quit while you still have a million left. That shouldn't take more than a year or so the way the market's been."

Butch walked toward the men's room and, seeing it empty, stepped inside and locked the door. Taking his own phone from his belt, he quickly scrolled through the menu until he found the number he was looking for. Dialing the number, he waited until he heard the familiar voice of one of his oldest friends, Kevin Knox.

"Hello, Fat Boy," Butch said into the phone, "I'm sure you know who this is, but I don't want to use any names. I'll explain later. For now, just answer yes or no, and don't mention any towns or places. Understand, Fat Boy?"

"Yep," came the answer. "There's nobody who would call me Fat Boy, except for one. That's because I'd whoop anybody else's ass. Go ahead."

"OK," Butch told him. "First and most important is that I have your assurance that you'll do exactly as I ask. I need a huge favor. One that could get you into a lot of trouble, but absolutely necessary."

"I owe you," Kevin told him. "Whatever it is, I trust you to keep me out of trouble if at all possible. Just ask."

"I need you to pick up someone for me," Butch told him. "They may not want to go, but it is vital that they get out of town and taken somewhere safe. I can't say much more right now, but this is critical."

"Who?" came the response.

"Now, remember, no names. Just think of where you get your hair cut. It's a 'blank' shop. Understand?"

"Yes."

"Next, the first name is the same as someone, female, that we both knew when we were going to those team sorting things a couple of years ago. You remember the one that kept getting drunk and falling off her horse?"

"Sure, got it."

"From now on, use the word 'mare' when discussing this individual. She lives in the town just about seven miles east of you. I want you to get over there as soon as possible and convince her to leave with you. Tell her you know me, and as a result of the man she was with on her birthday when she met me, she is in very grave danger. She has to get away from there."

"I'll take care of it," Kevin told him. "When are you going to fill me in on what's going on?"

"As soon as I can," Butch told him. "Now, regarding the man she met that night, we will call him the 'gelding.' Tell her that her contact with him must be kept absolutely quiet. She must not make any contact with anyone regarding him, that night, or me. Make sure she understands. This could be as serious as that little incident you were involved in about twenty-five years ago in that nice little country your Uncle Sam sent you to. This is going to be a very serious issue from now on."

"OK," Kevin told him. "Anything else?"

"Yeah, I want you to get as many prepaid disposable cell phones as you can. Don't buy more than one or two at any location, but get at least ten for now."

"Then what?"

"I want you to keep five for yourself, write down the numbers of the other five, and make a list of the numbers you have for me. I want each of your phones to call only one of mine, so match the numbers for me. We'll only use any of the phones once, regardless of who calls who. Understand?"

"Perfectly."

"OK, once you get the mare, take her to your house for now. Make damn sure she has no phone and there are no keys to a car or anything she can use while you're gone. Once you get her safe, take my phones and go to the biggest store in the large town about twelve miles north of my house. You know what I'm talking about?"

"Pretty sure, you do mean where the fat girls congregate, don't you?" Kevin asked.

"Yep. When you get there, go in and buy something. Doesn't matter what, maybe more phones if you need to. No more than two, and put all my phones in the plastic bag you get. Then, wait until you see my truck. Once I get there, I'll go inside. Just wait somewhere around the front of the store, maybe by the ATM until I get what I need and pay. Once I finish paying, I'll come by you and use the ATM. At that point, I'll take your bag and leave. You go out the other doors and go back home."

"When are you going up there?"

"I'll leave here in three hours. That should give you enough time to get the mare out and safe. Park somewhere out from the store where I can see your truck. If you aren't there when I get there, I'll be where I can see you come in. Just bear in mind, buddy, this could turn out to be some no-shit problem if either of us are discovered. Especially since someone is very, very interested in finding the mare. I just hope we aren't too late right now."

"Who is this someone you're referring to?" Kevin asked.

"Later, but they are closely related to that uncle that gave you that little vacation a few years ago."

"Got it. Guess I'll see you in a few hours. I suppose I don't know you when I see you?"

"Exactly. You better hope that our 'somebody' never sees us together, or you'll probably end up in one of those little cells where you have to decide whether you want to be the husband or the wife. Enough for now. Get your ass moving and make sure the mare is gone within the next thirty minutes. I don't care if you have to kidnap her. Just get her out. And thanks, buddy," Butch told him gratefully.

"No thanks needed, good friend. You've saved my ass before. I owe you, but this may just square the deal. See ya," Kevin told him.

"You too," Butch told him as he hung up and unlocked the men's room door. Walking back to Mikey's table, he handed him the phone and thanked him.

"You're welcome," Mikey told him. "The girls staying around much longer?"

"Nope," Butch answered. "I can't afford to keep those two around more than a day or so. They seem to think that I own the Jack Daniel's distillery. Between my whiskey bill and the amount of food those girls go through, I could have a covey of a dozen pretty ladies living with me. Take care, buddy."

Butch went searching for Mischelle and Jeannie in the rear of the restaurant. Finally spotting them already eating, he walked up and took the seat across from both. As he sat down, the waitress came up and handed him a menu.

"What'll it be, Butch?" she asked.

"Well," he said, "since my wonderful little children couldn't wait for me, I guess I need something you can bring in a hurry."

"How about a chicken fried steak, mashed potatoes, corn, gravy, a fresh jalapeno and a Dr Pepper?" she asked.

"What makes you think that's what I want?" Butch asked with a smile on his face.

"Well, it could be that you've ordered that here at least 90 percent of the time when you come in. Or it could be that your girls have already ordered for you, but made me wait to bring it out. What reason do you want to believe today?"

Laying the menu back down, Butch looked at each of the girls whose heads were down. Finally, not getting their attention, he looked back at the waitress and said, "Well, women trying to run my life again. What's new? Just bring me what you think I need, and I'll try not to seem upset."

"Oh, Butch. You're way too easy," the waitress said as she picked up the menu and sat a bottle of Dr Pepper down. "I'll be right back with your food. I picked the best jalapeno for you, just so you know. We may try to run your life, but you need all the help you can get."

"Why, thank you so much. All of you. I just don't know how I've managed to survive all these years without every one of you. Good thing I don't have to worry about another thing now. Just sit back and let ya'll take care of me. What's next, the rest home for broken-down cowboys?"

"Oh, come on, Poppy," Jeannie said, grinning. "You know you would have ordered exactly what we did for you. Even the waitress knows what you'll pick from the daily specials. You've been coming here way too long. Even if you don't know, we know what's best for you anyway."

"That's right." Mischelle nodded. "Besides, we need to practice so when we put you in the home, we'll know just how to do it."

"Worthless little urchins, that's what both of you are. Why couldn't I have just gotten a good dog instead of two ungrateful children," Butch said as he smiled at the girls.

"What took you so long anyway?" Jeannie asked.

"Oh, just saying howdy to a couple of people I know," came the response.

"Just a couple?" queried Mischelle. "I think you know just about everybody here. Must be only a couple that you wouldn't talk to."

"You could be right, little missy," Butch said. "A man's real wealth is in the number of friends he has, you know. If you two had just half the friends I have, you'd been more than rich. Now, enough. After we eat, I have a couple of errands to do, and I want ya'll to get busy finding a way to get home."

"Can't we come with you?" asked Jeannie. "I'm not sure if the airlines are running yet, and I think it would be a waste of time to try to get a flight right now. According to the news, it may be a week before flights start again."

"Nope, you can't come with me. If you want, you two can take the Corvette and go shopping or something. How about calling some of the people you knew when you were going to the University of North Texas that I paid for of course?"

"I don't know if any of them are still around," answered Jeannie. "But I would like to drive over to Lewisville and look around."

"That's a good idea," Butch said as his meal was delivered. "It'll probably take me all afternoon to finish what I have to do. How about we meet back at the house about seven tonight? We can clean up and go over to the Avondale VFW. Be interesting to hear what some of those folks have to say about this terrorist thing."

"Sounds good to me," said Mischelle. "I need to go to a mall to get some stuff anyway."

"All right, I know this is going to cost me," sighed Butch. "Just how much do you need? I mean, just the essentials, right?"

"Oh, I guess a hundred each should do it," laughed Jeannie. "If you want to get rid of us, it'll cost you."

"Hell, if I'd known that I could get rid of you two for only two hundred dollars, I'd have done that years ago," Butch told them as he took a bite of the fresh jalapeno.

TM

Chapter 6

Just a few miles outside Bowie, Texas, Kevin was searching through the phone book at a truck stop. As he scanned the pages looking for the name he had been cryptically told, he finally spotted it. Leslie Barber did indeed live in Bowie, and luckily he knew the area. Her house would be almost out of town, just off the road leading to the city dump.

Kevin climbed back into his pickup and headed directly toward the address he had written on the back of a business card Butch had given him several years ago. The Equestrian Center of Aurora Vista card had Butch's home and cell phones written on the back. Having the card might have some value when he approached Leslie.

He still wasn't sure what was going on, but he knew Butch well enough to know that this wasn't a game. Kevin had known him for too many years to remember, and Butch had saved his ass on several occasions. Regardless of what he had asked, Kevin would do everything possible to make sure it was done.

He knew from the way Butch had talked that someone was after this Leslie girl. The mention of the incident back in Vietnam alone told him that the government was involved and probably meant a cover-up of some kind. His three tours in that country had shown him the extent the government would go to in order to keep certain programs from ever reaching the public's knowledge.

As a member of one of the special teams that clandestinely removed those less-than-friendly tribal leaders, Kevin knew that public knowledge of those operations would have proven that our government did indeed sanction assassinations. On numerous occasions, he and his team had snuck into a village during the middle of the night and exterminated the designated target. As only one of several of these highly specialized teams, he knew firsthand what length the government would go to. That included removing anyone who attempted to compromise the information.

Kevin drove through the town named after Jim Bowie, famous for his legendary knife and his stand at the Alamo. As he reached the road to the city dump, he watched closely for the street he had to find. Finally, after almost reaching the last road on the east side of Bowie, he saw it. Leslie's house was right on the corner, and he could see a car in the driveway.

Looking quickly around, he pulled in beside the car and got out, leaving his pickup running. As he rang the doorbell, he listened for sounds within the house as well as keeping an eye on both roads. If anyone happened to see him, he would pretend he was lost and looking for another address. After no answer, he rang the bell again and firmly knocked on the door. From within, he heard footsteps coming toward the door.

As the door opened and he looked at a thirtyish lady still wearing what looked like yesterday's clothes and her obvious unbrushed hair, he asked, "Leslie Barber?"

"Yes," came the answer. "Who are you?"

"I'm a friend of Butch North. Do you know him?" Kevin asked as he pulled the card from his shirt pocket.

"Kind of," Leslie told him. "I just met him last night. What has that got to do with you?"

"I don't have a lot of time to explain everything," Kevin told her. "But Butch sent me to tell you that the young man you met with him just may cause you to be in a lot of trouble. He asked me to get you out of town until he can find out what is going on, but he insisted that you come with me for now."

"Just what kind of trouble?" Leslie asked, now fully awake and trying to comprehend what was happening.

"I'm not positive, Butch only had a couple of minutes to talk," Kevin told her as he handed her the card. "I know you don't know me, and you may not know Butch very well. But when that man gets worried about something, it's time to be worried. And for now, all you need to know is that he thinks you are in danger and asked me to get you to safety. You need to grab a couple of changes of clothes and come with me now. I'm sorry I can't tell you any more than that because that's all I really know."

"What does this have to do with Gene?" Leslie asked him. "Is he in trouble or something?"

"Don't know," Kevin answered. "Butch will take care of him, I'm to try to take care of you for now. Please, we don't have much time. Just get your things, and we'll go. I'm sure Butch will call me later, and maybe we can figure out what's going on. For now, just trust me. Someone is undoubtedly looking for you, and I don't think you want them to find you. Please, Leslie, this is serious, and you need to trust Butch's judgment on this. He's not the kind of man to jump to conclusions without good reasons. I've known him too long. Again, please let's get out of here. Not only are you in danger, if I'm caught getting you away, I'll be in as much trouble as you. Not to mention Butch."

"OK, come on in," Leslie said as she turned away. "I'll grab a couple of pairs of jeans and things. Just wait there."

Kevin watched as she started toward the back of the house. Sensing that something wasn't going well, he quietly followed her toward her bedroom. As he watched from beside the open door, he saw her reach for the telephone sitting beside the unmade bed. The minute he saw her hand touch the receiver, he quickly walked in and placed his had over her mouth and wrapped his other arm around her arms and waist.

"Well," he said as he easily lifted her off her feet, "I guess we'll just have to do this the hard way. I really do mean you no harm, Leslie. I'm sorry to have to do it this way, but you are coming with me. If you'll just be quiet, I won't have to tape your mouth shut and tie you up. But either way, you are coming with me."

Leslie continued to struggle as Kevin carried her back through the house. Weighing well over two hundred pounds, and very little of it not muscle, he had no problem whisking her toward the door. Stopping to decide just what he needed to do, he quickly slipped his hand from her mouth and dropped his arm to place her neck within the V formed by his forearm and bicep. Applying just enough pressure to cut off her breathing and momentarily blocking the blood flow to her brain, she slowly became limp in his arms.

Laying her gently on the sofa, he walked back out to his truck and pulled the ever-present roll of duct tape from behind the seat. As he returned to the house, he glanced around again, looking for any sign of other people in the area. It appeared that everyone was either at work or busy in their own houses.

Opening the door, he could see Leslie slowly starting to move her head. Ripping an eight-inch piece of the tape from the roll, he stretched it across her lips, making sure that her nose was left uncovered. Pulling her hands across her stomach, he wrapped her wrists with two complete turns of the tape. Seeing her eyes flutter open, he told her to just be quiet while he taped her ankles together. Finishing, he shoved the tape into the front of his shirt and picked her up in his arms.

"Now, Leslie," he told her as he opened the door, "I'm really not going to hurt you, but you've forced me to do this. I promise that as soon as we are safely out of here, I'll try to find a way to explain. But for now, any more resistance will only make things worse for you. I just have to get us both out of here."

Kevin pushed the screen door open with his knee and looked around as he carried Leslie to the passenger side of the truck. Still holding her close against him, he freed one hand to open the door. After placing her in a sitting position, he closed the door and went back to the house to lock and shut her house door. As he returned to the truck, he could see her eyes and knew that this wasn't going to get any easier. He would have to take the back roads out of town as he drove back to his place. He couldn't have her noticed, especially with the shiny silver tape across her mouth. In a small town like this, that would surely bring attention; and right now, he needed as little attention as possible.

"Shit," he said as he climbed into the truck. "I hope Butch is right about this, or I'll be hung out to dry. Leslie, again, I'm sorry I had to do things this way. Now, if you try to get anyone's attention, I'll have to put you to sleep again and lay you in the floor board. Do you understand?"

After she nodding her answer, Kevin put the truck in reverse and backed out of the drive. Quickly turning onto the road to the dump and making a left turn on a gravel road he knew would get him out

of town, he noticed two black Chevy Suburbans just turning onto the
road he had left. He prayed that he would seem to be just another
pickup leaving the city dump if they had noticed him. *Crap,* he
thought. *Looks like ol' Butch had things right. Those don't look like locals,
and I think we just barely got out of there with our heads.*

Continuing down the gravel road as fast as he thought prudent,
he finally reached Highway 59. Making another left turn, he followed
it to the intersection with 287 which led him back to 174, the road
to Vashti and home.

"Just a few more miles now," he told Leslie as he followed the
curving road through the heavily wooded area. "It's not the Hilton,
but I'll try to keep you comfortable until Butch decides what to do
with you. If it were up to me, I'd throw you to whoever was driving
those black Suburbans I saw coming toward your house just as we
made the first turn."

He looked over at her and asked, "Now, if I take the tape from your
mouth, will you please just sit quietly until we get to my place?"

Leslie slowly nodded her head and stared back. He could plainly
see that the situation wasn't fully under control, but he had to gain
her trust as soon as possible. Reaching one hand toward her, he said,
"Just lean over a little so I can get that tape. At least then you can
talk, but the real question is, will you listen?"

Using two fingers, he grabbed a corner of the tape and pulled
it from her lips. As soon as the tape was removed, Leslie began to
yell. "Just what the hell do you think you're doing? If you don't turn
around right now and take me home, I'll make sure the cops have
your ass."

"That wouldn't be too smart," Kevin replied as he glanced at her.
"I don't suppose you saw those two cars I mentioned, did you? Well,
I can almost guarantee you that it wasn't the Seventh-day Adventist
that was driving toward your house. And I can just as assuredly tell
you that they were Government Issue. Now, I don't suppose you
would be willing to tell me what you know about this man you met?
Or what happened to get Butch involved?"

"I don't know anything except that I met him last night with Butch
and his daughters. Gay Lynn, the owner of Red's, told me Butch was
a decent man, and I trusted her. Guess I sure screwed up. Just how
did you find me anyway? I never told him where I lived. And why are
you here if he wanted to find me. I want some kind of answer."

"I don't know those answers," Kevin answered. "I just know that Butch, who by the way is a decent man, knows something that he can't tell me right now. And he told me that he thought you told him you lived in Bowie. As to why he didn't come, I'm not sure. Could be not enough time, or there was something else he had to do. If you'll just be a little patient for now, I'm sure we'll both get the answers soon enough. And right now, I'm not too sure I want to know just what's going on. I wish for once that I'd never met that man."

About ten minutes later, they pulled through the gates leading to Kevin's house. Still half mile from the house, they had lost sight of every road due to the heavy woods surrounding the land. As they approached the house, he saw two helicopters a few miles to the east. Both were painted with the distinctive markings of army Blackhawks. Though several miles away, he pointed and told her, "I'd bet my firstborn that those are a couple of more people heading toward your house. Are you starting to get the picture?"

Kevin turned off the motor just outside the garage and opened his door. "Now, I'm going to take you into the house and try to make you as comfortable as possible. However, I don't trust you. So I'm afraid I'll have to leave you tied up until I take care of a couple more things. Please don't make this any worse than it has to be."

He hit the remote and walked around the front of the truck as the garage door opened. Reaching the passenger door, he unlocked it and started to open it. Just as he started to pull on the handle, Leslie swung her legs around and kicked it with her strapped-together feet. The door slammed into Kevin's arm but moved no farther.

"OK," he told her as he pulled the door fully open, "if that's the way you want to play, I'll have to strap you to a chair. You've had your chance, and I'm not taking any more chances. Maybe a couple of hours sitting taped to a hard wooden chair will help you understand that you can't win. I've handled much tougher people and never lost one. It's been a few years, but I still remember how to immobilize someone. Let's get this going. I have an hour or two's work left, and I damn sure can't take you with me, so you'll just have to sit still until I'm done."

Kevin reached in and pulled her from the pickup. Slinging her across his left shoulder, he walked through the garage and opened the door to his house. Typical bachelor's furniture littered the living room as he sat her on the couch. Taking a straight-backed chair from the kitchen table, he returned and sat it directly in front of the television. Next he picked Leslie up and sat her on the chair. With the tape still in the front of his shirt, he pulled the tape from her ankles and taped each to a separate leg of the chair. Once her legs were securely fastened, he unwound the tape from her wrists and held one as he used the dangling tape to secure the other one to the arm of the chair. Finishing taping the other wrist, he added another round of tape to both legs and wrists.

"That'll hold you for now," he told her as he used the remote to turn on the television. "How about you just sitting there and watching the news?"

As he was turning toward the kitchen, he heard Leslie exclaim, "That's him! That's the man I met with Butch last night. I know that's him!"

Turning to look, Kevin watched as the newscaster showed the picture of a young man and described how they were looking for an escaped terrorist. He stood quietly as he listened to the story about an attempted hijacking gone awry while Leslie continued to shout that she knew him.

"What do you mean, you met him with Butch?" he asked her.

"He was at Red's last night. That's where I met Butch and his daughters. That's where I met Gene, the guy on the television."

"Well, well," Kevin said, shaking his head. "Things are starting to fall into place. So that must be the gelding he's talking about. What the hell has he gotten into?"

"What do you mean, gelding?" Leslie asked as she continued to stare at the program.

"Just that Butch told me to never mention any names, places, or anything else that could be overheard. I'm supposed to say mare when I talk about you and gelding when I talk about that guy, whoever he is. One thing I'm pretty sure of, if Butch is trying to protect him, he ain't no terrorist."

"Do you think that the reason you think somebody is after me is because of having met Gene?" she asked.

"Well," he told her, "I'm not sure just why they are looking for this Gene fellow, but whether or not he's a terrorist, if you've had any contact with him, someone wants to talk to you. I'm positive that is why Butch is going to all this trouble. He's worried about what would happen to you if they were to find you. And as I've told you, he doesn't get worried unless there is probably a need to. Now, I'm still going to leave you in that chair while I finish what Butch asked me to."

"Can't you just take the tape off so I can go to the bathroom or something if I need to?" she pleaded. "I think I kind of believe you now, and I promise I'll stay here until you return."

"Sorry, I can't take any chances now. Especially since I know that if you are found, my ass is on the line too. And I sure don't want to be in the middle of a terrorist hunt. They are liable to shoot first and sort out the dead later. Nope, you can just stay as you are for a couple of more hours until I find out what the plan is."

Kevin turned and walked toward the door as Leslie continued to watch the news program, still unable to believe the man she had met was now under a nationwide manhunt.

TM

Chapter 7

        Mike and Paul were sitting in Dos Gringo's Restaurant waiting for their lunches to be delivered. The ride from the NAS/JRB had been very quiet. Both men were wondering how things back in Washington were being evaluated. Besides having their careers on the line, both of them were still professional about their responsibilities; and regardless of the future, they wanted to get Gene back. They knew the ramifications of his discovery and their duties still included following the directives from MJ 12 and that of the president of the United States.

    "Mike," Paul started as he looked thoughtfully at him, "what do you truly think our chances are of locating our project before he is discovered?"

    Both men knew to never speak directly regarding the program or its products. Only within the security of the facility itself would they ever mention by name or inference to what was actually happening. Even a small slip, the wrong name or reference to something could be heard by the wrong person.

    "Well, sir," Mike answered as he looked directly into Paul's eyes, "I know we've suffered a major setback. However, I think it seems far worse than it really is because we thought we had it controlled late yesterday when we discovered his location. Had we not gotten our

60

hopes up so quickly, I think we would still be in the same situation. Granted, we found him. At least we found where he had been.

"But we found where he had been when he was first spotted at the Downey place. Just as happened there, we arrived too late. Now, we at least know the direction he went. And just as Colonel Amy Moore predicted, he headed for the area associated with his genetic makeup. Some of the DNA was from the Aurora alien."

"I suppose you're right," Paul told him as the waitress was placing their orders on the table. "I guess the letdown is affecting our spirits right now. I'm sure everything we did will eventually lead to our success, and I'll convey that to my bosses when we get back. However, I want to make sure we have a good plan in place before I tell them anything else to get their hopes up. I especially think we need to have a firm location of the two ladies in question."

"I completely agree." Mike nodded. "I'm positive that Rick and the others are using every method at their disposal right now to pin down their location. With all the tools available to them, we should know within a couple of hours if the names were real. If so, we can find them. Between the IRS, FBI, CIA, Texas driver's license bureau, and all the other data banks held on every citizen, we'll soon find them."

Mike and Paul finished their meals quietly and prepared to leave as Mike's pager sounded. Glancing at the number, he quickly walked out of the restaurant and removed his cell phone. Dialing the number, he identified himself and listened quietly. After hearing the message, he disconnected and returned into the restaurant just as Paul was getting his change from their bill.

"I guess you're going to tell me that was not planned. I swear, Mike, how you get someone to call you just as the bill arrives, I'll never know." Paul smiled as he walked back to the table and left a tip.

"Well, if you have to know, I've programmed my pager number into my cell phone. Then all I have to do is hit the preset number and it sets off my pager. The rest is easy. You'll never know who taught me that trick," Mike laughed as they walked back toward their car.

"Never mind," came the reply. "I know I told you about that when I showed you how to get out of staff meetings early. I should have known. From now on, you'll have to figure out your own sneaky little ways."

Once in the car and driving back toward the base, Mike told him of the call. The air force car was routinely swept for electronic devices, and they felt relatively secure in discussing sensitive issues while driving. Paul did make sure the radio was on but not loud enough for them to have to raise their voices as they talked.

"That was Rick," Mike started. "They have confirmed that the names of Leslie Barber and Stacy Hyden are real people. Also, the address of each is as we were told. Leslie resides in Bowie, Texas, and Stacy is from Arlington. Just as Mr. North and his daughters told us."

"Mr. North may have been honest with his answers. But I'm almost positive that he wasn't being as forthcoming with his answers as I would have liked. I don't think the man would lie to us, but I'd bet a year's salary that he knows much more than he told us. Maybe he doesn't actually know anything, but he sure suspects something," Paul told him.

"I'm sure you're right about that. But we would have been hard-pressed to have pushed him or his daughters any further. I'd much rather deal with a stupid man than one like him. Stupid people don't know when to shut up, and they are always anxious to show you what they think they know," Mike said as they approached the gate leading into the base.

The guard at the entrance stood quickly to attention as he saw the two stars attached to the front license plate holder of the blue sedan. Holding his salute as the car passed, he only relaxed when they were safely some distance from his booth.

Arriving at the facility's parking area, Paul and Mike went quickly to the guarded entryway leading to the underground complex. Noting that the double-gated entrance was manned and security cameras aimed at each gate, both knew that the recent modifications made would increase the overall procedures to prevent another incident such as the one causing their concern at this time.

As they stepped from the elevator at the first level down, Colonel Erickson met them as they were approaching General Nelson's office. All three entered the foyer where Mike's secretary, Kathy Blevins, was busy at her computer.

"Kathy," Mike told her as they passed her desk, "could you please see if we have any cold Dr Pepper in the refrigerator? I think if we have some of those Dublin Dr Peppers, I'd like one. How about you two?"

"Sounds good to me," Paul responded. "Guess it's a little early for Jack Daniels, although I know I'll need some of that before this day is through."

"Certainly, sir," Kathy replied as she got up from behind her desk and walked toward the kitchenette located just off her office. "I'm positive we restocked this morning. Cory Romine knows better that to let you get low on your Dr Pepper. He's just hoping he'll get promoted from major if he keeps you happy."

"Well, he certainly won't if he lets me go thirsty. Just bring them on in when you can, please," Mike told her as they entered his office.

"Any good news, Rick?" Paul asked as they waited for Kathy to deliver the drinks.

"Yes, sir," came the response. "I'll fill you in after Kathy leaves."

Kathy came in just as they were all taking their seats. Handing each of them a Dr Pepper, she asked, "Will there be anything else, General?"

"No, thanks, Kathy," Mike responded. "Please hold any calls for now. We shouldn't be too long."

He paused while Kathy walked back toward the open door. The office was decorated with various awards and plaques commemorating all the years of his service. The one he treasured the most was a picture of an F-4 flying over Vietnam painted by Keith Ferris. The trail of a ground-based missile streaking toward the aircraft depicted the hazards of flying missions over the North during the conflict. Beneath the picture was his squadron patch and the signatures of every member of his squadron.

As Kathy shut the door, he asked, "What do you have, Rick?"

"Well, sir," he began. "We have the addresses of both ladies, Leslie and Stacy. All records confirm the names to be genuine, and the addresses were crosschecked with tax records. Even the birth records coincide with Leslie's birthday as the Norths stated."

"Have you located them, or just their addresses?" asked Paul.

Turning to General Modelle, Rick responded, "Sir, I have sent a team to each of the addresses and dispatched a helicopter to cover the area in the event of an escape attempt. The ground team should be arriving in Bowie and Arlington within the hour. I did not want to involve the local police because that could lead to providing answers to questions I don't want asked."

"I agree," Mike told him. "Our plan of using the locals for identification only worked well during the initial search, and no unwanted questions arose. I am in favor of keeping anyone other than our initial team as uninformed as possible. As far as I'm concerned, we're just a day later in solving the problem."

"Rick," Paul told him as he looked directly into his eyes, "Mike and I have discussed this. Our initial enthusiasm was premature. All that has happened is that we have to continue the same level of effort that located the product the first time. I am sure that when I make my next report to Washington, they will agree that this is no more than a minor setback. We just anticipated success way too early. Now, we know to hold off until Gene is actually back on the property."

"What else have you learned or done?" Mike asked.

"We have completed maneuvering the satellite into position. One of its sensors is focused on Mr. North's house and the stables. Two are trained on the general area around Bowie and Arlington. We are holding the rest in reserve, including the infrared systems. We can lock either to any designated target and place another to provide area monitoring. All systems will be linked to our communications rooms, and a secure feed will be going to mobile command posts once we complete equipping the vans."

"Who is manning the vans?" Mike asked.

"I have directed four of the search teams from Washington to take them. One will be standing by to roll toward Arlington, the other to Bowie. Along with them are two teams in our Suburbans. If necessary, we can divert the Bowie team toward Boyd or wherever we may need. They can each receive relayed data from the main communications center here. We will filter the data to make sure they get exactly what they need and not clutter their screens with nonessential information," Rick told them. "Also, Karyn is encrypting and recording all the data, including voice receptions from all the phones we discussed. All the numbers are now logged into the program to monitor any incoming or outgoing calls."

"Sounds good. Let's take about an hour while I brief my people back in Washington. I'm sure they will be receptive to keeping the initial team in place, and I'll make sure they are apprised of our ongoing plans," Paul told them as he stood. "Meet in the conference room in an hour?"

"Yes, sir," Mike told him as both he and Rick stood. "I'll have the same team as before ready for any further updates."

TM

Chapter 8

Butch and the girls finished their meal, and after declining the peach cobbler, Butch left a tip and headed toward the cashier. As a longtime resident of the Aurora area, he knew just about everyone in the restaurant. Aurora had gained some notoriety because of the rumored crash of an alien spaceship in 1897. Since that time, lots of visitors to the area had come to see the site and the local cemetery where the body of the alien was supposedly given a Christian burial.

Tater Junction, the only restaurant in Aurora, was a central point where the visitors sought information regarding the incident. The two nearby towns, Boyd to the west and Rhome to the east, also supported Tater Junction due to its reputation for excellent home-cooked meals. It was also a convenient stopping point for the numerous rock trucks taking material from the quarries around Bridgeport and Chico into the metroplex of Dallas and Fort Worth.

Seeing strangers in the restaurant was certainly normal, but with the recent events, Butch was extremely watchful as he walked through the restaurant. Although he saw several new faces, most of them looked as if they were either tourists or some of the new people moving into the Aurora Vista addition being developed just south of his home. He knew he would have to be extra careful whenever he was in there and not say anything that would arouse suspicions, especially if there were any faces that seemed out of place.

As he collected his change, Butch handed his keys to Jeannie and told her, "You guys go on back to the house. I have to talk to Mikey there for a minute. I'll just climb over the fence and walk across the pasture when I'm done. And don't forget to start looking at finding some way to get home."

"Sure thing, Poppy," Jeannie said, taking the keys. "How about the money for our shopping trip?"

"When I get to the house, you go on now," he told them as he walked back to the table where Mikey was still sipping coffee.

"Got a minute?" Butch asked as he took a seat across from Mikey.

"Sure thing, I got nothing but money and time," came the response. "What can I do for you now? Need the phone again?"

"Nope," Butch told him. "How're things up on the KC Ranch? Still pushing that 'Raising Beef for the Elite' marketing concept?"

"You bet," Mikey answered. "Hell, I've got the finest herd of cattle this side of the King Ranch. And I'm not sure if their cattle are as good as mine. I make it a point to name each and every one of them just to show them I care. Biggest problem is that I've had to start adding numbers to their names. I think I'm up to T-bone 23 and Sir Loin 64. Not to mention Prime Minister Rib 102."

"Yeah, those names sure fit your cattle. I'm surprised that you haven't used Ground Round or Ham Burger."

"Now, Butch," Mikey told him, "that just wouldn't fit with my 'Beef for the Elite' brand. Those cheap cuts might fit ol' Mad Mike Jackson's herd. Of course, he buys and sells up at the Bowie Livestock Commission. They just don't get the quality of beef my customers expect. Even that grouchy old som-bitch tries to get me to sell through his auction, but those low-rent ranchers he deals with just don't appreciate the quality of my cattle."

"I'm sure they don't, I'm sure they don't," Butch told him. "I know you think you should get at least an extra dollar a pound for the fine quality of bovine that you produce. That being said, have you got some place out there somewhere that I could park a little camper trailer for a while? If it has water and electricity, it would help, but I can manage without it if necessary."

"Trying to run away from your kids, or is some jealous husband after you again?"

"Neither, at least for now. I may need a place for a friend to stay for a couple of days. I'd prefer if it were well hidden. And, good buddy, don't say anything about this. I'd appreciate it if it was left to just between you and me. I'll explain later. For now, I just need a quiet out-of-the-way place that won't be noticed for a week or so."

"Well," Mikey told him as he sipped a little coffee and looked questioning at him, "I've got an area about two miles north of the house. It's in a pretty small area, only about two hundred acres, with lots of trees and some distance from any road. I don't think anyone would ever see it, unless they were back there looking for cattle."

"That would probably work just fine. I can bring a generator out for electricity and buy five-gallon jugs of water."

"Not necessary," Mikey told him. "We just finished drilling a well up there last year so we can have water for the cattle when we move them to that area. We can tap into the electrical line, and you can use that."

"Great," Butch said. "I'll get with you later if I do need to put the trailer up there. And again, not a word to anybody. Especially your wife."

"Hell, if she knew I was putting a trailer up there, she'd hire a private eye to watch it. She'd be afraid that I would have a senorita or two living there. Say, can I have the trailer when you're done? I just may need a place like that. Just as a hunting cabin, you know, nothing else for sure, just a hunting cabin."

"No problem, Mikey," Butch said, laughing. "I bet I know just what you'd be hunting. And I'm sure those deer don't have four legs either. Anyway, I'll get back to you on this. Thanks."

"Glad to help a friend, just let me know what you need," Mikey told him as he shook his hand. "Anything you need, I mean it."

"Appreciate it," Butch told him as he shook his hand. "Good to have friends like you."

Butch turned and walked back to the cashier. "Put that man's bill on my tab when he leaves, please. I'll be back later and take care of it."

"Yes, sir," the cashier told him as she made a note on Mikey's bill.

Butch quickly walked out of the restaurant and climbed the fence separating the restaurant from his ranch. The short walk back to his house across the pasture would give him time to go over what he would need to do to get Gene hidden. The issue of Leslie was still unknown, but he would have to wait until he got to Decatur and make contact with Kevin. Speed was crucial, but he had to make sure there were no obvious flaws in the initial plan.

With his background in the military, this was not unlike planning an operation that required secrecy in preparation and execution. His work within the black world of aviation would serve him well in the development of this operation. The worse thing was that the caliber of men he would be opposing would be an enormous obstacle. He held no illusions as to the difficulty and the risks of failure.

Once arriving at his house, he entered the back door and hung his hat on the handmade horseshoe hat rack. He noticed the blade of grass was no longer against the screen door, but knew it would have been displaced by the girls coming in. Continuing into the house, he walked into the living room where the girls were watching the news on television.

"Daddy," Mischelle told him, "they're still showing pictures of Gene and calling him a terrorist."

"I know, don't worry about that any more. We've done all we can, and there's nothing more we can do. You guys ready to get over to Lewisville?"

"You bet," Jeannie said, leaping up from Butch's recliner. "You got the money, we got the time."

"Worthless urchins," Butch told them as he pulled his money clip from his jean's pocket. "Here's two brand-new, never-been-spent hundred-dollar bills. Try to save some for our supper tonight."

"Never been spent?" Mischelle replied. "How did you get them, print them yourself? If you got them from anywhere else, somebody spent them before."

"I meant, never been spent by me. The reason I got them was to spend them, and now I'll never get to."

"Whatever," Jeannie said as she handed the truck keys to Butch. "Where are the keys to the Vette?"

"In the middle drawer under the counter. By the way, watch your speed. The speedometer is a little off. It shows about 20 percent slow. If it says fifty, you're going sixty. So just be careful. The cops always seem to think that a 1962 red Corvette is going too fast anyway," Butch told them as he turned the TV off.

"I've got to get busy, so you kids get out of here. Call me when you start home."

Jeannie and Mischelle ran to their bedroom to get their purses and took a couple of minutes to make sure their hair and lipstick were just right. As they were gathering their things, Butch went to one of the drawers under the kitchen counter and pulled a couple of stacks of one-hundred-dollar bills from under a bunch of loose papers. He knew he would need enough money to take care of several purchases, and he couldn't be pulling too much money from his bank accounts. That would probably set off alarms that he wanted to avoid.

As the girls left the house, he heard the engine of the Corvette fire up. As Jeannie backed from under the carport, he heard the unmistakable sound of the wheels spinning in the gravel. Next came the awaited squeal of the tires on the asphalt drive as they speed out toward the road. Butch just shook his head and headed for the back door. As he closed and locked it, he again placed a blade of grass just under the bottom. If the door were to be opened, it would displace the grass and tell him that someone had been in the house.

Climbing into his truck, he placed the two stacks of hundreds under his seat and backed out and started toward the road. Still aware of every car and especially any helicopters, he saw nothing suspicious as he turned onto Farm Road 718 for the short drive to Highway 114. Instead of taking the more scenic route through Boyd and north on 730, he headed east toward Rhome where he would take Highway 287 north to Decatur. It would save at least five minutes going that way, and he wanted to get to Wal-Mart as soon as he could. He didn't want to keep Kevin waiting if he was there. Plus, seeing him would let him know that Leslie was safely hidden for now.

The drive north on 287 proved uneventful, and as he approached the turnoff for Highway 51 and the entrance to Wal-Mart, he had not seen any vehicle following him. As he passed the entrance, he turned into the Tractor Supply parking lot and parked while he continued to watch the traffic pass. After a couple of minutes to make sure there was no one following, he cut across the parking lot toward Wal-Mart. As he drove between the rows of cars, he spotted Kevin's red truck parked almost by itself at the far end from the entrance.

He found a parking spot two rows from Kevin's truck and only slightly closer. Stopping, he sat slowly looking around as several cars came and went. Once satisfied, he got out and locked the truck. The hundred-yard walk to the entrance gave him another opportunity to observe the cars and drivers around him. As he neared the entrance, he turned and walked along the front of the store to the next door down before he entered.

Passing the greeter, obviously a retired fighter pilot, Butch thought, he walked directly toward the Wells Fargo branch office where he knew the ATM was located. As he came closer, he saw Kevin sitting on a bench as if he were waiting for his wife to finish shopping. Butch continued past him and stopped in front of the ATM behind a lady trying to get some money for her shopping.

As soon as he slipped his card into the machine, he felt something brush his foot. Never looking down, he extracted $300 and pulled the receipt from the front. Folding the receipt and placing it into his wallet, he noticed Kevin walking toward the exit. Quickly reaching down, Butch picked up the plastic bag and walked to the other exit and went directly to his truck.

Once in the truck, he dumped seven cell phones onto the passenger seat and started the truck. At least now he knew that Kevin had taken some action regarding Leslie. Exactly what had happened, he did not yet know. After starting the truck, he drove back to the road and made a right turn heading south on Highway 51. About a mile down the road, he pulled into David's Western Wear, the home of National Ropers Supply. He often shopped there and knew that his presence there would appear normal if he was being watched.

As he sat in the parking lot, he picked up each phone and looked at the numbers Kevin had written on each. Selecting the phone with a number 1 written on the face, he dialed the number he saw just below the 1. As the phone began to ring, he watched the traffic passing on the road. Not sure exactly what he needed to be wary of, he still tried to tell if any one car or truck seemed out of place or passed by his location repeatedly.

"Go ahead," came the voice over the phone after only a couple of rings.

"Did you get the mare?"

"Yeah, but it didn't go pretty. She was rather hard to load. Once I got her to the corral, I had to leave her tied to the fence. Are you sure you want this particular horse? I'm not sure you want the trouble that she could cause you," Kevin told him as he was heading back to Vashti to check on Leslie.

"I don't really want to be in this horse business at all, Fat Boy. But somebody needs to take care of them. Guess I'm just a dumb-ass to worry about someone else's problems."

"That's always been your problem—you get involved in too many of other people's difficulties. Maybe you ought to take all of your modeling money and retire to the Bahamas."

"Can't do that. At least not now. OK, here's the next step. I'm working on a new location for the gelding I have. He needs lots of pasture, and I think I've found the right spot. Do you remember where we scattered some ashes a couple of years ago? The previous owner of the only bar where I live?"

"I do."

"There is a small camper trailer for sale beside 730 south of where you just left. I need you to buy it and take it home with you. Don't worry about the money, I'll make it right. What do you think about the mare's condition? Can she be trained?" Butch asked as he got out of his truck and walked toward the entrance to David's.

"I think so. Do you know how much I'll need for the camper? I may need to get some more from an ATM."

"I'd guess less than a thousand."

"Not a problem, I've got enough with me for that. Say, I saw something on TV right before I left the house. That sure came as news to me as *we* watched it. That may help," Kevin told him.

"Good, maybe everyone involved in this horse trade needs to know what kind of rodeo we're entering," Butch told him as he entered the store. "For now, knowledge is going to be limited. I'm not exactly sure who has signed up, but there appears to be some pretty tough competition. Whoever it is, we still need to try to win this one. I need you to see if you can at least halter-break that mare. I'll call you later this afternoon on 2. You might need to soak 1 in the horse trough, and it wouldn't hurt if you happened to run over it. Later, Fat Boy."

"Thanks, I think. And watch that Fat Boy talk, I'm not sure I really like you right now," came the answer as Butch hung up the phone and placed it in the left pocket of his Wrangler shirt.

Chapter 9

As General Modelle entered the conference room, everyone there quickly came to attention. Walking to the head of the long polished table, he stood behind the chair as he looked directly at each of the officers standing there.

"First," he began, "let me assure you that there is no plan to replace any one of you here. General Nelson and I have discussed what has happened, and I have talked to the other members of my group back in Washington. We all agree. Now, let's take a seat and continue our efforts to bring Gene back as quickly as possible."

Everyone took their seats and waited for Paul to start the meeting. Regardless of his initial statement, each knew the enormous pressure that was mounting with each passing hour that Gene remained within the civilian community. Each one of them knew that unless positive results were made quickly, Paul's reassurances would evaporate with a single phone call from MJ 12's membership.

"Rick," Paul said as the staff tried to mask their concerns, "bring Mike and I up to date on where we are on looking for the two women and the measures you have taken to monitor them and Mr. North."

"Certainly, sir," Rick began. "Major Fleenor has completed the satellite assignments. I'll ask him to give you the specifics in just a couple of minutes, but it has been assigned and dedicated to our search."

Jerry pulled several sheets of paper from his briefcase and placed them on the table. He also placed the remote control for the television screen that hung at the far end of the room beside his briefcase.

"Colonel Lynch will have completed the necessary steps to encode and transmit the required data to our mobile command vans that we dispatched toward Bowie and Arlington. Those vans are in constant contact with the two teams accompanying them. Karyn will fill in the details following Jerry," Rick continued. "Do you want a briefing on the security issues we discussed earlier?"

"Not at this time," Paul told him. "I think we need to catch the chickens before we worry too much about the locks on the hen house. This implanting program still has me a little concerned, but we'll attack that problem later."

"Yes, sir," Rick told him. "Now, we discussed a way to get close to Mr. North. That seems to be in our best interest with a long-term value in the event we don't find Gene at either of the lady's locations or do not get any useful information from them. However, we must approach the 'friendship' issue with Mr. North very carefully. As we discussed, he will be very suspicious of a chance encounter with someone not immediately associated with the local area."

"I agree," Paul stated. "We definitely need to have someone close to him if he remains involved, and we don't find another avenue to locate Gene. But as you said, that's more the long-term goal, and it could take us weeks, if not months, to gain his confidence. Let's talk about that later. I'm more concerned right now with the location of the ladies and our tracking efforts."

"Jerry," Rick said, "go ahead with you brief."

Major Fleenor passed a couple of sheets around the table and waited as each one of them glanced through the material. He then pointed the remote at the screen and began.

"What you have before you is a depiction of the coverage areas upon which we are concentrating. The actual location of the satellite is directly over the stables where Gene was working. That will give us an almost-perpendicular view of what I believe is the central location of the search area," he told them. "If we determine that Gene is in another location, we can maneuver within a specific area as shown on page 1 of the material I just gave you. Anything outside that area will infringe on other satellites operating over the location."

Jerry then changed the screen to provide the current visual images of the stables as he continued, "As you can see on the screen, we have a perfect view of any activity on this location."

He changed the picture again and continued, "Here is an example of the capabilities this system possesses."

The screen again changed to show a close view of Butch's truck parked in front of the barn. The digital image showed the items in the truck bed with enough clarity to read the label of an empty oil can lying near the front as well as the numerous pieces of pipe, chains, and other material scattered within the bed.

"We have one of the cameras concentrating on Bowie and another on Arlington. Due to the differences in the viewing angles, they will not provide the detail of this one. But they will still be able to read the license plates of any car within the radius of our coverage," Jerry said as he changed the screen several times to show the details available from each camera.

"What about tracking a moving object?" Mike asked.

Jerry changed the screen again and told them, "If you'll turn to page 2 of the handout, I'll show you how we can track and record movement of any specific individual or vehicle."

As the television screen began to show a black Suburban traveling along a four-lane road, he said, "This is the lead of our team on its way to Bowie. From this angle, we can read the license plate from the rear and the data on the lower right corner is the latitude and longitude of the car, as well as its speed and direction of travel in relation to magnetic north."

Everyone paid close attention as the car traveled, passing others and rounding curves. The focal point of the car never changed as the exact location depicted with the scrolling numbers and the direction and speed varied with each turn.

"The actual tracking mechanism uses an infrared system that once is locked to a specific signature that will follow that heat source regardless of where it goes. The slaved imager will remain married to that same source and can be zoomed as shown on the static picture we viewed at the stables," Jerry told them as he turned the screen off.

"We have also planted transmitters on all of Mr. North's vehicles and will do likewise with any others we deem necessary. That will enable us to find them if we have not previously obtained an infrared lock. That will give the satellite's imagers a location to hunt for the lock if we have to change which sensor we need."

"What about the phone taps," Paul asked as he placed his handout back on the table in front of him.

"It has been accomplished," Karyn told him. "In addition to Mr. North and his daughters' phones, we have programmed the computers to search for certain key words used on any phone within the area using specific telephone relay or cell phone towers. For example, any telephone conversation using the words *alien, Gene, Leslie, Butch,* or any of our people of interest will immediately record the call. I have a team that will provide instant review and notification if one appears to be connected with our program. All will be digitally recorded regardless of the content in case we need to reexamine them."

"That all sounds good," Mike told them. "What are you tracking right now, and when does the telephone monitoring program begin?"

Major Fleenor spoke first and told him, "As of right now, we have locks on the lead Suburban of each team as they head toward the listed residences of Leslie and Stacy. That will give us pinpoint accuracy with the initial focus of the imaging cameras. We are also locked onto Mr. North's truck and his Corvette should they become mobile. We also have one additional system trained in the general location of the stables in the event Mr. North attempts to leave in a different vehicle. We can lock that one and still leave the other cars locked onto."

Colonel Lynch followed him by saying, "Our phone taps are currently in operation, and the word search criteria has been entered into the computer. We are trying to refine the breadth of the search to make sure we include enough to obtain the calls we need, but to filter out extraneous information. We have cross-coded to ensure any combination of the key words will not be ignored, but those whose contents don't trigger another programmed criteria will be dropped from monitoring, but still be recorded."

She continued, "You'd be surprised at the number of times the word *alien* is used around the Aurora area. Most of the time it is some

tourist calling home to tell someone that they are standing in front
of the Aurora Cemetery where the alien is supposed to be buried.
To counter that, we are attempting to enact a voice recognition
program that will immediately lock a voice we want to hear and delete
monitoring of any we don't. That will also enable us to intercept a
known voice regardless of the phone that's being used."

"Do you have that capability?" asked Paul her.

"Yes, sir. We do. It's still in the experimental stage right now. We,
meaning our sponsors, have contracted with the civilian world to
develop the program. If I am not mistaken, the initial methodology
came from a piece of material removed from one of the objects
stored up in Area 51. It's not perfected as of yet, but our trials have
shown it to be over 90 percent reliable."

"Well, I'll be damned. There just seems to be no end of what we
can extract from those old crashes," Paul said as he gathered the
papers he had been given. "Well, I better get back on the phone
and let our people in high places know just what we are doing and
how far we have come. Let's take an hour or so off and meet again.
I guess the monitoring systems are tied to your communications
room, Mike?"

"Yes, sir," Mike told him. "Why don't we meet there in an hour?
Karyn and Jerry can bring us up to date on the progress, and
hopefully we will have located our very interesting ladies."

They all stood as General Modelle and General Nelson rose to
leave. Still standing after the door closed behind them, Rick looked
at each and gave a slight smile as he seemed to finally breathe a sigh
of relief. Slowly each gathered their material and somberly left the
room.

TM

Chapter 10

"Hey, Ronald," Butch said as he walked into the tack shop of the store. "I need some roping gloves. What do you have for a poor ol' cowboy with no money?"

"Afternoon, Butch," came the reply. "The way you rope, you don't need gloves. You have to catch one before you worry about the rope burning your hands. How long has it been since you managed to get a head loop on a set of horns anyway?"

"Well, I managed to hit close to 90 percent the other day. Not too bad for an old man," Butch said as he glanced out of the window toward the parking lot where his truck sat.

"Sure," Ronald joked. "I'm not talking about that roping dummy you have sitting in the yard. I mean a four-legged running steer."

"Guess that's been a while," Butch acknowledged. "It's either been too wet in the arena, my horses are lame, or the cattle have gotten too big. I just can't seem to string enough days together to practice much. Now, if you don't mind taking care of business instead of berating my roping, where are the gloves?"

"Right in front of you, if you can still see. Do you need to borrow my glasses?"

"Nope, just wanting a little special customer assistance. I am special, you know," Butch said as he picked up the package of cotton gloves.

"Yes, you are special," Ronald laughed as Butch walked to the counter to pay. "At least that's what the school you attended said. Special Education."

"You're a funny guy," Butch said as he paid and got his change. "I think I'll start shopping somewhere folks don't make fun of me. I have enough trouble getting my kids to be nice to me. I don't need harassment from anybody else."

"Hell, there isn't a store within fifty miles where people won't make fun of you. They know you too well," Ronald told him as he handed him his change. "Want me to count this out for you, or can you tell the difference between a penny and a dime?"

"I'll just trust you, this time," Butch replied as he pocketed his change and started for the door. "Take care."

"You too. See you next time."

Butch returned to his truck and headed back past Wal-Mart and turned onto 287 headed south. As he passed James Wood Motors, he exited onto 730 south toward Boyd. He needed to confirm that the small camper he had seen a couple of days ago was still for sale. If not, he would have to revise the still-developing plan.

About five miles south of Decatur, he saw the trailer still sitting beside the road with the For Sale sign still taped to the side window. *Not the most luxurious of accommodations,* he thought. *But it will have to do for now.*

Continuing on toward Boyd, the traffic was light and consisted mainly of pickups and the occasional truck hauling thousands of gallons of water to the ever-present drilling rigs probing for the bounty of natural gas located deep beneath the ranch land. Now, just about everywhere you looked, the horizon was cluttered with the spindly towers of each new well.

As he reached Boyd, he made a right turn on 114 and headed west through town. After going through the one stop light in town, he pulled into the parking lot of the Southern Delight Restaurant. Parking and walking in, he saw that almost no one was sitting at the tables eating. Not surprising, given the time of day. He could see Nannette Bost back in the kitchen area as he approached the warming trays behind the glass shields.

"Hey, miss," he called out, "can you spare a little food for a poor, broke, hungry man?"

Nannette looked up and smiled as she saw him. "Sure, mister. We try to help the needy anytime we can. But what you're needing, we don't serve. What can I get you, Butch?"

"Oh, how about a six-piece chicken tender, a biscuit, and some gravy?" he answered.

"I suppose you want your usual Dr Pepper and a jalapeno."

"Of course," he said. "Any meal without a Dr Pepper and a jalapeno would be just eating. When you have them, it's fine dining."

"I'm sure. You gonna eat it here?"

"Nope, don't have the time. Make it to go, please."

"Sure thing, headed somewhere exciting?" Nannette said as she boxed the food.

"You bet," he told her as he walked to the cash register. "I get to go feed horses and clean stalls. How exciting is that?"

"You? Cleaning stalls? Where is your hired hand?" Nannette asked him as she rang up the bill.

"That sorry cuss ran off and left me to do all the work. Hired help nowadays think they get more time off than the boss. Whatever happened to riding for the brand?"

"I know what you mean. I can't seem to get anyone who wants to come to work on time, doesn't complain constantly, and then leaves as soon as they have enough money for their drug use. I'll tell you one thing. Once they do that, I'll never take them back."

"Got that one-strike rule, do you?" Butch asked as he handed her a hundred-dollar bill. "Can you change this, please?"

"Barely, now how do you get off telling me you're poor and broke when you have money in your pocket?" she said as she counted out his change.

"It's not how much money you have that makes you poor. It's how much of it you get to keep after your kids get done with it." He smiled as he took the change.

"Speaking of your kids, how are they? Are they going to get to stay long this time?"

"Well, I'm not sure. With the way the airlines have had to stop flying after the World Trade Center thing, I just don't know. I'm trying to get them home somehow as soon as I can. I can't afford those two beggars around much longer. I *will* need charity if they keep going through my money the way they do," he said as he walked toward the door. "Take care."

"You too. See you next time," she said as she returned to her work.

Butch started the truck and headed back east toward the stables. Again, just the usual pickups, water trucks, and rock haulers were streaming along Highway 114. As he passed the turn to his house, he could see that Mischelle and Jeannie had not gotten home yet.

Turning onto Old Base Road, he noticed a helicopter passing overhead. It wasn't that unusual since numerous helicopters flew through the area every day. With the NAS/JRB located to the south, Care Flight, the Sheriff's department, and the local news people flying around the country, it would be difficult to determine who was who. Especially if they used one of the civilian birds instead of a military one.

Pulling into the stables, he noted that there were no cars around. If no one had come out to ride or check on their horses, Gene should still be safely hidden. As he walked from the truck to the barn doors, he again saw the helicopter pass overhead, this time headed in the opposite direction. Immediately he knew that something wasn't right.

Hurrying down the aisle, he paused only long enough to drop the used cell phone into one of the water buckets hanging in a stall. As he entered the area where Gene was hiding behind the bales of hay, he noticed that the lock was still in place.

"Gene, you still back there?" he asked as he unlocked and opened the sliding cage door.

Gene's head appeared above the front row of bales as he replied, "Yes, sir.

"Anybody been here since I left?" Butch asked as he climbed onto the lowest row of bales.

"No, sir," came the response as Gene slid from behind the hay. "I was starting to worry that you weren't coming back or that you had called someone to come and get me."

"Not yet," Butch told him as he handed him the paper sack containing the food he had brought. "Here, eat this while I bring the horses in and get them fed."

Gene eagerly took the sack and returned to his hiding place. Butch began filling a wheelbarrow with pellets and checking the list of supplements each horse was supposed to get each day.

As he walked through the main barn dumping a scoop of feed into each stall, he pulled the now-wet cell phone from the bucket. Returning down the aisle, he stopped by the tack room and took a hammer from the shelf. Smashing the phone, he picked up the shattered pieces and dropped them into the wastebasket just inside the kitchen area.

Finishing putting the required feed and supplements in all of the outside stalls, he returned the wheelbarrow to its place within the hay storage cage. As he cut the three strands of string that held a bale of hay, he asked, "How's the chicken?"

"Good. I was getting pretty hungry. Do you want me to help you?" Gene asked as he chewed.

"No, I don't want you out of your cozy little room up there. When I finish this, we need to talk some more. I need to know about anything that happened between you and either of those two girls you stayed with when my kids and I left last night," Butch told him as he pushed the load of hay into the barn aisle.

Placing a flake of hay into each rack in the stalls, he continued outside to finish having each stall ready for the horses once he let them in. As he put the hay into the troughs, he again checked the individual watering systems for clean water and proper operation of the floats and the connecting hoses.

Finally, after returning the wheelbarrow to the barn and walking to the gate that connected the stalls to the pasture, he saw all the horses gathering around the entrance to the aisle that led them to their respective stalls.

He opened the gate and let two of the horses run past him before he shut the gate. The remaining horses jockeyed for position as he walked to where each horse was stomping in front of their stall wanting to get to their feed. As he shut the stall gates behind the two horses that had been first, he returned to the pasture entrance to let a couple more in. Sorting the inside horses into pens beside the aisle, he finished locking the stalls before he picked up a lead rope and began taking the remaining horses into the main barn.

As he was taking the last horse through the front doors, he saw a white pickup turn into the drive that lead to the barn. Quickly shutting the stall door on the horse, he hurried down the aisle to where Gene was visible on top of the stack of hay bales.

"Get your ass behind those bales right now! Somebody just drove up. And get that sack and cup out of sight too," Butch told Gene as he turned and headed toward the front where he saw the truck stopping.

As he exited the barn, a man wearing a well-worn felt hat was getting out of the truck. Acting as nonchalant as possible, Butch walked toward him and said, "Howdy. Can I help you?"

"You Butch North?" came the answer.

"Yes, sir. At least what's left of him. How're you doing?"

"Fine, I suppose. The folks over at MD Resort told me you might be able to put up a couple of horses for a day or two. My wife and I are going to be staying there this weekend, and we wanted to do a little riding. My name is Roy, Roy Martinez. My wife, Margarita, is looking over at the cabins to make sure she's happy with them. You know how women are. Gotta have all the comforts," he said as he stuck out his hand.

"Yeah, I know. Sure, we can help you with the horses. You riding locally or headed up to the LBJ Grasslands?" Butch asked as he shook Roy's hand.

"We'd like to ride a little here, if that's all right. The horses haven't been ridden too much lately, and I'd rather have some soft dirt to fall in if they're too spunky. Then, maybe go up to there and ride the trails if the weather cooperates."

"Not a problem," Butch told him as he started walking toward the covered arena. "I've got some stalls by the arena we use for overnight horses. And you're welcome to use any of the facilities while you're here."

Butch let him into the arena area and showed him the row of stalls he would be using. As they continued down the aisle, Roy asked, "What do you charge to stay overnight?"

"It's $20 per night for each horse," Butch told him. "We furnish all the feed, hay, and shavings, unless you want to use your own feed."

"That's reasonable," Roy said as he looked at the arena. "Do I need to make a deposit or anything?"

"Nope," Butch said. "Just when you come out, pay for how many days you'll be staying. When do you think you'll come out?"

"Probably just after noon on Friday," came the answer.

"No problem. I'll have fresh shavings and clean buckets for the feed and water when you get here. Just pick any of these stalls you want, and I'll take care of it."

"How about these two here," Roy asked as they approached the connecting aisle to where the hay and Gene were.

"Sure," Butch told him as he stopped just before the turn into the hay storage area. "Let's go out here, and I'll show you where you can park your trailer."

They turned and walked back down the aisle as they continued to talk about the boarding arrangements and the local trails available to the boarders. Although Butch was sure Gene was safely hidden from sight, he wanted to get Roy out of the barn and on his way. Trying not to appear in any hurry, he pointed out the quarter-mile track and the other areas available for riding on the property. After a few more minutes, Roy stuck his hand out and told him he would be back sometime Friday afternoon.

"Thanks, Roy," Butch told him as the truck started. As soon as Roy had started out of the drive, Butch returned through the barn and went to where Gene was still out of sight.

"OK, Gene," he told him, "let's discuss last night. I need to know exactly everything you told those girls and what happened after I left. If you expect my help, you better tell me everything. Understood?"

"Yes, sir," Gene said as he climbed from behind the bales as sat on the bottom row. "I tell you everything."

TM

Chapter 11

         Kevin immediately took the next turn around after hanging up the phone. Although only a few miles north of Decatur, this latest request from Butch was going to take more time than he wished. He was anxious to get back home and see how Leslie was doing. Maybe by now she would have settled down a little. Seeing what she described as the man she had met on TV and hearing him described as a terrorist had certainly seemed to change her attitude.

    Heading south on 287, he was careful not to speed enough to draw the attention of the numerous Texas Highway Patrol officers that maintained a very visible appearance along this stretch of highway. If there was one thing he didn't need right now, it was further delays or having his license plates broadcast across any police network.

    The traffic was fairly light, and as he crossed beneath Highway 380, he slowed back to 55 mph. The Wise County Sheriff's main office was just a mile down the road, and numerous police cruisers passed through there going back and forth during their normal duties. In addition to the concentration of deputies, the Decatur Police kept a close eye on 287, the main road through Decatur. Not to mention a highway patrol station beside the road.

    As he neared the cutoff for Highway 51 south toward Boyd, he pulled into the used car division of James Wood Motors. Parking

84

and walking into the sales office building, he waved at one of the salesmen that had gotten up to greet him.

"Don't need a car right now," Kevin told the man. "Just need to use your restroom. Hope that's all right?"

"Sure thing," the salesman replied. "If you need anything else, just holler."

Kevin went into the men's room and placed the used cell phone into the sink and turned on the water while he used the urinal against the wall. Finishing, he washed his hands in the still-running water; and after drying them, he turned the water off and picked up the wet phone. He attempted to turn it on a couple of times, and after ensuring that it was not operating, he placed it in his shirt pocket and left the restroom.

"Thanks," he said as he walked toward the exit. "Maybe next time I'll need another truck."

"You're welcome," came the reply. "We'll be glad to help any way we can. Come again."

Kevin climbed back into his truck and pulled back onto the road for the half mile to the 51 exit. As he continued south, he kept watch for the camper Butch had told him to look for. About five miles down the road, he saw it. Sitting along with numerous pickup grill guards, camper tops, and various other car and truck parts, it sure didn't look like something he would want to own. Still, this was what Butch had asked him to get.

As he parked and walked toward the small camper, an elderly man came walking toward him from the brick house beside the used parts displayed on his front yard.

"Howdy, mister," the man told Kevin. "What can I help you with today?"

"Howdy," Kevin replied. "How much for this little camper here? Looks like it might make a reasonable hunting cabin for a place I have leased out around Jacksboro."

"Oh, I guess I'd take $900 for it. She's not real pretty, but there's no leaks and everything works. There's propane tanks for the stove top and the heater. I've checked the electrical system, and it all works too. Open it up, and take a look."

Kevin opened the door and stepped inside. Across the front was a small kitchen table and bench seats that he could tell that it would convert into a bed if necessary. Turning toward the back, there was a small refrigerator and sink on the right side of the camper. On the other side were the stove top and some counter space before it ended at the wall of a very small bathroom. The bathroom had a sink, toilet, and a small shower.

Just past the bathroom was a closet on the left and the door to the bedroom which was standing open. Inside the bedroom was a small bed that would certainly make for cozy sleeping if two people of normal size were to be in it together.

Kevin walked back toward the only door exiting the camper and looked at the well-worn flooring and cheap cabinets. The window coverings appeared to be hastily made from old sheets and towels. "Not quite a honeymoon cottage," he said as he stepped down from the trailer. "But sure good enough for a couple of smelly deer hunters."

"Yes, sir," came the reply. "I bought that old thing back in the fifties for my wife and me. We spent a lot of time down in the Big Bend area on vacation. We just loved to go down there in the winter or stay at Terlingua for the big chili cook-off. You ever go down there?"

"No, sure haven't. But I've heard it's quite a party. Cookers from all over the country," Kevin said as he inspected the tires and the hitch. "I make it to the Boyd cook-off every year, but I can't see driving over a thousand miles for some chili."

"Oh, it's not just the chili, young man. You should go down there sometime. The country's beautiful and lots of interesting people. Hell, one time we drove up to Marfa to see if we could see those Marfa lights everyone talks about. Supposed to be UFOs or something."

"Really? Did you see anything?" Kevin asked as he continued around the camper.

"Nope," the man laughed. "Me and the missus just sat out there in the middle of nowhere and drank beer. I think that's why those folks see those things. Dark nights and cold beer will make you see lots of things that aren't there."

"I know what you mean," Kevin said as he finished his inspection. "I've seen quite a few beautiful women in the dark while full of beer. The scenery sure changed when the sun came up and I was sober. How about $500 for this poor ol' thing?"

"Can't do that, young man. But I'll knock a hundred off just to give the old girl a new place to live. How's that sound?"

"It's a start. I'll have to get new tires before I pull it over to Jacksboro, that'll cost me at least $100. I'll go as high as $600."

"You sure are trying to get in my pockets. Tell you what. I'll take $700. That's the very best I can do. You know you're going to starve a poor old man, taking advantage of my good nature."

Kevin stood with his hands on his hips as he looked from the camper to the man waiting for his answer. "Sir, there's nothing I'd like better than to stand here and bargain with you. But I've got to get back to work. I can give you $650 in cash and tow this pretty little camper off right now. How about it?"

The old man scratched the grey stubble decorating his face with one hand and stared at Kevin. "You sure drive a hard bargain, young man. If my poor old bones would let me, I'd still be hauling this thing down to the Big Bend country and live out my last days in the warm sunshine. But since the missus has passed and I'm too old to do it alone, guess I'm stuck here dickering with yahoos like you."

Kevin smiled at the man's sales technique and reached into his jean's pocket. Pulling his money clip out, he peeled seven one-hundred-dollar bills off and handed them to him. "Mister, you're skinning me like a rabbit, but I'm in a hurry today. Here's your $700. I don't guess you have a set of trailer tags or a title, do you?"

Pocketing the money, he told Kevin, "Got some farm trailer tags that are only a couple of years' out-of-date. No title, haven't seen that since I bought this thing. It that a problem?"

"No, not really," Kevin said as he walked toward his truck. "Just help me get hitched and toss the tags into the bed. I'll stick to the farm roads when I leave. Most of the trailers out here haven't seen new tags since the first ones they had."

Kevin backed his truck as the old man guided him to get the hitch directly over the ball on the heavy-duty receiver mounted beneath the bumper. As he stopped at the signal, he set the parking brake and walked to the rear. After lowering the trailer and locking the hitch, he shook hands and said, "Thanks, mister. I may just come back one of these days and get one of those grill guards, if you don't try to rob me like you did this time."

Shaking his hand, the old man grinned and told him, "You come on back any time, young man. Been a real pleasure. Take it slow on those back roads, those old tires won't hold together with too much speed over some of that gravel you'll run across."

"I'll certainly do that, sir," Kevin replied as climbed into the truck. You have a good day, and I'll look forward to seeing you again."

Heading back north on 730, he knew he could never make it going through Decatur with no tags, and probably no brake lights. There were several roads that would lead him west before he reached the city limits, and from there, he knew several back roads that would lead him back to Vashti. As he turned onto a narrow dirt road that would help him circumnavigate his way home, he stopped and took the used cell phone from his pocket. After placing on the rear bumper of his truck, he took a hammer from within the bed and smashed the phone several times. Gathering up the pieces, he walked to the shallow drainage ditch running beside the road. Using the claws of the hammer, he dug a small hole and placed the remains of the phone in it and covered it.

Using the back roads would take at least an extra thirty minutes, but he would probably be unnoticed along the way. Traffic, if any, would be ranchers or hired help; and the dust he stirred up as he drove would prevent anyone from seeing who he was. Still, he wanted to avoid any further contact with anyone until he found out just what sort of problems Butch was going to cause him.

Chapter 12

          Major Jerry Fleenor was on the phone when General Modelle entered the communications room after spending more time discussing the situation with his counterparts of MJ 12 back in Washington DC. As he entered the room, he could see several screens of the monitor board depicting views of residential districts and others of vehicles both moving and parked.

    Colonel Karyn Lynch was busy talking to General Nelson as she pointed to one of the screens. The image in question was concentrated on a neighborhood of numerous average brick homes with the normal yards and trees. Centered within the image was a house where a small white car was parked just outside of the garage and two black Suburbans were located on the street in front.

    "How're things going?" he asked as he approached the screens.

    "Our Bowie team just arrived, sir," Karyn told him. "As you can see, they are just now approaching the door."

    As they watched, one man exited each of the Suburbans and walked up the sidewalk leading to the front door. Major Fleenor turned to watch with them, and as he spoke into the phone, the image zoomed in to show distinctly the men's faces and the closed door. After ringing the doorbell and waiting, the men rang it again and simultaneously knocked on the door.

After a few seconds, one of the team left the door and walked around the house, peering into the windows as he went. Returning after completing his examination of the rest of the house, he spoke into the transmitter now in his hand. His voice sounded over the conference room speakers as he stated that no one appeared to be home and they were attempting to call the listed phone number.

A white van marked with the logo of a satellite television installer pulled into the driveway beside the parked car. As a sliding door opened, a man in grey coveralls exited the van and walked to the front door and spoke briefly to the two black-suited men that had preceded him. As they watched, the man in coveralls pulled a small leather case from his back pocket and began to work on the lock of the door. Shortly, he pushed the door open and stepped back. As the first two men entered the house, he walked back to the van and entered, closing the door behind him.

After only a few minutes, the speakers told the results, there was nobody home. As the two men closed the door and returned to their cars, the phone conspicuously sitting on the table in front of the screen displays rang.

Karyn picked it up after the second ring and said, "Colonel Lynch." As she listened she looked from the screen back to Mike.

"Thanks," she told the caller and hung up the phone.

"What did they find?" asked Rick as he rose from his chair where he had been busy on a computer.

"Well," Karyn reported, "as you heard, there was no one home. However, it appears that the bed had been slept in or left unmade from a previous night. There was a purse sitting on a coffee table in the living room and a jacket lying on the couch."

"What does the team think?" asked Paul.

"They think that Leslie was there within the last few hours, but unless she has another car, she must have left with someone else. It is possible that the other woman, Stacy, spent the night, and they left together this morning prior to our arrival," Karyn told him as she moved to look at another screen.

"This image is of Arlington where Stacy is supposed to live. That team should be arriving within a few minutes," she continued as one of the screens showed the progress of the black Suburbans followed by another white van identical to the one back in Bowie.

Glancing from one screen to another, they followed the progress of the vehicles as they wound through the residential streets. Finally arriving at the reported location, the overhead view zoomed to the house they were interested in. The garage door appeared closed, and there was no noticeable activity around the house.

As the Suburbans parked along the street, the van remained out of view somewhere behind them. The doors of the cars opened, and two men walked to the front door. After ringing the bell, the door opened, and a woman dressed in blue jeans and a sweatshirt stood before them.

They could monitor the conversation over the speakers dedicated to each team's transmitters as they asked her if she was Stacy Hyden. As they listened to the conversation, Rick asked General Nelson if he thought they should pick her up.

"Let's see what she has to say first," Mike told him as he watched the scene unfold before them.

After confirming that she was indeed Stacy, the team asked her if Leslie Barber was with her. Hearing that Leslie was not there and now knowing that Stacy had not spent the night in Bowie, Rick picked up a phone and tried to call the Bowie team again. As soon as he made contact, he told them, "Go back into the house and do a detailed inspection. Your subject may have left something that will help us locate her. Make sure you leave no traces of being there, but be damned sure you don't miss anything."

"Does Ms. Barber have another car?" Paul asked as he watched the Bowie team return to Leslie's door with the man in coveralls.

"None on record, sir," Jerry told them. "Our search of the Texas Motor Vehicle records only show one car registered to her. Unless it is a recent purchase and not yet registered, she has only the one white car parked in the driveway. We confirmed the tags after the digital image of the car first became available."

As they watched, the team reopened the door and entered the house. They could hear their movement as they searched the rooms, and after a few minutes, one of the team informed them that he had found a business card that might be of interest.

Leaving the house, the agent walked to the van and entered the open sliding door. Almost immediately the phone began to ring, and Karyn answered it before it could make a second ring.

"What did you find?" she asked.

After listening for a couple of seconds, she said, "Leave the card with the van. They can scan it and send it here. I want it physically brought here after you leave, but I want to see the information immediately."

After hanging up, they watched the agent return to the house to finish their search. As they continued to watch the Bowie screens, the computer on Jerry's desk lit up with a picture of the business card they had found. Clearly visible was the front of the card belonging to the Equestrian Center of Aurora Vista with Butch North's name and the phone numbers associated with the stables.

Next came a view of the back of the card where they saw two phone numbers handwritten. They did not need a directory to know that the two numbers belonged to Butch North. One was his home phone number, and the other was for his cell phone.

"Son-of-a-bitch," Mike said as he looked at the computer monitor. "Why did that bastard give her his phone numbers? And when?"

"He may have given it to them at Red's last night," Paul told him. "But why didn't he mention that when we talked to him this morning?"

"One thing is for sure," Rick told them. "Butch either gave her the card because he knows something we don't or expected her to contact him."

"It could be that it was completely innocent," Karyn said. "Maybe he just gave it to them in case they were going out to Red's again. Or maybe he hoped for something more romantic than sinister."

"It doesn't matter. Either way, Mr. North didn't tell us everything about that night. I think we better have another conversation with him, and maybe just be a little more forceful than we were last time," Mike replied. "It's beginning to look like he may be more involved than he lets on."

"Let's not bet on that horse before we see the vet's report," Paul told him. "Where are we on placing a transmitter on his truck?"

"We put a transponder with an exact location transmitter on it while it was parked at Tater Junction. We also inserted a voice transmitter beneath the dash," Jerry told him. "We will be able to monitor any movement within less than three feet of his location at all times. We can also hear any conversations taking place within the truck."

"And his house, have we wired it also?" Paul asked.

"Yes, sir," Jerry told him, "we had several placed within the house at the same time we did the truck. They will pick up any conversations in any room of the house."

"Good," Paul responded. "Make sure we have good recordings of any of his conversations. I want to know anyone he calls as soon as contact is made. He may be using any of his friends to help him and may not be letting them know what they are getting into."

"What about Stacy?" Rick asked. "Should we bring her in?"

"I don't think so," Mike told him. "If we don't locate Leslie within an hour or so, we'll get back to her with some more questions. Maybe tell her that Leslie is missing and we're part of the investigation that's trying to find her. I don't want to arouse her suspicions at this point. Make sure we have some way of monitoring her phones and her movements though."

"Should we involve the Montague County Sheriff?" Karyn asked. "We can phone in a missing person report and make sure they are on the lookout for her. It will also help establish a cover story in case we find her and she still has Gene."

"That's a good idea," Mike told her. "It will also help to have the local Bowie police to call Stacy later to establish the story with her. Then when we question her again, she'll certainly believe that we are just trying to find a missing person."

"I agree," Paul told them. "For now, let's make sure we keep a real close eye on Mr. North. Keep those cameras trained on his two vehicles, and don't miss a word of any of his conversations."

TM

Chapter 13

Gene sat on one of the hay bales as he began to tell Butch of what he knew of his past. Telling him about the rooms where he had grown up and his relationship with Vicki Grubbs and how she had taken him from the facility. Butch asked very few questions as he listened to the story. Finally after Gene had finished, Butch got up and walked around the area in front of the storage cage.

"Tell me again about the testing," Butch said. "Did you ever hear them say what they were looking for?"

"No," Gene replied. "They never actually told me anything, but I know they were expecting me to know something that I don't think I knew. I had watched some programs on ESP and stuff and read about people who could tell what was on a card they couldn't see. But I never really believed that."

"What about those trips you say they took you on? What were they showing you?" Butch asked.

"Those came more in the last couple of years," Gene told him. "Most of the testing stuff was earlier, but we made more trips as I got older. Although they never told me what I was looking at, they kept asking me if I knew what something did or what it was."

"You're referring to the things you saw after you had been taken from the facility and flew for a couple of hours during the night, aren't you?"

"Yes, sir," Gene answered, "although a few times they would bring something in for me to look at. I remember once they had some clear wire or something. It looked like a bundle of small flexible plastic connected to a metal box. They turned on a switch on the box, and the wires would glow in different colors that changed as they moved a dial."

"Did they bring anything else that you remember?" Butch asked.

"Sometimes it was something that looked like a remote for a television or maybe a video recorder. They would show it to me and asked if I knew what it did. They would try to make it work by pressing buttons or moving the knobs, but I never saw it do anything. Once I felt a kind of buzz, kind of like a vibration. When I told them that, they seemed interested, but when I asked if they felt it, they changed the subject."

"What about having talked to Vicki about the alien thing?" Butch asked as he returned to sit beside Gene.

"Like I told you, she seldom mentioned it. When she said something about it, I thought she meant like the Mexicans or something. You know, illegal aliens."

"What made you come out here?" Butch asked him. "Were you aware of any reason to go north instead of another direction?"

"Not really. When Vicki dropped me off at the place where Mr. Downey found me, I didn't know where I was but just looking for any way to leave as Vicki told me."

"What about after, when I brought you up here? Anything strange about that?" Butch asked again.

"Nothing definite," Gene answered. "But sometimes I get this feeling. Kind of like feeling that I have been here before, but I know I haven't. Sort of like I keep expecting to see something or someone I should know. I don't really know how to explain it."

"Back to your trips, you say you always got in the airplane that was in a hangar. And that it was always at night. Who was flying the airplane, was it people you knew?"

"I never really saw the pilots. But the airplane was always in the hangar that we got to from the elevator, and it was always at night, about the same time."

Butch sat for a moment, thinking. It sure reminded him of a program he had been involved with while stationed in California.

While there, he had known about the development of the F-117 and the training of its pilots. That program had required moving men and material from Air Force Plant 42, located in the Mojave Desert just south of Edwards AFB, to a remote site reported to be in Area 51. Each of the flights were arranged to be during the night when there was little or no moon in the sky above. It was also coordinated to avoid known satellite coverage. That extremely black program existed for several years before public knowledge finally occurred.

"Did they ever tell you that you might need special treatment in case of an accident?" Butch asked as he again stood and began pacing.

"No, but only certain doctors or nurses ever saw me. I really never got hurt or sick."

Butch stopped in front of Gene and stood looking at him for few seconds. Now he was sure that Gene had no ties to the bunch of radical Islamists or any terrorist group. The entire story he had seen on the news and had been told during his interview was proving to be a lie. Although he didn't fully understand the situation, he was positive that Gene had to be moved, and it had to be soon. His initial plan to hide him on Mikey's ranch seemed to still be the best option for now. He needed to contact Kevin and make sure the camper trailer would be in position as soon as he could devise a way to move Gene without being seen.

Even more than before, he was positive that he would be closely watched and needed to try to get his girls away from here as quickly as possible. If there was going to be any trouble, and he was just as sure that it would be sooner or later, he did not want them involved.

"Gene," Butch said, looking directly into his eyes, "I'm not sure what is going on. But I believe you. Right now those people Vicki thought would be after you are watching this place and more than likely looking for those girls you met. Is there anything that happened that night after I left? I thought I saw you go out to a car in the parking lot before I drove off."

Gene lowered his eyes and sat silently for a couple of minutes. Finally he confessed, "Yeah, something happened."

"What?" Butch asked.

"The one named Leslie, you know, the one having the birthday? She said she wanted a special present. Then she whispered something to Stacy, and they both started laughing. She stuck her hand out toward me and told me she was going to get a great present and give me one too."

"Is that when you went outside?" Butch asked, already knowing where this was headed. If he was correct, Gene had joined the infamous parking lot club.

"Yes," Gene mumbled. "She took me to the car, and we started kissing. Not like when Vicki kissed me or held me. This was a lot different. It really felt strange. Good, but strange. Then, she put my hand on her breast and started rubbing me between the legs."

Butch slightly smiled as he listened to this account of another man's first sexual encounter. He could still remember the first time he had been introduced to a girl's pleasure. Years long past, but the memory was indelibly etched into his memory. He needed to know if they had actually had sex, but hesitated in asking so personal a question.

"Did you take your clothes off?" Butch asked, trying to keep a smile from showing on his face.

"We both did," Gene answered, his head still hanging down. "She took off her shirt and pushed my face to her breasts. Then she started unzipping my pants. Before I knew it, we were naked."

Gene finally raised his head and looked at Butch. "I didn't know what to do. She just kept on doing things. I liked it, but before I knew it, we were naked lying in the backseat. Then she got on top of me and stuck me in her. It didn't last long, but all of a sudden she started smiling. Then she said, 'Kind of a quick shot, aren't you little cowboy?'"

"Anything else?" Butch asked, just barely able to keep from laughing.

"Yeah, we lay there for a couple of minutes, and she started kissing me again and playing with me. Then, she made me get on top, and we did it again. After that, she started putting her clothes on and told me to get dressed. As soon as I had my clothes on, we went back into the bar."

Gene lowered his head again and said, "I know what we did. I didn't mean for that to happen, but I couldn't stop once she started."

Butch shook his head and put his hand on Gene's shoulder. Trying to sound like a father to his son, he told him, "Don't worry about it. That's almost the same thing that happened to me a long time ago. But now I know that we've got to get you away from here as soon as possible, and I have to find Leslie. Those people looking for you will really want to find her if they ever learn about this. Make sure you never tell anyone about your little backseat adventure if you're ever caught. You can't let anyone know about that. Do you understand?"

"Yes, sir," came the reply. "I know all about girl's reputations and how you're supposed to be married and stuff. I promise I'll never say a word."

Butch shook his head and smiled as he said, "It's not so much her reputation. And I doubt that she had any intention of marrying. The real problem is if the people back at your old home find out. If what I'm beginning to think is true, Leslie could be in more trouble than you can imagine."

Gene raised his head and looked up. "I'm so sorry. I never meant for her to get into trouble. She just seemed determine to do that, and although I really liked it, I wouldn't have tried anything. She seems like such a nice girl. I really liked her."

"Yeah, you can say you really liked her, at least twice," Butch replied, almost bursting trying not to laugh. "But the fact remains that there will be intense interest in that lady if anyone ever finds out about how much you *liked* her. For now, you just stay hidden, and I'll see if I can't figure out how to get you off this property without being spotted. Just sit tight, and I'll be back as soon as I take care of a few things."

Gene climbed back to the top of the bales of hay and crawled behind the front row. Locking the cage doors, Butch walked back down the aisle of the main barn toward his parked truck. He knew now more than ever that time was running out. Not only did he have to find a way to hide Gene, he would have to make sure that Leslie was never found. Although he wanted no one else involved, getting Gene from the stables to the camper when it was parked would require at least one additional person. And he knew just the right person for the job.

He got into his truck and started the engine. As he pulled out of the drive and onto Old Base Road, he pulled his cell phone from its case on his belt. Selecting the number he needed, he called Levi Wilson, owner of Southwest Hay Exchange.

TM

Chapter 14

       Kevin wound his way through the back roads that he had traveled often over the past several years. There were occasions when the unfortunate deer just *happened* to attack his truck during the early-evening darkness. It was usually fortunate that he always carried an old 30-30 Winchester that had once belonged to his father. It was on those *rare* occasions that he would have to defend himself and protect his truck. Of course a little fresh back strap on the grill erased most of the remorse he sometimes felt.

    Out here, the game warden was the most likely law official that you would run into. This part of the country was still considered remote, and the dirt roads ran through wildly overgrown post oak and briar. You would be lucky if you could see over fifty feet from the road into the heavy brush that lined each side. It was not abnormal to see forty or fifty deer crossing the road soon after sundown.

    As he pulled across the cattle guard that lay on his property line between the stretches of fence that followed the line around his place, he stopped and watched the road behind him. The dust from his travel still hung heavy in the air, making visibility down the road less than half of a mile. After a few minutes of seeing no dust rising down the road, he continued around the curving driveway to where his house lay virtually invisible from outside of his property.

He stopped well short of the garage to leave room to turn the camper around when he needed to leave. Leaving the truck unlocked, he hit the garage opener and took his remaining phones into the house with him.

"Honey, I'm home," he called out as he closed the door connecting the house to the garage. "What's for dinner?"

Leslie was still taped in place where he had left her. He could tell that she had not even tried to move the chair. That indicated that she had either given up or had decided to hear what was going on. Either way, it was a good sign. He had half expected to see her lying on her side, struggling to extract herself from the chair.

"Well," he began, "are you ready to listen?"

"Yes," came the reply as Leslie turned and looked at him. "I'm not sure what is going on, but you must think that I'm connected with some terrorist group."

"No, nothing like that," Kevin told her as he pulled a chair from the kitchen and sat facing her. "What I think is that somehow you got mixed up in something that you weren't aware of. What can you tell me about meeting Butch and Gene?"

"Well, Stacy and I went out to Red's to celebrate my birthday. We always get together for our birthdays, and since it was mine, she came and picked me up. That's where we met Butch and his daughters and Gene."

Kevin watched her eyes as she talked. Over the years, he had developed his own version of a lie detector. It had worked very well when he had done some field interrogation during his tours in Vietnam. Even back in the civilized world, it helped when dealing with cattle buyers or horse traders.

"What happened there?" he asked.

"Nothing really, we just danced and drank. You know. Just celebrating."

"Did you leave with Butch or any of them?" Kevin asked, wondering just how well his friend Butch knew this girl. He knew that Butch had an eye for the ladies, but this one didn't seem to fit the standard profile. Plus, having his daughters with him usually meant that he would pretty much behave himself.

"No," Leslie said, "we just stayed there pretty late, and then we came home."

The slight hesitation in her voice told Kevin that there was much more to the story than this first rendition. "Really, then where was this other lady when I came to your house?"

"Oh, she dropped me off and went home."

"And what about Gene?" Kevin asked as he leaned forward to place his face directly in front of hers. "Did he leave with Butch?"

"Uh, no, he kind of came with us," Leslie said as she lowered her head. "Stacy took him back home early this morning when she went back."

"Stacy took him home with her?" Kevin asked with a tone of unbelief in his voice.

"I don't mean home with her. I meant she took him to his place on her way home," she replied, still holding her head down.

"I think there's probably a lot more to this story than you're telling me. But I don't really care about that," Kevin said as he rose from his chair. "I guess Butch knows that Stacy was involved also, so I better make sure he has a plan to get her somewhere safe too."

Kevin pulled a couple of cell phones from his bag and selected the one marked number 2. Dialing the number he had written on the face, he waited as it rang. The television still replayed the pictures of a man dressed in Middle Eastern attire and showed the picture he had come to know as Gene beside it. If he hadn't known better, he would have sworn that Gene was indeed the purported rag-head that was attempting to hijack another airplane as the other assholes had done.

Finally hearing an answer, he said, "Hey, good buddy. What have you gotten into? And more importantly, what have you gotten me into? This horse business may ruin me."

He listened for a couple of minutes and then responded to the question he had been asked, "Yeah, I got it. It's here at my house as we speak. And as we speak, that mare sure has settled down. I'd like to see her pedigree—I'd bet it is real interesting. I don't suppose you'd care to share that little bit of knowledge, would you?"

As he spoke, he would occasionally glance to where Leslie was quietly watching the news and shake her head every time Gene was shown or there was a mention of the hunt for him.

"Yeah, I can take the mare in my trailer out to the ranch. Where do you want to stable her?" Kevin spoke into the phone.

A couple of seconds later, he said, "Sure, I remember who you're talking about. We had this conversation just a short while ago, are you getting senile?"

Still smiling, he replied, "Yeah, I can get the number. Does he know I'm coming?"

Kevin listened for another minute or two and told Butch, "OK, I'll load up and head over there. I'll call again when I have the mare unloaded and stabled for the night. By the way, I'm sure you know that there is another mare available."

He listened as he heard Butch explain why he couldn't take care of that one, he knew nobody he could trust there, and he sure couldn't take the chance of trying it by himself. She would just have to make it on her own.

"All right," Kevin finally said. "I guess you're right, but that may cause some problems later. You know how those mares are when they are separated. Anyway, I'll call you when I'm done with this little chore. Why the hell don't you just get out of the horse business? It sure is causing you a lot of problems, and me."

Kevin disconnected the call and walked into the kitchen. Filling the sink with a couple of inches of water, he held the phone under for several minutes while he thought of how to get Leslie and the trailer out to Post Oak and Mikey Carmichael's place. Getting there would be no problem; he'd use the same back roads he had taken to get home. The real problem was in the timing. He didn't want to be sitting around some rancher's land. Lots of these old ranchers would be more than helpful if need be. But you certainly didn't want to cross the property line uninvited.

Taking the wet phone from the sink, he turned to Leslie and asked, "Do you think you can at least behave now? I told you I wasn't going to hurt you, and it was for your safety. Do you believe me know?"

Leslie turned and looked at him. "Maybe, I'm still not sure what is going on, but at least I know you aren't trying to hurt me. I still don't understand why they think Gene is a terrorist. I sure don't believe that."

"I don't either," Kevin said as he sat down in front of her again. "Neither does Butch. I don't have the entire story, and I may never hear all of it, but he thinks the same people that are looking for Gene are looking for you. Probably looking for your friend Stacy too.

Right now, all I need from you is a promise that you'll at least trust me and do as I ask. Believe me, I don't want to be involved either. But a very good friend of mine asked me to help, and something has him concerned for your safety."

"Why does Butch think I'm in trouble?"

"He hasn't told me. But I know that I saw those black cars I told you about as we were leaving your house. And I know that Butch said that it has something to do with the government. From that, I'd say that those people certainly have an interest in you, probably wanting to know how you know Gene. That appears to be the only tie to you. Just how they know about you, I'm not sure."

"What do you plan to do now?" Leslie asked.

"I bought a camper that Butch asked me to get," Kevin replied. "He has made some sort of arrangement with another friend to park the camper on his ranch and wants me to take you there and get everything set up. But as I said, I need your promise that you won't cause any more problems."

"Where are you taking me?" she asked.

"There's a ranch a few miles from here where we'll park the camper," he told her. "It's not the prettiest thing, but at least you'll be hidden until Butch finds better arrangements. This ranch is owned by another of his friends, and I'm sure it will be well hidden. There's some pretty rough country out there. And lots of rattlesnakes. So I wouldn't try to sneak off if I were you."

"How long do you think I'll have to stay there? Can I at least call my mom or Stacy?" Leslie asked.

"Not a chance. Butch is pretty sure he is being watched, and he made me get throwaway phones so we can talk. If anyone else finds out where you are, all of us will be in trouble. When we leave here, the only people you will probably see are Butch and me. Again, do you think you can behave, or do I have to keep you taped and carry you?"

"I guess I'll do as you ask, but I want to find out why somebody is after me. I don't know how they found out or why they would think that I have anything to do with that terrorist thing," Leslie told him.

"Maybe Butch will let you know when he can. For now, I'll cut the tape loose, and we'll try to get out to Post Oak without being seen," he said as he started removing the tape that held her to the chair.

"Just remember, I'll smack you in the head and put you to sleep if you try anything."

Kevin finished setting Leslie free and began loading cans of food and drinks into bags. As he gathered up all the things he thought she would need for a few days, she came walking into the kitchen with several rolls of toilet paper and some soap. Placing them into another bag, she told him that she would need toothpaste, a brush, and hopefully a couple of T-shirts.

They finally carried several bags to the trailer and loaded them inside. Kevin found two full bottles of butane for the heater and stove which he put in the bed of his truck. Loaded at last, they climbed into the truck and started out toward the road that would take them to the next hiding place.

Chapter 15

Colonel Lynch was on the phone while everyone else watched the screens depicting the movement of their teams and the truck belonging to Butch North. Every screen on the display wall showed a different location or vehicle movement. Karyn replaced the phone and turned toward the group.

"Well, we may have a problem," she told them. "We've received information regarding a conversation Mr. North had while we tracked him in Decatur. As you recall, the transmitter we placed in his truck monitors all of his conversations. The tap we put on his cell phones monitors those. In this case, we listened to a conversation within the truck that appears to be a phone call, but it was not on his personal phone."

"Exactly what are you getting at?" Rick asked as he turned to look at the screen showing Butch's truck still sitting at the stables.

"It appears that he was using another cell phone," Karyn answered. "Either he has another phone that we are unaware of or he borrowed someone else's."

"Is it possible that he was talking to someone standing outside of the truck?" asked Mike.

"No, sir," answered Major Fleenor. "We looked at the images that match the time of the conversation, and there is no one around his truck. If you would like to see it, I can rerun the images and play the conversation simultaneously."

"I think we better take a closer look at it," Paul told him as he turned to look at Jerry and Karyn.

Both Karyn and Jerry picked up the phones they were using and relayed their requests. "Recorded images will be coming onto the lower right screen in just a minute," Jerry told them as he replaced his phone.

Almost immediately the scene showing Butch's truck stopping at David's Western Wear began appearing on the screen. As it parked, it froze with a date and time stamp flashing on the image. Karyn read the time codes measured in hundredths of a second into her phone and waited.

A few seconds passed as they waited for the voice recorder to synchronize with the digital image. As the image once again showed movement within the area, the speaker beneath the screen clearly provided the conversation they were concerned with. Listening to Butch asking whether or not a mare had been found and further conversation regarding a gelding, everyone watching remained quiet. As soon as the conversation ended, they watched Butch get out of his truck and walk to the entrance of the store.

"What do you think he is referring to about the mare or gelding?" Paul asked.

Mike looked from the screen to General Modelle and told him, "It could be something to do with the stables. Possibly some horses that are coming out to board or maybe he's locating potential purchases for someone."

Karyn shook her head and said, "I don't think so, sir. If you paid close attention, he never spoke any names that would identify either the other person or names of horses. I would be willing to bet that he has developed some code to use."

"Why would he be using a code? It's not like he has to answer to anyone about his activities," Mike told her.

"I'll tell you why," Paul said as he looked at Mike. "That man believes that he is being watched. You saw the way he acted during the interviews. And being suspicious, he is assuming that we will try to get information from him that he didn't want to tell us."

"I'm sure you're correct," Rick answered. "One thing that I noticed toward the end of the conversation was a reference to calling on 2 and soaking 1. I'll bet that when we determine the phone he used, it will turn out to be a prepaid."

"When can you find the number of that phone?" Paul asked Karyn.

"It will take a while," she answered. "We will have to search all of the transmissions that were made through the surrounding towers during the exact time Butch was talking and isolate the numbers involved. Then we can delete any numbers that are known to be registered to other people. We may be able to cross-reference any number provided to prepaid systems."

"If he has resorted to using prepaid numbers," Mike announced, "I believe he will destroy each phone after it is used. That would be consistent with him saying to soak number 1 and call later on number 2."

"Son of a bitch," Paul said, shaking his head. "We've sure underestimated this man. Not only has he found a way to prevent us from hearing his phone calls, he makes sure we can't find out who he is talking to. And that code, I'm sure the mare he is referring to is one of the ladies we are looking for."

"More than likely, it will be Leslie," Rick told them. "I'll bet that he has contacts all over that area. It would be less likely if he knows enough people in Arlington where Stacy lives to attempt contacting her."

"And don't forget that we found one of his business cards in Leslie's house," Mike said. "The fact that she wasn't home and her car was still there tells me that someone beat us to her. If she didn't get the card from Mr. North while at Red's, and we know he didn't go there himself, someone else must have given her the card to convince her that Butch was involved."

"Why would Leslie leave with anyone that she didn't know," Karyn asked. "I don't think any woman would willingly let a man, or woman, that she didn't know take her from her home."

"Let's not discount the people that Mr. North knows in that area," Paul told them. "It's possible that he sent some other woman that knew Leslie to take her away from the house."

"I don't think so," Rick said. "Whoever he was talking to about the mare was most likely a man."

"What makes you think so?" Paul asked.

"He called him Fat Boy," Rick answered.

"That's right," Mike replied.

"What about that remark concerning a trailer somewhere on 730? He told him to buy it. Whoever he is talking to must be a close friend and is willing to spend his own money, trusting he will be repaid," Karyn told them. "Everything points to it being a man that has long ties to Mr. North. Combined with the use of codes for names and using different phones, I'd say that he is trying to locate and remove Leslie."

"We'd better get one of the teams down 730 and see if we can locate this camper he referred to," Paul said. "Let's send one of the Bowie teams as quickly as possible. If we have any luck, we'll find it before it can be moved. We may even catch the man Mr. North is plotting with."

"I'll get them on their way, and I'll have the chopper that's up there swing down South to see if they can locate it," Rick said as he walked to a phone on the desk.

"What do you think he means by *gelding*?" Paul asked while Rick was talking on the phone.

Mike looked again at the screen showing the stables. "I would guess he's talking about Gene."

"Probably so," acknowledged Paul. "If that is true, he must be planning on moving him. That would be why he needs a camper. Now, we need to make sure that we find that camper before it's moved out into the country. It could take months to search every spot in some of that area."

"Don't forget that there are probably hundreds of trailers or campers scattered across thousands of acres up there that are used for hunters during deer season," Rick said after hanging up the phone. "The chopper is headed back to Decatur. He'll pick up 730 toward Boyd and see if he can spot any camper trailers along the road."

"What do we do about Mr. North?" Paul asked. "Do you think we should pick him up again?"

"No, I don't think so for now," Mike told him. "If we go back out there this quick, he'll really suspect something. And if we tip our hand on the surveillance, he'll know for sure we have taps on his phones. He may suspect it, but he may not think about one in his truck. Where is the Corvette now?"

"It has gone east on Highway 114," Jerry told him. "The two daughters left in it shortly after they left Tater Junction. There's a location transmitter on it, but we didn't have a chance to put a microphone inside."

"I'm not too worried about what the girls may be saying," Paul told him. "I'm sure they told us everything they knew. It's Butch I'm concerned with. With all that has happened since we took them home, it seems that he has made a lot of effort in hiding his actions. That tells me he suspects that the terrorist story isn't entirely true."

"Let's just hope that he doesn't find out the real reason we're trying to find Gene," Mike responded. "I know he would have been completely cooperative if it had been a terrorist. I was worried about that aspect of the story when we reviewed his background."

"Well, it's too late to change the story now," Paul said. "Now, we have to catch Butch moving either Gene or Leslie. Without that, we don't have much of a chance in getting him to volunteer any more information."

"What if we went out there and just had a talk with him?" Rick asked. "What if we were honest and told him we needed to find Gene but couldn't tell him why? Do you think he would be more cooperative?"

"I doubt it," Mike told him shaking his head. "Unless we're ready to tell him why we need Gene, I don't think he'll help. Even if we told him the full story, I can't be sure he'd want to help. Let's just concentrate on finding the camper and determining who he's working with."

"I agree," Paul said. "Let's just sit back and see if he makes a mistake. We still don't know where Gene is, but if he is anywhere around Mr. North, we'll soon find out. With the satellite coverage, we can see if anyone comes to the stables and count heads when they leave. If he shows up there, he can't escape without us knowing."

TM

Chapter 16

Butch was headed west on 114 toward Boyd when he finally got Levi Wilson on the phone. "How you doing for good-quality horse hay, Levi?" he asked.

"Oh, you know," Levi told him. "Same excellent stuff I've been selling you for years. How much do you need?"

"That depends on the price," Butch said. "I need about fifty bales of coastal Bermuda and twenty-five of alfalfa. And I expect the family discount."

Levi laughed as he answered, "I think we've got too many members in this family. I don't think any of the five families in New York have as many as we do in the Boyd family. I can't afford to give all of you that discount."

"You think I joined for the goat barbeque? I expect some financial benefits," Butch replied. "When do you think you could deliver?"

"For you, maybe next week. Anybody else I can deliver today, if I don't have to give them any discount," Levi said.

"Next week is too late, I need some today. Those damned horses just seem to eat it as fast as I can buy it," Butch told him. "Are you in town?"

"Yeah, I'm just pulling into Rock Island Express for some diesel."

"I'll meet you there, but if I have to pay $4 a gallon and fill this hog of a truck, I may have to get the hay on credit."

"I think I can trust you for a day or two," Levi said. "I know this gas station wouldn't just take your word that you'd pay. They need folding money and big bills!"

"I hear you. I'll be there in a couple of minutes. Just hang out until I get there. We may have to argue about the delivery charges you keep throwing on my bill."

Butch passed through the stop light at 718 and hurried on into Boyd. After crossing the railroad tracks, he took the first left into the parking lot behind Rock Island Express. Parking his truck, he went into the back entrance and saw Levi sitting having a cup of coffee.

"Another cup of coffee, please," Butch told the attendant at the Subway counter. "Regular and black will be just fine."

As he waited for his coffee, he looked back down the road and glanced around the shopping area. When the coffee was delivered, he pulled his money clip from his jean's pocket and put a dollar on the counter. With his cup in his hand, he walked toward the tables where Levi sat.

"Anything new in town?" Butch asked.

"Not much," Levi told him. "Still one bar full of rock truck drivers. Hell, I haven't seen any new women since you made your daughters move out of town."

"Well, I didn't want them involved with the available single men around here," Butch said, sipping his coffee. "There's as few quality men in this town as there are women. That's why I tend to head east for my romance. I like to have at least one county line between me and them."

"Not to rush you," Levi said, "but I don't have all day like you retired folks. You really need hay today?"

"No, but I do need something today. I need a favor."

"What do you need?" Levi asked looking at Butch.

"I need you to have someone drive a load of hay to the stables, unload about half of it, and take the rest back to your barn."

"Why do you want me to haul hay to you then haul half of it back?"

"I need you to transport something from the barn, and I don't want anyone to know I've done it," Butch told him.

"Just what do you need taken from there?" Levis asked, puzzled.

"I'd rather not say," Butch answered. "You just have to trust me on this. I just need you to send a truck that has plenty of bales, a couple of hundreds, and take 125 or so back. I just want it to look like you sent a large load, gave me the seventy-five I asked for, and took the rest back to your barn."

"I trust you. I guess you have your reasons, no matter how ridiculous it sounds," Levi said, shaking his head. "Anything else?"

"Yeah, once you park the truck, make sure it is inside the barn. Then have the driver leave it there until I see you again. I need you to do it as quickly as you can, preferably within the hour. Can you handle it?"

"I suppose so," Levi answered. "I may have to drive it myself though."

"I'd rather you get one of your drivers. It would help if that driver was sent to California or wherever for a load immediately after he parks the truck in the barn."

"I don't suppose you're going to tell me anything more about this, are you?"

"Not right now," Butch said. "One more thing I'll need."

"Oh boy, what now?"

"I don't want anyone around that truck until I say it's OK. There will be a pickup come by as soon as I can arrange it to take care of the package. Just make sure no one stops him. Let's just say he works for me."

Levi looked Butch in the eyes and said, "Let me see if I have this correct. I'm to send a driver with two-hundred-plus bales of hay to your barn, unload seventy-five, drive the rest back to my barn, park the truck inside, leave it, and then take another truck somewhere to get more hay. And I'm not to let anyone get near the truck except a pickup that you send. Have I got it right?"

"Pretty much," Butch said nodding. "Just make sure your driver backs the trailer under the roof at my place to unload. I'll be there to help. Think you can do it?"

Levi sat his empty cup on the table and stood up. "You know, if I didn't know you so well, I'd think you're smuggling drugs out of that place. Just tell me that isn't true."

"No, no drugs. The horse business doesn't make as much money as drugs probably do, but as least I know the horses' asses when I see them. Thanks, Levi," Butch told him as he finished his coffee and took both empty cups to the trash can beside the door.

"I'll be at the stables waiting for your driver. Thanks again, and I'll probably see you at the bar Friday night."

Butch walked out onto the sidewalk and sat down at one of the outdoor tables. Sitting under the umbrella that shaded the table, he pulled a phone from his pocket. Dialing the number written on the face, he waited for an answer. As he waited, he watched the road and glanced around the sky. Normal traffic continued to flow along 114, and the cars and trucks parked there around his appeared normal.

Just as the phone was answered, he saw a helicopter coming south just over 730 as it intersected 114. Watching it turn back northbound as it circled, he heard Kevin's voice.

"How's it going?" Butch asked.

"Pretty good, all things considered," Kevin replied. "I've got the camper, the mare, some food and stuff, and headed for the ranch. What's up with you?"

"Not too much," Butch said. "I need you to do something else after you get things set up out there. You got a few hours?"

"Oh sure," came the answer, "I've got nothing but money, fine clothes, and time. And I'm beginning to believe that you're taking all of them. When are we going to have a chance to talk about this?"

"Not for a while. We'll have to have a chance meeting in a day or so, somewhere like where you left the bag. For now, I just need you to park the camper, settle the mare down, and drive down here as soon as you can. How long before you can break loose up there?"

"I should be set up on the ranch within the hour. It will take me another hour to drive down there. Where do you want me to go when I get there?"

"You know where I buy my hay?" Butch asked, knowing that Kevin had gone with him before to pick up a few bales.

"Sure."

"There will be a truck parked in the big barn. Within the bales that are on the trailer, you will find a package. I want you to park your truck beside the trailer and get the package stored in your truck before you drive out from inside the barn. Then, go back to the camper and put the package with the mare."

"Is this package what I think it is? Maybe a gelding?"

"Sure is."

"I had a chance to talk to someone on the way to the ranch," Kevin said as he turned into a gravel drive leading onto a thick oak—and briar-covered road. "There may be some things you aren't aware of regarding your package and mine. I really think we need to talk."

"I think I may know what you're referring to. I had a little talk with mine and learned some very interesting facts of life so to speak," Butch told him.

"Sounds like we may be reading the same book," Kevin said as he approached a clearing about one and a half miles from where he had turned in. "Anyway, I've reached the campground, and I'll get things set up. I should be down that way in an hour or less. By the way, this little mare is turning out to be a lot calmer than I originally thought. A certain show on TV seemed to take a lot of starch from her, if you know what I mean."

"I do. Call me when you get the package," Butch told him. "And I guess we'll need a few more phones. See if you can get another ten or so. I'll figure out how to get them later."

"All right. You know, this is starting to be fun," Kevin said. "Reminds me of some good old times. You know, sort of clandestine."

"I know. Talk to you later. Say, why don't you just happen to be at the Avondale VFW tonight? I'm taking the girls, and I know they would like to see you. Might be a chance to talk. I'll be there about nine or so."

"I'll give it a try. See you later."

Butch hung up the phone and slipped it into his shirt pocket. As he stood and walked toward his truck, he saw the same chopper coming back south over 730. Now he was positive he was being watched. Making his decision, he started the truck and headed back toward the stables. As he came to 718, he turned south and then into his driveway.

Leaving the truck running, he walked to the back door and looked. Sure enough, the blade of grass was gone, and this time there should have been nobody around the house. If they had been in the house, he thought, they had probably placed microphones or other devices inside. Turning and looking at his truck, he said, "Shit, they probably wired my truck too."

Shaking his head, he went back to the truck and started back toward the stables. From now on, he would make sure he didn't talk in the truck unless absolutely necessary, and he'd make sure the radio was as loud as possible.

TM

Chapter 17

Kevin pulled out of his drive and turned south down the same gravel road he had traveled while bringing the trailer to his house. The grey dust from the road turned all the vegetation along the sides almost white as it covered the leaves of the trees and vines that covered the land behind the usual barbed wire fences common in this area. Some of the fences had been standing so long that the trees had grown into the barbed wire.

The hackberry trees and briar vines helped to ensure that anything more than fifty feet from the fence was invisible to anyone driving down the road. Even the cattle were so hidden that unless you actually went onto the property, you'd never know they were there.

A great place for the hundreds of deer that lived in the sparsely settled country, and if they didn't come out at night to look for food or water, they were never seen. This part of Texas was well-known for the quantity of deer and wild hogs. Those areas that were unfit for cattle were generally leased to hunters. It was common to see hunting cabins scattered down well-worn trails where small clearings held deer stands and feeders.

Kevin knew that if this camper was seen from the air, it would appear the same as the hundreds of others across North Texas. He knew the area well where he was headed and was positive that was why Butch had picked it. His biggest concern right now was getting there unseen. He would have to join Highway 59 shortly for a mile of so. Although the traffic between Bowie and Jacksboro was usually light, he'd rather have been able to stay entirely on the dirt roads which even the ranchers avoided unless necessary.

After a mile on 59, he made a right turn onto Farm Road 2127 that would take him toward Mikey Carmichael's KC Ranch. He had been there when an old friend's ashes were spread across a small hill deep within the ranch. The memorial had been erected just off the main drive to the ranch house. Both he and Butch had been there as they gave him his last farewell. Everyone attending had toasted their departed friend as they said goodbye.

Three miles down 2127, he saw the dirt road leading to the ranch. There had only been one pickup on the road during the drive, and it was just another of the dusty old trucks that couldn't pass the state inspections and had been placed on the ranches to carry feed or materials around the property. Whoever had been driving that truck was just as keen to be unseen as he had been.

Leslie had been extremely quiet during the ride. She had sat silently on her side of the truck, resigned to her current fate. It appeared that she had finally accepted the fact that she had become involved with someone that the entire United States was looking for. She may not fully trust Kevin right now, but it was a long way from the resistance she had shown when he first arrived at her house. Although it was only a few hours ago, it felt as if it had been years.

Kevin had been worried that if they had seen another vehicle on the road, she might have attempted to draw attention to them, but she showed no signs of wanting to move when the only pickup had met them. He wasn't sure that had been a good sign, but he would have a chance to talk to her more once they got the camper set up.

Still a couple of miles from the ranch, his phone rang. As he looked at the number 3 phone, he pulled slightly to the side of the road and answered it. Looking at Leslie watch him, he said, "What's up?"

Butch was standing just inside the main entrance of the barn, making sure he was completely hidden from anyone flying overhead. Much farther in the metal sides and roof would make it difficult to get a good signal, and he needed to be here when Levi had the hay delivered.

"Not much, how's the move going?" Butch asked as he watched the road.

"Going good, and the mare has really gotten quiet. I think you may want to come see her sometime," Kevin answered as he looked at Leslie. Placing his hand over the phone, he whispered, "It's Butch."

"Not even a chance, my friend," came the response. "I'm afraid that you'll have to tend to that until I can find a buyer. I just hope that those two horses can get along until I do."

"I know what you mean. I'll do what I can, but there's no telling what will happen when you put two horses in the same pen. I have a feeling that these two will come to some arrangement that will work out in the long run," Kevin said, still watching for Leslie's reaction.

"Well, they always seem to sort it out eventually. Have you had a chance to call the head honcho of that place where you're heading?"

"Not yet, he is sure I'm coming, isn't he?" Kevin asked.

"I talked to him earlier and told him you were coming, but I haven't had a chance to smooth out the details. I need you to call him from your real phone and let him know you're helping me. He can tell you exactly where you need to be," Butch told him. "I'd rather not have him involved any more than necessary. All he knows is that I wanted a place to park a trailer for a friend. When you talk to him, just make sure he understands that absolutely no one, including him, should be in that area until we let them."

"I'll relay the message," Kevin said, shaking his head. "Kind of pushing it a little, aren't you? Asking a man to stay off his own property isn't the most polite thing to do."

"I know, but that man understands that I wouldn't ask unless it was absolutely necessary," Butch acknowledged. "And I'm sure he will make me do some horrible favor for him someday just to get even. Hell, he may even make me dance with that crazy ex-wife of his."

Kevin smiled as he nodded and said, "I know exactly which one you're talking about. Not to change the subject, but is the other package ready?"

"It will be when you get there. Have you explained the situation up there?"

"Not yet, I've been waiting until we get settled," Kevin answered as he looked at Leslie again. "I'll do what I can."

"Good," Butch told him. "I've got to get busy down here for the next step. Make sure you get more phones. We're going through these faster than a fat woman goes through a dozen doughnuts."

"OK." Kevin smiled. "I'll get back with you after I get the package. By the way, you really owe me. You do know that. And I'll do more than make you dance with a loony. This will cost you large."

"You know I'll always help a friend. All a man has to do is ask. Take care," Butch said as he hung up the phone and walked down the aisle toward the kitchen area.

Kevin hung up his phone and put it into his shirt pocket. Taking his normal cell phone from its case on his belt, he dialed Mikey's number. While waiting for the answer, he motioned for Leslie to look out of the windshield. There crossing the road less than twenty-five feet in front of the truck was a large rattlesnake. As it slithered across the dusty road, he told her, "Lots of those out here in the woods. You gotta be careful when you step out doors."

Leslie sat watching as the five-foot-long diamondback made its way across the road and into the brush along the fence. As it disappeared, she sat back in the seat and hung her head. If it wasn't enough that she had been kidnapped and drug away from her home, seeing where she was going to be kept further deepened her depression. Those pictures of Gene and the massive manhunt for him had been a shock, but she had thought that she could explain that to anyone involved. That chance seemed long gone now.

"Hello, my friend," Kevin said as the phone on the other end was answered. "I'm calling about a place for a hunting cabin. I believe a mutual friend spoke to you earlier."

On the other end, Mikey replied, "Yeah, sure did. Are you looking for the best spot?"

"I reckon so, I'm about a mile from the entrance to the ranch house right now. Which road should I take to get the trailer dropped off?"

"You should be just about there," Mikey told him. "There will be a cattle guard on your left that has a chain across the road. It's the only one between 2127 and the road to the house. If you haven't seen it yet, it can't be more that one hundred yards in front of you. The key to the lock is behind the Southwest Cattle Raisers sign on the fence to the right of the crossing."

Kevin put the truck in gear and started forward slowly. Less than fifty yards down the road, he saw the cattle guard and chain. The road disappearing into the brush looked as if it hadn't been used in months. The dust on the brush matched the color of the road, and had the cattle guard not been somewhat clear, it would have been easy to have passed it unseen.

"Got it," he told Mikey. "Is this the only road in there?"

"No," came the reply. "There's another one that comes into the back side. But I was told that you need a quiet place with no interruptions. I'll make sure nobody comes there from the ranch. If you keep the chain locked, you'll be left alone."

"Great," Kevin told him. "If you don't mind, I'll keep the key for now. I wouldn't want someone poaching your property. If you need any more information, you know whom to talk to."

"I sure do," Mikey laughed. "But I bet he'll keep his mouth closed as tight as a frog's butt. I guess I'll just have to wait and keep my curiosity under control for now."

"I reckon so," Kevin responded. "I'm not sure exactly what that man's up to either, but I'm sure he has something in mind. One of these days, we'll have to get him to buy us a beer and get the real story. Thanks though. I've got to get this thing off the road before anyone comes by. I'll talk to you later."

"You too. Take care, there's still a few snakes looking for their winter homes, you know," Mikey told him as he hung up.

Kevin stopped just short of the cattle guard and walked to the metal sign hanging beside the steel post that provided the starting point for the barbed wire fence running along the road. Getting the key from the hook screwed behind the sign, he stepped onto the four-inch pipes that comprised the bottom of the cattle guard. Careful not to catch his boots in the four-inch spaces between the pipes, he unlocked the chain and lowered it.

Returning to his truck, he slowly drove across the six-foot expanse of pipes. Each bump could be felt, and he was still concerned about the tires of the trailer. Once across, he stopped and replaced the chain and hooked the open lock through the links to hold it in place while he was parking the trailer. Once back in the truck, he followed the winding road down a slight hill and across several dry streambeds. After half mile or so, he topped another hill and spotted the clearing he had been searching for.

Surrounded by heavy brush and post oaks, there appeared to be three or four acres of clearing with a single pole on one side. The wires leading to it ended where the water well had been drilled. Dirt from the well still lay around the covered hole, and a single pipe ran to a large metal tank that would provide water for any cattle in the area.

Kevin pulled the trailer beside the water tank and backed it beside the electrical pole. Parking the truck, he told Leslie to wait until he had unhitched. As he stepped down, he looked at the area around the camper and decided that this was probably exactly where Butch would want it parked. The trees and hills completely hid the area from the road, and even the slight overhanging trees beside the well helped hide the trailer.

Walking to the rear of the truck, he placed a piece of an old railroad tie beneath the jack on the tongue of the trailer and began screwing it down. Once satisfied that it was fairly level, he picked up a couple of rocks and blocked the tires to ensure that the trailer would not roll. Then opening the catch that held the trailer attached to the ball on his truck, he raised the tongue to clear it when he pulled forward.

He walked around the trailer and looked closely at the grass and dirt in the immediate vicinity. Looking for fire ants, open holes that might lead to a snake den, and any other hazard, he opened the door to the camper and stepped in. Everything that he had loaded was still where he had set it down. Taking one of the propane bottles, he returned to the front of the trailer and set it in the brackets where the hose from within the camper lay.

Satisfied that Leslie would be as comfortable as possible, he opened the passenger door on the truck and told her it was all right to get out. She reluctantly stepped down, looking apprehensively at her new home. The sight of the rattlesnake that had crossed the road earlier remained on her mind as she walked toward the trailer.

"I'm afraid that this will have to do for now," Kevin told her. "I'll hook up the water and electricity later. There's plenty of food and drinks to last you for a while."

They both entered the trailer, and Leslie sat on the bench that doubled as dining area and living room. "How long do I have to stay here?" she asked, looking at the cramped quarters.

"I'm not sure," Kevin told her as he sat opposite her across the Formica-topped table. "I have to go somewhere in a few minutes, but I think we need to have a little discussion before I leave."

"Where are you going?" she asked with surprise in her voice. "You aren't going to leave me out here alone, are you?"

Kevin leaned back and looked at her for a few seconds before he spoke. "Yes, I'm leaving you alone here for now. However, you will have company later this afternoon."

"Who?" she asked.

Kevin paused and then told her, "Gene."

A surprised look came across her face, and she leaned back speechless. "How do you know where he is?" she asked. "The news said that the police, FBI, and everybody else are looking for him."

"I know," he told her. "From what I can figure, Butch has him and is trying to get him away from the people that are looking for him. He doesn't think that Gene is a terrorist and is attempting to hide him until he figures out what to do."

"What does he know about it?" Leslie asked.

"I'm not sure. I think he wants to meet me later tonight. Maybe I will know more after that," Kevin told her as he started to get up. "And I'm pretty sure I'll get a little information from your friend Gene when I get him up here."

Kevin walked to the door and turned to look at her. "Now, I'm not going to lock the door. I've got to trust you sooner or later. I guess it's sooner. If you decide that you want to leave, go ahead. But I better warn you that if you try to leave, either the snakes or those people looking for Gene may get you. I may get in trouble for trying to help, but I really doubt that it will be anything like the trouble you will be in because of your contact with Gene."

"I'm not about to try to walk back through this place," she told him. "I need to tell you something."

"What?" he asked her as he turned from the door.

Leslie lowered her eyes and hesitated. "We had sex."

Kevin's face registered the surprise. "You had what? Who with?"

Her face still almost hidden, she told him, "Gene, we had sex."

"Oh shit," he exclaimed. "Who else knows about this?"

"Just Stacy and of course Gene," she mumbled. Lifting her head, she looked at him. "I didn't mean for it to happen. It's just that it was my birthday and I got a little drunk. And I thought that Gene was such a cute little guy, so we kind of went out to Stacy's truck and it just happened."

"Does Butch know about Stacy?"

She looked puzzled and then told him, "Of course, we were all at the same table. Butch even danced with both of us."

"I better tell him about this," Kevin said as he shook his head. "He may want to try to get her away also. Crap, girl, you may have really stepped in it. I hope no one else knows."

"I'm sorry if I've caused you a problem," Leslie said, almost crying. "God, I wish I could have that night back. And now, you tell me that he is going to be living here. I don't know if I can face him. What will he think of me?"

Kevin walked back and put his hand on her shoulder. "Look, I'm not the one to tell you what to do or criticize what you did. You're a young lady, and maybe you made a mistake. You certainly aren't the first one, and I'm sure you won't be the last. For now, let's just try to make the best of this. You and Gene can talk about it when I get him here, but both of you have to stay here for now. Understood?"

"Yes, sir," Leslie said as she wiped her moist eyes.

"Good," Kevin said, walking to the door of the trailer. "While I'm gone, you need to think real hard and make sure there isn't anything else that either Butch or I need to know. Whether or not you realize it, this isn't a game. You may have to learn a lot of things that most people will never have to know. I'll be back in a couple of hours. If you want to start putting away all the food and stuff, it might make it a little less crowded in here."

Kevin shut the door behind him and walked back to his truck. As he started and drove back across the clearing toward the narrow road that led off the ranch, he watched in the rearview mirror to see if she would leave the trailer. He saw the curtains open and saw her watching him leave. *Well,* he thought. *There's nothing more I can do for her until I get back. I just hope for all our sakes that she sits still until I find out more about this.* He continued back up the drive, and as he crossed the cattle guard, he stopped and relocked the chain across the road. Slipping a small blade of grass into the keyhole of the lock, he placed the key in his pocket and headed for Boyd.

TM

Chapter 18

The atmosphere within the operations center at the facility was subdued as they continued to monitor the numerous satellite images and waited for either phone conversations or those from the taps they had placed in the truck and house.

The screen dedicated to monitoring the activity at the stables showed Butch's truck sitting outside the main barn. They could clearly see the horses moving about the pasture grazing. As they watched, several of them walked to an oval track that ran through one of the pastures. Upon arriving at the sandy track, each would sniff the ground; and finally after selecting a certain area, they would kneel down and slowly lay on their side. Then, they would roll from side to side and slightly twist their bodies as they rolled.

"Amazing, the clarity of these pictures," Paul said as they stood in front of the wall of monitoring screens. Asking Jerry to zoom in on the area, they watched as the view contracted from about one-half mile square to only a couple of hundred yards. "You can even read the brands on some of these horses," he noted.

"Sure is," Mike responded as he watched the horses rise up and shake the dust from their backs. "Wonder why they do that? And why they pick a certain spot?"

"I think I can answer that one," said Lieutenant Colonel Mark Mallory as he stepped into the room. "Now, I'm not positive as to why they pick a certain spot, but they roll to coat their backs with sand. It helps in dislodging insects and provides some natural repellant. The rolling also is a way of stretching their back muscles and getting the kinks out. Somewhat like we do when we twist or turn. At least that's what some of the old-timers tell me."

Rick turned as Mark was talking and nodded, "I've heard that too. A lot of the time they say that the layer of sand or dirt they pick up provides some protection from insect bites. Where do we stand on recruiting Bob Wilson?"

"We've got him." Mark smiled as he continued to the screens and watched the horses wandering around the green pasture. "Bob will stop by Red's Take 5 Sports Bar every afternoon for the next week and get to know a few of the people out there."

"What sort of cover story does he plan to use as to why he suddenly shows up in the area?" Mike asked.

Mark turned from the screen and looked at General Nelson as he answered, "Sir, since there are hundreds of new people in that area working on the gas wells and pipelines, he'll tell everyone that he's involved with supplying some of the various chemicals or materials needed in that field. We've had business cards printed, and since most people never meet the men that deliver the actual material, he should be able to convince them. The company name we've used is similar to one around that area, so most people will associate it with one they've heard of."

"What if someone checks it out?" Paul asked. "How can we ensure that his company can back up his employment?"

"Well, sir," Mark continued, "we've used a local number on the cards as well as an address in Bridgeport. He has already rented office space and will hire a secretary to answer the phones and transfer any calls to his cell phone."

"Won't that involve risking the secretary talking to someone and saying that the business isn't real?" Rick asked.

"No," Mark told him. "We've printed several blank order forms and will have filing cabinets full of 'placed and delivered' orders. We will also call in orders during the day, and she will be filing those that are subsequently 'filled.' It will appear to be a normal sales operation to her."

"What about why she was hired to start with?" Karyn asked.

"She will be told that Bob's wife was the former secretary but had to quit because she needed to return to San Antonio and take care of their kids," Mark answered. "This is supposed to be a new business that has only opened within the last month or so. I don't think we will have any problems with the secretary. The salary is reasonable, and she'll probably be glad to have the job."

Mark took a stack of business cards from his pocket and handed one to each of them. "With any luck, Bob will get friendly with a few of the clients, especially Gay Lynn, the owner. She knows Butch very well, and once she knows that Bob also ropes, she'll be eager to introduce him to Butch."

"How do we know Butch will want to get to know him?" asked Paul. "Since we know he's suspicious right now, he may not be willing to befriend anyone new."

"We'll have to take it slow of course," Mark told him. "But you know how it is at the bar. Sharing a common interest, like team roping, will get the conversation going. Bob will tell him that he hasn't roped in years, but would like to help if Butch needs someone to run the chute or assist in wrapping the cattle. I'm sure this plan will work."

"Just make sure we take it slow," Mike told him. "We can't afford to spook Mr. North any more right now. If we don't find either Gene or Leslie within the next couple of days, he may be our only lead."

Turning to Rick, he asked, "What about Stacy? Was she any help?"

"Very little," Rick responded. "She said they were at Red's, met Butch and his kids with Gene, and then she dropped Gene off at the stables before she took Leslie back up to Bowie. After that, she drove back to Arlington and went to bed."

"What did she seem to think about Gene being a terrorist?" Mike asked.

"She hadn't seen any of the news programs until we showed her the pictures and had her turn on her TV set. She was genuinely surprised that Gene was suspected to be wanted in connection to the series of attacks," Rick said. "She told the team that she never suspected that he was from the Middle East and that he seemed more like a Mexican."

"Did she mention what time she dropped off Gene at the stables?" Paul asked him.

"She said that it was somewhere between twelve thirty and one o'clock that morning," Rick answered. "And that Gene had drunk quite a bit, or at least he appeared to be pretty drunk when she let him out. She also said that it would be strange that a Muslim would drink alcohol since she had heard that it's against their religion."

Mike slightly smiled and told them, "Well, there are a lot of things that they aren't supposed to do, including killing innocent people. They seem to pick and choose what parts of the Koran they want to follow when it's convenient. I've seen them drinking and whoring every time they get the chance. They are one of the most two-faced cultures I've ever met."

"Hey," Karyn called out. "Butch is on the move. He just got in his truck and is headed up Old Base Road."

Everyone turned to watch the satellite image remain locked on the truck as it came to a stop at the intersection with Highway 114. A string of rock trucks and tankers hauling their loads of water stretched for over a half mile from the west as Butch waited at the Stop sign. Finally moving again, he appeared to be heading toward his house.

"He's on his phone," Karyn announced as they heard the dedicated speakers come to life.

They stood quietly listening to him talk to someone named Levi Wilson. As they monitored the conversation, they watched him pass through the light at 718 and continue toward Boyd. Hearing him mention buying hay and wanting the family discount, they looked at one another with surprise.

"What do you think he means?" Paul asked. "What family is he referring to? Our records show no family in this area. Are we certain that we haven't missed someone?"

"I don't think we've missed anything about his family," Rick answered. "It must be some sort of reference to getting a better price on his hay. I'm positive that he has no family around here."

"Let's get more information on this Levi Wilson," Mike told him. I want to make sure that we haven't missed any connections. There may be some loose alliance between the two that we need to know about."

"That reference to the New York families seems to indicate some sort of Mafia connection," Karyn remarked.

"Not a chance," Rick told them. "I'll double-check with our people with the organized crime force in the FBI, but there's no way they have any operations out here."

As they continued to listen, Butch's truck arrived in Boyd and pulled into the Rock Island Express gas station and convenience store just as he had mentioned to Levi. They saw Butch park and enter the back entrance of the building.

After watching for several minutes, the screens showed him leaving the building and then disappear under an umbrella. While they wondered why he hadn't returned to his truck, Jerry answered his phone.

As he listened, he glanced at the wide view of the area and then thanked the caller before hanging up. "That was from the choppers flying down from Bowie. They have searched 730 from Decatur all the way to Boyd and did not spot any camper or trailer that might resemble what we are looking for."

Everyone turned to look at the screen. They saw the helicopter turning back north and head back toward Decatur. The view of the area they were watching showed the entire stretch of 730, and there appeared to be only one area that might possibly have several items for sale along the road.

"Can we zoom in to that area?" Paul asked as he walked closer to the screen and pointed to a spot on the east side of the road about halfway between Decatur and Boyd.

"Certainly," said Jerry as he picked up the phone. Within seconds, the screen filled with what looked like numerous pickup truck bumper guards, several pieces of farm equipment, and some small utility trailers that might be used to haul lawn mowers or other light loads.

"That is probably the area we were looking for," said Mike. "Can we review the last half hour or so to see if there was a trailer there?"

"Yes, sir," Karyn answered as she walked to her computer. Quickly typing in her instructions, the screen began running the previous filming in reverse.

As they watched the date and time stamps rewinding, they saw each vehicle travel backward until there appeared a truck backing into the area with a camper trailer attached.

"Right there," shouted Rick. "There's our trailer. Go on back until the truck arrives and restart it."

Karyn continued rewinding the images until the truck pulled into the lot beside the road. They watched someone get out and walk to the trailer. While the man from the truck inspected the camper, another person came down from the house. Silently they watched the entire process as Kevin was arranging the purchase and finally drove off.

"Can we zoom in on that truck?" Paul asked as the truck headed north.

"No, sir," Karyn told him. "We can zoom in on the current images, but we can't go back in time to those frames."

"Let's get someone out there to talk to the man that came out of the house," Rick said. "Maybe he will know who took the trailer and where he was going."

"Call your helicopter," Mike told him. "See if he can land around there and get the information."

Rick picked up his phone and spoke rapidly as he relayed the general's request. Listening for a couple of seconds, he hung up and turned back to the screen showing the helicopter almost back to Decatur. As they watched, it turned south and slowly approached the area where they had seen the mysterious truck leaving with the camper trailer they had heard Butch tell someone to buy.

Within minutes, the helicopter landed across the road from the trailer's previous location and someone from inside climbed out and ran crouched beneath the still-turning blades toward the road. As he was crossing it, they saw the door open to the house and what appeared to be the same man they had previously seen come walking down to meet him.

TM

Chapter 19

Butch left his house and turned left onto 718. As he passed the fence that marked the southern end of his property, he approached the entrance to Aurora Vista. The newly developed property was almost completely covered with houses ranging from $300,000 up to over $750,000. Where he used to ride his horses, now BMWs and Lexuses roamed the streets. Most of the deer and coyotes had left the area with the influx of people.

Thinking back to the days before the migration of people into the area, he missed seeing turkeys and deer grazing in his pastures in the early mornings and late evenings. It had been a long time since he had sat on his back porch and listened to the coyote pups calling for their mothers.

This latest development, centered around Gene, made him wish for the days now over. He had moved out here to get away from the complexities of dealing with large groups of people and missed the quiet country he had known before developers began replacing the ranches with thousands of houses. Now the old ranches were renamed Rancho Verde or Wild Horse Ranch Estates.

This new breed of "ranch" owners had never seen beef unless it had been processed and wrapped in cellophane. The only doggies they knew were lap dogs that wouldn't make it through the week if left outside where the coyotes would carry them back to their dens.

As he drove through the development and onto Old Base Road, he knew that he couldn't turn back the time. Now he had to deal with the situation that had been forced on him and make the best he could of the hand he had been dealt. Right now that included taking care of the mounting problem of what to do with Gene until he could figure out why the government wanted him so badly.

After the conversation he had with him earlier, he was coming to the conclusion that Gene had some connection to the projects rumored to be taking place in a location in northern Nevada. He had known about Area 51 for years. Although having never gone there, he had worked with programs that used the area. Talk of UFOs and alien beings were something that he had never really believed, although he did not discount them.

Everything Gene had told him pointed to that area. The flying time from the NAS/JRB to there was about as Gene had said. The country would appear as he had described. And just as importantly, the method of transporting during certain periods of darkness and the limited exposure to public scrutiny lead him to believe that he had been involved with a project as black as some he had worked with while in the air force. Nothing really made sense, but if there were alien spacecraft and if there were bodies recovered from the crashes as so many people believed, it would stand to reason that the government would not want any information to get into the public's hands.

Pulling into the stables, he finally decided that what he was doing would place him, his daughters, and his friends in grave danger. He had no doubt that the government would go to any length to keep knowledge about Gene from becoming public. He had to get his two kids out of here. And he had to make sure that he protected his friends as much as possible. He had already placed Kevin in a situation that could possibly endanger his life. Even Mikey Carmichael could be in jeopardy if Gene were discovered on his property.

As much as he dreaded placing his friends in situations that could mean dire consequences for them, he knew he couldn't do this alone. All he could do now was to limit their exposure and make sure they didn't know any more than absolutely necessary. He was sure Kevin would discover the truth, if what he suspected was indeed the truth. But of all his friends, Kevin would be the best equipped to handle the situation.

He parked in his usual spot beside the hitching rail that stood in front of the main barn, and after taking one stack of hundreds from under his seat, he stepped from his truck. Standing in the open, he took his cell phone from its carrier on his belt. Suspecting that he was now under constant surveillance, he would use it to his advantage whenever possible. Any misdirection or misinformation that he could generate might raise their suspicions, but it would at least allow him to keep their attention on him while he got Gene to the safest place he could for now.

As he waited for Levi Wilson to answer the call, he watched the road and listened for the telltale sounds of any helicopters in the area.

"Hey, Levi," he said. "When do you expect that load of hay to get here? I don't have all day, and if you want me to help unload, you better chap up and ride."

Pausing to hear the response, he walked around the side of the barn and made sure the two sliding doors that led to the hay storage area were fully open. "Sure," he finally said as he stood in front of the open doors, "I'm here right now, and I'll make sure your driver takes the rest of the load to your big barn. Just make sure you send me the bill when he confirms what I bought."

Butch looked inside the barn at the still-locked hay cage. As he watched, he saw Gene poke his head above the top layer of hay. "No," he continued, "I can't come over there and help unload it in your barn. I'm a busy man, Levi. I still have to find my poor, almost-orphaned daughters a new mother. You'll have to take care of that problem on your own. Gotta go now. You take care."

Butch hung up the phone and replaced it into its carrier. Walking into the barn, he took his keys from his pocket and opened the chained cage doors. Sliding one side open so he could help unload the hay, he told Gene to come down from his hiding place.

"Gene," he told him. "I'm going to move you. I can't take care of you here, and before long, I think those people who are looking for you will be back to search this place again."

Gene climbed down the layers of bales stacked in half of the storage area and sat on the lowest row. "Where are you taking me?"

"Somewhere that I hope nobody ever thinks to look," Butch said as he sat down beside Gene. "And I may have to leave you there alone for quite some time."

"How will I live? Will there be a house? What about food?" Gene asked as he began to worry about what was going to happen to him.

"I'll take care of all that," Butch told him as he put one hand on his shoulder. "You won't have the best of accommodations, and the food will be pretty basic. The main thing for now is to get you somewhere that they won't find you while we figure out a better long-range plan."

"I don't want to go back there," Gene said, shaking his head. "I'd rather live out in the middle of the country and eat whatever I could find than go back."

"Don't worry," Butch said as he stood up and walked to the open doors of the barn. "I won't let either of those happen. But you need to pay attention very carefully to what I want you to do."

Turning back to face Gene, he told him, "There will be a truck arriving in a few minutes. The driver will back the trailer into here, and I will help him unload some of the hay that's on the back. You have to stay hidden until the driver gets back into the truck."

Looking at the large wheelbarrows used to haul the shavings from the large container beside the barn to the inside stalls, Butch told him, "I want you to stay behind this wheelbarrow until I come get you. Once we've unloaded some of the hay, I will leave a hole in the middle of the remaining load. As soon as the driver walks back to the cab, you climb up here, and I'll put a couple of bales over the hole where you'll be hiding. You have to stay there until someone comes to get you. It may take some time, but you have to promise me that you'll just stay under the hay until then."

"OK," Gene said as he walked over to help Butch roll the wheelbarrow on its side and against the wall of the barn. "Will you come get me?"

"No, I'm afraid that I'm being watched and that would lead them to you if I came. The man coming to get you is named Kevin. He is one of my closest friends and is the only one that'll know where you'll be taken."

"Is he going to stay with me?"

"No."

"You mean that I'll be left all alone?" Gene asked with near panic in his voice.

Butch sat Gene down behind the wheelbarrow and made sure he wouldn't be visible from where the truck would be parked. "No, you won't be left alone," he said. "As a matter of fact, Leslie will be with you."

"Leslie?"

Butch turned and looked at him. "Yes, is there a problem?"

"No, I just never thought that I would get to see her again."

"Well," Butch said as he looked out of the doors to see if the truck was arriving. "You'll get to see her. I'm afraid that she'll be in almost as much trouble as you are if they ever find out about the sex thing. What you and she did could complicate things more than you'll ever know."

"I didn't mean to cause any trouble for her," Gene said worriedly. "I really liked her. She seemed to like me too. Other than Vicki, she's the only one that paid any attention to what I want."

"Well," Butch smiled. "I guess she *really* paid attention to what you wanted. Now, get back behind there. I think I just heard the truck pulling up out front. Remember, stay behind there until the driver goes back to the cab. I'll be on top of the trailer throwing the bales down to him. I'll let you know when to climb up here."

Butch walked out and saw the semitrailer backing down beside the barn toward the open doors. He stood to the left side and motioned the driver to continue backing until the rear of the trailer was under the roof and close to the stack of hay. Signaling for him to stop, he walked to the cab and waited for the driver to climb down.

"I'll climb up and throw the bales down," Butch told him. "I want to stack them on top of those already there. I know I told Levi that I wanted seventy-five bales, but I think I'll just take the coastal and none of the alfalfa."

"That's fine," the driver told him as he pulled on his gloves. "Levi told me what you wanted and to do anything else you asked. I'll stack these new bales down here in front. Then if you decide you need more, we can just go on top of them."

"Sounds good," Butch told him as he climbed up the back of the trailer and waited for the strap holding the bales to be loosened. "Just make sure there's room to slide the cage door closed. There should be plenty of room for fifty bales. If not, just stack them over by the alfalfa."

Once the hold-down strap was removed, Butch began to pick the 125-pound bales up and toss them down to the driver. He made sure he removed enough for it to be noticed if anyone had watched the truck come in. He was fairly certain that his request for fifty bales had been overheard, and it needed to look as if he had taken a routine delivery.

Each row on the back of the trailer held ten bales, and as soon as he had removed four rows, he began to take some from the top of the sixth row to make a hole for Gene. Once the bales were unloaded, a two-foot-wide hole running five feet within the center of the remaining bales was created. The bales to cover the hole and block the end were sitting where the unloaded bales had been.

Standing on the floor of the trailer, Butch told the driver, "I'll stack these back in a minute. There were a couple of bales in those first rows that looked a little off-color. Tell Levi that I can't feed hay that isn't nice and green. If you'll go get a ticket made, I'll restack these and tie them down. I'll come up to the cab to get the ticket."

As the driver walked out of the barn and got into the cab of the truck, Butch motioned for Gene to come from behind the wheelbarrow and climb up onto the trailer. Motioning for him to be quiet, he showed him where to crawl into the opening.

Once Gene was well into the hole, Butch began placing the loose bales over the top and in front to look exactly as if the back five rows had been removed. Reaching into his back pocket, Butch pulled the stack of money out and handed it to Gene, whispering, "Give this to Kevin. And tell him I said thanks."

He shoved the last bale into the slot to complete the replacement, and he reminded him to remain perfectly quiet and still until Kevin came to get him. "Sorry, little fellow, I may not get to see you again for quite some time. Just do exactly as Kevin asks, and we'll get you out of here."

After pulling the strap across the last row of bales, he climbed down and tightened it to the side rails of the trailer. Once satisfied that everything looked normal, he walked to the cab and waited for the driver to step back down.

"Thanks," he told him. "Make sure you let Levi know that I appreciate him getting me this hay so quickly. I'm expecting several of my customers to need some to take on a trail ride later this week, and I can't afford to run short for the horses that are staying here."

"No problem," he was told as the driver handed him the ticket showing delivery of fifty bales of coastal. "After I drop this off back at the hay barn, I've got to head to Arizona for another load. Thanks for your help unloading."

As the driver started the truck and began pulling out of the barn, Butch walked outside and took out his cell phone. After his call was answered, he said, "Hey, Levi, I've got the coastal. The alfalfa had a little too much stem for me. Let me know if you get another load, and I'll look at it. I won't need it for maybe a week or so."

After he heard the reply, he followed the departing truck back to the front of the barn and climbed into his truck. As soon as he saw the truck turn north on Old Base, he left the barn and headed back to his house. Once there, he took one of the remaining numbered phones and walked down to his barn there to feed his two rope horses. Whistling for them to come down, he waited until he was under the roof before he dialed the handwritten number on the face of the phone.

Chapter 20

                         Kevin turned south on 59 and drove the twenty miles or so down to Jacksboro. Butch had asked him to buy some additional cell phones, and he knew from the way they were using them, it would take at least four every day. He planned to stop at every convenience store, truck stop, or grocery store all the way to Boyd and get as many as he could.

    Each store he picked had an adequate supply of phones, and he always bought something else that he knew Leslie could use. He was careful not to buy too many things or items that might make him stand out as anything other than a local hunter or someone picking up a few things for his wife on the way home.

    Leaving Jacksboro and heading east on 114, he entered Bridgeport and continued his traveling buying spree. After getting two Styrofoam coolers, he filled one with milk, lunch meat, eggs, cheese, and any other thing that would last for a couple of days after the ice melted. In the other one, he placed several quart bottles of Dr Pepper and then filled them both with two bags of ice he bought at the service station after filling his truck with fuel.

    Continuing east on 114, he glanced to the right as he approached the edge of town. Sitting just off the road, he saw Red's Take 5 Sports Bar. Tempted to drive in and see where Gene and Leslie had first met, he decided that it would not be a good idea to show up there in case any of his acquaintances might be inside. He did not need to be explaining why he was down here when he very seldom went to any of the local bars. *Still,* he thought, *here is where Gene unknowingly got himself, Leslie, Butch, and who knew how many others into this mess.*

As he passed through Paradise, one of the cell phones lying beside him in the seat began ringing. Reaching down and picking it up, he did not need to look at the incoming number to know that Butch was on the other end. "You're a sorry asshole," he spoke, "I think I must have adopted a family. Good thing my last ex-wife left me a little something, or I couldn't afford a stepson like you."

"Love you too, buddy," Butch told him, standing inside the barn waiting for his horses to get into their stalls. He watched them come loping down through the trees and seem to race each other as they neared the open gate that separated the two pastures. "I just sent you a birthday present. It should be arriving as discussed earlier within the next fifteen minutes. You about ready to get it?"

"I'm about ready to beat the shit out of you, that's what I'm about ready to do. You and your little project are taking all my time and most of my money. I suppose you'll want me to keep track of these two horses and keep them in food and water."

Butch smiled as he listened to Kevin complain. "Sure do. Hell, I take care of lots more than that over here at the stables. I figure that if I get $400 a month, you should be happy with half that much since you only feed half as much. So $200 each should be about right. Why don't you just send me a bill every month for $400, and we'll call it even."

"You are one worthless human being," Kevin laughed. "Hell, even if I don't put out as much feed, it costs lots more than that cheap hay and pellets you buy. Make it about $4,000 a month, and I might not hate you so much."

"Just bill me what you think is right," Butch replied. "I'm sure a fine gentleman such as you wouldn't try to cheat a poor ol' broken-down cowboy like me. And don't forget, I'm a veteran. Have some pity."

"I'll make it right. My time and energy costs a lot more than you're offering. And when I send the bill, it just may take you the rest of your life to get it paid."

"No problem," Butch told him. "If this little program is ever discovered, there may not be much left of the rest of our lives."

Kevin somberly nodded his head and said, "I know what you mean. We really do need to have a face-to-face. I don't want to stay on these phones any more than necessary. You still planning on the VFW?"

"Yeah, I'm going to try to get the girls to stay in Lewisville tonight. I don't want them out here any more than necessary. I'll try to be there by nine o'clock."

Kevin was approaching the west side of Boyd and slowed to turn into the IGA grocery store. "I've got a few more things to buy, and I'll pick up the package. Anything else?"

"Nope," said Butch as he poured a scoop of pellets into each horse's feed bucket. "I'm feeding my horses here at the house, and then I'll head back to the stables. I have to get their feeding schedule back on track. This day has been way too long, and I do need a big tall Jack and Coke."

Kevin sat in his truck as he finished the conversation. "I sure know that, I'll be a little later getting there. It's a long road back and forth, you know. But I wouldn't miss this little talk for all of the world. I'll let you know if I have any problems with our new horses. I suppose you know that gelding is proud cut?"

"Yep," came the reply. "I just hope there aren't any problems that could arise from that gelding. Sure wouldn't want a colt, you know."

"Could further complicate the situation, that's for sure. Anything else?" Kevin said as he reached for his door handle.

"Nope, but if you've got any new phones, put them in a bag and leave them somewhere in my town that I can find," Butch told him.

"I'm there now," Kevin said. "I'm going into the only grocery store you have. I'll leave them with the store manager."

"Thanks, see you tonight."

Kevin hung up his phone and wrote the new numbers on all the phones he had bought. He then put them into one of the plastic bags he had received when he bought them. Placing the last one used on the ground beside his truck, he stepped on it with all his weight. The plastic made a cracking sound as it broke. He picked up the pieces and dropped them into a five-gallon bucket in the bed of his truck.

Entering the IGA, he bought several candy bars and some apples. Taking these up to the manager's window for quick checkout, he asked the lady behind the cash register if she knew Butch North. After she replied that she did, he handed her the bag of phones and told her that he would be by later to pick them up.

As she sat the bag to the side, Kevin pulled his wallet from his pocket and waited while his items were scanned and bagged. After paying, he thanked her and headed back to his truck. Tossing the bags in with the rest of the food in the coolers, he glanced up and down the road. Rock trucks continued roaring through the center of town, ignoring every speed limit posted.

He stepped into the truck and pulled back onto 114, heading east toward the intersection with 730 leading back north to Decatur. *Hell,* he thought as he pulled into the left-turn lane, *I was only about seven miles north of here a couple of hours ago getting the trailer.*

Driving north for a mile, he came to the gravel road leading to the storage barns for Southwest Hay Exchange. As he approached the largest barn, he saw the trailer parked inside still loaded with hay. He drove into the barn and parked beside the end of it.

Climbing from his truck onto the bed of the trailer, he walked to the last row of hay stacked and tied there. He reached down and released the straps that crossed the last rows and began lifting them off and setting them onto the rear of the trailer. After removing three from the center of the rows, he saw an opening and stopped as he watched a face appear from within the semidarkness of the stacks.

"You Gene?" he asked as he looked at the young face staring up at him.

"Yes, sir," came the answer. "Are you Kevin?"

"Only what's left of him," Kevin said as he lifted the last bale from over Gene. "Come on out of there. Butch asked me to give you a lift up north somewhere. I hope he told you what was going on."

"Yes, sir, he did," Gene told him as he began to brush loose hay from his face and hair. "He said for me to do exactly whatever you say."

"Good," Kevin told him. "Are you ready to get out of here?"

"Yes, sir, I sure am. Oh, Butch told me to give you this," Gene told him as he handed him the stack of hundred-dollar bills.

Kevin took the money and shook his head. "You know, that man never fails to surprise me."

Climbing down, he told Gene, "Jump on down and get in the truck. I need to get you put away and try to make myself a drink before I talk to your good friend Butch."

He watched Gene climb down from the trailer and thought to himself, *So this is the reason for all the problems.* Looking closely at Gene's face as he opened the passenger door and climbed into the cab, Kevin asked him, "Where are you from?"

Gene turned to him as he shut the door and replied, "I don't know. I've told Mr. North everything I know, but I've never been told where I really did come from."

"Doesn't matter," Kevin said as he started the truck and began to back from the barn. "For now, please get down in the floor board and try not to be seen. There was only one person in this truck when it came in, and there should be only one when it leaves. I'll let you know when you can get up."

Gene slid down off the seat and sat with his back against the door and watched Kevin drive. Once again, he thought, he's heading into an unknown future and depending on strangers to help him. Granted, everyone he had met out here in the country had befriended him and no one ever seemed to care where he was from. As long as he did what he was told to do, they all seemed to want to help him.

It was certainly very curious the way these people worked together. There wasn't any formal structure to their interactions, but they each seemed to treat each other with the same respect he had seen the subordinates back at the facility show their bosses. Here, there were no bosses, yet they all respected each other. Sometimes it seemed that they showed it even more than back within the hierarchy of the facility. He wondered how such diverse people could come together and do the things he knew must be going on to get him away and to safety.

After what seemed like hours of being covered in hay or cramped almost beneath the dash of Kevin's truck, he was told that he could get up and sit in the seat. Looking out the windows, he could see miles of pasture with barbed wire fences stretching along the sides of the road. The land was becoming rocky and tree covered as they sped down the gravel road, leaving a hanging cloud of grey dust behind.

The short stretches they spent on black-topped roads was kept to a minimum, and even in the fading sunlight, Gene could see that it would be very difficult to see more than a few feet into the land laying beside the roads. The hills seemed to be more frequent and marked with steep rocky slopes. It had been miles since he had seen the last house, and it had been at least a mile from the road as they passed.

Finally, Kevin stopped the truck in front of a chain that ran across the small gravel road that seemed to disappear into the heavy brush. He watched as Kevin inspected the lock before inserting the key and unlocking it. Dropping the chain and returning to the idling truck, Kevin told him, "Well, you're almost home. I guess you know who's waiting."

"Yes, sir," Gene replied. "Mr. North told me that Leslie would be there. Is she going to be staying there with me?"

"That's the plan, do you think there will be any problem with that?"

"I don't know," Gene said as he looked down into the fast-developing darkness. "I'm not sure if she wants me to be around her."

"Well, either way, you two are stuck together for now. Let's just try to make the best of this and see what we need to do later."

They sat in silence as they wound through the heavily wooded area and watched as several deer crossed the road in the beams of the headlights. Several stopped and stared at the approaching lights, and Kevin had to slow to give them time to bolt out of the road as they came within several feet of the stationary deer.

Finally arriving at the camper trailer sitting in the dark, Kevin wondered what he would find inside the dark interior. Taking a large flashlight from under his seat, he told Gene to wait in the truck while he checked out the trailer. He shut his door and walked to the closed door of the camper and knocked. "Leslie," he called out. "It's me, Kevin. I need to come in, so make sure you're dressed.

The door swung outward, and Kevin looked with relief at Leslie as she stood in the doorway. He could tell that she had probably spent most of the time alone crying. Her eyes were red and puffy, and he could see where the tears and mucus from her nose had run down her face. He shone the light inside as he stepped in and slowly shut the door.

"Leslie, I know that this has all been a nightmare, but I'm sure we're doing the right thing. Now, I've got Gene in the truck, and I need to get him in here. I hope you've had time to consider how you'll act when you see him. I just want you to know that he is probably as scared of seeing you as you are of him."

He watched Leslie wipe her face with the sleeve of her shirt and shake her head. "What will he think of me?" she cried.

"I think he's more worried about what you'll think of him," Kevin told her as he put his hand softly on her shoulder. "There's a lot neither of us knows about him. But I do know he's got Butch's trust, and I've never known the man to be wrong about a man's basic worth."

Kevin stood motionless for a couple of minutes while Leslie tried to wipe the tears from her face. "What do you think? Should I go get him, and let's see where we stand? We can't let him sit out there all night, and I need to get back to talk to Butch."

Leslie nodded her head and told him, "OK, bring him in. I guess we'll have to sort things out for ourselves."

"Yeah, I guess you will. Like Butch always says, you're over twenty-one and weigh more than a hundred pounds. You get to make your own decisions and live with the results."

Kevin opened the door and lowered the beam of the flashlight to the ground as he walked back to his truck. Approaching the passenger door, he told Gene to get out and follow him. As soon as Kevin shut the truck door, he stopped and looked at Gene.

"Son," he started, "there's a mighty scared little lady inside that trailer. I know you're scared too, but she's worried about what you'll think of her. Probably because of what happened the night you met. Now I'll tell you, women feel different about these things than men normally do. So regardless of what you really think, make sure she thinks that you still respect her and care about her. Can you do that?"

Gene's face took on a puzzled look as he answered, "What do you mean? She didn't do anything that would make me think any less of her than I would any woman that treated me nicely. I don't understand what you're talking about."

Kevin shook his head and told him, "Well then, don't worry about a thing. Just keep on thinking she was nice to you, and you be as nice to her as you can. I think this might work out better than I expected. Let's go in and say hello."

Kevin again knocked on the door and waited for Leslie to open it to let them in. As the door opened, he made sure he didn't shine the light in her face to help her hide the fact that her emotions were plain to see.

"Please come in," she said as she walked backward into the kitchen area of the little trailer.

Kevin stepped in and told Gene to come inside. As he shut the door, he kept the light shining on the floor. "Gene, I'm sure you remember Leslie. And, Leslie, you know Gene. Now, why don't you two sit down there at the table, and let's get a few things out of the way."

Leslie walked to the front of the table and sat on one of the bench seats that would later make into the small bed in the front. Gene reluctantly sat down opposite her with the table between them. Both sat and looked at each other in the dim light as the questions in their minds raced about.

Kevin stood quietly for a couple of seconds and then told them, "Folks, I've got a long way to go and a short time to get there. I need to get a few things from my truck for you, and then I'll leave you alone to sort out the situation."

He took his flashlight and opened the door to leave the trailer. Shining the light on the ground, he walked to the bed of his truck and took one of the coolers back to the trailer. Knocking on the door, he pulled it open and sat the cooler inside.

"Please put this somewhere for now, and I'll bring the other one in."

Returning to his truck, he thought of the scene he had just seen. Both of them were sitting motionless with their heads down, afraid to make eye contact with each other. *Poor kids,* he thought as he removed the remaining cooler and walked back to the camper.

As he placed it inside the still-open door, he had to shove the previous cooler aside. Neither of them had moved. He stepped inside and waited before he spoke, "Kids, I'm going to leave this flashlight over there on the counter by the sink. I don't have any spare batteries with me, so use it sparingly. I'll be back out here tomorrow morning and see if we can't get you hooked up with water and electricity. Until then, just try to relax and get some sleep. This has been a long day for all of us."

Kevin left them sitting in the faint glow of the light he had purposefully pointed away from them. As he shut the door and walked back to his truck, he shook his head and wondered what he would find when he returned tomorrow. He started the truck and turned around. It was just after sundown, and the woods around him were completely dark. Leaving the trailer behind, he saw a faint glow in the windows as he headed back to the road to Jacksboro.

So far, so good, he thought as he sped east on 114. Within the hour, he should be at the Avondale VFW and get a chance to have a very private talk with his good friend Butch. As he passed the edge of town, he saw another helicopter heading north on 730. *Sure are a lot of choppers around here today,* he thought as he sped toward Rhome where he would take 287 south to the VFW and hopefully get some answers from Butch.

TM

Chapter 21

Back at the facility on the NAS/JRB, they watched the short conversation with whoever had sold the trailer they were searching for. After only a couple of minutes, the team member that had approached the man turned and headed back to the waiting chopper.

As the helicopter began to rise, Jerry's phone began to ring. Stepping to his desk to answer it, he kept his eyes on the screen showing the helicopter heading back north toward Decatur.

"Major Fleenor," he said and waited for the caller to relay his information. After only a couple of minutes, he thanked the caller and hung up.

"They got no information on the buyer," he told the waiting members. "The man who bought it paid in cash and only told him that he needed it for a hunting cabin. When he left, he was going toward Decatur, and that's all the man knew."

General Modelle asked, "Is there any way we can back up the data from now and see if we can determine where the trailer went?"

"Sure," Jerry replied. "We can start at any point and watch in reverse until the truck and trailer are spotted. Just give me a minute."

He picked up his phone and dialed the number that connected them to the technicians that controlled the images and directed the satellite. Within minutes, the screen showed the view that stretched from Bowie to the north down to Boyd on the south. As they watched it scroll backward, they finally saw the truck and trailer enter the picture in reverse.

"OK," Jerry said into the phone, "pause it there and then take it forward slowly until I tell you to stop again."

Everyone watched the screen as the red truck with the camper inched its way north on 730. After traveling only a few miles, the truck and trailer turned west on a gravel road. As it began speeding up, they could plainly see the dust cloud trailing them down the road.

"Let's get someone out there to see what road that is and where it goes," Colonel Erickson said. "All we have to do is count the number of roads from where he left, and we can send the helicopter back there to get the number, probably noted as a county road."

Karyn nodded and quickly picked up the microphone and relayed the instructions. As she replaced the microphone, they saw the chopper again turn south. It flew down to the same area where the trailer had started its journey and slowly began to fly back north.

Jerry had finished counting the roads that intersected 730 from the west and told Karyn that it should be the fifth road north. She relayed the information and waited for the pilot to reach the designated road. As it approached, it hovered for just a few seconds and reported that it was CR 4073. The pilot then continued westbound along the road while everyone returned their attention to the truck still shown on the screen as it made its way down the dusty road.

As they watched, it turned north for a mile or two and then returned to its western track. Several times they lost sight of it when it passed below the tops of some of the hills or was obscured by the dusty cloud it was leaving behind. The farther west it went, the harder it was to keep it in sight. Finally, it entered an area that was so heavily wooded that it could no longer be seen. Only an occasional glimpse of the dust rising behind it or from some other vehicle could be faintly seen.

"Never mind where that road goes," said General Nelson. "That man is switching roads and seems to know that country better than I know my own wife. I doubt if we could ever track him now."

"Well," Rick told him. "We know he is a friend of Mr. North and must be the one that obtained all the prepaid phones. Why don't we start at Decatur and see if we can determine where he bought the phones."

"That's a good idea," Mike told him. "But I remember Butch telling him to just buy a couple at any location. There must be a hundred places he could have purchased them."

"Yes, sir," Rick replied. "It will take a lot of footwork, but sooner or later, we will isolate a couple of stores, and if they have a security video, we can identify any person that bought phones at several locations."

"Sir, if I may," Karyn said. "If that is the same person that took Leslie, and I think he is, then we should start at Bowie. There aren't that many stores up there that would carry prepaid phones. Also, if he is from that area, one of the store clerks may just happen to recognize him."

"OK," Mike told her. "Contact the team up in Bowie and have them start. I doubt if he would get too far off the road leading to Decatur, so have them concentrate on those along the highway."

As Karyn was contacting the Bowie team, Rick pointed to the screen showing the stables. "Look, there's a truck with a flat bed trailer pulling in. It looks like it is loaded with hay."

Everyone turned their attention to the screen and watched the truck pull down the gravel drive and then backed down the side of the barn. As they watched, they saw Butch come from the barn and talk to the driver. Then, they both went into the barn where they could not be seen. Finally, after about thirty minutes, they saw the driver come out and climb into the cab. About five minutes later, they watched Butch come out and take a small piece of paper from the driver.

As the truck began to pull forward, they could see that the rear of the trailer was now empty. "That must have been the hay that Mr. North ordered from Levi," Jerry said as they watched the truck depart the stables and head back north on Old Base Road.

Almost immediately they watched Butch walk out and pull his cell phone out. As he made the connection, they listened to him tell Levi that he had gotten the hay. Closing the phone, they saw him get into his truck and follow the departing hay trailer. He followed the truck until passing Tater Junction and then turned south on 718 and into his house.

After parking, they saw him walk down to the barn just south of the house and had two horses following him. As he disappeared into the barn, they waited for him to make his next move.

"While we're waiting, what's the status of our undercover man, Bob Wilson?" Paul asked.

"He plans on being at Red's tonight and start spreading his cover story. If he goes there for the next several nights, he should be able to get to know Gay Lynn, and she'll be sure to introduce him to Butch," Mark answered.

"Well, the way things are going from our high-tech imaging systems, we may have to rely on some old-fashioned footwork. It may take us several days or weeks, but our best chance does seem to be getting Mr. North to slip and say the wrong thing," General Modelle said.

"Are we going to give up on Stacy Hyden?" Rick asked.

"Not entirely," Karyn answered. "We have her phone tapped, and if she attempts to contact Leslie or gets a call about her, we'll know."

"Is there anything else we can do for now?" General Modelle asked. "If not, I need to make a few calls and let the folks up in Washington know how we're doing."

"For now, sir, about all we can do is to continue watching Mr. North. He has to make physical contact with someone sooner or later," Mike told him. "The only other options we have are to bring him in or to hope we get the identification of the man who bought the camper."

"What about his kids?" Rick asked. "They went to Lewisville in his Corvette and haven't returned."

"Let's just monitor their phones and keep the car locked onto in case they don't come back to North's house this evening," Paul said as he prepared to leave the room. "Be sure to let me know if anything promising comes up. Right now, I'd like to have some good news to report."

"Certainly, sir," General Nelson told him as they all came to attention. "Colonel Erickson will remain here for the next couple of hours while I run home and get cleaned up. Then I'll take over while he heads home for a little sleep."

They remained standing while Paul left the room. Relaxing slightly, everyone breathed a slight sigh of relief. The pressure was still heavy on their shoulders to find Gene quickly before the folks up in Washington changed their minds and sent a new team down to replace them.

"I'll have Kathy send some sandwiches and drinks in," Mike told them as he walked toward the door. "Call me if you need to, I want to know what you find before we disturb General Modelle."

Colonel Erickson nodded his head and told him, "Yes, sir. I'm going to watch the tapes again and see if there isn't something unique about the truck that picked up the trailer. Like Karyn, I think he's probably from up around Bowie. Maybe we can identify him from that truck."

"Why don't we see if there are any former air force or other military personnel up there that may have served at the same time as Mr. North?" Major Fleenor asked. "I can have the Pentagon run a program that shows the location of any discharged or retired members. It's always possible that they are using our hospitals or other facilities and would have left their addresses."

"That sounds good, but again, it is going to take a lot of time," Mike told them as he opened the door. "However, right now we seem to have lots of time to pursue any option that might lead us to whoever is helping Mr. North. I'll be back in a couple of hours."

Chapter 22

Butch finished feeding the horses and again destroyed the phone he had just used. Leaving the horses to eat, knowing that they would return to the pasture when they had finished, he started walking back to his house. As he closed the gate separating the house from the pasture, he took his cell phone from its holder and dialed the stored number for his youngest daughter Jeannie.

He stood watching the longhorns graze in the pasture while he waited for the call to be answered. The ten steers were roaming loosely as a group as they nibbled on the last remains of the summer growth of Bermuda. *Looks like it's about time to buy a few round bales,* he thought as he noticed the short stems remaining for them to eat.

"Hey, young lady." He smiled into the phone. "You wreck my car yet? Or have you gotten caught speeding around town trying to impress all the local boys?"

"Hey, Poppy," Jeannie told him as she answered. "I haven't wrecked it yet, but Mischelle keeps waving at all the guys and giggling. I'm not sure I want to be seen with her any more."

"Well, too bad. You're stuck with her. Ya'll find any of your old friends?"

"Yep, we're going to Chili's here in Lewisville to have a beer and eat with two of the girls I went to school with up in Denton," she told him. "Not sure what time we will be heading back there, probably won't get home until midnight."

"Well," Butch said. "The lights on the Vette aren't the greatest and if you've had any beer, I'd rather you guys stay in town until tomorrow."

"We talked about that," Jeannie replied. "Sonsura, she's one of the girls I knew at the University of North Texas, lives here in Lewisville. Her house is just a couple of blocks from Chili's, and she asked us if we want to stay with her for the night."

"That sounds good, but if Mischelle would rather stay at a motel, go ahead and get a room. I'll take care of it when you get back," Butch said as he watched one of the horses walk out of the barn.

"Oh, she wants to stay with Sonsura," Jeannie said as she laughed. "That little midget is a party animal. I can't get a word in edgewise with her around. You'd never know there were so many words packed into her tiny body."

"I know," Butch acknowledged. "I think she stores up her party mode until she gets down here. And you don't help either. You keep her wound up."

In the background, he could hear Mischelle singing her rather unique version of "Girls Just Want to Have Fun." He smiled as he remembered how shy Mischelle had been growing up and how she became more expressive as she got older.

Shaking his head, he told Jeannie, "You girls just enjoy yourselves, but please take the car to Sonsura's house before you start partying. I'd rather not have you driving it around after you've been drinking."

"You do!" Jeannie said. "I used to see you coming home from the club after you and your fighter pilot buddies had been drinking and telling lies half the night."

"First," he said, laughing, "there were absolutely no lies, just facts with a little embellishing maybe. Second, and more important, it's my car. You want to wreck yours, that's your choice. Mine, you don't drink and drive. Got that, you little poopy butt?"

"Sure, we've already parked it at Sonsura's house," came the response. "We're with her on our way to eat right now. Don't worry, Poppy, we'll take care of your precious little car. Besides, it will be mine shortly after you kick the bucket."

"We'll see about that. I may just want to be buried in it."

"When you're dead, you don't get to make the decisions any more," Jeannie laughed. "Mischelle and I will decide what to do with your worthless carcass."

"Sorry little urchins," Butch said as he continued walking to the house, "You know I want my hide tanned and made into a ladies saddle. That way I'll be between the two things I love most, a pretty woman's legs and a fast horse. Just be safe and let me know when you get ready to come back tomorrow."

"OK, we'll give you a call in the morning."

Butch hung up his phone and glanced down to see the blade of grass still hanging where he had placed it. As he opened the door, he heard the unmistakable sound of another helicopter in the distance. The increased activity was no longer a surprise and deepened his feeling of being watched.

Inside, he showered and changed into a clean starched white Wrangler shirt and stiffly creased jeans. Taking his favorite black hat from its place on the rack made from old horseshoes, he expertly placed it on his head. After so many years of wearing a hat, it naturally fell into place on his head. Grabbing a light jacket, he paused in front of the mirror in the bathroom just off the kitchen and confirmed that the hat sat exactly as he wanted it.

As he closed and locked the door, he again stuck the blade of grass back where he wanted it. Getting into his truck, he backed out and headed down the driveway. Glancing at the fuel gauge, he crossed the road and pulled up to the diesel pumps at Kountry Korner. Shaking his head at the latest increase in fuel prices, he began pumping the liquid gold into his almost-empty tank.

Once full, he drove to the entrance of the combination feed and fertilizer store, diner, and gas station. He had been coming here since he had moved to the area over ten years ago and tried to buy all his gas or feed from the owners since then. The proximity of the store and the friendliness of the owners made it convenient to trade here.

After paying and making a little small talk with the cashier, he headed toward Boyd. Always watching the traffic for unusual vehicles, he noticed the familiar red truck belonging to Kevin Knox headed east on 114. As they passed, both drivers raised their left hands and gave a typical wave as most of the local people did as they passed each other.

Now smiling as he was reassured that things were going somewhat smoothly, he quickly passed the only stop light in Boyd and pulled into the IGA parking lot. Dropping his keys into the cup holder, he opened his door and walked briskly into the grocery store. As he approached the manager's window, he saw a plastic sack with its top tied together sitting on the counter beside the cash register.

"Evening," he said as he leaned on the counter. "How's business?"

"Oh, you know. Kind of slow so far," came the response.

"Did you happen to get a package for me?" Butch asked.

"Sure did," the manager said as he picked the plastic bag up and handed it to him. "The fellow that left it said to tell you hello and that he would see you next time he got to town. Where's he from, I thought he looked familiar?"

Butch took the sack and answered, "Oh, he's just an old friend of mine from down around Azle. We were supposed to meet and have a beer over at the Double K, but he had to get home to that mean old woman he's married to. Thanks for helping."

"No problem, glad to be of help when I can. You headed over for a beer?"

Butch headed toward the door and told him, "No, guess not. I've got to get back to the stables. Supposed to be some new boarders coming out to check on their horses. Thanks again."

He walked quickly to his truck and placed the phones on the passenger seat as he started the engine and pulled back onto the highway. Reaching under the seat, he pulled a couple of hundred-dollar bills from the stack he had taken from the house earlier. Putting them into his left shirt pocket and snapping it closed, he headed east to meet Kevin at the VFW.

TM

Chapter 23

Kevin pulled off Highway 287 and joined the service road that provided access to the few businesses along the road. A few truck-related shops and a couple of trailer parks dotted the roadside. The closed buildings stood darkly in the night as he approached the small lighted sign denoting the location of the Avondale VFW.

Once he had parked in the row closest to the road, he locked his truck and walked to the front entrance. Several cars and trucks sat in the parking lot, but it was obvious that there wouldn't be too many patrons inside. That could be good or bad. If there were more people, he wouldn't stand out as much. But if it was too crowded, it would make it difficult to have any real privacy to carry on a conversation without risking that someone might overhear it.

As he entered, he signed the guest register to the left of the door. Glancing at the names written in the log, he almost wrote his name before deciding that he didn't want any record of having been here tonight. Smiling, he wrote "Won Dum Phuc" in the next open line. If anyone happened to see that name, he doubted it they would connect it to him. The only other person who would know what it meant would be the man he was here to meet.

He walked to the bar and took a seat near the far end where there would be several stools between him and the other patrons.

As the bartender came over, he asked for a Budweiser and placed a twenty-dollar bill on the bar.

As he sat there watching the other people talking and paying him little attention, he sipped the beer and waited for Butch to show up. He had immediately recognized the big maroon dually truck as he had passed it on his way here. Glancing at his watch, he figured that he would be here within the next fifteen or twenty minutes. Shaking his head, he recalled the long friendship and anxiously awaited his arrival.

The Avondale VFW was like most organizations of its type across the country. A couple of dartboards and pool tables filled the front bar area along with a few video machines. The tables around the room were occupied primarily by an older crowd, and the noise from the juke box was much lower than in other bars. Most of the patrons were former members of one of the branches of the military.

Kevin felt right at home around the veterans drinking and relaxing after the long and rather interesting day that had begun with the cryptic call from Butch. He was wondering what new information that he would receive tonight and how his life would be further disrupted. Ordering another Budweiser, he checked his watch and glanced at another couple entering the room.

As he took his change from the bartender, he heard the door close and looked into the mirror behind the bar. Finally, he saw the familiar black felt hat and the back of the man signing in that he knew would soon occupy the seat next to him. Leaning back slightly and sipping from the long-necked bottle, he appeared as relaxed as any other off workman.

Butch walked over and took the open stool and looked around the bar. Two open stools rested between him and the next man sitting with what appeared to be his wife. They were engrossed in a conversation that he could barely hear, other than an occasional laugh. Turning to Kevin, he stuck out his hand and said, "Hello, Kevin. Had a good day?"

Kevin just shook his head as the bartender asked Butch for his order. Ordering two Budweisers, Butch laid a twenty-dollar bill on the bar and told her to make sure not to let Kevin drink too much, but any more beers he ordered would be on him.

As soon as the beer arrived, Butch picked his up and tipped it toward Kevin. Both nodded silently and tapped the necks of the bottles in familiarity. As Butch took his first sip, he looked into Kevin's eyes and apologized.

Setting the beer down, he said, "Thanks, old friend. I hated to get you into this, but I didn't know anybody else that could have pulled it off. I think you'll understand when I tell you the story."

Kevin sat his beer down and returned the frank look that two men have when they both respect the other and know that a serious issue is about to be discussed.

"Glad to be of help," Kevin replied. "How serious is this little deal?"

"Pretty damn serious. I may be wrong, but I think I've stumbled into what should never have been known outside the government, and probably most of them don't even know the extent of the program."

"You sure this is worth the risks?" Kevin asked.

"Yeah, I think this is worth it. It's going to take a few minutes, but I think you'll understand when I finish. I'm sure you remember some of the 'interviews' you had after some of those late-night missions you had back in Vietnam. You know how much effort the military went to just to make sure word of the specifics never reached the public."

Butch paused and glanced into the mirror to see if anyone was paying attention to them. "Well, this has the same feel. It reminds me of some of the black programs I dealt with when I was stationed out in the Mojave at Palmdale. Only much darker."

He then quietly told the story of how he had met Gene, his time spent working with him, and how he had taken him to Red's. As the story progressed to the point of the helicopter ride to the base and the suspicious actions of the two officers that had monitored the interview of him and his daughters, he stopped and sat back.

Taking another drink, he then told Kevin about the team that had been sent to capture the supposed terrorist. "You've seen enough missions to know the force normally sent to pick up a high-value target. They don't send nurses."

Pausing to let Kevin envision the situation, he continued, "You've seen the broadcasts and seen the outrage over the attacks on the World Trade Center, the Pentagon, and the others. Now, who in the world would send a small team in to capture such an important target as Gene is supposed to be?"

Kevin shook his head knowingly and turned slightly on his stool. He too kept a close eye on the people around them to detect any unwanted attention.

"Now," Butch continued, "the only reason to keep the team small is to minimize the attention they would get and the number of people knowing about the mission. If Gene was indeed involved with the hijackers and with the attention spread across the country, you would think that his capture would warrant national coverage."

Leaning slightly toward Kevin, Butch lowered his voice slightly and said, "I'm positive that the fifth hijacker story was a government cover-up of a program that involved only Gene."

"What makes you think that?" Kevin asked. "They have already captured others of the team that didn't succeed in hijacking another airliner."

"Really?" Butch asked. "How many times can you think of when the government released information about a program that had absolutely no relation to the actual one. Hell, I've been involved with more misinformation or misdirections on programs that were fairly black in nature, but this one seems to be one of the blackest I've ever seen."

Kevin looked closely at Butch and asked, "Have you finally become one of those conspiracy idiots that see the evil hand of government in everything?"

"No," he replied. "I'm fully aware that certain programs or information do not need to be shown to the public. The reasons may be to prevent our enemies from knowing our capabilities, or it may be due to political sensitivity. Back in the sixties, I worked on planning nuclear missions against some of our best allies. If they had known, or if it had become public, it would have resulted in major shifts in political alliances. I have no problem with contingency planning and fully support the security needs of this country."

Sitting back and crossing his arms over his chest while holding the Budweiser in his right hand, he asked, "How do you feel about alien life-forms being here on earth?"

"Oh shit," Kevin exclaimed. "Where is this coming from?"

"OK, I'm not going to say that aliens are living among us and planning on colonizing the world. What I'm asking is, do you think that there is a possibility that there is life outside of our little planet?"

"Well," Kevin answered thoughtfully. "We've had this discussion before, and I agree that we would be awful arrogant if we believe that we are the only thing in the galaxy that can add two and two. But I think it is improbable that an intelligence that could travel light years would visit backwoods Bubbas looking for intellectual enlightenment or to find suitable breeding material."

"Yeah, I agree," Butch said as he took a sip of the half-empty bottle. "But what if through mechanical problems, one of these visitors happened to crash here. What if they are exploring other planets just as we are, but with much more advanced capabilities? Hell, we're still wearing diapers compared to where other societies may be. Even our rate of technological advancement demonstrates the rapid advances achieved as we progress."

Still wary of unwanted attention, both men watched to see if their conversation would be overheard. Kevin now faced Butch and could quickly see if anyone behind them was showing any interest.

"Just look at what has happened in computers or aircraft in the last fifty years," Butch told him. "From the time that the Wright brothers first flew in 1903, the speed has gone from Mach 1 in the late forties to hypersonic. Computers that used to take up thousands of square feet now fit into your watch. What if another species was only a thousand years ahead of us? Think of the advancements that could take place in our next thousand years."

"OK," Kevin acknowledged. "I'll go along with that, but what does that have to do with Leslie and Gene? Have we gone to all this trouble and expense because there may be alien life somewhere? Even if there have been crashes, such as Roswell, what bearing does that have on this?"

"Just a theory I have," Butch told him. "But what if our government does have the remains of alien life-forms? And let's take it one step further. What if they have been experimenting on these bodies? What if they are trying to figure out how their spacecraft worked? There is a shitload of information out there that supports some of these theories."

"Granted, but information is a long way from proof," Kevin replied. "I would like to see something solid, something physical before I subscribe to the UFO phenomenon. Programs on the history channel or Jerry Springer's exposé of trailer park trash having alien babies ain't going to make it."

"Solid physical proof, do you really want it?" Butch asked. "Well, you may have just got your wish."

"What are you talking about?" he asked incredulously. "Surely, you aren't talking about Gene. Granted, I have my doubts about the terrorist story after meeting him, but how can you stretch that into some wild-ass story about aliens. I think you better take it a little easier on the Jack Daniels, my friend."

"All right, I'll admit that it sounds too far-fetched right now," Butch countered. "But let's analyze the facts. This publicity about a fifth hijacking team, where did that information come from? And how did they manage to catch all the other members so quickly? Especially up north where there is a lot more population to deal with. Now, here we have a single individual, hours and hours of publicity, and no mention of his not being found or information about where they saw him."

After pausing for a second, he continued, "Next, remember the makeup of the team sent to get him? There should have been every state trooper, county cop, and a shitload of military personnel. No, they send a couple of Suburbans and a frigging nurse. Were they afraid that they would need first aid? I don't think so."

"All right, I'll grant that was strange, but I just can't get my mind to accept little green men or whatever you think Gene is."

"Just wait," Butch told him. "I've had a little time to talk to Gene. The story he told was a little vague on the details, but the areas he was taken to and the environment he was kept in are eerily familiar to some of the things I've known for several years. I'm not saying that I know there are spaceships up in Area 51, and I'm not saying that little green men are lying on autopsy tables somewhere while we experiment on them."

"Just what is it you're saying then?" queried Kevin. "Are you implying that Gene is the product of some government program involving extraterrestrial beings?"

"Kind of, but I want you to take some time and talk to him about where he came from and some of the things he's seen. If you're not positive that he isn't part of some terrorist plot, and even some of his story makes you wonder where he came from and why the government is especially concerned about finding him, then you tell me what is going on," Butch told him.

Looking around and remembering to keep his voice down, he continued, "How would the government try to find someone, solicit everyone's assistance, yet not reveal what they were actually trying to accomplish? Give them something the public will get behind and make them believe that it's raining while they're pissing on their boots."

Kevin sat back and finished the almost-warm beer he had been holding. Placing the empty bottle on the bar, he motioned for the bartender to bring another round. Both of them sat quietly as their fresh Budweisers were placed in front of them and the bartender had moved on to care for the other customers.

"All right, I'll spend a little time talking to him," Kevin finally said. "But I'm still not buying this alien thing. Speaking about that, what do you intend to do with those two while we're figuring out what is really going on? They can't live out there forever without being seen shopping or whatever."

Butch leaned back and smiled. "Well, good buddy. I want you to adopt them."

"What do you mean, adopt?" Kevin questioned.

"I mean, I want you to take care of them as if they were your family. Make sure you take them the food, get the water and electricity hooked up—you know, take care of them."

"I suppose that you don't want anybody knowing about any of this for the next, what, twenty years?"

"I don't think it will take that long," Butch replied. "But yes, nobody can ever find out what we're doing for now. At least until we know for sure what we're dealing with. I almost hope that you're right. It would be a lot easier if Gene were a terrorist, we could just duct-tape his little arms and legs together and leave him in front of the Boyd Police Department."

"And why can't we do that anyway?" Kevin asked. "We don't know why the government is looking for him. And it's not any of our business."

"I know it isn't any of our business," Butch responded. "But what if we've discovered a secret that hundreds of people have searched for since the Roswell incident? What about your sense of adventure?"

"I'm not sure I want this type of adventure," Kevin told him. "Sure, I was stupid and wanted to go bear hunting with just a spear. But this could get us in more trouble with the feds than you can believe. Especially if you're right, which I'm not too sure of."

"Speaking of getting into trouble," Butch asked. "Have you noticed any increased helicopter activity around the area?"

"Yeah, come to mention it. Especially up and down 730 between Decatur and Boyd," he said. "I figured it was something to do with one of the local drug dealers."

"Well," Butch said, "I figure it has to do with looking for Gene. And I figure it involves more than a few helicopters and cars driving around. That is one of the reasons I've tried to keep our conversations on the prepaid cell phones and never use names.

"I think my house has been searched and probably the phones have been tapped. I would guess that my truck has been targeted and at least a microphone stuck somewhere inside," he continued. "And I would bet that sooner or later, they will come looking for you."

"Why would you think that?" Kevin asked. "As far as anyone except you, Gene, and Leslie knows, I'm not involved at all."

"And I plan on keeping it that way," Butch told him. "I'll go one step further. If this is as black of a program as I believe it to be, then I would use every system available to find where Gene is and I'd concentrate on who came in contact with him. That would include me, my girls, and the two ladies he met at Red's. I would concentrate on them for now."

"You know," Kevin said as he shook his head, "I thought this might have something to do with trying to help out a friend that was being looked for. You know, someone's ex-husband or something. I never expected to be trying to hide someone from the government. But it may explain the two black Suburbans I saw when I left Leslie's place."

"When did you see them?" Butch asked.

"As I was leaving, they were just coming from around where 287 passes through Bowie. And I do recall there was a helicopter that arrived right after that."

"So," Butch remarked, "you think that some ex-husband would have those assets? Think about the scenario, kind of having a black ops feel, doesn't it?"

"Yeah, sure does."

"Now," Butch asked, "how much do you remember about the satellite operations from Southeast Asia? How many photos did you have showing the activity of those little villages they sent you into?"

"Quite a few, and pretty damned accurate."

"If you were trying to find something or someone out here, what would you use to track and monitor them? How good do you think today's systems are compared to what we used over thirty years ago? And how long do you think we have until one of us makes a mistake that highlights us?"

"I guess you're trying to tell me that Big Brother is in the sky and watching our every move," Kevin replied.

"I'd say they have developed a large interest in me," Butch told him. "And I'd say they will develop the same interest in you if they find out you are involved. I'm trying to keep them from ever knowing about you, but it wouldn't surprise me to find out that they know I'm working with someone, and it may not take them long to sort out who that is."

"What do you suggest?" Kevin asked.

"First, make sure we always use the phones as we have. Never call me on any other phone to keep them from getting your name from the number of the phone you used," Butch told him. "And get another truck to use when you're taking care of our guests. Get some old used thing that would look like any other ranch truck, and keep it hidden when you're not using it. Try to keep it down to once or twice a month."

"Also," he continued, "make sure our guests understand the rules and the consequences of breaking them. I don't mean what we would do, but what the government might do if my initial theory about Gene's origin is correct."

"What about them wanting to contact their families?" Kevin asked. "Leslie has already asked if she could."

"Absolutely not," Butch said. "And I think you'll find out that Gene has none. At least none that he is aware of. Hell, his mother may have been a petri dish, and his father may be just pieces of a long-deceased visitor."

"Let's just withhold our judgment until I have a little more information," Kevin told him. "I'll go along with this for now, but I expect to do a lot of questioning before I subscribe to your alien theory."

"Fine," Butch said as he finished his beer. "Take your time, but keep your mind open. You know as well as I do that there are things that just couldn't be years ago, but are readily accepted today."

Butch stood up and pushed the remaining money to the edge of the bar. "I'm heading home. I hope we don't have to get together again for quite some time, but if we do, it has to be short and in some public place like Wal-Mart where we won't be noticed. Otherwise, use the prepaids as sparingly as possible. The less contact the better for now."

"OK, Butch," Kevin said as he sat back on the barstool. "I'll do as you've asked. I've trusted you for too long to quit on you now. But I want some firm answers."

Butch turned to go and said, "I think you'll get some of those answers after you have that little talk with Gene. Like I said, keep an open mind and question why things are happening as they are. Take care, and I really mean it. Take a lot of care."

Kevin sat and watched Butch wave at the bartender and walk out the door. Shaking his head, he wondered just what was going to happen next.

TM

Chapter 24

Colonel Erickson was sitting in one of the more comfortable chairs watching the scenes unfold on each of the screens. Activity in Bowie was now concentrated on convenience stores and truck stops lining Highway 287. Leslie's house had been thoroughly searched and the phones had been tapped. The microphones planted in each of the rooms would pick up any sound and alert them to any activity. Her car had been wired, and a location transmitter installed. For now, there was nothing more to do at the house.

Stacy's house had also covertly been searched and wired exactly the same as had Leslie's and Butch's. It seemed that she had no further useful information, but could possibly be the one that Leslie might contact.

Karyn Lynch was talking on one of the numerous phones on the desk and discussing ways to get copies of all the security camera tapes from the stores where prepaid cell phones had been purchased. Several of the stores had sold the phones throughout the day, but there did not appear to be any one where more that two had been bought.

Major Fleenor was on another phone with his counterpart in Washington trying to get a list of former service members that lived within a hundred miles of Boyd. He was amazed at the number of retired members or those that had served, some as far back as Korea. There was even a couple that had been in World War II. These, he dismissed and directed them to concentrate on service between 1960 and 1980.

Having seen Mr. North's service record, he tried to limit the scope of the search to as few possibilities as necessary to ensure everyone in the area was covered. Even with the enormous amount of data available, finding many of these people was proving to be impossible. Information on those that had served only the basic three—or four-year commitment was sketchy and unreliable after so many years.

He had finally decided to have the state records of driver's licenses cross-referenced with military records and help narrow the search parameters to a more manageable amount. Even so, there were thousands of former army, navy, marine, and air force personnel living in the area.

The people at the Pentagon had tried to match those identified as residents within the search area with being stationed at the same bases as Mr. North during the same time frames. Several of these were found, and a cursory investigation yielded no promising individuals. Most of the matches were current or retired airline pilots that had known Butch during his time in the air force. There were none that matched his time in the navy.

One of the problems with this system was that it did not cover all of Butch's numerous short-time assignments to special projects. Unless they could pinpoint every pilot that had participated in a Red Flag exercise or one of the Team Spirit exercises, they were virtually impossible to locate.

One of the many problems that could not be resolved was who he had known during the Vietnam era. Working in Naval Intelligence, he had contact with people in all branches of service and had information about many others. The entire project would take months to complete and, even then, might not provide the name of the man who had bought the phones.

Kathy Blevins had brought in a tray of sandwiches that Major Romine had picked up from the officer's club and occasionally called to see if they needed anything else. As General Nelson's secretary, she didn't have full knowledge of the situation, but was certainly aware of the importance of their mission. Kathy had been in the facility for several commanders before Mike, but he was certainly one of her favorites.

Rick sat staring at one of the screens, thinking that there was something that he was missing. He had just watched Butch leave his house and drive toward Boyd. As he saw him pull into the IGA parking lot, he realized that the reason for the feeling was that there had been a familiar vehicle on the same road moments earlier. Not only had it been there, he thought, but he could swear that he had seen it only a couple of hours before in the Boyd area.

"Major Fleenor," he said as he turned from the screen, "could I get you to rerun a couple of these views for me?"

Jerry replaced his phone and walked over to stand beside Rick. "Certainly, which ones do you have in mind?"

"Let's start with the one of that truck that was seen pulling the trailer. I think I have seen that same truck at least once since then," Rick told Jerry.

Jerry picked up the phone and dialed the number for the technicians that controlled the systems. Telling them to replay the tapes they had reviewed earlier, he had them freeze the frame that had the best image of the truck as it sat just in front of the trailer.

Looking at the image on the screen, Rick told them to replay the one he had just been watching, starting with when Butch left his driveway and stopping when he parked at the IGA. As the images began to roll across the screen, Rick pointed to the truck that passed Butch's on the road headed in the opposite direction.

"There," he exclaimed. "I think that is the same truck as in these pictures at where the camper trailer was bought. Now, let's reverse the tape and see where that truck came from.

Watching the traffic in reverse, they saw the truck in question backing into the IGA parking lot. As the screen continued, a man got out of the truck and walked backward into the store. Several minutes later, they watched the same man walk backward to the truck, get in and back out heading west.

Now playing it forward, the truck drove in, parked, and the man got out, went in, and came back out after a few minutes. He then left the parking lot and once again passed Butch's truck as he headed toward Boyd.

Jerry spoke into the phone issuing instructions and then hung up. "We'll have both shots of the truck isolated, enlarge the images, and overlay them with computer enhancement in just a couple of minutes," he said as he returned to the array of screens. "Did you say that you thought that you had seen the same truck another time?"

"Yeah, I think so," Rick said thoughtfully. "I'm sure it was after we saw it with the trailer since that's the first time we paid it any attention. So somewhere between then and this shot, I think we'll see it again."

"OK," Jerry told him as he again picked up the phone. "I'll have them rerun the overhead view and search for any truck that fits the same description. The computer can digitally match the general description and isolate the scenes that contain possible matches."

Speaking quickly into the phone, he relayed his request and waited for the reply. Nodding silently, he waited until he got the answer and then hung up.

"We should have some potential matches within the next fifteen or twenty minutes," he said. "We can then look for matches ourselves, and after we think we've found them, the team will use their programs to match any distinguishing features to either confirm or deny the identity."

Karyn had finished her conversation and was standing just behind Rick's chair. "Do you think you've found our mystery man?" she asked.

"Not sure," Rick replied. "But I think I've spotted the truck in question a couple of more times around Boyd. Granted, there are a lot of trucks out there, but red isn't the favorite. If it had been white, as at least 90 percent of them are, I might not have noticed."

"Do you think we should call General Nelson?" she asked.

"Not yet," he replied. "I don't want to raise any expectations yet. And identifying a truck doesn't give us much more than proving what we already know. Someone is helping Mr. North. Unless we can identify the man, the truck isn't of much benefit."

Several minutes passed while they waited for the technicians to produce the scenes showing several trucks that roughly fit the description provided to the computer. Jerry's phone finally rang, and after answering it, he turned and told them on which screen the images would appear.

Hanging up and walking back to stand beside Karyn, he waited with them for the first of several shots of various trucks. After almost one hundred pictures of trucks ranging in color from almost pink to a dark maroon, Rick again pointed at a particular truck on a highway.

"That one," he told Jerry. "Have them isolate the time frame and run the tapes involving that one."

Moments later, one of the screens showed the truck coming east on Highway 114 and pass through Boyd. Passing almost through town, it turned north on 730 and headed toward Decatur. About one mile after turning, it turned right onto a gravel road and then entered an area notable for two large barns. As they watched, it drove into the largest one and disappeared.

They sat watching for several more minutes until it suddenly backed out and headed back toward Boyd. They followed its progress until it passed through Bridgeport and became lost in the traffic and was obscured from their view due to buildings and the angle from the satellite.

"OK, Jerry," Rick said. "Let's have them compare that truck with the other two. Karyn, have one of your people find out what the area with the barns is used for and why he was there."

Excited now by what could be a major break in the search, Rick picked up his phone and called General Nelson. Mike was due back within the next few minutes, but Rick wanted to inform him of the potential good news as soon as possible.

"General Nelson will be here in about five minutes," he told them. "In the meantime, let's see if we can't produce an image that will show us who this man is. Jerry, please have your people start at the scenes of the truck entering the barn and run backward to see if there was any other activity that might warrant our attention."

"I don't think it was a coincidence that the very same truck was at the same IGA within minutes of Mr. North. I'll bet that if we get a firm match, we can have the computer review every scene we have, and that truck will show up again. And I want to start with Leslie's house just before we got there if possible," he said as he removed a fresh Dr Pepper from the small refrigerator and took a long drink.

Chapter 25

          Butch walked out of the Avondale VFW and started his truck. He knew that what he had told Kevin sounded impossible. Normally a down-to-earth, matter-of-fact type of person, he had just verbalized something that he himself found hard to believe. Sitting in the parking lot waiting for the engine to warm up, he wondered how much of the alien story Kevin would really believe.

      Finally, pulling out of the lot and onto the service road, he drove south to the Stop sign where he turned right and followed Farm Road 718 north toward Newark and ultimately his house. Normally he did not use this route, but he wanted to divert any possible attention away from the route that he knew Kevin would take back toward Vashti. He wasn't sure he would be followed or if they were using some satellite system, but he would take every precaution possible.

      The drive up the two-lane road was slightly slower than if he had used 287, but he needed time to think and sort out the thoughts that were running through his mind. Just south of Newark, he passed the road that led to where the Copeland Ministries occupied more land than most of the local ranches. He had never been on the property, but had heard numerous stories about the armed security guards that roamed the compound.

Wondering why a church should require a fleet of aircraft and more protection than most military installations, he recalled the numerous religious organizations, especially televangelists, which had proven to be nothing more than con men with Bibles. Though never really religious, he always felt that every person should treat others with respect and help those less fortunate. He did draw the line at enabling those that only wanted to take from others instead of trying to make their own way.

Passing through the small town of Newark, he decided that when he got home, he would see what information he could find on the Internet regarding UFOs or alien life. *Damn,* he told himself, *Kevin may be right. I may be losing my mind. All these years of only believing what I could see or touch. Here I am about to try to prove right those same people that I used to scoff at.*

As he approached the intersection with Old Base Road, he quickly decided to take a run by the stables. Usually he would drive by when he was out even if he had no intentions of stopping. Just to see if there were any strange vehicles or one of the boarders checking on their horses. Now, with his full-time hand gone for the next few days and no one staying in the mobile home there, he felt he needed to keep a closer eye on the property.

The night security lights shone through the trees and revealed an empty parking area. He drove in and parked in front of where Gene was supposed to have spent the night. He had not been back inside since he had been here with the team that had picked him and his daughters up. Walking up the steps to the porch, he noticed that the glass storm door was slightly open. Cautiously, he tried the door that led inside. Unlocked, it swung open and revealed the dark interior.

Butch felt along the wall just inside the door to find the light switch and flipped it on. The ceiling light illuminated the living room and part of the kitchen area. Glancing around, everything appeared normal. He walked down the narrow hall to the bedroom where Gene was supposed to have spent the night. There on the floor were the clothes he had been wearing when they first met.

Butch picked up the pants and checked the pockets for anything that Gene may have left. Finding them empty, he dropped them back on the still-made bed. There didn't appear to be anything here that would help him determine where Gene had come from or who he really was.

After a quick check of the bathroom, he departed and locked the door after he shut it firmly. With no one staying there for a few days, he left the light on to discourage anyone from coming in. As he stood on the covered porch, he took a cigarette butt from the ashtray on the small table sitting there. After making a small tear in the paper around the filter, he placed it against the bottom of the closed door and watched it roll out. Satisfied that it would be moved should anyone open the storm door, he put it back and securely closed the door.

He debated going into the barn, but knew that if he opened the doors and turned on the lights, the horses would be disturbed and would be expecting to be fed. Instead, he got back into his truck and swung around to head back out. Everything appeared as usual, except he wondered about the storm door having been open. He couldn't be sure that it had been securely shut before, but he wanted to know if anybody came there again.

Pulling into the driveway to his house, the lights of the truck showed the cattle lying beside the fence. They raised their heads and watched him pass without showing any concern. He had been roping this set for a couple of months, and they were used to him driving by or riding among them. Unlike longhorn cattle that roamed free across hundreds of acres, these were completely used to human contact and rarely displayed any of the aggressive nature that made the huge horns so dangerous.

All of these cattle had their horns tipped twice already, and it would be necessary again soon. Since they continued to grow, he had to occasionally cut a couple of inches from the ends so they would fit through the roping chute. Remembering the first time his cousin's husband had come to help, he smiled. The poor man was unaware of the amount of blood that came spurting from the cut end, and he had been covered with the spray that shot out.

After parking and walking to the back door, he glanced down to see if the blade of grass still rested against the door. Satisfied that no one had been in the house, he entered and walked directly to the desk where his computer sat. He took off his hat and sat it upside down on the floor beside the chair while he waited for the screen to light up. Flipping on the light, he retrieved his hat and walked back toward the kitchen. As he passed the entry for the front door, he placed the hat back on the rack mounted on the wall.

Taking a can of Coke from the refrigerator, he filled a glass with ice and moved to the countertop where the glass decanter of whiskey sat. Removing the stopper from the Jack Daniels, he poured almost half of the glass with the golden brown liquid. As the familiar fragrance of the whiskey reached his nose, he added a splash of Coke. After swirling the mixture around with his finger, he raised the glass in a silent toast to friends and family before taking the first sip.

Returning to the computer, he sat the glass on a stone holder and began his search for answers. He looked for any site that would provide information on UFOs, alien life, or anything that might relate to either proving or disproving what he thought might be the real reason for the desperate hunt for Gene.

He was amazed at the volume of information available that dealt with every facet of aliens or UFOs. Searching for specific data when he did not know exactly what he was looking for proved to be more difficult and time-consuming than originally thought. Web sites that dealt exclusively with reported crashes littered the pages.

Hours into the search, he began to focus on the more notable occurrences. He reviewed the one that dealt with the 1897 crash here in his home town of Aurora. He had already seen most of the information, and his review was complete within minutes.

The site involving the Roswell crash in 1947 had much more information and mentioned that the remains had been taken to the Fort Worth Army Air Corp Base. That base today was named the Naval Air Station/Joint Reserve Base (NAS/JRB), the very one where he and the girls had been taken.

Most of the reports later told of the materials being shipped to Wright-Patterson AFB, but some mentioned hangars at the NAS/JRB that were used for storage. Of course, there was a lot of discussion relating to Area 51 as well.

One of the more interesting things he discovered was an article that pertained to an organization known only as the Majestic Twelve, or MJ 12. Further research on the organization alluded to their involvement with managing the UFO phenomenon. Reading various articles, Butch discovered that it was obvious that disagreement among the different groups was the norm. Some claimed to have documentation proving its existence, while others claimed that the group existed only to spread disinformation about the government's knowledge of extraterrestrial activity.

Hours later, Butch finally turned the computer off and rubbed his neck. Hunched over the keyboard for all this time had provided him with sore shoulders and no definite answers. He had not expected to find absolute proof of any alien existence, but the research had done little to provide any more insight to the situation than before he had begun.

Turning the computer off and taking his empty glass back to the kitchen, he wondered how anyone could keep secret things that so many people had sworn to have seen. So many sightings, so many different stories, and so many reasons for why it hadn't happened. Believing in UFOs was like believing in a supreme being. You just had to either believe or not, there was absolutely no proof of either beyond written words.

Heading back toward the bedroom, he turned off the lights and rechecked each door. It was going to be a short night, and tomorrow he needed to get busy working on numerous chores at the stables. He just hoped that Kevin would take care of the business he had dropped in his lap.

TM

Chapter 26

Kevin finished the beer he had started while Butch was still there. By now it had warmed and tasted rather flat. Motioning for the bartender, he asked for one more. Waiting for her to bring him another Budweiser, he thought about what Butch had said. It was very strange, labeling Gene as one of the terrorists that was supposed to hijack an airplane and fly it into who knows what.

He hadn't dealt with a lot of Middle Easterners, but he was fairly certain that Gene wasn't from that area. Matter of fact, he looked more Asian, at least his eyes. And no facial hair. Shaking his head, he realized that he was trying to rationalize what he had done and was going to be doing.

One thing for sure, he knew Butch well enough to know that when his hair began to stand up on the back of his neck, something was definitely wrong. They had trusted each other for many years and respected each other's hunches. Strange, the way their minds usually ran in the same direction. Must have been that they were raised by poor families, served during the same demonized Vietnam war, thus earning the disrespect of their peers that had remained at home.

Even now, they both looked at life pretty much the same way. Take care of your own and your friends. Never turn away from a challenge and help those that deserve it. Bottom line here was, Gene needed help. Regardless of his previous situation, whatever that was, Gene seemed to be a genuinely good kid and had gotten caught up in something where he had no control.

This beer had to be the last one. He still had to drive home and prepare for a long day tomorrow. Turning the bottle up, he wasted no time in sucking the last of the cold brew. His throat still aching from the wet coldness that had almost given him a brain freeze, he sat the bottle down on the bar. Taking $5 from his pocket, he laid it on the bar and walked to the door.

The air was crisp and clear as he started his truck. After a moment to let it warm, he headed north on the service road until he came to an access road that led him back onto 287. Careful to maintain the speed limit, he used the hour required to drive back to Vashti in thought.

Parking his truck in the garage and shutting the door, he went into his house and prepared for bed. As he finished undressing and brushing his teeth, he mentally reviewed what he would need to connect the electricity and water to his 'new' family's residence. Maybe he could take a few things there to make life a little easier for them. They may be sitting there for a very prolonged time.

Slipping into bed, he turned out the small table light and was sound asleep as soon as his head touched the pillow. The strain and constant movement had taken its toll. It did not, however, prevent him from some of the strangest dreams he had ever had. Somewhere during the night, he imagined he watched flying saucers land in his pasture and small men came out to look at his cattle.

He was up before the sun had even tried to peek above the horizon. Entering the garage, he took the stack of hundred-dollar bills from under his seat and realized that Butch had given him $2,000. Shaking his head, he went back through the house and started a pot of coffee.

While the coffee was brewing, he walked the hundred yards in the dark down to his barn. Sitting there was the old pickup that he hadn't driven in over a year. He spent a few minutes checking the tire pressures and fluid levels. Pulling the door handle, it creaked and groaned but did open.

Sliding behind the wheel, he turned the key that was always in the ignition and prayed for the battery to have enough charge to crank the engine. The resulting click told him that his luck had ran out. He got out and opened the hood again. The battery showed enormous corrosion, but the cables seemed to be serviceable.

The battery charger was still sitting on the shelf where he had placed it after its last use. With two tractors, lawn mowers, and his trucks, there were always one or two batteries that would go down from lack of use.

Connecting the leads to the terminals, he flipped the switch to high charge and returned to the house. There the coffeepot was full of the dark brown liquid that he needed to jump-start his own batteries. Taking a cup, he sat in his recliner and used the remote to turn the TV on. Still tuned to the news station he had left for Leslie to watch, the same scenes depicting Gene in Middle Eastern attire with a beard and beside it a picture of him as he was today.

Now paying closer attention, he saw exactly what Butch had said about how he would look, if he could grow a beard. Absolutely certain that Gene hadn't shaved the day he had picked him up at the hay barn, he realized that these pictures weren't real. Somebody somewhere had altered Gene's photos to make him appear as they wanted the public to think.

More and more, he came to think that Butch was on to something. He still wasn't ready to believe the alien story, but he was sure that some sort of cover-up was taking place. As patriotic as he was, he just didn't believe in deliberate lies from his government. Trying to keep information from reaching the public was absolutely necessary, but unless you were from Oklahoma or a fighter pilot, you didn't lie.

Now in a hurry to talk to Gene and Leslie, he poured the remainder of the coffee into a large thermos and grabbed three clean cups from his cabinet. Pouring one cup full of sugar, he put the cups into a plastic bag and headed back down to his barn.

After putting the coffee and bag in the seat of the old truck, he again tried to start the engine. Enough time had passed that the battery had taken some charge, and the extra power from the charger provided enough to turn the motor over. As it cranked over and over, he decided to shoot a little ether into the carburetor. After removing the air filter cover, he sprayed a small amount of Quick Start and again tried to start the engine. This time it caught and began to rumble through the almost-nonexistent muffler.

Giving the old truck a few extra minutes to blow out the blue smoke that resulted from too many months of sitting unused, he pulled on the lights and was relieved to see that all of them appeared to be working. Now, if the tires hadn't dry rotted, he would soon be able to see what he would learn from his adopted kids.

He quickly loaded a couple of rolls of electrical wire, a can of connectors, several joints of PVC pipe, various couplers, cleaning solvent, cement, and the tools required to tie the water and electricity to the trailer. Climbing back into the truck, he backed out of the barn and headed out his driveway.

This time he drove straight to Highway 59 and took it all the way to the Post Oak exit. This early in the morning, there were few vehicles on the two-lane road. Most of them were local hunters heading out to their deer stands or some ranch hand sleepily going to feed his cattle somewhere.

As he approached the chain that crossed the cattle guard leading to the spot where the camper was sitting, he stopped and took out his flashlight. Before he stuck his key in the lock, he saw the blade of grass sticking out. Nodding silently, he unlocked the chain and dropped it down between the pipes that made up the bottom of the cattle guard.

The winding gravel road was still blanketed with darkness as he slowly crunched his way. Several deer and a couple of wild hogs crossed in front of him as he snaked his way up and down the hills. Finally reaching the camper, he saw no lights but had expected none. The lone flashlight he had left would have used all its battery power long ago if it had remained on throughout the night.

Keeping the truck running and its lights shining on the front of the camper, he got out and walked to the single door. Knocking loudly, he called out, "Let's rise and shine, folks, Santa Claus is here with hot coffee."

From within the trailer he heard sounds of movement. *That's good*, he thought. At least they didn't run away. Seconds later, the door swung out, and he saw Gene standing there bare-chested and barefooted in a pair of jeans.

"Well," Kevin asked, "are you going to invite a poor ol' cowboy in for coffee? Especially the one that brought the coffee?"

Gene hesitated for only a second and responded, "Yes, sir, please come in."

"Thanks," Kevin replied. "I'll just go back to the truck and get the coffee since you're gracious enough to invite me in."

As Kevin returned to the truck, Gene thought about how strange these people are. Leaving the door open, he found his shirt and snapped it closed. From the back of the trailer, he heard Leslie climbing out of bed.

"Who's there?" she asked sleepily.

"It's Kevin," Gene answered. "He brought coffee."

"Great," she said. "I'll be out in a minute."

Kevin turned the lights off on the truck and used his flashlight to walk back to the trailer. Entering, he placed the light on the small countertop so that it shone on the ceiling and provided just enough light to avoid running into anything in the cramped interior.

"Here's the coffee," he said as he pulled the cups from within the bag and sat the thermos on the counter. "I believe you have some milk, and there's sugar in one of the cups. Help yourself."

Gene busied himself converting his bed back into a table with two bench seats. Putting his sheets and blankets on the floor, he walked over and poured an empty cup full. Not seeing a spoon, he poured a little sugar into his coffee and took the milk from the cooler sitting on the floor.

"Here, son," Kevin told him as he pulled a ballpoint pen from his pocket. "You can use this to stir you coffee. Don't worry, it's been days since I used it to pick my teeth."

As Gene was stirring the coffee, Leslie came in wearing jeans and a sweatshirt with a blanket wrapped around her shoulders. As she poured some sugar into her Styrofoam cup, Kevin watched Gene's reactions. *Damn,* he thought, *this kid's in love.*

After filling her cup, Leslie said, "Thanks, I'm glad you're here. I really need to talk to you."

"While you're up, would you mind refilling my cup?" Kevin asked.

"Sure," she replied. "How about that talk?"

"No rush, little lady," Kevin remarked. "I think we all need to have a heart-to-heart. I especially need to ask a few questions and see exactly what kind of situation we are going to have to tolerate."

Gene slid over on the seat, and Leslie sat down as far from him as she could without falling off. Kevin sat quietly and watched them as he sipped his refreshed cup.

TM

Chapter 27

Rick was watching the screens as several depicted previously recorded scenes. The truck they were looking for seemed to be a vital clue to who Butch was working with to prevent them from capturing Gene. The computer specialists were busy feeding various images into their programs to identify any unique marks or details that would provide positive identification of other images.

General Nelson walked into the room and asked, "What's got you folks all excited?"

Rick turned and told him, "Sir, we have identified a truck that has appeared around Butch's truck or at the same location too many times to be a coincidence. We are trying to profile it so we can be absolutely positive that it is the same one. We also think it is the truck that was seen pulling the camper from the lot south of Decatur."

"Have you notified General Modelle?" Mike asked.

"No, sir, not yet," Rick answered. "We want to make sure that is the same truck before we make our official recommendation. Especially if it's the truck that picked up the camper."

"I agree," Mike said. "We sure don't want to be chasing several trucks that have nothing to do with this case. How long before you can get confirmation of the truck?"

"Maybe as soon as an hour," Major Fleenor told him. "The biggest problem we're having is the time delay due to the technicians being back in Washington and having to relay data back and forth."

"I think I may have that problem solved," announced General Modelle as he walked into the room.

He continued over to the array of screens and looked at the images showing trucks that all looked to be the same. Although each view was slightly different, some from one side and others from the opposite side, they did all appear to be the same vehicle.

"I just got off the phone with my council members, and they are in agreement that we need assistance. They are sending a complete unit of computer technicians and another unit that will have complete control of our satellite. That way, we can instantly change which system is looking where and move the satellite from one location to another if we need to get a different angle on the subject," he told them.

"When do you expect them to arrive?" asked Mike.

"They should be airborne within an hour," he said. "The president has made arrangements with the FAA to open the airspace for this mission, and Air Force Two will be bringing them down. Mike, you need to contact General Brown over at NAS/JRB and alert him. The cover story is of a security team's inspection prior to an official visit to President Bush's ranch. Once the plane has landed, there will be a caravan of vehicles that will off-load the various teams and head south."

"Yes, sir," Mike told him. "Will our team be going south with them?"

"No, they will be directed to our area to provide backup if any of the initial teams have any problems," he answered. "We need to provide a space for the satellite controller within this room. It would also help if we could accommodate the computer folks too."

"We can move Karyn down to the main conference room," suggested Jerry Fleenor. "Most of her work involves communication with the field teams. We can still provide timely information to her and take her folk's reports."

"That sounds OK," Mike told him. "Karyn, what do you think? Can you operate there with minimal impact?"

"Certainly, sir," she answered. "Most of my work involves land vehicles or the two choppers we have in the air. That will also give me more space to plot their progress on the survey to find the stores that sold the phones."

"Good," Paul told them. "Now, just where are we on following Mr. North?"

Rick walked to the screen showing Butch's truck sitting outside of his house and said, "He went from his stables into Boyd, where he stopped for a couple of minutes at the IGA, the local grocery store. Then he drove south to the Avondale VFW where he spent a couple of hours. Following that, he drove north on 718 and cut off just north of Newark toward the stables."

As he was talking, he pointed to the overhead satellite view of the area. "Then he turned into the stables and spent some time in the house trailer where Gene was supposed to have been. After that he went back to his house and has been there ever since."

"What about phone calls or anything picked up from the truck transmitters?" Mike asked.

"None," Rick answered. "The only thing that he did after he got home was get on his computer for a while before he apparently went to bed."

"Can we get into his computer to see what he was doing?" Paul asked.

"Yes, sir," Karyn answered. "Along with the phone taps and hidden microphones, we were able to patch in and monitor his Internet use."

"What do you have from that?" Mike asked.

"Just a second, sir, and I'll have that information," she told him. "I have to go through Washington still for that."

"Well, let's hope that we can shorten this process when the new folks arrive," Mike said. "It seems that we've been just a few minutes behind everything Mr. North has done. If we can cut the delay out, maybe we can get a step ahead of him for a change."

"How many places have you placed this mystery truck so far?" Paul asked Rick.

"Sir, we just started reviewing the tapes after I saw the truck passing North's truck as he went to the IGA," Rick explained. "Since then, I think that truck was also seen going into a large barn just north of Boyd. Karyn is checking into whose barn it is. Karyn?"

"I just heard from one of the Bowie men," she answered. "That barn belongs to Levi Wilson. I believe that is the same man Mr. North ordered hay from earlier this afternoon."

"Let's have a look at that hay delivery," Paul directed. "It seems a little coincidental that our suspicious truck would be in the same location that was suddenly asked to deliver hay. Did anybody watch the truck after it left the stables?"

"No, sir, we didn't," answered Rick. "We were concentrating on Mr. North. He pulled out right after the hay truck and returned to his house. The last time we were monitoring the truck stopped as North turned south on 718. The hay truck continued west on 114."

"Let's look at it now," Mike told him. "Rerun the overhead view from when Butch turned off 114. Let's see if we can determine where that truck went."

"I remember seeing it leave," Paul told them. "Unless I'm mistaken, it drove in loaded and left shortly after that with some bales missing from the rear of the trailer. That all seemed normal."

"I remember it too," Mike said. "But what if there was something added? We didn't really look at the cab since it was always in view, but maybe we missed something that was placed on the part of the trailer that was under the roof of the barn."

"Son-of-a-bitch," Paul said. "Do you think that Gene was hiding in the barn and got onto the truck? We searched that place before we brought North and his kids in. It has been under surveillance since then. How could he have gotten back there?"

"I don't know, sir," Rick answered. "But our search didn't really include every hiding place there. The report only said that they walked through and opened the office, tack room, and did a general inspection of the rest. There are lots of places where Gene could have hidden."

"OK," Paul told them. "Let's not start second-guessing ourselves. If we missed something that morning, we still have the same goal now. If Gene was hiding in the stables, he may have escaped with the hay truck. First, let's send someone to do a complete inspection of the trailer house again. There may be something there, if North didn't find it when he stopped back by. Then hit the stables and check everywhere he could have hidden. Maybe there will be something left behind."

"I'll send the team that went to the hay barn," Karyn told him. "They're still in the area. It shouldn't take more that a few minutes for them to get there."

"Sir," Jerry announced, "here are the tapes from when the hay was delivered and forward."

As they watched the now-hours-old data scroll across the screen, they saw the truck leave the stables, Butch following, and his subsequent left turn as he went home. They concentrated now on the load of hay as it continued west on 114. Watching it slow and make a right turn at 730, they followed it directly into the large barn now known to belong to Levi Wilson and the Southwest Hay Exchange.

"Let's fast-forward this," Rick said. "I want you to see if you think the red truck I noticed is the same one as I saw going into that same barn."

As the accelerated movements flashed across the screen, they saw the driver of the hay truck walk out of the barn. After what seemed an eternity, they saw the red truck drive into the barn and delay for several minutes before it left."

"Damn," Paul said. "I'll bet you my next year's paycheck that our boy Gene is in that truck. I'm damned positive that it's the same truck. Can we follow it now?"

"I don't think so," Jerry answered. "If it goes as far west as before, we'll lose it in either the hills or the trees again. We would have to have the satellite moved about fifty miles west to get the vertical angles we need."

As they watched, the truck ultimately got lost in the low-lying hills and increasing trees. Shaking his head, Mike said, "That satellite driver better get here quick. We've probably just witnessed at least twice, if not three times, that if we could have followed that truck, we'd have our man."

"How would he move the satellite that quickly?" Rick asked. "Won't it disrupt its orbit if we slow or speed it?"

"You can speed it some without affecting its geosynchronous track," Jerry told him. "It's a little more difficult to slow it without causing a change in the altitude. Normally, if they need to reposition toward the west, they do a series of north and south moves. Sort of like S-turns that will allow it to keep its speed, but slowly shift to a farther west location."

As they talked and watched the screens, it finally arrived at the time of Butch's arrival at the VFW. As they looked, Rick's eyes opened wide. "Look," he said as he walked closer to the screen. "Right there, that's the same truck. I know it's dark, but when Butch turned in, the lights flashed across it. I'd bet on it. Right there, those two got together, I just know it. I'm beginning to understand this man."

"If you're right," Mike told them, "and I think you are, that sly son-of-a-bitch has been managing to outsmart us. But that's going to change. Once we get our communication and satellite delays taken care of, he won't have the luxury of a head start."

"Sir," Karyn said as she put down the phone, "I think I have some news that won't make any of us any happier."

Turning to look at her Paul asked, "Just what is that?"

"I just got off the phone with the computer folks that reviewed North's Internet use," she answered. "He spent over an hour researching UFOs. He opened almost every site that dealt with alien life, UFOs, or spaceships."

Paul looked at Mike and announced, "I think our friend has learned something. If he hasn't, he's certainly running fast in the right direction. Let's revisit our decision not to pick him up. We may need to be a little more persuasive this time."

"Sir," Mike responded, "I think we should wait until we see if we can find the man working with Mr. North first. And we still have the option of getting that sheriff deputy to try to get some information."

"Maybe you're right," Paul told him. "But if we don't get some results by tomorrow, I want to look that man in the face and let him know that we aren't going to keep playing games."

"Yes, sir," Mike replied. "We'll see what tomorrow brings."

TM

Chapter 28

Butch woke early the next morning. The sun had not lightened the sky as he threw back the covers and headed for the kitchen. A quick stop by the bathroom to relieve himself, a pause in the hall to turn the heat up and he was soon rinsing the coffeepot and measuring out the Folgers he enjoyed most. Having tried the fancy blends when visiting his daughters, he still preferred regular black Folgers.

After the water and grounds had been put into the coffeemaker, he poured one-half cup of orange juice into his mug and walked into the living room. Sitting back in his recliner, he picked up the remote and tuned in CNN. Still showing Gene's picture and retelling the stories about the terrible carnage brought about by the terrorists, Butch watched to see if there were any updates on having found Gene in the remote regions north of Fort Worth.

Seeing nothing there, he switched to Fox News and waited for any news of any spotting of this desperate terrorist that the entire country was looking for. After a few minutes, he switched to the local news. Watching channel 4, he again saw no mention of Gene having been seen around Aurora or Boyd.

Pretty strange, he thought. *Here the nation is on high alert for this man, and after he is spotted in one area, they never mention it.*

Finishing the orange juice, he rinsed the mug and filled it with the now-steaming coffee. Taking his cup into the room where the computer sat, he waited for it to come to life and checked his e-mail. Nothing of interest, just the same old forwarded jokes or 'If you love America, pass this on' messages.

After finishing most of the pot he had brewed, he began searching for any information on genetic manipulation. The wealth of information available rolled down his screen as he quickly read the different types of DNA transference. The applications used on plants and animals resulted in new species of hybrid plants or animals with genetic-altered features.

Everything from cloning to inserting DNA strands to make plants disease or insect resistant. As soon as the idea hit him, he sat back and stared in amazement at what was being done. He knew that if the civilian world had progressed this far, there was no telling what the super secret government programs had developed. This made some of the most bizarre sci-fi movies seen entirely too possible.

He shut down the computer and returned to the kitchen. The possibilities continued to bounce around his brain as he rinsed the cup and turned off the coffeemaker. Walking back to the hall to lower the thermostat so that the house wouldn't stay too warm while he was gone, he decided that he would have to call Kevin and tell him what he was now thinking.

After grabbing a coat and his hat, he shut the door and placed a small stone inside the storm door that would roll out if the door was opened. Glancing at the breaking daylight, he headed down to his barn to feed his two horses. As he whistled for them, he pulled a cell phone from his shirt pocket and looked at the number written on its face. As soon as he was under the roof of the barn, he dialed and waited for Kevin to answer.

Both horses came running into the barn and stood in their respective stalls, waiting for him to pour a scoop of pellets into the buckets attached to the corners of each one. Kevin answered just as he was locking the tack room and preparing to return to the house.

"Hello, Fat Boy," he said. "Did you get a good night's sleep?"

"Not worth a shit," Kevin answered. "Long days, short nights, and strange dreams. You've really screwed up my life, and you'll certainly pay for it. By the way, thanks for the down payment on taking care of your horses."

"Don't mention it," Butch told him. "I'll get you another installment as soon as I can arrange a meeting or a drop-off."

"Whenever, I know where you live anyway," Kevin replied. "But I'm sure you didn't call just to ask me how I slept. What's up?"

"Well, now that I've got you out of bed, I have a theory," Butch said.

"Wake me? Hell, I've made coffee and taken a short drive to visit some dear old friends. We're sitting here all cozy and sipping some of my fabulous brew," Kevin answered.

"How's the crew? Getting friendly yet?"

"Half and half. I'll fill you in when we can discuss it further," Kevin said.

"If it's too crowded where you are, maybe you better find a little breathing room so we can finish this conversation. I need to know what's going on, and I want a little privacy for you when you hear my latest wild-ass theory," Butch told him as he watched the sky becoming much lighter.

Kevin motioned for Leslie and Gene to wait, and he opened the door to step outside. As he was stepping down, he noticed Leslie get up and move to the seat he had just vacated.

"OK," he told Butch as he walked over to his truck and got in. "What do you want to know?"

"What do you mean by half and half?"

"The gelding seems to wish he was still a stud, but the mare apparently isn't in heat," Kevin said, smiling. "She must have been in season too early and now shows no interest."

Butch shook his head and told him, "I'm not going to worry about the breeding yet. After what I found out, he must have been proud cut, and there could very well be a foal in the oven. God, I hope not."

"Me too," Kevin replied. "Now, what's this new, gotta be some real off-the-wall shit theory?"

"What do you know about genetic manipulation?"

"Some, I tried some genetic-altered coastal Bermuda a couple of years ago. It grew like a son-of-a-bitch, but couldn't take the dry climate up here. Why do you ask, Ol' Inquisitive One?"

"I think that we have a product of some program that experimented with what we were discussing the other night. I think we have got us a whole new hybrid."

"You've done lost your whiskey-soaked mind, Kemo Sabe," Kevin laughed. "Where in the world did you come up with that bullshit?"

Butch paused a moment and placed a fresh dip of Skoal in his cheek. "I had a little spare time last night and did a little research on that and the articles I could find on aliens, UFOs, and stuff."

"And naturally you added two and two, and came up with five. Hell, it may even be six or twelve, maybe even fifty on the 'you gotta be shitting me' meter," Kevin almost laughed.

"Nope, I'm serious," Butch told him. "Think about it, we've been altering plants and animals for years. Ever since they mapped the human genome, the civilian world has taken pig DNA and combined it with bovine DNA. If transparent universities or research centers are doing this, what is our friendly government doing? Sitting on their asses and letting civilian technology beat them? I don't think so. I would bet that most of the advances made in the real world don't come close to what the black programs have done."

"This is going to take a little time to simmer in my head," Kevin said somberly. "Just how do you plan on proving this theory? Ask the good doctors out at the base in Fort Worth?"

"No," Butch answered. "But I think it does explain some of the answers I got the other morning. I want you to slide around the issue subtly when you're up there and see if any of it fits."

"Sure, I'll just slip it into the conversation. Kind of like, say, are any of you made from alien parts?"

"Whatever, just ask a few questions and see what seems to fit my theory. Even if you don't get a complete answer, you do the math," Butch told him. "You've had to deal with unknowns and devise an answer before. Do it now."

"OK, what do you want me to do about the civility of our guests?" Kevin asked as he got out of his truck.

"Just explain again that we will try our best to take care of the current situation, but it certainly won't be over in the next day or two. They need to quit drawing lines in the sand and daring each other to step over it."

"I don't think it's that bad," Kevin remarked. "More like a cold front just blew in, and only one of them is standing out in the wind."

"Just work it out, please," Butch told him as he prepared to walk out of the barn. "Pretend you're the ambassador to the Middle

East and you've got to get a Sunni to marry an Israeli. I've got to go to my other job and feed. Let's plan on another call later this afternoon."

Almost hanging up, Butch asked, "Say, did you get the utilities connected?"

Kevin was walking back to the trailer as he answered, "Not yet, hell, the sun's just now peeking over the trees. I'm not about to go crawling around under this thing with rattlesnakes as long as my pecker roaming around."

Butch laughed and told him, "Hell, if that's your unit of measurement, you must have seen an earthworm. Take care."

Hanging up, Butch took a hammer from the workbench and broke the phone into several pieces before he shoved it into his jacket pocket. Walking back to his house, he watched a very black Suburban drive north on 718 toward Tater Junction Restaurant. Paranoid or not, he just knew that he was being watched and decided that since leaving town was out of the question for now, he would have his girls come back and try to appear as if nothing was out of the ordinary. Kevin would just have to take over the entire operation for now. And his stable hand would be back tomorrow. That would allow him to spend a few days with his daughters and maybe show that he had no further interest in whatever the government was doing.

Chapter 29

Kevin walked back to the trailer after he smashed his phone with a hammer from the back of his truck. As he opened the door and stepped inside, he could tell that Gene and Leslie had done nothing except sit and drink their coffee. He walked over to the thermos and refilled his cup before turning to them. Leslie made no move to either slide over or move back to the side where Gene sat staring at his cup.

Standing at the head of the small table, he looked from one to the other and finally said, "Now look, kids, this isn't going to get any easier. And it's not going to be over for at least several days. So please, let's try to be congenial for a change. Leslie, would you like more coffee?"

She looked up at him and said, "I'm trying to be as nice as I can. I'm just not used to being kidnapped and held hostage out in the middle of nowhere."

"First," Kevin told her, "I didn't really kidnap you. I was just trying to get you away from a dangerous situation. Yesterday you said that you knew something was wrong, that you couldn't believe that Gene was a terrorist. Now, you go back to the kidnapping thing. What do you want me to say? I've tried to tell you everything that I know, and I'm still willing to share any information that I have."

Gene looked at Leslie and told her, "I'm so sorry if I got you into this. I never meant for anything to happen to anyone." Tears began to run down his face as he continued, "I just had to get away from that place. Vicki told me that I must not ever go back there."

Leslie looked into Gene's face and saw the shame and sorrow plainly written there. As her face softened, she said, "This isn't your fault, Gene. I'm sorry if I made you feel as if I blamed you. I'm just scared and don't know what to do right now."

Gene lifted his eyes and wiped them on the sleeve of his shirt. "Please, Leslie, don't be mad at Kevin either. Both he and Butch are only trying to keep me safe. I'm just so sorry that you got involved."

Kevin stood quietly while the two seemed to suddenly develop some glimmer of understanding. After a few seconds, he spoke, "All right, let's start all over. I'm going to tell both of you some things that may seem very strange. Hell, I'm not sure if I believe half of it myself."

He eased over to Gene's side of the table and sat beside him. As he turned his head and watched for his expression, he asked, "Gene, what do you know about your parents?"

"Nothing," he said. "Like I told Butch, I never knew them. The only person that treated me like a real person was Vicki. She was the nurse that took care of me. And she took me out of that place where I was living and told me to get as far away as possible. The only other people I ever saw were doctors or scientists. They just kept giving me tests or asking me what I thought about things that they took me to see."

"You never knew your parents?" Leslie asked.

Gene looked at her and replied, "No, I don't even know who they were. I never saw any photos, and no one ever talked about them. Not even Vicki."

"That must have been so hard on you," she told him.

"Regarding where you were kept," Kevin interrupted, "what type of house was it?"

"It wasn't really a house, more like a couple of rooms on one of the floors."

"Floors?" Kevin asked. "Like a large apartment building or a hospital?"

"I guess it was more like a hospital," Gene answered. "I only got to see a couple of the different floors, and there weren't any windows. Also, when we would leave, we went up to get to where the airplane was."

"Now, Gene, I'm going to ask you something that may seem strange but is a theory that Butch came up with. Did anyone ever say anything to you about aliens?" Kevin asked.

"Kind of, like I told Butch, I thought they meant like illegal aliens. You know, from Mexico or something," Gene replied.

"Well, I'll be damned," Kevin said as he sat back. "That son-of-a-bitch may have just figured this out."

"Figured what out?" asked Leslie.

"Figured out why the government is so intent on finding our little boy here, missy," he answered. "He just told me about it while I was outside. He asked me to try to find out if there was anything alien about Gene, and I think we just got the answer."

For the next several minutes, Kevin told them what Butch had been doing and how he came up with his theory. Shaking his head as he talked, he told them about the search on the Internet and how nobody seemed to know that Gene was seen in the area. "I've never really believed that there were any alien visitors," he told them. "But I'm starting to believe that our friendly government has been holding out on us."

"You mean that you think Gene is some cross between us humans and some outer space thing?" Leslie asked incredulously.

"That's exactly what I mean," Kevin told her. "Now before you get your panties in a wad, let's look at what we know."

Leslie shrank back in her seat, staring at Gene. "I just can't believe that," she said. "I can't believe that there's some alien sitting right here looking at me. Oh shit, I can't believe what I may have done. Oh shit, no!"

"Hold on," Kevin told her. "I'm not saying that Gene is an alien. What I'm saying, or rather Butch is thinking, is that he is the product of some genetic manipulation program that the government was running."

Gene sat speechless. He had never in his wildest dreams thought of that. Now, looking back, it made sense to him. All the testing, the blood analysis, the questions, the strange trips. No wonder Vicki was concerned. Now he knew why.

"I'm sure you know that we have been using genetic work for years now," Kevin offered. "We've programmed plants, cloned animals, changed the genetic codes to help eradicate diseases, and improved life for everybody. If Gene is truly a genetic product, it doesn't mean that he isn't human. It's no different than if you had a liver transplant from some man. That doesn't make you any less female. All this means is that he may have some genetic material that wasn't originally part of him."

"I don't know about that," Leslie told him, shaking her head. "I'm not sure what it means."

"Would you ever have thought he was anything other than normal?" Kevin asked. "Isn't he exactly like you and I?"

Gene sat with his head down, ashamed to look at either of them. He had just been handed the worst information possible. *Now,* he thought, *I'm just some experiment. I'm not even human.* He laid his head onto his hands on the table and began to silently weep.

Kevin looked from him to Leslie and asked, "Doesn't that seem human? Is that what you'd expect from some alien life? I don't care who his parents were, he's the same as you and I. Maybe smarter, maybe with some extra special gifts, but still as human as either of us."

Leslie watched him softly crying, and her heart suddenly went out to him. For as long as she had lived, she had always had a tender spot for every animal she had ever seen. She had worked tirelessly to find homes for stray dogs and cats. She never questioned how they came to be lost, only that they deserved a good home. That same instinct now made her look at Gene in the same way. *Here,* she thought, *is a poor thing that has no home, no family, and is scared to death.*

"Excuse me, kids," Kevin said as he stood. "The sun's up, and I have work to do. I'm sure you'd like some electricity and water here in your vast mansion. Ya'll just sit and think about this while I take care of a few things outside."

Kevin closed the door behind him and retrieved all the material he had brought from the back of his truck. Starting with the water connections, he saw that he could simply connect a hose to the faucet that was attached to the pipe feeding the large metal tank. Screwing the hose on, he then strung it back toward the trailer. There on the side was a female fitting that would supply the entire trailer.

Next, he examined the electrical panel that supplied the power for the well pump that had been installed not long ago. Opening the panel, he decided to splice into two of the wires and fasten a plug end where it would fasten to the trailer. Over the next couple of hours, he busied himself as much to get the job done as to leave Leslie and Gene alone together. *Unless I am mistaken,* he thought, *those two will end up being at least friends.*

Inside the trailer, Leslie reached out her hands and touched Gene's arms that lay folded under his face. "Gene," she said softly, "please look at me."

Gene slowly raised his head and, keeping his eyes down cast, said, "I can't. I'm so ashamed. I'm not even a human, how can I ever be anything to anyone if I'm not even human. Maybe Vicki was wrong, maybe I deserve to be kept locked up and kept away from normal people."

"Now you listen to me," Leslie told him sternly. "You're as much human as anyone. Vicki may have been the only one to have seen it back there, but I see it too."

"No, you don't," Gene whispered. "You even said that you regretted what you did the other night, like it was disgusting."

"That's not what I meant," she replied softly. "I was just so shocked. What I really mean is that I'm sorry that I've hurt you too."

Gene raised his eyes and looked at her. "You mean that you don't hate me for what I did?"

"No, I don't hate you," she told him, shaking her head. "It's not what you did, it's what we did. And if there is any fault here, it's mine."

"Leslie," Gene stuttered, "I've never had anyone except Vicki care for me. I thought that when we did that, it meant that you cared too."

"I do care," she answered. "It's just that what happened was so sudden, and we were both drunk. I'm not sure what would have happened otherwise, but I do know that you're a very nice man. Even drunk, I'd never have done that with someone that I didn't like."

Gene's face lit up, and he almost smiled. "You mean, after hearing this, you still like me?"

Taking his hands in hers, she said, "Yes, Gene, I still like you."

Kevin pushed the door open to tell them that he was going to test the water and electrical systems when he saw them holding hands with tears running down both of their faces. Silently, he closed the door and walked down to the tree line behind the trailer. Searching the ground for fire ants or snakes, he squatted and leaned back against one of the slender post oaks that covered most of the land out here.

Lifting his head and looking at the few puffy white clouds floating overhead, he said aloud, "Just wait until Butch hears about this. He's gonna shit."

Chapter 30

           As the sun came up over the horizon, Rick was rubbing his tired eyes and trying to decide how best to use the satellite information that would now give them nearly instantaneous repositioning and provide better views of the area. Especially since it appears that the majority of the focus had shifted westward. If Gene had been moved as they suspected, everything pointed to the area north and west of Boyd. At least the red truck they were interested in had disappeared in the clutter in that direction every time.

As he walked into the small cafeteria room just off the main conference room, he flicked on the lights and began to prepare a pot of his "cowboy coffee." Taking a pot and filling it with water, he plugged it in and put in a handful of grounds. It floated on top until the water began to boil, then it slowly settled to the bottom. After filling his cup, he returned to the operations center and glanced at the multitude of screens. He noticed Butch walking back from his barn in the early-morning light.

All of the tracking and imaging had only proven one thing as far as he was concerned. They could tell you what had happened, what was happening; but the thing they need most, knowing what was going to happen, was still beyond anybody's technology. After all the spook-and-spy stuff, it was still the human mind that solved the puzzle.

As he was wondering just what he would do if he were Butch, Karyn came in and placed a small stack of paper on the desk. "Good morning, Rick," she said as she looked into his cup of coffee. "That looks suspiciously like that mud you call cowboy coffee."

Smiling, he said, "You bet. Puts hair on your chest, care for some?"

"No, thanks. Hair is one thing I certainly don't need on my chest." She smiled back. "I'm going to get some real people coffee. You might want to take a quick look at what came in from intercepting Butch's early-morning Internet travels."

As she turned and walked out, Rick sat his cup down and picked up the papers she had left. Each page showed what site Butch had logged on to, what time on and off, and a brief description of the information he had been reading. Page after page, he read in awe of the progress Butch had made in unraveling the mystery of Gene. Although it was clear that he was certainly getting the theory right, at least there was no proof of how right he was.

"What do you think?" Karyn asked as she walked back in the room with a cup of coffee. She kept her eyes on Rick as she gently blew across the steamy cup.

"I think Mr. North is getting way too close to what we've done," he answered. "This just may have sealed his fate once the generals find out just how close he is. They can't take any chances of his having Gene and also knowing, or at least suspecting, what he really is."

Karyn sat her cup on the table and told him, "That's exactly what I thought. I've gone along with this program for years because I believed in our mission. But when we start targeting civilians, I have a real problem."

"I know what you're talking about," he replied. "But we've sworn to prevent disclosure of any sort. People before him have made the mistake of letting information slip about this place. We can't make exceptions now."

"What exceptions?" Major Fleenor asked as he walked in. "Did I come in at the middle of the movie? If so, how about bringing me up to date?"

Rick handed him the papers he had been reading and waited for Jerry to quickly glance through them. It was evident that he was as shocked as they were about how close Mr. North was to discovering what they were searching for.

"What do you think?" Karyn asked.

"I'm not sure," he answered. "So he's been doing a little research. I agree that it's pointing to the right answer, but he'll never get proof. As far as what the rest of the world will think if he happens to try to go public, he'll just be another crackpot seeing things that go bump in the night."

"I hope you're right," Rick said doubtfully. "I'm not so sure the upper level of this program is willing to take that chance. I'm just glad it's not my decision at this point."

"Do you think we need to tell them?" Jerry asked. "As far as his Internet use went, it actually had nothing to do with our search for Gene. What if he had been visiting a porno site, would we need to tell them that?"

"That's not the same, and you know it," Karyn told him. "This has a direct bearing on his knowledge of our program and could lead to further complications. I think it is absolutely necessary to tell both General Nelson and General Modelle what we've found out."

"Is this connected in any way with finding Gene? I don't think so," Jerry replied. "As I said, I don't see any direct connection. He may have even been researching DNA for his interest in horse breeding. I think this could be taken way out of context and have dire results."

Rick looked at each of them and finally said, "Look, right now I'm in charge of the operation. It's still my decision as to what information is or isn't applicable to our mission. Simply stated, the mission is limited to finding Gene and bringing him back here with as little civilian impact as possible. Anything that would highlight our program is against the basic premise which has guided all these related projects."

"I agree," Jerry said. "If we start bringing in civilians because they believe in UFOs, alien abductions, or any of the thousands of things they think are going on in the world, we will do no more than reinforce those beliefs."

Rick picked up his cup and stared briefly into the grounds resting on the bottom. Finally looking up, he announced, "Thank you, Karyn. I'll take these, and when I believe it becomes a factor in our search, I will give them to General Nelson. He can then decide if it is important to our mission. In the meantime, let's concentrate on finding that red truck. For now, that's where our concentration is needed."

Pausing before he walked back for another cup of coffee, he asked, "Are there any questions? If not, let's see if the satellite driver has put the eye in the sky over our subject area."

Karyn stood, shaking her head as she watched Rick leave the room. "I think he's making a mistake," she told Jerry. "If it turns out that the information he withheld had any bearing on finding Gene, his career is definitely over."

"That's his decision," Jerry replied. "I don't necessarily agree with him, but I think we need to look beyond the narrow scope of our current mission. What if we brought him in and questioned him about this research and it turns out that it had no bearing on Gene? That alone would arouse his suspicions and more than likely confirm what he's thinking if it does have to do with our project."

Rick was returning to the room as Jerry finished. "Not only that," he remarked, "it would also let him know that we are watching his computer. He obviously suspects we're listening to his phones and probably thinks we're tracking his vehicles. This would just confirm those suspicions. As long as he thinks he can use the computer with impunity, he may let slip some information that would help us."

"I follow your reasoning," Karyn told him. "But I still think that the information needs to be passed on to at least General Nelson. Rick, I won't go over your head, but if it comes out that you withheld information, I can't deny that I gave it to you."

"You also need to think about what would happen if they didn't get this information," Jerry added. "If I were to advise you, it would be to turn it over to them and try to use your rationale as to not acting on it. At least that way you've protected yourself."

"You both may be right," Rick acknowledged. "I've always supported my commanders, right or wrong. But I'll certainly try to make them see the possible downside of confronting Butch. As I said, I don't see where this improves our chances of finding Gene, but it would be wrong of me not to give them every piece of the investigation that I find. Thanks, both of you. I'm glad to have people working for me that will let me know when I've crossed the line. I really do appreciate you're not just some yes-men. Hell, even I make the wrong decision every now and then."

Both Karyn and Jerry breathed a sigh of relief. Neither wanted Rick to keep information from their bosses, but they didn't want to have to go behind his back. Karyn nodded and headed back to the conference room where she was controlling the various teams scattered throughout the area.

"No problem, Rick," she said as she turned away. "I've always known you to listen to different points of view. And you've always made the right decisions, even if it wasn't your idea."

"I agree with Karyn, again," Jerry said as he sat down on the desk. "Now, let's see if our computer team has a usable profile of that red truck. We could be lucky enough that it is sitting in somebody's driveway and waiting for us to drop in for early-morning coffee."

"I wish it was that easy," Rick replied. "When do you expect to hear from them?"

"I'm calling them right now," he answered. "If it is ready, I'll have them review every image we have and highlight each sighting. I would like to have that available when General Modelle gets here. I have a feeling that he needs some good news."

"You're right about that," Rick said. "Personally, I think General Nelson needs it more. He probably needs it more than any of us."

"What kind of good news?" Mike asked as he walked in. "Do we have something positive for a change?"

Standing, both men turned to acknowledge General Nelson's arrival. "Not yet, sir," Rick said. "But Jerry is about to find out if we can isolate any frames that contain the red truck. We're hoping that we can find out who owns it by where it may be parked."

"Is it ready?" Mike asked Jerry.

"I'm just calling, sir," he answered. "I should know in a couple of minutes."

"That your cowboy coffee?" Mike asked, looking at the dark, black liquid with grounds floating on top in the cup.

"Sure is, want a cup?" Rick responded.

"I'll get the regular, thanks," Mike told him as he turned to go get himself a cup. "I'll be right back."

Major Fleenor listened as he held the phone in one hand and sipped his coffee with the other. After a few minutes, he told them thanks and asked for the images to be placed on one of the screens within the operations center. As he hung up, the screen on the lower right showed an image of the red truck they were interested in. Several arrows pointed to various locations on the truck and notes describing each abnormality.

Mike came back carrying his cup and stood beside Rick as they watched the surrounding screens depicting the same truck with notes showing the matching details noted in the first picture. Depending on the angle and side of the truck, there were numerous points where minor things were described. The pattern of mud spray on the rear fenders, a small scratch on the right front fender, some gravel damage to the hood, and numerous items in the bed of the truck made it obvious that each truck was the same.

"Sir," Jerry told General Nelson, "we've got a match in several scenes. The first time this truck was within the field of view of our overhead shot was at Leslie's house only moments before our team arrived. We're extremely fortunate to have that information. The satellite was only activated minutes before we sent the team to Bowie."

They all watched as Kevin carried Leslie out to the truck and put her in the passenger seat. Although they could see the action, the angle of the shot did not provide enough detail to prove that it was Leslie, but there was no doubt that they were watching her disappear just as they were about to arrive.

"Can we follow him from there?" Mike asked.

"No, sir," Jerry told him. "Again, he disappears behind houses on his way out of town, and he gets lost among the trees once he leaves the major roads."

They sat and watched each time that Kevin's red truck came back into the center of the satellite's vision. Shaking their heads, they saw it at Wal-Mart in Decatur, again moving the camper, entering the Southwest Hay Exchange barn, and finally at IGA in Boyd before they lost it in the dark. Each time in came into view, it was coming from the west and returned westward each time it left.

"There is still one time that we don't see that truck," Rick told them. "That was at the Avondale VFW. I can't prove it, but I'm sure I saw it in the flash of Butch's truck lights like I said earlier."

"One other thing that we now know," Jerry remarked. "If you'll look at the scene from Wal-Mart, you'll see Butch's truck arrive shortly after it does. That makes at least twice that Mr. North and the driver of that truck have had made personal contact."

"Have we sent anyone to visit the Avondale VFW to check on who was there that night?" Mike asked.

"I'll have Karyn send someone out there right away," Rick answered. "I'm not sure when they open, but we'll be waiting."

He picked up his phone and dialed the number for the conference room. After telling her that she needed to come in for a minute, he hung up the phone and picked up the papers she had provided.

"Sir," he stated, "Karyn's team also intercepted some more information on Butch's computer use. He spent some time early this morning researching genetic information. I doubt if it will help us find Gene, but I thought you ought to see it. Jerry has seen it also, and both of them think it could be important."

Mike took the papers and swiftly read through them. Finishing, he asked, "You said that Karyn and Jerry think it's important, what do you think?"

"As I told them," Rick answered, "I don't see how this will help find Gene. It may have absolutely nothing to do with him. Also, if we take any actions based on this alone, we'll disclose that we're monitoring his computer use."

"But," Mike asked him, "taken with his previous research on alien life earlier, aren't you concerned that he may discover the purpose of our facility?"

"No, sir," he said, shaking his head. "He knows nothing about this facility. He wasn't taken anywhere he could have possibly seen it. He very seldom visits the base, and this looks just like the other hangars around here. It would be impossible for him to tie Gene to this facility."

Pausing while Mike was thinking, he continued, "Additionally, should he ever discuss what would be pure speculation, nobody would believe him without proof. And the only proof available to him is Gene. That's why I think that it would be better to concentrate on our search and deny him the only thing that would possibly prove any theory he may have."

"You're probably right," Mike told them. "I don't see how this affects our current mission. But we must make absolutely certain that Mr. North never gets his hands on Gene again."

Karyn walked into the room and asked Rick, "What did you need?"

"Good morning, Karyn," Mike said. "Rick was just about to ask you to send someone down to that VFW where Butch went to see who was there."

"Good morning, sir," she answered. "I see you've seen the computer info from Butch's research. Very interesting choice of Internet use, isn't it?"

"Interesting," he responded. "But I'm more interested in who was at the VFW. If I'm not mistaken, everyone must sign in when they arrive. That includes members and visitors. Let's get somebody down there quickly."

"I'll take care of it right now," she answered as she turned to return to her current center within the conference room. "I'll get a copy of the sign-in sheet as soon as they open."

As Rick turned back to the screens, they saw that the satellite had indeed been repositioned. As the sun rose higher in the sky, they saw it was now centered over an area just north of Bridgeport. Still hidden in shadows, the numerous dirt roads and pastures surrounded by trees were barely visible. The images locked onto Butch's truck showed it still sitting at his house. Those of his Corvette were now at such an angle that it was lost among the houses in Lewisville.

"Well, folks," Mike told them. "I'll be in my office for an hour or so. Somebody still has to run the rest of this place while you play cat and mouse with a red truck. Call if anything develops." He turned and left them watching the scene unfolding as the sun erased the shadows and showed more detail of the rugged ranch land where the search had moved.

Chapter 31

When Butch got back to the house, he got into his truck and headed for the stables. It was still a little early for the horses to be fed, but he wanted to get it over. There had been a couple of notes from people wanting to ride this morning, and also one had scheduled the veterinarian they normally used to come out this morning. He wanted to make sure that the horses had finished eating when the customers arrived. He hated to have them standing around waiting while their horse finished its feed.

As he turned the corner onto 114, he saw the black Suburban sitting in the Tater Junction parking lot. There were several pickups there also. The usual crowd was having breakfast or just sitting around drinking coffee and telling the latest rumors that abound in a small community. He was tempted to go in and see what the driver of that particular vehicle looked like. But he decided to pay it no interest, and he didn't feel like having any more coffee right now.

As he pulled into the drive leading down to the main barn, he saw a familiar car sitting on the parking pad beside the trailer. He was surprised to see that his stable hand, Steve Rose, was back. He hadn't expected him until sometime tomorrow. The lights were still out in the trailer, so he continued down to the barn. If Steve and his wife, Sheril, had gotten in late, he didn't want to wake them.

After parking in front of the double doors, he slid one of them back and flipped on the interior lights. As soon as the lights came on, the horses began neighing and stomping around in their stalls. Continuing down the aisle, he turned on the lights for the other end and opened the door leading to the hay and feed storage area. After unlocking the storage cage doors, he dumped fifty pounds of pellets into the wheelbarrow and pushed it back into the barn.

Adding supplements as requested by some of the owners, he quickly put a scoop into each one's feed bucket. Returning the wheelbarrow, he threw a bale of hay into another one and went back to give the horses a flake of hay. Several of them were shaking their buckets against the wall as they shoved their heads into it, trying to get at their feed. Some of them would grab the edge and jerk it outward to shake the feed out and onto the floor of the stall.

Over the years, he had noticed that most of them would pull the hay from the rack attached to the side and drop it on the ground before they would eat it. Since horses normally graze, it made sense that they would be more comfortable eating off the ground, even in their stalls. After finishing the horses in the main barn, he reloaded the first wheelbarrow with another fifty pounds of pellets and went outside to feed those in the stalls out there. Again, he returned the empty wheelbarrow and put another 125-pound bale of hay in the other one and gave it to them.

As he was relocking the feed cage, he heard Steve walk in. "Good morning, Butch," he said as he stood in the open doorway and watched.

"Good morning to you," Butch replied. "I didn't expect you to be back until tomorrow."

"Got bored," Steve told him. "Besides, I was worried that you would have this place so screwed up that it would take me a month to clean up after you. Speaking of that, where is the guy you hired to do this?"

"I'll tell you about that when we get to the office," Butch answered. "You had coffee?"

"Not yet, I heard that noisy diesel of yours and decided to make some down here instead of waking Sheril. I'll go make a pot. I don't suppose you have any doughnuts down here, do you?"

"Nope, afraid not," Butch told him. "But if you're hungry, we can run over to Tater Junction and have breakfast while we wait for the horses to finish eating."

"That sounds good," Steve answered. "I can handle one of those huge omelets they make. That and some hash browns would put a big smile on my face."

"You got it," Butch said. "I just want to take a quick look at the board to see when Diamond W is coming out and which horse they're looking at."

They continued down the aisle and stopped in front of the board where boarders left requests or notes regarding farrier or vet appointments. Glancing at the note, Butch saw that one of the English riders had scheduled an appointment with Diamond W Equine Services for ten o'clock. All of those wanting to ride this morning were supposed to be out between nine and ten o'clock, so they had plenty of time.

Once out of the barn, Butch slid the door closed before going to his truck. After starting the engine, he asked, "Did you happen to see the news about the terrorist they are looking for in this area?"

"Sure, that's about all that's been on the local news," Steve replied.

"I don't suppose that the one that's still loose reminded you of anyone?"

"You mean the one that sort of looked like Gene?"

"That's exactly the one I mean," Butch told him. "You wouldn't believe what happened the morning after you left."

"What?"

"Early that morning while I was having coffee at the house, I had just seen the picture on TV when a couple of cars and a helicopter showed up."

"No, shit? What did they want?"

Butch looked over at him and said, "Gene."

"You mean that it was really him? The guy that was supposed to try to hijack another airplane?"

"One and the same," Butch told him. "Not only did they come to my house, they took me and my kids to the stables to look for him. When we didn't find him, they took us to the base down in Fort Worth and asked us all kinds of questions."

"What about? Did they think you were part of some plot or something?"

"No, but they were certainly interested in why Gene was out here and wanted to know where he was," Butch said as he stopped before turning left on 114.

"So where was he?"

"I don't have a clue. The last I saw of him was when the kids and I left Red's. There were a couple of girls up there that took a shine to him. They were supposed to bring him back here after they finished their little birthday celebration."

Butch was almost positive that all of this conversation was being monitored and recorded. He wanted to seem clueless to where Gene was or what had happened to him. Knowing that it probably wouldn't convince the people watching him, it might give him a little less attention. If he could just shift it elsewhere for a while, he would be less likely to have to deal directly with them.

As they pulled into the parking lot of Tater Junction, Butch saw the black Suburban still sitting there. *Good,* he thought. *I'll make sure we sit where whoever that is can overhear our conversation.* Stopping between two white pickups, they got out and went into the restaurant.

Looking around, Butch recognized most of the customers. Nodding to those he knew, he saw a table open across the aisle from two men wearing suits. He pulled out a chair there and took a seat. Steve sat opposite and looked around while they waited for the waitress to bring the menu.

"So," Steve asked as the waitress was approaching, "what do you think happened to him?"

"I don't know," Butch answered as he took a menu. "Like I said, he was dancing and having a good time with those girls, and they wanted him to stay with them. Gay Lynn seemed to know them, so I figured that he would be safe. Besides, he's over twenty-one and weighs more than hundred pounds. He makes his own decisions and lives with the consequences."

"Coffee?" the waitress asked Steve. "I know what you want, Butch, black and a glass of water."

"You know me too well, you pretty little thing," Butch replied. "I'll have the Spanish omelet with picante on the side, hash browns, and toast."

Steve laid his menu down and told her, "Make it two. If that's what keeps Butch so handsome, I'll do the same."

"Who said he was handsome?" the waitress said as she picked up the menus. "All I said was that I knew what he wanted. He may be nice, but I wouldn't go so far as to call him handsome. Barely cute if you ask me."

She turned smiling and walked away. Butch could see out of the corner of his eye that the two men in suits were not talking and obviously listening to them.

"Anyway, as I was saying earlier, they took us down to the base and questioned us for over an hour," Butch said as their coffee was being brought. "I looked for Gene after I got back, but the only thing I found was the clothes he had when he first came out. Hell, maybe those girls kidnapped him. The one from Bowie seemed to be especially sweet on him. Of course, she was looking at him through her whiskey goggles."

"Do you think we actually had a terrorist working out here?" Steve asked as he added a packet of sugar to his coffee.

"I don't know," Butch answered as he held his hands around the warm cup. "I wouldn't have thought so, but they had lots of evidence and seemed to know a lot about him. They even told me about his family back in California and how he had attended a Muslim mosque out in San Francisco. I knew he didn't look like other Middle Easterners, but what they told me made sense."

"Shit," Steve exclaimed. "All this excitement, and I'm off visiting my wife's family. What do you think they'll do now?"

Butch paused before answering and noticed that the two men were still intently listening. "Well, if it was me, I'd keep an eye on the area and try to find those girls. He may even be with one of them right now. Or he may have gotten spooked and headed back to California."

As their omelets were delivered, Steve remarked, "I don't see how he can get far, with all the publicity. Unless he's caught a ride with some trucker that's never seen the news for the last few days, he doesn't have much of a chance."

"I agree," Butch said as he poured the picante over his omelet and hash browns. "He'll be seen somewhere, and they'll get him. I hope they fry his ass if he's like one of those gutless shitheads that were involved in the other crashes. Let's eat and get on back. The vet's due out at ten o'clock, and if they send that doofus Lamper, I'll have to show him which end of the horse to look in. He tells me his specialty is teeth, but sometimes it looks like he's going in from the wrong end. I keep telling him it's a lot shorter distance if he'll just start at the mouth. I like the boy, but he's just not right. God bless him. He's just not right."

After paying, Butch sat in his truck and waited. It wasn't long until the two men he had seen inside came rushing out and got into the Suburban. Parked between the white pickups, he watched as they sat using their cell phones. Maybe their report would create some doubt about his intentions. He certainly hoped so.

Chapter 32

Kevin had been sitting under the tree for ten or fifteen minutes when the door to the trailer opened. Gene stepped out and waited for Leslie to step down to the ground. Shaking his head, Kevin watched Gene holding his hand out to help her as she came out. *Amazing*, he thought. *Just minutes ago, she wouldn't even sit close to him. Women, who can figure out what they want? Certainly not me, I'd have figured she would have kicked him out when I first started talking about him being part alien. Now, here she is holding his hand. Who'd a thunk it?*

"Come on over and have a seat," he called out. "It's a little chilly, but it looks like it'll be a beautiful day."

"There aren't any snakes or crawly things, are there?" Leslie asked as she looked around on the ground.

"None that I've seen today. It's a little too cold for them right now. You might see one or two later this afternoon when it warms up some."

"I don't want to see one," she protested. "Matter of fact, I want to make sure that I don't."

"I'd like to see one," Gene said as he surveyed the grass and brush close to where Kevin as sitting. "Are they poisonous?"

"The rattlers damn sure are," Kevin said as they stood in front of him. "The copperheads are too, but nothing like those diamondbacks or the cottonmouths."

"How do you tell the difference?" Gene asked.

"Well, the diamondback and cottonmouth are pit vipers," he explained. "They have a sort of triangle head, you know, broad in the back. The copperhead doesn't have that head or the long fangs the others do."

"That's real nice," Leslie remarked. "Let's not have any of them around. Isn't there anything you can do to keep them away?"

"Well, generally they'll stay away from people. They primarily eat rodents, so if you stay away from the places where you might find mice, you'll probably never see one. Unless he's traveling either to or from his meal."

"Are you finished with the water and stuff?" Gene asked. "I'd like to take a shower, but I didn't bring any of my stuff."

"Don't worry about that," Kevin told him. "I'll run into Bridgeport in a little while and get anything you may need. Make me a list of the things both of you need."

Kevin stood up and started walking back to the trailer. Leslie kept watching the ground, afraid she was going to step on something, and Gene watched to see what he could find. The grass was relatively short and had turned brown and crunched softly beneath their feet as they walked.

As they arrived at the door, Gene bent down and looked beneath the trailer to see if any mice or snakes may be under it. Seeing nothing that peaked his curiosity, he went inside with the others.

Kevin turned on the faucet over the kitchen sink and watched the water come sputtering out. As it spewed into the sink, it looked brown and rusty. "Oh yuck," Leslie exclaimed. "You don't expect us to use that nasty stuff, do you?"

"Of course not," Kevin told her. "It just needs to run for a while to wash the rust and dirt out of the hose I used and the pipes of this trailer. Go turn on the faucets in the shower and bathroom sink. Then keep flushing the toilet until it looks clear."

He left the water running and stepped out of the trailer. Walking around to the back, he pulled the drain hose from within the bumper and slipped it on the drain valve. Pulling the shutoff valve open, he waited for the holding tank to start draining. Once the water came flowing out of the hose, he moved it so that the water would run back into the wooded area.

Returning to his truck, he took out a shovel and began digging a large hole for the hose to dump into. Finally watching semiclear water running out of the hose, he left the shovel and went back inside.

"How's it look now?" he asked.

"It seems OK," Gene told him. "I tasted of it, and it was all right."

"Good," Kevin said. "Now, let's see if the lights work in this old thing."

He flipped the switch beside the door, and the ceiling light came on. As he continued through the trailer, he tried each light. Although some did not come on, it appeared that the entire system was all right, probably just a couple of burned-out bulbs.

"Put down lightbulbs on your list," he told them. "I'll get a small microwave for you and another bottle of propane. Let's see if the stove works."

Turning on one of the burners, he looked around for some matches. Seeing none, he turned the burner back off and told them he'd be back in a minute to see if he could light it.

Getting a pack of matches from his truck, he headed back inside. As he was stepping back in, he heard a helicopter somewhere in the distance. Pulling the door closed, he again tried to light the burner.

After a couple of seconds, he could smell the gas, and it quickly produced a nice symmetric flame. Trying each one to make sure they all worked, he put the matches in the counter beside the stove and walked to the table where Gene and Leslie were now sitting.

"There's one thing you need to be very careful of," he told them. "As you already know, you are both being hunted. I want you to spend as little time as possible outside. I just heard a helicopter somewhere to the east and that's what I would use to search a lot of this area."

"Do you mean we have to sit in here all day and night?" asked Leslie.

"No, that's not what I mean," he replied. "What I said was to spend as little time possible outside, and it would help if you would wear jackets and ball caps when you do go out. And never look up if you hear a helicopter. You don't want them to see your faces. You need to look like two hunters out here for a couple of days."

"What if somebody comes by while you're gone?" Gene asked. "What are we supposed to tell them?"

"Just tell them that you're out here for a couple of days to clean up the trailer and get it ready for me," Kevin answered. "Tell them that I'm supposed to be coming out here next weekend with some friends to hunt hogs."

Kevin turned to leave and looked around the cramped trailer. Shaking his head, he looked back at them and said, "Look, guys, I'm sure you won't have to be here very long. I'm going to try to find somewhere that has a little more room, but it may take a few days. This was the best we could do on short notice. Maybe if you'd just tidy up a bit, it wouldn't seem so bad. I've got a couple of things to do back at my place, but I'll be back in an hour or so. If you'll have your list ready, I'll get what I can when I return. OK?"

Gene nodded and replied, "Thanks, Kevin. I know you and Butch are trying to help us. We'll do whatever is necessary."

Leslie reluctantly agreed, "Please do find another place. I don't know how long I can stand sitting around in this little place. Especially with the snakes and things when we go outside."

Kevin pushed the door open and stepped out. He walked quickly to his truck and climbed in. After he had started the engine, he backed up and headed down the road, leaving a slight dusty trail rising from his rear wheels. After arriving at the cattle guard that marked the entrance to the property, he saw the chain still hanging loose and lying on the ground. After driving across, he stopped and pulled the chain back and relocked it. Thinking that he had better remember to keep the chain in place even when he was on the property, he stuck another blade of grass in the lock.

Back in the trailer, Gene got up and poured a little more coffee into his cup. "You want any more?" he asked.

"No, thank you though," Leslie answered. She looked up at him as he stood filling his cup with the now-cooling coffee. "Gene, can I ask you some questions?"

"Sure," he said as he returned and sat across the table from her. "I'll try to tell you anything you want to know."

She hesitated, trying to figure out how to broach the subject of their first night. Finally she sighed and began, "What do you think of me?"

"What do you mean?"

"I mean, after what happened that night at Red's. Do you think I'm bad?"

Surprised and slightly confused, he asked, "Why would I think you're bad? You didn't do anything to me that would make me think that. I still don't understand what you mean."

She kept her eyes downcast and said, "I shouldn't have had sex with you. I really don't do that kind of thing. It was just that it was my birthday, I had too much to drink, and things just happened."

Gene reached over and took her hand. "Look," he told her as he pulled her hand toward him, "I don't know much about how normal people act. I've never done that before, but I know what it means. They taught me a lot of things back there, but there were a lot of things that they never could."

Leslie looked up as he continued. "Like I said before, Vicki was the only person that cared for me. She was my teacher, nurse, mother, and friend. But I know there were things she didn't talk about. She did tell me about how she and her husband met and fell in love. The only thing I ever learned about sex was that it was how people reproduced, but she said it was something special between two people. It was more than just for making children, like cattle do. She said it showed that two people felt more for that person than others."

Gene watched as Leslie's eyes began to water. Tears slowly began to slide down her cheeks, and she said, "I do feel differently about you. That night isn't the real reason. That was just something I did because of why I said, but I was sort of attracted to you. I can't say why, but it had something to do with the way you are."

"Do you mean because of me maybe being some kind of alien?" he asked.

"No, of course not," she quickly answered. "I certainly didn't know that back then. It was because you're kind of cute and so nice. You don't seem to have any bad feelings for anyone and just enjoy everything. I really don't know how to explain it, but I think I would have liked to have met you even if I hadn't been drinking that night."

"If that's what's bothering you," he said softly, "I just want you to know that I like knowing you. That other part was different than anything I have ever known. But even if we hadn't done it, I know I would have liked you. Besides Butch, and now Kevin, I haven't had much of a chance to get to know people after Vicki."

Leslie gripped his fingers and asked pleadingly, "Can we just forget that night and start over? Kind of like we just met today?"

"Leslie," he said as he held her hands firmly, "I'll do anything you ask if it'll make you happy. I don't know how to explain it, but you mean more to me than even Butch or Kevin. If I ever get caught and have to go back, you'll be the one thing that I'll regret losing most of all."

TM

Chapter 33

Major Fleenor was on phone with his counterparts in Washington when Karyn walked into the room. She stood quietly watching the images from the repositioned satellite. *God*, she thought, *there's thousands of acres in that area. With all the hills, trees, and brush, we'll be lucky if we spot anything. No wonder the satellite couldn't track that truck without being directly overhead.*

Jerry hung up the phone and turned to her. "Anything new?"

She walked over to his desk and handed him a single sheet of paper. "Here's the sign-in sheet from the Avondale VFW. As you can see, Butch North signed in late in the evening. There are several signatures above him that obviously got there earlier."

Jerry read down the list of names, looking at both members and nonmembers. As he came to the name just three above Butch, he said, "Well, I guess we better start looking for Mr. Won Dum Phuc."

He laid the sheet on the desk and smiled at Karyn. "Kind of makes you wonder, doesn't it?"

"What do you mean?" she asked.

"Just what sort of people we are dealing with," he answered. "We already know Mr. North is rather intelligent. Just looking at his past is enough to make you admire him. Now, this new guy, Mr. Phuc, he can't be some dumb-ass either."

"What makes you think that?"

"Read it again as fast as you can say the words," he told her.

She read the name out loud, and after hearing herself, she began to smile. "I know what you mean. These guys would probably be a lot of fun to know, if we had the opportunity. What a sense of humor Mr. Phuc has."

"Yeah," Jerry said thoughtfully. "I'd be willing to bet that those two would have been quite a pair when they were in the military."

"How do you know that Phuc was in the military?" she asked.

"That name. It was one of the names given to Vietcong when one of them did something particularly stupid," he told her. "For him to have used that name, he more than likely spent a tour or two over there."

"I imagine that North got quite a kick out of seeing it written there when he signed in," she remarked.

"I imagine so," Jerry agreed.

"You know," he said thoughtfully. "Sometimes I wonder if what we're doing is really the right thing to do."

"Why would you say that?" Karyn asked incredulously.

Jerry walked to the door and looked down the hall in both directions. Shutting the door as he came back to his desk, he sat down and looked at Karyn. He knew this could be very dangerous. What he was thinking would certainly not help his career, especially since he was talking to a senior officer.

"We're violating just about every constitutional right that Mr. North has," he started. "As far as we know, he did nothing illegal. Oh, maybe he did think that Gene was an illegal and hiring an undocumented alien is against the law. But that happens out here every day. Just look at the place where Mr. Downey found him that morning that Vicki dropped him off."

Waiting for her to recall the convenience store where Gene had been picked up, he said, "There are all sorts of jobs out there that need a hand for a day or two. Lots of them will never get done unless there is a certain amount of day labor available."

Continuing, he told her, "If that is the only crime we have on Mr. North, why are we monitoring his phones and tapping into his personal computer? Hell, if they were doing that to me, I'd be mad as hell."

"I think you've got this all out of balance," she said. "The only reason we're watching him is to find Gene. It has nothing to do with him personally."

"Bullshit," he stated. "Look at how we were acting when we thought he might have discovered our secret. I was beginning to worry about his safety and maybe that of his children. How far are we willing to go to find Gene? Does it include harassing or maybe even incarcerating a man that did nothing more than to try to help another man?"

"I agree with you, to a point," she answered. "When he was brought in here and questioned, he could have avoided all of this just by telling us where Gene was."

"What if he didn't know at that point? What if he only learned of his location after he returned home?"

"Then, he had the opportunity to turn him in. If he's been singled out for our scrutiny, then it's his own doing," Karyn said emphatically.

"Come on, Karyn," Jerry pleaded. "You know as well as I do that he didn't believe the story we told him. Both of the generals agreed that he was suspicious of it and became rather uncooperative. Based on this man's past, I'd say he would have reacted pretty much the way he has. He doesn't trust anybody that lies to him, and we certainly lied."

"So you think that is a good reason not to watch what he is doing when it has become very obvious that he has Gene and Leslie? Besides, I think that taking Leslie would qualify as kidnapping, and that's certainly against the law."

"I don't think a court in the world would convict him of kidnapping," Jerry said. "He certainly wasn't there. We have the proof on our tapes. And we can't prove that our mystery man had anything to do with Mr. North."

"What about all those encounters? How many times does the same pickup have to be in the same location as North before you see that it isn't a coincidence?" Karyn asked.

"I'm not saying that there isn't a shitload of circumstantial evidence, but we have no complaining party to kidnapping. And we really have no proof of him doing anything with Gene," he countered.

Seeing that he was failing to persuade Colonel Lynch, he told her, "All I'm saying is that if Mr. North was to go public, and if he found our microphones in his truck and house, which he just might have, I don't think we could stand the investigation. We've worked for years to keep the spotlight off this facility and our mission. I'd hate to see it jeopardized because we got carried away with targeting him."

Karyn relaxed as she thought she had been mistaken as to Jerry's meaning. "Well, I don't think he will go public. If he had been inclined to do that, he probably would have called one of the newspapers or television stations after he found out that the man everybody is looking for was at his place."

"I guess you're right," Jerry said, thinking that it had been a mistake to take Karyn into his confidence. "Maybe I'm just worrying too much about what damage he could do to us and how it would look if it were public knowledge. He certainly doesn't seem to be the sort to take it lying down."

"You're right about that," Karyn said as she started to leave. "Well, I'll be in my new office. When do you think Rick or the generals will return?"

"Not sure," he told her. "I think Colonel Erickson is still around and General Nelson should be in his office. Is there anything I can help you with?"

"No," she answered. "I just wanted to know where they wanted me to use the teams that are just sitting around right now. The only ones working are the ones looking for the stores where the phones were bought."

Turning and walking to the closed door, she said, "Please have them call me if they want to move the teams or come up with any new ideas."

"Sure, I'll let them know," Jerry said as she left.

Colonel Erickson walked into the room with a cold can of Dr Pepper and stood looking at the display of screens. "Anything new?" he asked.

"Well, a car came into the stables late last night and parked by the trailer," Jerry answered. "There were two people in it, and they carried some suitcases inside. They didn't come back out until Mr. North arrived at the barn this morning. Then a man walked down and stayed there as Butch was feeding the horses. After that, they went to Tater Junction for about forty-five minutes. Right now, they're back at the stables."

Jerry turned and picked up the sheet of paper that Karyn had brought in and handed to him. "Also, Colonel Lynch just got this. It's the sign-in log from the VFW."

He stood silently as Rick read down the list. Watching his expression as he read, Jerry was waiting for the minute Rick recognized the fake name. When he saw no reaction, he asked, "Did you see anything that looked out of place?"

Rick looked again at the list and then saw the name. "Smart-asses. I should have known they wouldn't use their real names. I'm a little surprised that Mr. North actually used his."

"Probably because they know him," Jerry responded. "I would bet that the other man, Mr. Phuc, doesn't go there often enough for anyone to know him."

"Probably," Rick acknowledged as he laid the paper back on the desk. "Well, this doesn't give us any new information. Anything new from the phones or North's movements?"

"Not that I know of," Jerry told him. "I'll check with Karyn. I need to take a short break, and I'll stop by and ask her to come in."

Rick turned back to watch the images on the screens and noticed that Butch North's truck was at the stables. As he was watching, Karyn walked in.

"Jerry just told me you were in," she said. "I have something from the team that's in the Boyd area."

Turning, Rick asked, "What's that?"

"They just had breakfast at Tater Junction, and while they were there, Mr. North came in with another man and sat close enough that they could overhear the conversation," she answered.

"Anything of value?" he asked.

"Just kind of surprising," Karyn told him. "According to the team, Mr. North told the other man about being taken to the base and how we were looking for Gene. He then told him that he didn't know where he was but hoped we would find him."

Rick looked at her questioningly and asked, "Do you think that North knows nothing?"

"I'm not so sure of that," she answered. "There've been too many unexplained things that are suspicious. It doesn't add up, all the times his truck was with the red truck, the coded phone calls. No, I think he still knows more than he's let on."

"I think so too," Rick acknowledged. "I don't know why he would be telling someone about all this but not tell them about not believing us."

"Me neither," Karyn said. "Jerry and I had a conversation about this whole issue earlier. I think he's worried that North will do something to jeopardize our operation."

"What does he think Mr. North will do?"

"He was just wondering what would happen if North were to go public," she answered.

"I wouldn't worry about that," Rick told her. "That would be about the same as if he started talking about spaceships, aliens, or abductions. The end result would probably be the same. No, I'm not overly worried about that."

"Yeah," she said. "That's kind of what we decided, if he hasn't done it by now, he probably won't."

As they finished the discussion, they saw a white pickup pulling into the stables. This one had the entire bed covered with what looked like a molded fiberglass lid with several doors on the sides and back. As it pulled around to the side of the barn, they saw Butch come out through the wash rack with somebody by his side.

The driver's door of the pickup opened and a man with "A&M" on his ball cap got out and shook Butch's hand. After a brief period, they all turned and went into the barn.

"Who do you suppose that is?" Rick asked. "Let's keep an eye open to make sure that truck doesn't leave with more than it came with, just in case."

"I'll make sure the satellite people keep it in sight," Jerry said. "But I can tell you that I would bet it's a veterinary's truck."

"What makes you think so?"

"Well, you can see the medical symbol on the cover on the bed," Jerry answered. "And that ball cap? It's from Texas A&M, and most of the really good vets go there. But I'll make sure it gets watched closely."

Chapter 34

Butch started his truck and drove back to the stables. He pulled in and let Steve out beside the trailer. "I'll meet you down there after you get Sheril up," he said as Steve shut the door. "No rush, I'll let the horses out that aren't going to be ridden or not scheduled for the vet."

Driving the short distance to the main barn, Butch took out his cell phone and called Jeannie's number. Parked in front, he waited in the truck for her to answer.

"Well, you little shits up already?" he asked, smiling. "I guess you stayed out late and now want to come back and lay around while I work. Right?"

He sat listening to her tell him about the fine time they had out with all of her old friends. Finally after several minutes, he said, "I'm glad you had fun. I've had to work like a cur dog while you played. Anyway, that's not the reason I called. I'm thinking about running out to Red's tonight and have a beer. Why don't you girls get any shopping done that you haven't finished and plan on being home by five or so?"

After hearing that they would be back a little after five o'clock, he hung up and went into the barn. Walking down the aisle, he picked up a lead rope and opened the first stall door. Throwing the rope over the horse's neck, he led it out to the gate that opened into the pasture. He repeated it for every horse in the barn and then went to the outside stalls.

Opening the gate that connected them to the pasture, he proceeded to open each stall gate and let the horses run down the sandy aisle through the gate. After each horse, except the ones that were going to be ridden and the one the vet was coming to see, had galloped across the pasture, he shut the gate and returned to the barn.

As he was hanging the rope on the horseshoe holder, Steve came strolling down the aisle. Butch went into the office and turned on the computer. Finding the name he wanted on the list of horses and owners, he had the page printed so that when the vet arrived, he would have all the information he needed.

"So," Steve said, "other than having to do all the work for the last day or so, what else is new?"

Butch turned the computer off and turned around. "Not much," he said. "I had a guy stop by the other day that wants to bring five or six horses out for a month or so. He wants them over on the arena side."

"What kind?" Steve asked.

"Quarter horses," Butch answered. "They belong to his son, and he wants us to get them in shape for the Ranch Horse sale sometime next month."

"Are we going to ride them or what?"

"No, we're supposed to just swim them," Butch told him. "We'll have to start as soon as they get here, probably just a couple of laps the first day. We need to have them up to at least ten minutes by the end of the second week."

"Have they been swimming before?" Steve asked.

"I don't think so," Butch told him. "I'll get them for the first few times to make sure everything is going OK, then you can have them once I get them past three or four minutes. They're supposed to be in fairly good shape, and since they've been working on the ranch, they shouldn't be much of a problem."

"I'm glad you're starting them," Steve told him. "I don't like it when they try to climb out of the entry ramp and on top of you."

"Well, I'll want you to be there the first couple of times to make sure that doesn't happen," Butch told him and smiled. "You can be responsible for making sure they stay off me. Just remember, if I die, you're out of a job."

"Haven't you written me into your will?" Steve joked.

"You know it," Butch replied. "After my kids get all the money and property, I told them to let you have all of the pile of horseshit and shavings we've piled out there in the pasture."

As they were talking, they heard a pickup drive up beside the barn. They both went out to see who had arrived and what they needed. As soon as they got to the open wash rack, they saw the familiar white pickup belonging to one of Diamond W's vets. Butch told Steve to go get the horse that was scheduled for the vet and walked out to meet him.

"Morning, Doc," Butch said as he stuck his hand out and shook the vet's.

"Good morning, Butch," Matthew Lamper said as he stepped down from the pickup. "What do we have this morning?"

"I thought you knew," Butch told him. "Didn't your office schedule you to look at a horse here, or are you just coming by to showoff your pretty Texas A&M hat again."

"I'm supposed to look at one horse's teeth," he answered. "But I know you always add a horse or two to the call."

"Not this time," Butch told him. "Just the one you already know about. Steve's going to get him now and will bring him into the wash area."

"Do you know what the problem is?" the vet asked.

"I think the owner just wants you to check and see if the teeth need to be floated," Butch told him. "I know how much you like to clean the sheath, but you're stuck with just the front end this time."

"I'm a full-service vet," Matthew told him. "From one end to the other, I can take care of it all."

"Your only problem is knowing which end to start with," Butch laughed.

"Hey, I know where the horse's ass is." He smiled. "It's standing right beside me. But there's no known cure."

"That's my only charming attribute," Butch replied. "Most folks think I'm too nice anyway. I have to have at least one personality flaw."

Steve came into the wash area leading a large black mare. He stood her on the rubber mats and asked if the vet wanted her tied.

Standing well over sixteen hands, one hand being four inches, and weighing over 1,200 pounds, she calmly waited while they discussed how they wanted to work with her.

"No," Matthew said, "I'll sedate her and have you hold her head while I check out her teeth. If I need to float them, I'll bring in the stand. Just hold her there while I get the shot ready."

He returned to the truck and opened the rear compartment. Sliding one of the trays out, he selected the tranquilizer he wanted and filled a small syringe. After he returned to the mare, he quickly found the vein running along the neck, and after ensuring the needle was in it, he depressed the plunger and stepped back.

Within just a few seconds, the mare's head began to drop, and Matthew returned to his truck and got a stainless steel bucket and the device to hold the horse's mouth open while he examined the teeth. After filling the bucket with water and rinsing his tools with a mild solution to ensure they were germ free, he stepped to the horse's head and slipped the metal device into her mouth and fastened it behind her ears.

He spread the two halves open and locked them so that he could reach deep into her mouth and felt of the rear teeth with his hands. After checking the top and bottom teeth on both sides, he nodded and said they did need to be floated to remove the sharp points.

This time bringing a padded stand, he plugged in the cord for the tool used to grind down the rough points and asked Steve to hold the head steady while he worked. By now the horse's head was too heavy for them to comfortably hold it in the correct position for the time required.

"I'll leave you to your business," Butch said as he turned to leave. "By the way, Matthew, who's your latest female admirer?"

Matthew was busy holding the long handle of the grinding tool with one hand and guiding the abrasive end against the teeth with the other. "Nobody you'd know," he said. "This one has looks, intelligence, and knows that she doesn't want to hang out with a broken-down old cowboy like you."

"I don't imagine it will take her too long to figure out that you're never around most of the time," Butch said. "Just make sure you bring her out here sometime. I'm sure she would toss your sorry ass aside the minute I use my charms."

"I think she already has a father," Matthew said as he began to smooth another area of the horse's teeth. "I don't think she needs another one."

Butch laughed and started to walk away, saying, "I don't want to be her father, just her sugar daddy."

Shaking his head, Matthew told Steve, "Thank God there's only one like him. But sometimes I'm not sure if the world wouldn't be better if there were more people like him in the horse business. I swear 90 percent of the people I deal with are either crooks or just plain crazy. At least the man's honest and knows horses."

Steve smiled and held on to the halter keeping the horse's head straight and replied, "Yeah, he is one of a kind."

Butch went out to the equipment shed and started the tractor with a harrow attached to it. After the engine had warmed up sufficiently, he drove from under the shed and into the covered arena to make sure the ground was smooth and soft for the riders. After dragging the entire arena, he returned the tractor to the shed and returned to the wash area.

They were just finishing working on the horse as he walked up. "You done yet?" he asked.

"Just finishing," Matthew told him. "Just in time too. She's starting to wake up and resist my delicate touch."

As he started gathering his equipment and storing it back in his truck, Butch told Steve to put the mare in one of the stalls until she had fully recovered. Walking out to the truck, Butch asked, "Say, Doc, do you guys ever do DNA analysis?"

Matthew shut the rear of his truck and turned. "Yeah, sometimes we send a blood specimen to the lab to verify the pedigree. What do you want to know? Do you have a horse that's got questionable papers?"

"No," he told him. "I'm just wondering where I could go to get some information on the genetic makeup of some samples. Do you know if your lab will do the tests for private individuals?"

"That I don't know," Matthew answered. "But if you'll give the sample to me, I'll have it sent to the lab. They can compare it to their data bank of DNA to determine if it matches the registered sire or dam."

"What if it's unknown?" he asked. "Can they determine who the parents may be?"

"I guess if it matches anything they have on file," Matthew answered. "But it may take a lot of work to try to find a match if they didn't know where to start."

"What if I had just a cheek swab? Could they use that?"

"I'm not sure," he replied. "But there's a lab in Lewisville that does genetic profiling. From what I've been told, they can take anybody's DNA and determine their ancestors. I'd think that they could do the same for horses, if they have the right data to compare it."

Butch thought for a minute and asked, "What about getting the lab in Lewisville to work with your lab, would they be able to access their database and compare my sample with those already on file?"

"Possibly," Matthew said. "I'll ask next time we send a sample to them. I don't know if they share information. But I'm sure if you go through the American Quarter Horse Association, you might get their assistance."

"OK," Butch said as they walked to the front of the truck. "I'll let you know if I need your help. Thanks."

They shook hands, and Matthew got into his truck and left. Butch went back into the barn and told Steve that he was going to be gone the rest of the day. After being assured that everything would be taken care of, Butch got in his truck and left. Driving home, he went into the house and found a Lewisville phone book that Jeannie had when she was attending college in Denton.

Finally finding the number of the genetic lab, he wrote the number on the back of one of his business cards and left the house. Sorry now that he had destroyed the cell phone he had used that morning, he decided to go into Rhome and use one of the phones at the Woodhaven Bank where he had an account. *Maybe,* he thought, *I can find out where Gene came from. At least I may be able to verify my suspicions if there is some strange material in his genes.*

Chapter 35

Kevin drove back up to his house at Vashti and picked up a box of laundry detergent and some dish soap. After taking one of his rifles out of the tall safe in his bedroom, he found a box of ammunition and took it all back to his truck where he laid it behind the seat. Going back inside, he searched his closet and found a couple of pairs of old sweat pants and some sweatshirts. As he left this time, he locked the gate and placed another blade of grass in the lock.

The drive back down to Post Oak went smoothly, but he was aware of the unusual number of helicopters flying east of the area. They still appeared to be concentrated around the Bowie area, but he was becoming more alarmed at the frequency of their flights.

Stopping at the chain, he checked the lock, opened it, and left it open this time since he wasn't going to be at the trailer very long. Just enough time to drop off the clothes, take their dirty ones, and get the list of things they wanted. As soon as Gene and Leslie had taken off their dirty clothes and put on the ones he had brought, he told them he would be back as fast as he could. Quickly leaving, he drove out across the cattle guard, relocked the chain, and replaced the grass blade.

He then drove down Highway 59 to Jacksboro and turned left on 114 toward Bridgeport. As he approached Lake Bridgeport and

Runaway Bay, he decided to turn into the country club and have lunch. He used to play golf quite frequently there and still had several friends that spent most of their free time at the clubhouse known as the 19th Hole.

As he pulled into the parking lot, he recognized several of the cars and trucks there. The old truck he was driving didn't fit with the rest of the new BMWs and latest model pickups, so he decided to park close to the maintenance area so that his truck wouldn't stand out.

As he walked into the club, he saw an old golf buddy sitting at the bar by himself. As he took the stool beside him, he asked, "Nobody to golf with today?"

"I guess I got stood up," the man said. "What are you doing here this time of day? You normally only get out after two or three in the afternoon."

"I needed to run into town and get a few things," Kevin told him. "Thought I'd stop by and have lunch. Care to join me?"

"Reckon so, unless you'd rather play a round."

"Don't have the time," Kevin answered. "But I'll certainly take you on any other day."

"Sounds like a bet to me. If golf's out, I'll take the lunch. Maybe someone will show up that needs a partner or just wants to knock a few balls down the course."

Getting up, Kevin told him, "Let's go in the dining room. I need something more than the sandwiches they serve in here."

After they had taken their seats and placed their orders, Kevin asked, "Do you still have that place up north of Ringgold?"

"Yeah, I've still got it. You interested in buying it?"

"Not really, but I've got a friend that's looking for something up by the Red River," Kevin answered. "Did you ever build the house you were planning?"

"No, all I ever did was put one of those doublewide mobile homes up there and spend way too much fixing up the fences and the boat dock."

"Is there anybody living up there now?" Kevin asked.

"Nope, I guess the last time I was up there was over a year ago. I put it up for sale, but not a nibble yet."

"Have you tried to rent it or lease it for hunting?" Kevin asked.

"No, I don't want to rent it to somebody just for a hunting cabin. They'd tear it up, and I'd have to burn it down. No, thanks."

"How about if I rented it," Kevin asked. "I've got a friend and his wife moving out here from Missouri, and they need a place. He's going to be working at Sheppard Air Force Base, and they don't like living in town."

"When is he coming?"

"Actually, he's already here," Kevin told him. "They're staying with me for now, but the drive's too far, and to be honest, they're starting to get on my nerves. As much as I like them, I like my privacy even more. Just make it a reasonable amount, and I'll guarantee the payment."

"Well, I'm not much on renters, but if they're friends of yours and you'll be responsible for the payments and any damage, I'll do it."

"Not a problem," Kevin said. "You'll be doing me a huge favor. What do you want per month and for security?"

"How about $500 a month? And I'll take your word on the rest."

"That's fine," Kevin answered. "You sure that's enough?"

"Yeah, to be honest, I'd rather have someone living there. Keeps the druggies away. No, $500 will be enough. But they'll have to take care of the place."

"That won't be a problem," Kevin assured him. "This boy likes to work outdoors. He'll probably have it all mowed and flowers growing around the house."

"I don't expect that. But if he wants to do a little work, the boat dock needs some repairs."

"I'll make sure he takes care of it," Kevin said, pulling out his wallet. "Here's the first two months' rent. When can I get the keys?"

As he took the money, he said, "They're on the kitchen counter, I haven't locked the doors since I took it up there. You think he may be interested in buying it?"

"Could be," Kevin told him. "Once he gets settled in, who knows? He likes to live sort of solitary, and his wife isn't exactly the social type either. He may just decide that your place is just where he wants to stay."

"Well, when you get up there, let me know if there are any problems. If you need to repair anything, just keep the receipts for the materials and I'll take it off the next month's rent."

Their orders finally arrived, and Kevin rushed through his to get back to Leslie and Gene. When he finished, he took the check, left a generous tip and said, "Sorry to be rushed, but I've got to run. Do you know if there are many other people around that area now? It's been several years since I was up there, but you know how things are growing out here."

"Actually, the closest neighbor is probably seven miles away, and they pretty much stick to themselves."

"OK, thanks again, and we'll have that game sometime next week if you're not busy," Kevin said as he walked to the cashier. "I'll win this lunch back on the front 9 and win the bar bill on the back."

"You're on, and don't plan on winning anything. I've had lots more time to practice since the last time we played."

Kevin waved and replied, "I don't need practice to whup your ass. Take care."

After leaving the club, he drove on into Bridgeport and stopped at the Laundromat and put all of their clothes into the washer. Leaving them to wash, he went to the IGA grocery store and purchased all the items they had included on the list. The Movie Gallery was just a short drive away, and he picked up a couple of movies he thought they would enjoy. Next he stopped at Ken's Appliance and bought a television with a VCR and an antenna to take back to the trailer. After buying a roll of cable, he looked around to see if there were any other items he would need. Finally, he decided to wait until he had a chance to look at the doublewide he had just rented before buying anything else.

He returned to the Laundromat and took the clothes from the washing machine and put them into one of the dryers. While waiting for them to dry, he drove to one of the gas stations and bought a couple of five-gallon cans of gas. After loading them into the bed of his truck, he returned to the Laundromat and waited for the clothes to finish drying. Glancing at the TV on the wall, he saw repeats of the search for Gene. Shaking his head, he wondered as Butch had done why there weren't any broadcasts of the sighting in Aurora. Pulling the warm clothes from the dryer, he gathered them in his arms and went out to his truck, tossing them into the passenger seat before leaving.

It was still early afternoon when he arrived back at the entrance, and as he parked, he saw another helicopter flying to the east of the area. After checking the lock and seeing the grass blade still inserted there, he opened it and then relocked it after driving in. As he pulled up at the trailer, he saw Gene and Leslie walking back from the water tank holding hands and watching him. Smiling as they came toward him, they looked like schoolkids coming home from their first date.

"Get your asses over here and give me a hand," he told them. "I'm out running all over hell and back for you, and all you do is walk around enjoying the beautiful Texas weather."

Gene dropped Leslie's hand and walked over, saying, "I'll help you take everything in. We just finished cleaning the inside as much as we could and decided to go for a short walk. We've only been outside for a couple of minutes, and we didn't see anybody."

Handing him the clothes from the seat, Kevin said, "That's all right, I don't expect you to sit in there all the time. I've already said it's OK to go outside, but you should have put on a ball cap or something."

"That's my fault," Gene answered apologetically. "I was just going to dump one of the buckets of dirty water out when I saw this dog back at the water tank. I told Leslie to come look, and we walked down to see it."

"Except it wasn't a dog," Leslie said. "It was a coyote. It ran off as soon as we started down there."

"Yeah," Gene added. "I've never seen a coyote before. It was kind of neat seeing it for real and to get that close."

"You'll see lots of wild things out here," Kevin told them. "There're lots of turkeys, deer, some bobcats, and wild hogs. Just be careful, especially around the hogs. They can get pretty aggressive sometimes, and those tusks sticking out the sides of their mouths aren't for opening beer cans either."

"What do you want me to take in?" Leslie asked.

"Just grab the sacks from the other side and bring them," Kevin answered. "And I've got a little surprise for you two. Ya'll go on in, and I'll bring it inside when I finish something out here."

Leslie and Gene took everything inside and began to put it away while Kevin took the antenna and carried it to the side of the trailer where he had seen the U-bolts for holding it up. Taking his Leatherman from his belt, he slipped the short pipe into the U-bolts and pointed the antenna to the northwest where he thought it would pick up the stations out of Wichita Falls and tightened the bolts to hold it in place.

Attaching the cable, he ran it under the open window that was beside the dining area. As he slipped it into the trailer, he watched Gene sitting on one of the bench seats and gently folding Leslie's clothes. Shaking his head, he thought, *Talk about being whupped, that boy's gonna have hell to pay if he keeps that up.*

Returning to the truck, he picked up the television and carried it inside. "Here it is," he announced. "Now you can keep track of your favorite soap operas and see what the rest of the world has to put up with while you're on vacation."

He connected the cables, plugged it in, and turned it on. "Watch this, and tell me when you get the best picture," he told Gene as he went around to make any necessary adjustments to the alignment of the antenna.

Standing outside the window, he watched Leslie walk over and lay her hand on Gene's shoulder as they looked at the fuzzy picture. "Kind of snowy," she called out.

Kevin turned the antenna a little and asked, "Better or worse?"

"Worse," she said. "Now you can hardly see what's on the screen."

He turned it the other way and asked again. Finally after several adjustments, they were satisfied with the picture, and he retightened the bolts. As he was walking back to the door, he saw Leslie rub Gene's hair and return to putting things away.

Entering, he said, "Well, I guess you two have finally decided to be friendly. That's good because this will go a whole lot easier now. Just don't have any little temper tantrums and throw each other out in the cold. It's a long way to anywhere from here, and I'm not inclined to be a matchmaker or personal therapist."

Gene smiled and told him, "No, I think we can live here together for a while. If she gets mad, I'll just take a blanket and live with the coyotes until she calms down. She told me that since we don't have a dog house, that's the closest thing."

Smiling and shaking his head, Kevin said, "Well, you guys just do whatever you have to. I know it won't be easy, but I'll do my best to take care of you. I've promised Butch that you'd be OK, and I won't break my word to that man. Now, I've got to get home. I'll see you again tomorrow."

As he was walking out the door, Leslie sweetly told him, "Thanks, Kevin, and if you can, tell Butch we want to thank him too."

Kevin stopped and turned, saying, "I appreciate it, and I know Butch will too. Just remember, he's taking an awful chance helping both of you. But don't ever think he'll take anything for it. Your thanks will be plenty. See you tomorrow."

TM

Chapter 36

Rick and Jerry stood watching the various scenes from each of the satellite monitoring systems. Now that it had been repositioned west of its initial location, they had better visibility of the majority of the area between Bowie and Jacksboro. They were able to see excellent details of the people and vehicles in that area as well as Newark, just seven miles south of Butch North's house.

As they were concentrating on the vehicles at the stables, General Nelson came in and stood beside them. "Anything new?" he asked.

"Yes, sir," Rick told him. "We have the sign-in log from the VFW, and Mr. North had some people in the room that were very interested in his conversation when he had breakfast this morning."

He handed Mike the sheet and waited to see his response. As General Nelson smiled and handed it back, Rick said, "Not really much help. Now, one of Karyn's teams was at Tater Junction this morning when North went in. She can fill you in on the details, but basically he told another man with him about the 'interview' and how he had no knowledge of where Gene went after their night out."

"Really," Mike replied. "I don't think that I believe that story. I wonder if he's made our men and said all of that for their benefit. That reminds me, let's try to dress our men more like the locals from now on. They stand out too much and draw unwanted attention."

Turning to Jerry, he asked, "Major Fleenor, what do you think the chances are of using the same techniques we used on the red truck to help locate the missing camper?"

"I don't know," Jerry answered. "We don't have as many views and several of them were as it went down dusty roads which would have obscured some of the details. But I will ask the technician to give it a try."

Mike continued, "Well, I just thought that since that thing is rather antiquated, there probably aren't too many of them in the area. That should make finding it quite a bit easier."

"I agree, sir," Rick said. "But as Jerry mentioned, there may not be too many details, and I'll bet that there are more of those little campers scattered around the country than you'd imagine. They were very popular back in the fifties, and most of them probably wound up as hunting cabins or just rusting behind someone's barn."

"Well, either way," Mike responded, "I think it's worth a try as long as it doesn't tie up too much computer time. The other thing I want to try is to see if we can use the system for facial recognition."

"I don't think we have a face or good profile picture of our mystery man," Jerry said. "I'm sure we don't have enough data for it to prove worthwhile at this point."

"I'm not talking about him," Mike told them. "I'm discussing both Gene and Leslie. If we could find her, that may help. And if we were to stumble upon Gene, our search will come to a rapid conclusion."

"I know we can get photos of Gene that would supply sufficient detail," Rick answered. "I'm not sure about Leslie."

Jerry thought a minute and asked, "What about her high school pictures or in the local papers? There may be some available if we can locate them."

"Please ask Karyn to come in," Mike directed. "She can have the Bowie teams look around up there while they are canvassing the stores for the phones."

Jerry picked up the phone and told Karyn that General Nelson wanted to see her. Hanging up, he told them that she would be right in.

"Who's visiting the stables?" Mike asked as he looked at the screen showing the vet's truck.

"We think it's the veterinarian that Butch mentioned earlier," Rick answered. "Jerry said he recognized the emblem on the truck and the Texas A&M on the ball cap."

"Not to change the subject," Mike said, "does anyone think it worthwhile to visit the people listed on the VFW list to see if anyone recognized whoever was there with Mr. North? And I sure don't mean to ask if anybody knows a Dum Phuc."

"We could try," Rick told him. "I'll ask Karyn when she gets here."

Just as he was finishing the statement, Karyn walked in. "Whatever you are going to ask me, I'm here with an answer. And I have an answer to the question you haven't even asked."

Rick smiled and asked, "Just what is the answer to the unasked question?"

"The answer is, Butch North and his daughters are probably going out to Red's in Bridgeport tonight," she answered. "He just talked to his youngest daughter, Jeannie, and told them to come on home and plan on going there. Now, your question?"

"Can you get someone out to the Avondale VFW to talk to the bartender, waitress, or the night's guests that were there while Mr. North was possibly chatting with a friend?" Mike asked her.

"No problem, sir," she answered. "I'll have the same ones return and see if we can locate the people you're interested in. I suppose it's to see if anybody recognized our infamous Mr. Phuc?"

"Exactly," Mike told her. "How long do you think it would take to interview those on the list that signed in within an hour of North's arrival or while he was there?"

"The sheet doesn't have any times listed," she replied. "However, I think I can get the information from either the bartender or waitress. I'm sure the majority of the people there are regulars, and we'll probably find them there on any given day."

"Good," Mike told her. Turning to Major Fleenor, he asked, "Is our man ready to meet Mr. North if he shows up at Red's tonight?"

"I'll check with Lieutenant Colonel Mallory," Jerry answered. "He told me everything was in place, and Bob Wilson is ready. I'll make sure he knows that Butch and his kids will probably be there tonight."

"Is there anything else for me?" Karyn asked. "I need to get back and send someone to the VFW. I want them there as soon as it opens."

"One more thing," Mike said. "We need to have someone up in Bowie look for pictures of Leslie Barber. I'd like to use the recognition program of the computer to see if we can develop a profile to help find her."

"I'll call the Bowie team when I get to the office," she told him. "They have found a couple of tapes of a man buying prepaid cell phones, and I should get them later today. I'll have one of the helicopters pick the tapes up and ask them to start some research for photos of Leslie."

"Have we seen the red pickup again?" Mike asked.

"No, sir, not since Colonel Erickson thought he saw it at the VFW," Jerry told him. "I made sure the techs would let us know if they see it again."

"That's kind of strange," Rick told them. "It was everywhere up until yesterday. Now it's disappeared."

"I'll be back as soon as I get the tapes from the convenience stores," Karyn told them as she left.

"Have we seen Mr. North do or say anything strange lately?" Mike asked. "It seems as if he's no longer working with our Mr. Phuc, if he really was to begin with."

"No, sir," Rick replied. "I haven't even heard any conversations from his truck or house that would seem related to Gene or any other aspect of our search. It's as if he's no longer involved."

"Well, I still think he's involved," Mike told them. "He may have passed Gene to someone else and is letting them work the problem. I'd bet that he'll stay in touch even if it's just to get reports on him."

"Probably," Jerry answered as he returned from using the phone. "I just talked to our technicians, and they are going to develop a profile of the camper and run it through the computer, comparing it to everything on all the images available from when we lost it. They guess it will take a day or so to review all the tapes."

"What did they say about facial recognition?" Rick asked.

"That program is available right now," Jerry answered. "It will use the same computer model as the airports and other security offices are currently using. Except the new program is faster and will match faces using even fewer details than the current civilian programs require."

"How long will it take once we get them the photos of Gene and Leslie?" Mike asked.

"If we tie the computer up with the trailer, we'll have to wait at least two days before we can start," he said. "But if we run it first, it shouldn't take more that twelve hours."

"Why don't we start the program on the trailer," recommended Rick. "Then, when we get either Gene's photos or Leslie's, we can stop and run the facial recognition program. Since it will take some time to get Leslie's photo, if we get any good ones at all, we can probably review most of the images for the trailer."

"That sounds like a good plan," Mike said. "But I want Gene's photos run as soon as possible. It may very well be that he's out in the open and nobody has spotted him. We know for a fact that he's somewhere out there, and finding him is the mission. Finding Leslie may not actually help us, and the same goes for the trailer. So far, we have no absolute proof that there is any relationship between the two. Nor do we have proof that the red truck and Mr. Phuc are involved. It's very likely that they are, but we only know that Gene isn't at North's place."

"I agree with you," Rick told him. "But I don't want to relax any on watching Mr. North or trying to find Leslie, the camper, or the red truck. I believe they are more than just involved, I think they are an integral part of the situation."

"I'm not saying to drop any aspect of the search," Mike clarified. "I'm just saying that if we can run Gene's profile on the facial recognition, we'll absolutely know where he is if we get confirmation."

"Where's General Modelle?" Jerry asked. "I was hoping we'd have some positive news for him when he comes back in."

"He's been tied up with his counterparts back in Washington," Mike told them. "He said it will probably be tomorrow before he can get back with us. I'd like some good news for him too. If we can get identification from the tapes from Bowie or recognition from the VFW on Mr. Phuc, I think he'd see the progress we've made. Don't forget, he's under just as much pressure as we are, and he needs to show results to his bosses. Regardless of what he told us earlier, I don't think he can protect us if we don't get Gene back very soon."

TM

Chapter 37

Butch drove east from the stables toward Rhome. He checked his watch and saw that it was almost noon. Instead of heading directly to the bank, he crossed over 287 and pulled into Giant Burger for lunch. After parking, he went inside and placed his order. The owner was there as usual and welcomed him as always, "Hey, cowboy, where have you been? You haven't stopped by in a long time."

Butch smiled and told him, "I'm too busy most of the time. Even if you do make the best burgers in the county, I can't always stop and eat here. As a matter of fact, I'm kind of in a hurry and need to get back to work. But I will take time and enjoy one meal today, if you don't forget the jalapenos."

Butch sat at one of the tables where he could watch the parking lot and see the television that was always on one of the news stations. Waiting for his food to be delivered, he pulled his cell phone from its holder and called Jeannie again. After she answered, he asked when they would be back. Assured that the kids would be back in a couple of hours, he turned his attention to the huge cheeseburger and tater tots.

Sitting alone, he had time to contemplate how he would get a sample of Gene's blood or saliva to the lab in Lewisville if they would accept it. And more importantly, what it might show. If there was

some strange DNA, how would the lab treat it? Would they recognize
it as being abnormal? Probably so, but then what?

Finishing, he wiped the few crumbs from the table and put the
trash in the can beside the door. As he placed the tray on top, he
turned and said, "Another fine burger, but if I keep eating that much
every day, I'll be bigger than the ladies up at Wal-Mart. Thanks."

Taking his half-full cup of Dr Pepper, he returned to his truck
and headed for the Woodhaven Bank. As he pulled into the parking
lot, the next phone in the sequence of numbers Kevin had given him
rang. He stepped from the truck and walked into the bank before
answering it. Listening, he heard Kevin tell about the new location he
had found to board the horses. Agreeing with him that the current
stalls were too small for long-term use, Butch told him to do whatever
he thought would be best.

As he sat in the small lobby, he pulled his business card from his
pocket and dialed the number written on the back. As he waited for
it to be answered, he waved to one of the bank clerks behind the
counter. One of the reasons he kept an account in this bank was
the friendliness of everyone working here. He always made a special
effort to stop by on Fridays since they had a tray of cookies set out.
They knew his favorite was white chocolate macadamia nut, and it
was usually there. Now, if he could just convince them to have a glass
of cold milk to go with it.

Finally getting past the prolonged numeric menu, he was able to
speak to a real person. First, asking if they would do testing for the
public and hearing that they did, he asked what type of samples they
would require and how to deliver it. He was told that a cheek swab
would be sufficient but that it needed to be taken at their location.

Finally convincing them that it would be impossible to bring
the individual in, they agreed to accept a sample if it could be
kept absolutely uncontaminated. A Q-tip would be satisfactory if
it was untouched and kept in a new ziplock plastic bag. Butch also
questioned what became of the results of the test after they were
given to whoever requested it be performed.

They assured him that it was absolutely kept confidential and the
only access to the information would be granted to him. Satisfied that
he could get the sample and protect it from contamination, he asked
if it could be mailed and how long it would take to get the results.

After making sure he had proper procedures and providing a security code to retrieve the results, he thanked them and hung up.

After thanking them for letting him use the phone, he returned to his truck and put the used phone in the console until he could destroy it. Having given Kevin approval to move Gene and Leslie, he felt he was losing control of the situation, and he was beginning to feel quite nervous. Not being in charge of his own destiny was something that didn't sit well with him. He knew that he had to distance himself if they were to keep the military from finding Gene through him, but it didn't sit well at all.

Butch drove back home and stopped to check the mail. The latest issue of the American Paint Horse Association Journal was nestled within the mailbox along with several bills that had arrived since he had last checked. Gathering them, he continued down the asphalt drive to his house. Seeing all of the cattle resting in the pasture, he made a quick count to make sure one wasn't missing. Satisfied that they were all there and looking healthy, he checked the door and unlocked it.

Once inside, he walked into the living room and turned on the television to check the latest market numbers and see what was going on in the world. Sitting down in his recliner, he kicked the footstool out and laid the mail beside him. Selecting the magazine, he looked at the list of articles written for this issue. Nothing really interesting, but there was the latest clothing section, and he checked to see which of his pictures they had used. He had been modeling for them over the last couple of years and always wondered why they used him instead of the much younger guys they had available.

After a quick glance, he tossed the magazine aside and grabbed a throw pillow from the stack resting on the couch beside him. Before he slipped it beneath his head and leaned back to watch the news, he pulled his boots off and sat them under the coffee table. Within very few minutes, his eyes had closed, and he fell fast asleep.

The next thing he knew, Mischelle was tickling his feet and waiting for him to wake up. "Poor Poppy," she said. "Did you stay out too long last night?"

Slowly sitting up, he asked, "What time is it?"

"It's almost two o'clock," she told him. "How long have you been asleep?"

"Not near long enough," he replied. "When did you get home?"

She plopped down on the sofa and answered, "Just a few minutes ago. We carried our stuff back to the bedroom, and Jeannie's getting us a Dr Pepper. Do you want one?"

"No," he replied. "I just want to get a few more minutes of good nap time. Why don't you girls go play outside or do something for an hour or so. I know you'll want to stay up late tonight, and I need a little more rest. You kids are trying to kill me."

Jeannie came in and sat down after handing Mischelle a small bottle of Dr Pepper. "Well," she said, "look who's awake. What's the matter, Old Man? Can't run with the big dogs anymore?"

"I don't see any big dogs sitting here." He smiled. "Just a couple of pups with no manners. Who told you that you could have my Dublin Dr Pepper? There are plenty of cans of the regular ones, those are my private stash."

"I know," Jeannie told him. "Maybe you should have one now. You always say that it's at least 30 percent more refreshing, and you look like you need at least that much more than we do."

"I'll settle for a little peace and quiet right now," he answered. "You and your sister get out of here. Why don't you go wash the truck or something instead of bothering your poor old father?"

"The truck's too big," Mischelle told him. "We'll wash the Corvette though. Where's the stuff?"

"It's in the garage," Butch said. "Just make sure you dry it good. The water out here has a lot of minerals in it and leaves spots."

"Can we finish our drinks first?" Jeannie asked.

"Nope, you'll sit there and cackle like a couple of old hens," he answered. "I want to get back to my nap."

The girls finally got up and protested as they went out of the room. Butch again laid back and tried to get back to sleep, but it was too late. Shaking his head, he sat the recliner back upright and reached for his boots. As he was pulling them on, Jeannie came back in and sat down.

"Anything wrong, Daddy?" she asked. "You don't ever take naps."

"No, nothing's wrong," he replied. "Just a little tired. Steve's back though, so I won't have to go feed tonight, and we can go out and have a little fun."

"What about Gene?" she asked. "Have you seen him or heard anything? I saw on the news that they are still searching for him."

"Not a thing," he answered. "Maybe if they find either of those two girls we met at Red's, they can tell them what they did with him after they left."

"That's too bad," Jeannie said. "I still don't think Gene is a terrorist. I hope they don't catch him."

"That's not the way to be," Butch replied. "If he is a terrorist, he needs to be caught. If he isn't, then he at least needs to clear his name and let them find the real one. That's not our problem now, let's just forget about it and enjoy the next few days until you can get home."

"OK," Jeannie said as she got up. "Where do you want to eat before we go out tonight?"

"I think I'll cook a couple of steaks here," he told her. "There's three or four still marinating in the refrigerator. I'll let you girls make a salad, and we can make crunchy potatoes. That sound all right?"

"Sure," she answered as she started out of the room. "You going back to sleep?"

"Not a chance now," he told her. "You kids have once again ruined my life. I might as well get up and go over to the stables and make sure everything is going all right before we get cleaned up."

He waited until they were outside busy washing the Corvette and then he went into the kitchen. After pulling two more stacks of hundreds from the back of the drawer, he slipped them into the front of his shirt and walked out to the truck.

The girls were busy pushing the sudsy water across the hood of the car as he opened the door and got into the truck. "I'll be back in about thirty minutes," he told them. "Don't forget to change the air in those tires, it's been in there almost one thousand miles, and I hate to use stale air in such a fine vehicle."

The wet sponge hit the window just as he got the door closed. Laughing, he started backing up as Mischelle came running at him with the hose spraying the side window. He couldn't hear what she was saying, but just seeing them laughing was enough to make him happy. *Maybe,* he thought, *it's a good thing to get some distance between me and the problems with Gene and Leslie. I need to enjoy my kids in the few days left before they go home. Kevin's perfectly capable of dealing with the situation, and I know he's going to be enjoying the excitement for a while. Not to mention the stories he can tell when this is over.*

After he got to the stables, he could tell that Steve had been busy. The concrete aisle in the main barn had been washed, and the front of all the stalls had been swept to remove the spiderwebs that had built up over the last few weeks. He pulled the new cell phone from his pocket and dialed the appropriate number.

As soon as Kevin answered, he looked to make sure that Steve couldn't overhear the conversation and asked, "What's new, Jarhead?"

"Too much for your pickled brain to comprehend," Kevin told him. "I've done their laundry, bought their meals, given them a television—everything except wipe their butts."

"What? Did you forget toilet paper?" Butch laughed. "Or did you plan on using your left hand like a raghead?"

"Smart-ass," Kevin replied. "You weren't joking when you said I had to adopt them. By the way, I'm going to look at the new stable later tonight. If it looks good, I plan on moving the horses tomorrow. Speaking of that, we may only need a single stall. Those two are almost joined at the hip now."

"Well, I guess that's good," Butch remarked. "I have another special request, if you don't mind."

"What now?"

"I need you to get a sample for DNA testing," Butch told him. "Use a couple of clean Q-tips and put them in a ziplock baggie. I'll try to get them tomorrow sometime."

"What are you trying to prove?" Kevin asked. "Not to mention, who is going to do this testing?"

"I've got that worked out," Butch answered. "As far as proving something, I don't know. Maybe just trying to get some answers. We'll just have to wait and see. All you need are a couple of cheek swabs. Just keep them clean."

"I know how to do that," Kevin replied. "I had to do one a few years ago on a paternity case."

"You, a new daddy?" Butch snickered. "How'd an old warhorse like you get to breed anything?"

"You'd be surprised at what a real manly man like me can get done," Kevin laughed. "But thank God I wasn't the proud father of that one. I think she just wanted someone to help support her latest offspring."

"I thought you had that problem solved years ago," Butch reminded him.

"I did, and I even had a sperm count run after they took the swab," Kevin told him. "Both came back negative. Couldn't have been me."

"Good," Butch said. "I'm going out with a couple of lovely young ladies tonight. Give me a call when you get the move made. And thanks, old friend. You don't know how much I appreciate all you're doing."

"Kind of getting to be fun," Kevin said. "I've missed having something like this in my life. Not quiet as dangerous and exciting as back in Nam, but still keeps things from being boring."

"I know just what you mean," Butch told him. "There'll be an envelope waiting for you at the Boyd Feed Store later this afternoon. Just ask for it when you get to town. Take care."

"You too, I'll let you know how things work out tomorrow."

Butch hung up and walked into the tack room and destroyed the phone. Just as he was picking up the pieces, Steve came walking down the aisle. "What happened to that?" he asked, looking at the shattered phone.

"I got pissed off and smashed it," Butch replied, scooping the last of the phone from the concrete floor. "It quit working, and I can't stand something that doesn't work. You might remember that if you ever get to feeling lazy. I do have bigger hammers."

"What, then have to do all the work yourself?" Steve laughed. "I'm not too worried. I figure the few days I was gone showed you how much you need me."

"I guess you're right," Butch told him. "By the way, nice job on the cleaning. I didn't get a chance to really clean the aisle while you were gone. Thanks."

"Just doing my job, boss."

"Anyway, I'm glad you're back," Butch said as he headed out the door. "I'll see you tomorrow. Kids and I are going up to Red's tonight. Call me if you need anything."

Steve followed him to the door and told him, "Have fun, I'll take care of things here." Turning as Butch backed out and left, he started the process of filling all the buckets with pellets and placing hay into the stalls before he had to bring the horses in for the evening.

Chapter 38

        As Kevin drove off, he could see through the front window of the trailer that Gene and Leslie had sat together on one side of the table and she was changing channels. The occasional touch between them let him know that for now, everything was going to be all right. If all of his problems could be solved as easily, life would be so much simpler.

        After relocking the chain and adding his personal security measure, he headed east on County Road 2127 until it intersected with 59. Turning north, he drove back into Bowie and turned on 81 to complete the drive toward Ringgold. From that point on, he was traveling through very heavily wooded areas with unmarked gravel roads leading to the south bank of the Red River. Since leaving Ringgold, he had not seen a single vehicle and had barely caught a glimpse of a mobile home sitting very far back from the road.

        Several of the roads were completely covered with the tops of the trees that lined both sides of the narrow winding roads. The grey dust covered the vines and bushes that almost brushed the sides of his truck as he wound his way to where he remembered the trailer sitting. Finally after twenty minutes of wrong turns and dead ends, he recognized the Bulls for Sale sign nailed to one of the posts that marked the property.

Weeds and tall grass had almost overgrown the single-lane dirt road that led into the brush that covered the land, and he was almost on top of the mobile home before he saw it. He'd have to bring a lawn mower up and help Gene clean up around the home as soon as he could. Parking and stepping into the knee-high vegetation, he walked to the wooden steps that sat in front of the door. As he had been told, the door was unlocked and swung open as he turned the knob. Stepping inside, he felt for the light switch and was pleasantly surprised to find it worked as they came on in the living room.

He continued through the house and checked the water, lights, and tried to make a mental list of all the things they would need to clean it. If he had time, he would have hired someone to come do it, but he wanted them moved as soon as possible. Additionally, the fewer people who knew there was someone living here, the better it would be. Satisfied that everything was in working order, he found the keys lying on the counter and walked outside.

He returned to his truck and found the next phone he would use to call Butch and tell him about the upcoming move. Sitting on the open tailgate, he dialed the number and waited. Sitting there with his legs dangling, he watched a small group of deer crossing the open land just west of the house. They eyed him cautiously as they hurried back to the safety of the trees and headed for the river. He was almost ready to hang up when it was finally answered.

"Well," he said, "I guess you're surprised to hear from me so soon, but I think you'll like what I'm going to tell you."

Listening for just a second or two, he continued. "I found a very nice doublewide just south of the Red River. It has every comfort of home and is at an affordable price."

He listened to Butch ask a few questions about it and then said, "I plan on bringing them up here later this afternoon. I plan to have the beds made by sundown, and I'll stay for a day or two to straighten things up. Other than that, things are real cozy, if you know what I mean."

After hearing that he had Butch's approval for anything he thought necessary, he slammed the tailgate and returned to lock the front door. As he climbed into his truck, he wondered how things would be with him living with Gene and Leslie for a couple of days. It didn't matter, he decided as he drove back down the dusty road. Maybe it would keep them in separate bedrooms for a few days.

He drove straight back to Post Oak and stopped to unlock the chain. Still seeing that no one had been through it, he continued down to the camper. He saw Gene look out of the window as he pulled to a stop. Leslie was just sitting back down beside him as he got out of the truck and walked to the door. After knocking, he heard them invite him in, and Leslie opened the door to greet him. He could tell from the smile on her face that so far, Gene was still in her good graces.

"Pack it up, folks," he said as he closed the door behind himself. "You've been transferred."

"What do you mean?" Leslie said as she sat down. "We've just got things put away and cleaned up."

"Sorry about that," he replied. "I've found a much better place. It's got three bedrooms, two bathrooms, a nice big kitchen, living room, dining room, and already has all the furniture. Come on, I want to be up there before the sun goes down. It's kind of hard to find in the day, night would make it practically impossible."

"All right," Gene said. "Whatever you think we ought to do. Come on, Leslie, let's get to work."

Leslie gave him a less-than-pleasant look and jumped to her feet. "Fine, I'll just let you move me around the country like cattle changing pastures."

"Don't worry about it," Kevin told Gene. "Women need some stability in their lives, and she's made her nest here. Things will be fine once we get you moved."

Leslie sulked as she started throwing everything into the plastic bags and started gathering up her clothes. "Men, you all think alike. It doesn't matter where you throw your clothes at night. For once, I'd like to have some choice in the matter."

Kevin stopped and calmly told her, "Look, I'm not doing this for fun. If it wasn't for giving Butch my word to try to help you as much as I could, I'd leave you here until you were either found or starved. Just don't give me any crap right now, please."

Leslie continued piling their clothes on the counter and mumbling under her breath. Kevin just shook his head and started carrying everything out to his truck. As Gene came out with a load, he just nodded and placed it in the bed beside the other things. Within very few minutes, they had everything loaded.

"What about the television?" Gene asked.

"Leave it," Kevin answered. "There's one up there, and I want to leave enough things to make it look like someone might be using it for a hunting cabin. Take the videos, I'll return them in a couple of days. You may want to watch them tonight anyway."

With all the food, clothes, and other things loaded, Kevin reached behind the seat of the truck and took out his old deer rifle. Carrying it and a box of ammunition into the trailer, he put it into the closet of the bedroom and locked the door as he left.

This time as he left, he just locked the chain and didn't worry about whether or not anybody would come in after he was gone. Heading west on 2127, this time to avoid going through Bowie, he intersected Highway 148 and went north to Henrietta. Turning right on 82, he drove the fifteen miles to Ringgold and then went north on 81 until he saw the exit he needed.

Although he didn't think anyone would pay attention to them, he had made Gene and Leslie wear ball caps and jackets with the collars turned up. Once he was back on the gravel roads and away from other traffic, he relaxed and tried to smooth over the ruffled feathers he had caused earlier.

"I'm sorry, Leslie," he told her as he maneuvered the truck along the overgrown roads. "I just thought that if it were me, I'd like to have a little more room and a few more nice things than we could get back there. Since we don't know how long this is going to take, I want you two to be as comfortable as possible."

"I know," she said. "I do appreciate everything, and I know you're doing your best. It's just that every time I think I can settle down a little, you come in and force me to go somewhere that I don't know."

"Well, if it's any consolation, I'll be staying with you for a couple of days," he told her. "There's a few things we need to work on up there, and I'll need to get some equipment that Gene may not know how to use."

"Like what?" Gene asked.

"Like a lawn mower, a weed-eater, anything to clear out some of the grass and brush around the house," he answered. "Do you know how to use them?"

"No, but I can learn," Gene replied.

"I'm sure you can," Kevin told him. "But I'll have to show you how to mix the oil and gas for the weed-eater, bring safety glasses, and the other things that you've never done. Don't worry, you'll have plenty of time to learn how to do the work yourself."

As soon as they turned in at the Bulls for Sale sign, Gene asked, "Are there bulls out here?"

"No," Kevin said smiling. "There's always been a bunch of bull around up here, but not the kind you sell. That sign came from my place when I was running cattle. Now it just kind of marks the road for anyone coming out here."

As they drove up to the house, Leslie finally perked up a little. Kevin could tell from her expression that she would be happier here. Looking at Gene as they parked, he winked and said, "Home sweet home. Let's get to work."

It didn't take long for them to get their few things into the house, and as he was carrying in the last load, Kevin told Gene to stay at the truck until he got back. He placed the things on the kitchen counter and walked out the door as Leslie was wandering around the house, giving it her critical eye for cleanliness.

Kevin walked to the back of the truck and lowered the tailgate. As he sat down, he motioned for Gene to sit beside him. They both sat there in silence for a few minutes. The sun was just going down over the trees, and the sky was turning orange and gold. The few leaves left on the trees rustled softly in the breeze, and some finally gave up their hold and floated to the ground.

"Pretty up here, isn't it?" Kevin asked.

Gene looked around and told him, "Yes, it's beautiful. I've never seen country like this. Is this where we're going to stay?"

Shaking his head, Kevin told him, "I hope so. Like I said, I'll stay for a couple of days and help straighten things up, but then you'll be left alone. I'll still stop by every few days to bring you things you need, but you two will be on your own."

Kevin turned and looked Gene in the eyes and told him, "Now, I don't have a son to tell this to. And you don't have a father to tell you, so I'll just tell you like I would my own boy. There are a lot of things you need to know about women, and I certainly can't tell you all of them. Hell, I sure don't know all of them, no man does."

Gene watched Kevin's face as he was talking and listened to every word. He had never been talked to like he was someone's son, and he wanted to make sure he didn't do or say anything wrong.

"The best thing to remember," Kevin said, "is that no matter how right you think you are, Leslie may think differently. Women just look at things differently than we do. You may be different because you haven't been raised the way most boys were, but there will be times when you two don't agree on something."

"Like what?" Gene asked.

"Like anything, what television show to watch, what side of the bed to sleep on," Kevin answered. "Speaking of that, you guys are grown folks and make your own decisions, but I hope you know what can happen if you're sleeping with Leslie."

"Yes, sir," Gene replied. "And we've talked about that. She says she's taken care of the birth control thing and isn't worried."

"I hope so," Kevin replied. "But that can lead to complications that neither one of us are prepared for. Just be careful."

"We are," Gene assured him. "I guess we were kind of anxious after we met again, but I really do like her and she likes me. I don't see how what we're doing is wrong."

Kevin shook his head and smiled. "Man, you sure are learning things your mama didn't teach you. But just remember that when she gets upset about things, give her a little time to think and then see if there isn't some way you can resolve any little problem. It's generally the little things that upset people the most. The big things seem to work themselves out."

"Yes, sir," Gene said. "What else do I need to know?"

"More than I can ever tell you," Kevin answered. "Oh, I need for you to do something for me."

"What?"

"Just wait right there for now, I'll be right back," Kevin told him as he went back to the cab of the truck. Pulling the ziplock baggies and Q-tips from inside, he walked back and stood in front of Gene.

"I need to swab the inside of your mouth," he said. "Butch wants to try to get a DNA sample of yours to run. He thinks he may be able to find out who your parents are."

Gene opened his mouth and let him swab several times to make sure there would be sufficient material to send back to Butch. After it was done, he asked, "Will Butch tell me who they are? And will I ever get to meet them?"

Kevin sealed each swab in a separate bag and then placed them into another that was locked shut. "I don't know, he probably will if he can, but that may be too dangerous. Let's not worry about it for now. Let's see if we can go make Leslie happy and see if she'll make us a little something to eat. I need to put these in the refrigerator until I can get them to Butch."

It was almost dark as they returned to the house. The moon was rising above the trees, and several flocks of birds could be seen silhouetted against it. The sounds of the night were beginning to be heard as they closed the door.

Chapter 39

Colonel Amy Moore came into the operations center carrying a small disc. Her position as the laboratory commander of the facility meant that she was in charge of all aspects of the ongoing program dealing with the genetic manipulation of the embryos and care of the results. Gene had been her first and only real success. His disappearance had taken her prize from her grasp, and she was extremely interested in getting him back. Her reasons really had nothing to do with the security of the program, they were purely scientific.

"I have those photos you requested," she told Rick as she walked to the massive display of screens.

Rick turned and said, "Thanks, Amy. If you'll give that disc to Major Fleenor, we'll try to get a usable profile built."

Jerry came from his desk and asked, "Do you have every aspect of his face on this disc?"

"Yes, we have images of just about every part of his face and body," she replied. "The size and shape of his eyes are certainly one of the most unique traits, but if you use body and head proportion, you should be able to pick him out of any crowd."

"I just wish we could have him in a crowd," Jerry remarked as he took the disc. "So far, there has been no information of him being anywhere, and as you know, that only leaves him to be hiding somewhere around the area."

"Still no information from watching Mr. North?" she asked.

"No, we have lots of speculations," Rick answered. "But there has been no direct contact with Gene that we know of. As you heard, before you went back to run your lab, he claims that he last saw him at Red's."

"I'm sorry that I couldn't be more help," she said defensively. "But if the worst case happens, my lab is the only thing left that may provide us with the replacement."

"Sorry," Rick apologized. "I didn't mean to imply that you haven't been of any help. I know how important your work is, and I also know that you were the one that got us pointed in the right direction the first time. I guess we're all a little stressed right now."

"Don't mention it," Amy told him. "I know the strain is heaviest on you and General Nelson. I'm still worried about your jobs and careers."

"That may be the least of our worries if we don't find Gene," Rick admitted to her. "I'm sure you've heard the stories about what happened to some of the previous personnel problems."

"Yes," she said, nodding her head. "But those were more due to breaches of security. I sure don't think they would eliminate someone just because of this."

"You could be right," Rick admitted. "I'd just as soon find Gene and not have to contemplate what might happen. I hope General Modelle has enough juice to keep anything drastic from happening to any of us."

"I hope you're both right," Jerry said as he started back to his computer. "In the meantime, I'll get this entered and see what our magicians in the computer world can do to start the program."

"Do you have anything helpful?" Amy asked as Jerry started to walk away.

"Well," he said turning back. "They've been running the profile of the camper we think is involved. I hope they've made some progress there, at least it will either provide some clue as to where Gene went or rule it out so we can concentrate on other areas."

"We've also been looking for a red truck that has been in too many places to be coincidental," Rick told her. "But as Jerry discussed before you came in, it could be just that. We have no hard evidence linking the truck, the camper, a certain individual known only as Mr. Phuc with either Gene or Mr. North."

Jerry continued back to his desk and inserted the disc into the tray and began to transfer data to the technicians that were monitoring the recognition program and satellite positioning. Just as he was completing the data transmission, General Mike Nelson came in.

"Hello, Amy," he said cordially. "How are things down in the lab?"

"No real progress," she said. "I have a couple of prospects that seem to be developing normally, but it's too soon to celebrate. We've had others this advanced and lost them within a week or two."

"We'll just have to keep after it for now," Mike told her. "I appreciate you helping Rick and Jerry with the photos of Gene. I know how busy you must be right now, just don't let this little problem affect your work down there."

"No, sir," she said. "I'm just sorry I can't be of more help to you looking for Gene. I'll certainly provide any information I can get to help you."

"I know you will," Mike said. "If we need your assistance, I'll make sure you're brought in as soon as possible."

"Certainly, sir," Amy replied as she turned. "I'll be in the lab if you need anything else."

Mike stood looking at the screens, and after seeing Butch's Corvette moving west on Highway 114 between Roanoke and the Texas Motor Speedway, he asked, "Have you heard anything more on Mr. North going to Red's tonight? It looks like his girls are on their way home."

Rick stood beside him and looked at the same screen that had been dedicated to the car and answered, "Yes, sir. He's mentioned it to some other people, and we have Bob Wilson ready to be there."

"Has he had enough time to get to know anybody?" Mike asked.

"Not really," Rick answered. "He'll just have to play it by ear. From what I've heard, Red's is pretty friendly and welcomes just about anybody that comes in, as long as they don't start any trouble."

"I hope Bob doesn't push it too hard," Mike worried.

"I'm sure he knows what he's doing," Rick assured him. "He was in security enforcement for several years before we recruited him. He'll know how to play his hand."

"I don't think North will tell him anything meaningful tonight," Mike said. "So let's just make sure we have a long-term view of how we approach this. If North doesn't visit Red's very often, we need to make sure we get Bob somewhere he's more likely to visit other times."

"I'm sure if they hit it off, Butch will tell him about other places around the county," Rick said. "Bob can always go there when he thinks Butch will be around."

"What about any lady friends?" Mike asked. "Have we considered sending a female out in addition to Bob?"

"Not really," Rick admitted. "That might be a good idea. I'll ask Bob if he thinks it might help get some information."

"Well, we know most men like to brag around a pretty girl," Mike told him. "Maybe Butch will be more forthcoming with a good-looking lady."

Rick smiled and replied, "It's sure worked before. I'll see what we can come up with. But we'll probably have to bring in someone from out of county. I think he's seen just about everyone around here."

"What if we could put a microphone on someone he already knows?" Mike asked. "That might speed up the process."

"I don't think that would work," Rick told him. "I don't think he's the kind of guy who tries to impress people he already knows. To be honest, I don't think he'll tell anyone anything more that we've heard him say so far. But if you think it worth trying, I'll see what I can find."

"You're probably right," Mike admitted. "From what we've learned, he doesn't say much about himself or what he's done to anybody except very close friends, and they usually have to ask a lot of questions before they find out much."

Jerry came back from his desk and said, "General Nelson, we've entered Gene's images into the computer, and they're running the program right now to see if we can spot him anywhere in the previous tapes. They had to stop the program on the camper for now. It takes too much computer time to run them simultaneously."

"I don't suppose they ever found the red truck again, did they?" Mike asked.

"No, sir," Jerry answered. "It's just plain disappeared."

"Do you think our Mr. Phuc has Gene and has taken him out of the area?" Mike asked.

"That I don't know," Jerry admitted. "First of all, we don't know that Gene was ever in the truck. And after the night that Colonel Ericson saw it at the VFW, we haven't seen it again. So there's no evidence that he's taken him anywhere."

"I'm not talking about evidence," Mike said. "I'm talking about where we think these few leads are heading. What do you think would be a rational explanation for what we've seen?"

"I agree that it looks like our Mr. Phuc *is* involved," Jerry quickly answered. "But I'm trying to use every asset we have available before we commit to any course of action. I'd hate to make the wrong move right now and further alert Mr. North."

"I understand your position, Jerry," Mike said. "I don't want to spook him anymore that you do. But I think we may have to start expanding our thinking and investigate some of these coincidences a little more thoroughly."

"I understand," Jerry said, nodding his head. "I'll see if we can get another look for the truck, especially outside of the range of our dedicated satellite. They may be able to use data from other systems around our area and keep looking for the truck in areas where we don't have coverage."

"Good," Mike said. "Now, where do we stand on the images from the convenience stores and any of Leslie?"

"They should be here within thirty minutes," Rick said. "Karyn asked for them to be flown down just a few minutes ago. There are a few shots of people buying cell phones, and they've found a couple of Leslie's in her yearbooks."

"Can we run Leslie's photos and the convenience store photos concurrently?" Mike asked.

"Yes, sir," Jerry told him. "We'll add them to the search as soon as we get them profiled. We can run them and Gene's simultaneously since it's the same program. We'll just have to rerun the portion that has previously been run with Gene alone."

"How long will that take?" Rick asked. "I'd like to get back to the camper as soon as possible. I still think it is one of the central issues and maybe where Gene's been hidden. And Leslie too."

Just as they were finishing their discussion, Jerry's phone rang. As soon as he answered it, he thanked the caller and hung up. Turning back to Mike and Rick, he announced, "Well, Colonel Ericson, you may have just got your wish."

"What do you mean?" Rick asked.

"That was the computer geeks," Jerry answered. "They've found something that very closely matches your missing camper."

"How sure are they?" Mike asked anxiously.

"They say better than 95 percent," Jerry answered. "I think we need to get one of Karyn's helicopter teams to head out there and take a quick look."

"I agree," Mike told them. "Have her come in, and let's get the coordinates to the pilot as soon as we have them."

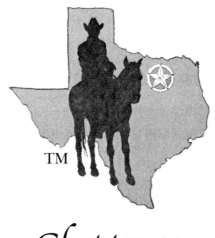

Chapter 40

Butch drove straight home from the stables and went into the house. After hanging his hat on the rack, he went into the kitchen. As he ran water from the sink into a bowl, he retrieved another stack of hundred-dollar bills from the rear of one of the drawers beneath the counter. After placing the pieces of the last-destroyed cell phone in the water, he let them soak for a couple of minutes while he checked his phone for messages.

There were none except a couple of calls explaining why he should apply for new credit cards or how much he could save if he would just change insurance companies.

After draining the water from the bowl, he placed the cell phone remains in the trash beneath the sink. He removed the bag and tied a knot in the top before setting it on the counter. Next, he walked through the house to the old rolltop desk where he kept a cluttered arrangement of notes, ledgers, books, and envelopes. He inserted the money into a legal-size envelope and sealed it. Looking for a pen, he opened one of the drawers and saw one of his father's old knives.

As he picked it up, he remembered the time his father had given him his first knife and that brought to mind him giving Gene one several days ago. It seemed like ages since he had first picked Gene up and taken him to the stables to work. So much had happened since then. His life had been disrupted, and he had involved some very close friends in helping him keep Gene from the people searching for him.

Finally finding a ballpoint, he wrote Kevin's name on the front of the envelope and carried it back through the house and grabbed his hat. After starting the truck and driving toward Boyd, he thought about how fortunate he was to have a friend like Kevin that would take over the task of keeping Gene safe until they could figure out what to ultimately do. Not only was Kevin willing to disrupt his own life, he was fully capable of taking control of the situation and ensuring it would be done as well as Butch himself.

The drive into Boyd was quickly accomplished, and as he turned into the parking area in front of the feed store, he pulled another of the prepaid cell phones from under the seat. Sticking it into his shirt pocket, he was getting slightly nervous about moving Gene and Leslie. Not knowing how it was going preyed upon his mind, and he wouldn't relax until Kevin called. If he didn't have the next phone available, he might miss it, and he wanted to know how it had gone before he went out for the evening.

"Looks like I just made it," Butch told the owner. "Looks like you're getting ready to close. I wish I had a job where I could sit around all day and take off whenever I wanted. It must be nice."

"What do you mean?" asked Robert as he stood behind the counter. "You're retired and just lounge around all day. Two retirement checks coming in and all that money you get from the stables, you never have to work another day of your life."

"You bet," Butch replied. "By the time the government gets through with my pay and the horses eat all my profit, I figure I keep just enough to let my sweet little daughters party it away."

"How's the hunt for a new mother for them going?" Robert smiled. "You've sure spent lots of years trying to find her."

"Lots of years and lots of money," Butch answered. "Maybe tonight I'll find the girl of my dreams. But in the meantime, would you hold this envelope for me? I promised to leave it here this evening, but he may not make it by until tomorrow to pick it up."

"No problem," Robert replied, taking the envelope. "It seems like I'm your personal financial center. Between you and ol' Mad Mike Jackson doing your cattle dealing through me, I barely have time to run my business."

"Yeah, we take all of your time," Butch said. "What, maybe twice a year I leave a check here for him when he buys cattle for me? With all the business we both give you, you should be calling us to see what you can do to help us."

"It's not your business that takes all of my time," Robert told him. "It's listening to both of you complain about everything from the price of oats to the lack of pretty women."

"Well, you know how Mad Mike is," Butch said as he turned to leave. "He's always had an eye for the ladies. Guess it's because he spends all his time up at the sale barn pushing cattle around knee deep in crap. Thanks anyway, I've got to get home and shine up a little. Trying to find the right woman is a tiresome job, you know."

"I'll bet," Robert laughed as Butch headed for the door. "I'll take care of this for you. Have fun tonight."

Butch waved and walked out to his truck. Quickly returning home, he headed straight to his room and threw his clothes into the hamper. As soon as he climbed into the shower, he heard Mischelle banging on the bedroom door telling him not to use all the hot water.

After he had showered and shaved, he pulled a freshly starched pair of Wranglers from the closet and pried the legs open. The heavily starched pants would hold their crease through a couple of wearings, but he had to force his legs into them the first time after they came back from the cleaners.

Selecting a white starched shirt, he finished dressing and carried his ostrich boots out of the bedroom into the living room. Jeannie was sitting in his recliner with a fresh Jack and Coke on the table beside her. Shaking his head, he sat on the sofa and started pulling his boots on.

"If you're going to steal my chair," he told her, "you could at least make your poor old father a drink."

"Oh no," she replied. "If I get up to make you a drink, you'll steal my seat. I know how devious you are. But I'm too smart for you now. You might have gotten away with that when I was little, but not now. Get your own."

He finished pulling his pant legs over the tops of his boots, stood up, and asked, "Well, can I get you anything since I have to get my own drink?"

"Oh, I guess not," Jeannie answered. "But I'm sure Mischelle will want something when she gets out of the shower. You can serve her like a good father should."

Butch went into the kitchen and took a glass from the cabinet. After filling it with ice, he poured it half full from the decanter on the counter. The remains of Jeannie's Coke sat close by, and he filled his glass with the rest of it. As he opened the door to put the empty can in the trash, he remembered that he hadn't replaced the bag, nor had he taken the old one to the Dumpster. Taking a Wal-Mart plastic sack from behind the trash can, he stretched it over the top of the can and dropped the can inside.

Mischelle was walking into the living room drying her hair with a towel as he came back in. "Hey, Poppy," she announced. "Did you have fun while we were gone?"

He sat down on the sofa and placed his drink on one of the coasters scattered across the coffee table. "You bet, everything I do is fun," he told her. "Maybe not as much fun as you two had last night though."

"It was great!" Mischelle exclaimed. "I haven't had that much fun in years. Sonsura was really funny. I think she can outdrink Jeannie and me put together. And there were so many people in all the bars. Too bad you couldn't have gone with us, you'd have liked it."

"Someone has to make a living," he answered. "I have to work twice as hard while you kids are here just to feed you and replace all my liquor you drink. Jeannie, you need to get ready. I'm getting hungry, and I'm sure Gay Lynn is anxious to see me later tonight."

Jeannie got up and picked up her drink, saying, "I'm going, but I want my chair back when I get back."

"We are leaving as soon as you're done," Butch told her as Mischelle hurriedly sat in the vacant chair. "I don't have time to cook right now, so we'll just eat up in Bridgeport at the Sagebrush Cafe."

After Jeannie had left, Mischelle asked, "Have you heard anything else on Gene?"

"No," he answered. "The only thing I've heard was on the news that he still hasn't been found. I wonder if they ever found either of those girls he was with."

"There're lots of places out there where he could hide," Mischelle told him. "It's not like in the city where there are people everywhere.

Out here, you can go for miles and not see anybody. It could take years to find someone out there."

"You're right," he replied. "But he has to eat, and he'll have to go into some town sooner or later. Maybe they'll find him then."

"I still don't think he was involved with those hijackers," she told him. "He was way too nice."

"You can't always judge people from how nice they seem," Butch reminded her. "Look at all those serial killers that the neighbors said were nice, quiet people. I agree that I don't think he was a terrorist, but we could both be wrong."

Jeannie finally finished dressing and came back into the living room with her empty glass. "I'm ready, let's get going. I'm fixing a roadie, Mischelle, do you want one?"

Mischelle jumped up and said, "Sure, just don't let Daddy have any more. Come on, Poppy, I'm starving."

Butch took his empty glass into the kitchen and placed it in the sink. "All right, I guess it's my job to be your chauffer for the evening. Come on, ladies, your carriage awaits."

Chapter 41

Kevin woke early the next morning. He had slept on the couch after Gene and Leslie had gone to bed. Regardless of what Gene had told him regarding her birth control, he worried about the possibilities. As quietly as he could, he started a pot of coffee and rummaged around until he found one of the old cups he had brought out earlier. As the coffee was brewing, he turned on the television after making sure the volume was as low as possible.

The local weather showed clear skies and moderate temperatures, the national station showed no real changes for at least the next week or so. That would give him plenty of time to clean up the yard and make sure there were no places for snakes or mice to hide around the house. He smiled as he thought of how Leslie would react if one of the large rattlesnakes found up this close to the Red River might crawl across the steps and she saw it. Better to prevent that instead of having to deal with her attitude later.

Getting a cup of coffee while it was still brewing, he sat and watched for any news regarding any further developments on finding Gene. Still nothing about any sightings, captures, or suspected locations. The longer he thought about it and the longer there were no changes in the news, the more he thought that Butch was right.

They desperately wanted Gene, but not enough to say he was seen in this area.

After he refilled his cup, he turned the television off, retrieved the baggie with the Q-tips from the refrigerator, and slipped out of the front door. The full moon was still hanging low in the sky, and the brightly light pasture in front of the trailer had several deer quietly grazing in the cool night air. As he climbed into his pickup, he hoped that he wouldn't wake them when he started the engine. As soon as it had warmed a little, he backed up and turned around. His headlights stopped several deer in their tracks as he drove out toward the road. Right now he wished he hadn't left his rifle back in the other trailer. There was some very tasty-looking venison just standing there waiting for him to shoot one of them.

He drove as directly to his house at Vashti as the scattered roads up here would allow. As he stopped and unlocked his gate, he checked to make sure nobody had been in since he had left. He left it open and continued down to his barn and parked. Leaving the lights on and the motor running, he used the illumination from the headlights to find one of the push mowers and a weed-eater. Putting them into the bed of his truck, he searched for a can of two-cycle oil. After a few minutes of scaring a few mice, he gave up and grabbed a couple of pairs of safety goggles that he tossed in the seat. As soon as he drove back to his house, he went inside and started finding things he knew they would need. All the small things that people use on a daily basis: dish soap, laundry detergent, bath soap, several towels, and washcloths. For almost an hour, he searched through the house and filled the passenger seat with everything he could think of.

Satisfied that he had just about all a family of two would need except for some food, he started the drive toward Boyd. As he entered Decatur, it was almost five o'clock, and the only place open was Wal-Mart. He turned off Highway 287 and parked in the nearly vacant lot in front of the store. After locking his truck, he passed through the automatic doors and took a cart from the front of the long line of them waiting for the morning crowd.

Starting at the produce section, he grabbed a supply of prepackaged salads, fruit, onions, carrots, fresh jalapenos, and potatoes. The next aisle had an excellent selection of breads and tortillas, and he selected several types. As he wandered through the remaining aisles, he put several cans of soups, boxes of Hamburger Helper, bottles of juice, milk, coffee, cheese, soft drinks, ground sirloin, bacon, and several packets of sandwich meats into the rapidly filling cart.

Next, he found the aisle with cleaning supplies and found room for several different types—a mop, a broom, several sponges, and some scouring pads. The next aisle held paper towels and toilet tissue, and he took one jumbo package of each. Continuing over to the clothing section, he guessed at the sizes needed and got underwear and socks for Gene, sweatpants and sweatshirts for both of them, and a couple of lightweight jackets.

He debated getting Leslie some underwear, but decided that it was too personal for him to guess at what she would want, and if necessary, she could wear some of the new tighty-whities he had bought for Gene. If she wanted something else, she could specify what she would wear, and he could get it some other time.

He started for the checkout lane and found two more prepaid cell phones that he knew would be needed. He decided that he would try to talk Butch into letting Leslie call her mother or someone else on one or two of them. He knew that her family would be worried, and he couldn't see why she couldn't use one to call them since it couldn't be traced.

Finally ready to pay, he pushed the overloaded cart into one of the open counters and began placing the items on the conveyer. As the items began sliding forward, he walked over to the line of waiting carts and pulled another one out. Knowing he had more than he initially thought about buying, he decided that it would be easier to take two carts. After the first one was reasonably filled, he pushed it out of the way and began filling the second one.

As the last item was waved across the scanner, the sleepy-looking teller asked him if there would be anything else. "No," he answered as he pulled the stack of hundreds from his pocket. "I think I've got enough."

"Well," she said. "That'll be $387.64."

Kevin peeled four fresh hundred-dollar bills from the stack and handed them to her. Waiting for her to verify that they weren't counterfeit, he glanced at his watch. It was nearly six thirty. By the time he got loaded and headed down to Boyd, the feed store should be open.

After taking his change, he thanked her and started trying to maneuver the two carts toward the exit. As he was struggling with the wobbly-wheeled carts, the official greeter walked over to help.

"Need a hand?"

"Definitely," Kevin said. "I didn't mean to buy this much when I came in. Guess I got carried away."

They pushed the two carts to Kevin's truck and managed to squeeze it into the floorboard and passenger seat. "Thanks," Kevin said as he shut the door and handed the man the ten-dollar bill he had received in his change. "I appreciate your assistance."

The greeter accepted the money and replied, "Glad to be of help. I'd bet you're ex-military, aren't you?"

"Yes, sir," Kevin answered. "Semper fi."

"I was air force," the greeter told him. "Flew F-4s for two tours in Nam back in the late sixties. Retired out here about fifteen years ago. Take care now."

"You too," replied Kevin as he got into his truck and started the engine. *Damn*, he thought, *Butch was right, the man is a retired fighter pilot.*"

He pulled out of the parking lot and rejoined 287 south toward Boyd. As he approached James Wood Motors, he took the exit for 51 and drove on through the slowly developing twilight. For the next twelve miles, he thought about the arguments he would use to convince Butch to let Leslie call her family. He still had no real reason in mind as he pulled up to the Stop sign at the intersection with 114. Just two and a half miles to the east was Butch's house, he knew he would be waking about now but decided that it wouldn't be too smart to be there if they were being watched. Finally, he made a right turn and drove west across the railroad tracks and made the next right to the Boyd Feed Store.

Robert was just pulling up as he parked in front. After getting out, he greeted Kevin and told him to come on in. As he walked behind the counter, he asked Kevin what he could do for him this morning.

"Butch North was supposed to leave an envelope for me last night," Kevin told him.

"Got it right here," Robert said as he pulled it from under the counter. "Anything else I can do for you?"

"Yes, sir," Kevin answered, laying the sealed baggie on the counter. "Could I put this in your cooler? Butch will come by later today and get it."

"No problem," Robert answered as he came from behind the counter and opened the cooler where various vaccines and medicines were kept. "Just put it on one of the shelves here, and I'll make sure he gets it. Anything else?"

Kevin laid the baggie on the shelf and told him, "Yes, sir, I need a couple of sacks of deer corn. I can load them myself."

"I'll have to open the feed area doors first," Robert told him as he walked back behind the counter. "Everything is locked up at night, and I haven't had time to get it out yet. That'll be $10.75."

Kevin gave him a twenty-dollar bill and looked around the store while waiting for his change. Seeing several small bottles of two-cycle oil on a shelf close by, he stepped over and got two. "I'll take these also, please."

"Sure," Robert said as he added them to the receipt. "That'll be $16 even. Do you need a sack?"

"No, thanks," Kevin told him as he accepted his change. "I'll just toss them in the bed of the truck."

They loaded the deer corn, and Kevin said, "Thanks, tell Butch I said hello." He got back into his truck and headed back to 114 for the drive north toward Ringgold. The roads were beginning to fill with rock trucks and early-morning commuters heading from the area into the metroplex. This country was sure filling up, he thought again as he watched the steady stream of vehicles.

The return trip took almost an hour, and as he pulled in front of the house, he could see the lights on and movement inside. As he stopped and turned off the engine, the front door opened, and Gene stepped outside. As he walked toward the truck, he waved and smiled as if he was welcoming home an old friend.

"Good morning, Gene," Kevin said as he opened his door. "You have a good night?"

"Yes, sir," he replied. "I guess we were so tired that we didn't hear you leave this morning. Leslie was kind of worried when you weren't here when she got up."

"I thought I told you I would be leaving this morning to get a few things," Kevin said. "Speaking of that, give me a hand carrying all this stuff into the house."

"Sure," Gene responded. "What do you want me to start with?"

"You take the stuff from the seat first. Leslie can tell you where to put it, and I'll get the things from the bed."

For the next few minutes, they busied themselves unloading everything Kevin had brought. Finally after removing the mower and other things from the truck, Kevin slammed the tailgate closed and walked into the house. As soon as the door opened, he could smell the bacon frying and saw a fresh pot of coffee on the counter.

"Breakfast will be ready in a few minutes," Leslie told him. "How do you want your eggs?"

"Over easy, please," Kevin said with a surprised look on his face. "I guess you've settled in now."

"Well, if I've got to live here, I may as well do it right," she replied. "By the way, thanks for all the food and stuff."

"No problem," Kevin said as he retrieved his cup from the sink where he had left it. "You guys just start another list of what you'll need, and I'll try to make sure you get it. Within reason of course."

Kevin poured a cup of coffee and sat down at the table. "What do you think about being able to call your family?"

Leslie stopped breaking the eggs into the pan and looked at him. "What?"

"Don't get too excited," he told her quickly. "I plan on discussing it with Butch later today. But I'll try to get him to let you make one call to tell them that you're OK. It's up to him, but I think we can convince him that one call will stop them from worrying and may help keep people from looking for you."

Leslie laid her spatula down and rushed over to him. "Oh, thank you, thank you," she said as she hugged him. "That will mean so much to me. Please make him see how important that would be."

"Whoa," he said, gently pulling her arms from around his neck. "I said I'll try. Just don't get too disappointed if he objects. He's always been open to advice or suggestions, but regardless of his decision, he'll think about it and do what he thinks is the safest thing for all of us. Do you understand that?"

Smiling as she returned to making the eggs, she said, "Of course, I just hope you'll convince him. Now, let's eat before it gets cold."

TM

Chapter 42

Colonel Karyn Lynch came into the operations center and asked, "Did you need me?"

"Yes," Mike told her. "We've found something that looks like it could be the camper trailer we're looking for. Major Fleenor is getting the coordinates right now. As soon as we have them, I want a helicopter out there to take a couple of pictures and get them back so we can confirm if this is the same one."

"No problem, sir," Karyn said. "How long before you have the coordinates?"

Jerry hung up his phone and quickly entered the data he had been given into his computer. Within seconds, a series of numbers appeared on the screen. "I have them right here," he said as he made a couple more computer inputs. "I'm sending them to your computer right now. They'll be there as soon as you get back to your office."

"Great," she said. "I'll get the chopper on its way."

"Karyn," Mike said, "all we want are photos of the top, sides, and both ends. We don't want to alert anyone inside that we're interested. Just make sure the crew uses some discretion and stays as far away as possible while taking the pictures."

"I'll make sure they know," Karyn told him as she started for the door.

"Major Fleenor," Mike said, turning to where Jerry was busy sending the data to Karyn's office, "are we still running the profile of Gene?"

"Yes, sir," he answered. "The possible match of the trailer just came in seconds before they were changing the search criteria. They're running Gene's profile through the entire data bank and won't stop until notified."

"Good," Mike replied. "Where do we stand on getting Leslie's photos into the system?"

"I'm not sure," Rick answered. "I'll go down to Colonel Lynch's office right now. The pictures were supposed to be here by now, I'll see if they've arrived.

Rick left them watching the overhead view as he headed for Karyn's office. The scene they were currently interested in showed a single helicopter leaving just north of Decatur and heading northwest. They continued to stare at it as it crossed Lake Bridgeport and flew over vast areas of open pasture and heavily wooded areas.

The destination of the helicopter was now highlighted on the screen, and they watched it overfly still on its original heading. After it had flown five or six miles away, it turned and reversed its flight path to cross the same spot. Again, it flew a few miles away and then circled north and began a run from north to south. Once again, it reversed its direction and crossed over the point headed north this time. Finally, it headed southeast, and they could tell it was coming directly back to the NAS/JRB.

It seemed like hours as the helicopter covered the fifty or so miles back to the base, although it was actually less than thirty minutes. As it approached, they could tell that it was being directed by the local radar approach control as it changed its heading and went slightly east of the runway centerlines.

Jerry's phone rang, and after answering it, he listened for a couple of seconds before he said, "Have the pilot bring the film directly to the facility entrance. I'll have someone there to bring it in. Thanks."

Disconnecting, he quickly dialed a number from his sheet of technical advisor contacts and waited for the answer. "Film's on its way," he spoke into the handset. "Have it converted to digital format and carried to the computer operators immediately."

As he hung up, he turned to Mike and said, "General Nelson, we should have it entered into the system in just a few minutes. They can compare the two images from all angles and verify if it is our trailer."

"Good," Mike told him. "Let's get a plan ready in case it is the one we're after. I want two teams out there as soon as we get confirmation. "Please call Colonel Ericson and have him come back as soon as possible and bring Colonel Lynch."

Jerry hadn't started to dial when the door opened, and Rick walked in followed by Karyn carrying an envelope she had just received. Jerry replaced the phone and walked toward Karyn.

"Are those the photos of Leslie?" he asked as he approached her.

"Yes," she answered. "They just came in, and I haven't had a chance to look at them yet."

Jerry accepted the envelope from her and pulled out three pictures of Leslie. One was from a newspaper story, and the photo was extremely grainy and showed very little detail. Another was a copy from what appeared to be her high school yearbook. The third had been taken from her last driver's license application.

Shaking his head, Jerry said, "I don't know how much good these will do, but I'll have them enhanced digitally and entered into the computer. We'll stop the run on Gene's pictures and run her up to the point we stopped."

"What's the status of your helicopters and the crews?" Mike asked Karyn.

"They're both refueling right now, and the crews are scheduled to remain on duty for another hour or so," she replied.

"I want them back in the air within fifteen minutes," Mike told her. "As soon as they're topped off with gas, I want you to send them back toward the location of the trailer and be prepared to land somewhere close."

"Sir," Rick told him, "it's going to be dark within an hour or so, do you think we need to send a car on its way if there's not enough light for them to see to land?"

Mike turned to Karyn and asked, "Where are your ground teams right now?"

Karyn turned to the screens and pointed to two of the Suburbans within a mile of each other parked along 287 just south of Bowie. "One is here at a truck stop, and the other is waiting to see if we want them to search a couple of small towns named Fruitland and Sunset."

"Get them headed back toward Bowie," Mike directed. "Rick, what's the quickest route from Bowie to that trailer's location?"

Rick turned and made an entry into the computer just behind where he had been standing. A detailed map appeared on one of the screens, and as he continued making entries, a red line began highlighting Highway 59 south and County Road 2127 west. As it approached Post Oak, it began tracking south until it stopped exactly where the helicopter had been crisscrossing.

"Have this transmitted to them immediately," Rick told Karyn. "Just make sure they don't go on any property until we give the word. And tell them that our subject may very well be inside the trailer when they get there."

"Yes, sir," she said as she started back toward the door. "Have you sent it to my computer?"

Rick nodded and told her, "Yes, and make sure both helicopter crews have the right coordinates and know that there will be some of our people traveling out there. I don't want any confusion if we have to enter the property."

"I'll make sure it's taken care of," she said leaving.

"Who owns the property?" Mike asked.

"I don't know," Rick admitted. "It's probably too late to do any research of the county records right now. And it might be leased to anyone else for either cattle or hunting. If we have to go on the property, I don't think we'll have time to get permission anyway."

"I'm not terribly interested in permission," Mike replied. "I'd just like to know if it's tied to our Mr. North or the infamous Mr. Phuc."

"I'll try to find out in the morning," Rick answered. "But it still might not tell us if it's been leased."

Karyn returned to the room a couple of minutes later and stood beside Mike and Rick as they watched. "Anybody keeping an eye on Mr. North or the stables right now?" she asked.

Rick shifted his eyes to the screen showing Butch's house and said, "The kids are back home, and there's been no activity in the last hour or so. One of the microphones within the house shows that they are getting ready to go out later."

"Are they going to Red's?" Mike asked.

"Yes, sir," Rick told him. "They've been talking about it and eating at a restaurant called the Sagebrush Cafe in Bridgeport before they go there."

"Has Bob Wilson been notified?"

"Yes, sir," Rick answered. "He'll be at Red's well ahead of them."

For the next few minutes, they stood and watched the Suburbans traveling along the depicted path, and the helicopters finally complete refueling. As soon as the choppers lifted off, they hovered for a couple of seconds awaiting clearance from the tower, and then they headed north out of the airport traffic area.

"What's the decision?" Mike asked Jerry. "Is it the same one?"

Jerry was still on the phone, and as he nodded and hung up, he turned and said, "Yes, they have an almost-perfect match on some scratches and dents from the front of the trailer. They've also matched several areas from both sides and the top. It's our trailer."

"Give them the word to go in," Mike directed. "And let's keep one chopper above them to monitor the activity and to follow anyone leaving that trailer."

In less than thirty minutes, the two Suburbans were driving across the cattle guard and down the dusty roads. The dust from the lead vehicle completely obscured their view of the second one. As they slid to a stop, one of the helicopters landed scant yards away in the clearing beside the water tank. As the other chopper hovered about one hundred feet above them, teams from both cars ran toward the camper.

The team from the sitting helicopter remained just outside the immediate area around the trailer as the ground teams surrounded it. One of the members stepped to the door and knocked loudly. After getting no answer, he knocked again and only waited a couple of seconds before trying to open the door.

As it swung out, he stepped inside and two other members followed him into the dark camper. Two minutes later, they stepped out, and one of them returned to his car to call in. Karyn changed the frequency on the monitor, and they heard him say, "It's empty. Looks like there's been someone in it recently, and we've found a rifle and some ammunition. What do you want us to do now?"

Karyn looked at Rick and Mike and asked, "Do you want a thorough search before they leave?"

Rick shook his head and told her, "Yes, have them look for any trash or anything else that might identify who was there."

She forwarded the request, and they watched silently as the orders were carried out. Soon, both Suburbans turned and headed back out, and the helicopter lifted off to join the other one.

"What's next?" Rick asked.

"We'll have to wait for anything they found," Mike answered. "Go ahead and put them to bed for the night. Let's hope that Bob has better luck than we've had. Shit, I thought we might be catching a break."

As he briskly walked from the room, Rick looked at Karyn and told her, "Even if Gene was there, we're still back at square one. You can bet there'll be some changes coming before long."

Jerry sat, quietly watching as she headed for the door and said, "I bet you're right. Neither General Nelson nor General Modelle will continue to play the game the way it's going. Guess I'll see you tomorrow."

Chapter 43

       Butch followed the girls out of the house and locked the door behind him. As usual, Jeannie ran to get into the front passenger seat, shouting "shotgun." Mischelle calmly walked to the still-open door and told her, "I'm the oldest, and you always get to ride up front. I want to this time. You go get in back."

    Jeannie stared at her for a minute and then reluctantly gave in. As she climbed out of the seat, she stuck her tongue out at Mischelle. "Bitch," she whispered as she opened the rear door.

    "Stinky Butt," Mischelle retorted as she shut the door.

    "Poopy Head," Jeannie replied as she slammed her door.

    "My, my," Butch said as he got into the truck. "You two have certainly grown-up to be such perfect little ladies. "Don't you remember any of the etiquette I tried to teach you when you were young?"

    "We remember," Mischelle answered. "That was as nice as I could be to such a stinky-butted twerp."

    "Nice toilet mouth, Poopy Head," Jeannie giggled from the backseat.

    "OK," Butch told them as he backed up and started down the driveway. "Let's just get it all out of our systems before we enter polite society. You know how disturbing it is when children are misbehaving in a public place."

"She started it," Mischelle complained as she turned and stuck her tongue out at Jeannie.

"Me? I didn't say anything, Daddy. You heard her, she started it," Jeannie protested.

"Oh, right," Mischelle said. "Just because you whisper and he doesn't hear it doesn't mean that you didn't start it."

Butch was sitting at the stoplight at the intersection of FM 718 and Highway 114 waiting for it to change to green. "I think you're both worthless little urchins," he told them. "But I try not to let my friends know how I feel. I'm always trying to make them think you two are wonderful children and pleasant to be around. Just keep this up, and everybody will find out how hard I work to protect your good names."

As the light changed and he began the left turn, he noticed a familiar black Suburban in the Tater Junction parking lot. *Still around,* he thought. They continued west, and the girls chatted about everything they had done and who they had seen in Lewisville for the rest of the trip into Bridgeport.

As they pulled into a spot along the street across from the restaurant, Butch pulled another cell phone from under his seat. There would be only three left after this one, and he needed to tell Kevin to get more of them soon. Placing it into the pocket of his Wrangler shirt, he snapped the pocket closed and followed the girls across the almost-empty street.

"Good evening, Butch," Doris, the owner, said as they entered. "You must be going on a double date tonight."

"Nope, I'm afraid not," he said as she led them to one of the empty tables. "These two lovely ladies happen to be my daughters, and I'm just so very proud to be their escort tonight."

"Well, welcome, ladies," she said. "You're certainly with the most handsome man in the county tonight. What would you ladies like to drink?"

"I'll have iced tea," Jeannie answered. "And not to be rude, but you must have left your glasses somewhere."

"Me too," said Mischelle.

"That's all right," Butch told Doris. "She's not used to being in public, and although born in Texas, she's now a Yankee. You just have to overlook her lack of manners. I've tried and tried, but she doesn't stay in Texas long enough for me to teach her proper behavior. And tea will be fine for me as well."

"Coming right up," Doris told them. "The special is written over there on the board. I'll take your orders when I get back."

"Come here often?" Jeannie asked. "How does she know you? This is a little far for you to go eat very often."

"I get up here every now and then," he told her. "Plus, I'm memorable and handsome."

"You're memorable all right," remarked Mischelle. "But handsome is kind of stretching it a bit. Not to mention how modest you aren't."

"How can you say that about your poor old father," Butch exclaimed. "I can't help it if I've been blessed. It's kind of like that song, 'Oh Lord, it's hard to be humble when you're perfect in every way.'"

"I know the song," Jeannie retorted. "Next you'll try to tell us that you wrote it."

"Nope," he replied, laughing. "I didn't write it, but I must have been the inspiration."

Doris returned and sat three glasses of iced tea on the table. "Ready to order?" she asked.

"I'll have the meat loaf, mashed potatoes, and green beans," Butch told her as he took a sip of his tea.

"Me too," Jeannie said, smiling. "And I apologize for saying you need glasses. I understand how all you people around here have to humor my father. It must be so very hard on all of you."

"I'd like meat loaf, green beans, and fried okra," Mischelle said as she also smiled. "And my sister and I do appreciate all of you being so kind to Daddy in his declining years."

"They're certainly your kids, Butch," Doris said. "Girls, you act just like you father. I guess I'd be shocked if you didn't. I'll be right back with your dinners."

"See," Jeannie said, "it's all your fault, the way we act. It must be bad genes."

"It could be genetic," Butch replied. "But it's not from my side of the family. All of the North family have good upbringing, except for a few that we don't talk about in public. Bless their poor little hearts."

Throughout the meal, they continued to joke and tease each other. At times Butch would have to remind them not to be so loud, but it was hard not to laugh as each tried to outdo the other. Finally, Doris came back and asked if there was anything else.

"No, thanks," Butch told her. "I've got to get out to Red's and have a quick shot of Jack Daniels. My nerves are about to unravel, dealing with these two."

"Well," Doris said as she placed the bill on the table, "it looks like the three of you are enjoying yourselves. I hope you have a good evening, and I'm sure you will."

Butch rose and pulled two twenty-dollar bills from his money clip. As he laid them on the table, he said, "Thanks, Doris. It was great as usual. I'll see you next time."

They left and drove directly to Red's. The short ride was made in silence as they relaxed in their seats. It was still fairly early, and the parking lot had plenty of spaces open beside the building. As they entered, Gay Lynn was standing at the front, checking membership cards.

"Howdy, Butch," she exclaimed. "It's been what, two or three days since I've seen you? What brings you back so often? You normally don't get up here more than two or three times a month."

"I just missed your smiling face," he told her. "You remember my girls, don't you?"

"Sure I do," she answered. "How could I forget two of the luckiest ladies in the world?"

"What do you mean, lucky," Jeannie asked.

"Just getting to be with your father," Gay Lynn replied.

Mischelle shook her head and said, "Boy, Daddy. You sure have all these people fooled. I just hope they never find out what you're really like."

"Don't pay any attention to my sorry little brats," Butch said. "I think the reason I'm back so soon is that they're driving me to drink. Speaking of that, how about a Jack and Coke?"

"Sure," Gay Lynn answered. "How about you girls, what would you like?"

"Jack and Coke," they said in unison.

"I should have known," Gay Lynn said as they followed her to the bar. "By the way, Butch, there's a man here that you might want to meet. He's fairly new in town and was asking about where there's any place to rope."

"Sure," Butch told her as he reached for his drink. "Bring him over to the table. I'll be glad to help him if I can."

They took their drinks and walked to a table beside the dance floor. As they sat there listening to the band, Gay Lynn came over, leading a man wearing a well-used black hat.

"Butch, this is Bob Wilson," she said. "Bob, this is Butch North and his kids."

Butch stood and extended his hand. "Glad to meet you, Bob. These two are Mischelle and Jeannie."

Bob shook his hand and replied, "Nice to meet you, Butch." Taking his hat off, he said, "You too, ladies."

"Would you like to join us?" Butch asked.

"I don't want to interrupt," Bob answered. "I was just asking about some place around here to practice roping, and Gay Lynn told me to talk to you."

"You're not interrupting anything," Butch told him. "Have a seat. The kids and I are just out for a little while tonight, and I need some adult conversation after talking with them for the last couple of hours."

"Well, if you don't mind," Bob said as he took a chair across from Butch. "I'd be thankful for some intelligent conversation myself. Some of those rock truck drivers can really get on your nerves. Gay Lynn said you were a fighter pilot before you retired. What was that like?"

"No, don't ask him that," Jeannie blurted out. "We don't want to hear how great fighter pilots are again and again. Can't you guys talk about how nice your wives are or how sweet your children are?"

"See what I have to put up with," Butch said. "How can I have a conversation regarding anything in my past with these two around? I certainly can't say anything remotely nice about a wife, and to call these brats nice would mean lying through my teeth."

Bob laughed and said, "Well, I do have a sweet little wife and two great kids. But I'd rather talk about something interesting. I've always wanted to be a pilot, but just never pursued it."

"Hell," Butch said. "It's like anything else, fun at first but just a job after a while. It's got its good points and its bad ones. But I sure did like some aspects of it. There's nothing in the world like high-speed low-level flying. And some of the most spectacular views in the world come from flying through the valleys between thunderstorms or watching the moon rise."

"Don't you miss it?" Bob asked.

"Sometimes I miss parts of it," Butch acknowledged. "But I don't miss the majority of the bullshit that goes with it. Now, what are you looking for regarding roping?"

"Well, I haven't had much of a chance to get back into it," Bob answered. "I'd just like to find some place that has a regular schedule so I can have a little fun practicing. I don't think I'll ever have time to get very serious about it. I just want to play a couple of times a week if I get the chance."

"I think the best place around here would be the arena that National Roper Supply built just south of Decatur," Butch told him. "It's a great facility, and they have classes, practice sessions, and I think they even have a little jackpot roping after the practice."

"That sounds like what I want," Bob said. "Who do I need to talk to?"

"Just go up to David's Western Wear in Decatur," Butch answered. "They can tell you the schedule and answer any of your questions. I'd just call them and see if their program fits what you want."

Bob got up and said, "I really appreciate it. I'll call and see what they have to offer. Nice to meet you and you girls too. I'll head back to the bar and let you folks enjoy the rest of the evening. Maybe I'll see you back here some other time. Ya'll take care."

As he left, Mischelle asked, "Why didn't you ask him out to your place when you rope?"

"If he's looking for some place with a regular schedule, I'm not the one he needs to rope with," Butch answered. "Besides, I just met him, and I generally don't let everybody that says they're ropers use my arena and cattle. I've had too many show up and leave their trash scattered around. Either that or they'll get there after I've brought the cattle in, wrapped the horns, and have them in the chute ready to start. Then, they'll have to leave before the cattle are unwrapped and put back out into the pasture."

"And don't forget that they forget to bring you beer," Jeannie added. "I know how you feel about guys coming out and not bringing enough beer for you."

"That's not the worst part," he told them. "I've had people show up, rope my cattle, drink my beer, and leave the empty cans scattered around before they leave without helping any at all with the cattle. Needless to say, they don't get invited back."

They sat and listened to the band for another hour or so, and finally Butch told them that he had to get back home. As they got up to leave, Gay Lynn came over and asked, "Leaving so soon? I was hoping for a dance or two tonight."

"Sorry," Butch apologized, "it's been a long day, and tomorrow will be just as long. I'd leave the girls, but I don't think you would want to put up with them once they get wound up. I better just take them on home."

Walking toward the exit, he stopped at the bar and told Bob, "Nice to meet you. I'll probably run into you again out here or up at the roping. I hope they can help you out."

"Nice to meet you folks too," said Bob as he stood up and shook Butch's hand. "Ya'll be careful driving home. There're more cops on that little stretch of road than I've ever seen anywhere else."

"You got that right," Butch responded as he turned to leave again. "See you later, Red."

TM

Chapter 44

It was almost noon when Kevin finished showing Gene how to use the equipment that he had brought. The grass had been mowed around their new home, and the bases of the few trees within the one acre area had been cleared with the weed-eater. Kevin had shown him how to mix the gas and oil in the proper amounts, how to check the oil in the mower, and the easiest way to keep the ground neat and clean.

Leslie had busied herself with cleaning the house and deciding how she wanted to decorate her new home. As the list grew longer and longer, she envisioned a life that was far removed from her friends back in Bowie. She still thought about them, but life here with Gene was giving her a satisfaction she had never known.

Kevin came in with Gene trailing him like a new puppy. As they took a seat around the kitchen table, Leslie poured three cups of fresh coffee and sat down with them. Quietly they sat there, each with their own thoughts. Finally, she sat her cup down and spoke.

"When are you going to talk to Butch?"

Kevin sighed and replied, "Sometime this afternoon. I guess you're anxious to talk to your family, aren't you?"

"Yes," she answered. "I just don't want them to worry any longer than necessary. I know I can't go back right now, and I'm not sure I'd want to."

"I've got to drive up to Wichita Falls later today," he told her. "I'll call him before I go and let you know what he says."

"Are we going to do any more work today?" Gene asked anxiously.

"No, we've done all that's needed for now," Kevin told him. "You've learned a lot and can take care of it from now on. It probably won't need much work until spring. Just pick up limbs that drop or maybe try to get all the rocks out of the yard."

Kevin sat his cup down and told them, "I'm going on into town and try to get all the things you've said you needed. But I'm not going to get everything you have on your list. Some of those things would be nice to have, but there's a limit on what we can do right now. Anything I don't get this time, we'll discuss it when I get back."

"Do we have to stay in the house now like we did before?" Leslie asked.

"No," Kevin answered. "I think we're hidden well enough up here that nobody will be looking too close. But make sure you wear a ball cap to hide your face when you're outside. And I'll get some sunglasses for you to wear."

He rose and walked to the door and told them, "If I don't come back tonight, don't worry. I need to go home sometime today and take care of some things there. If Butch does say it's all right for you to make a call, I'll let you know as soon as I can. Until then, just relax and enjoy your time together."

He quickly walked out and climbed into his truck. As he headed back out of the small clearing, he pulled one of the remaining cell phones from under the seat and dialed. As soon as he heard Butch's voice, he told him about the progress they had made and how everything seemed to be going.

"Thanks for the envelope," he told Butch. "I know this is getting expensive, and I want you to let me know when we've reached the limit. I don't mind pitching in, but I don't have the available funds that you do."

"Don't worry about that," Butch said. "My biggest problem right now is getting that sample to the lab in Lewisville. The money issue is more about how to get it without having it show up if they're watching my accounts."

"I have a favor to ask," Kevin said. "What do you think about letting a friend of mine have some limited family contact?"

"What do you think?" Butch asked. "You're more or less in charge of the entire operation right now. While we're on that subject, I want to start withdrawing from the situation. The less I do with ya'll will help take their attention off me. So if you think you can deal with it, do whatever you think best."

"Well, I'm going to allow it," Kevin told him. "I'll set strict guidelines and make sure nothing is compromised. Next, we need to talk about rendezvous points if contact is necessary."

"I'll work on that," Butch said. "For right now and the next few weeks or so, you need to stay away from this area. I'd say only go to Gainesville or Wichita Falls in case there's someone's husband around here looking for you. It might be wise to find another horse and keep it hidden just in case."

"I've got a cousin over at Henrietta that has a little bay horse that he's been trying to sell me for months now," Kevin said. "I'll see if he'll let me keep it there for now and promise to pay him when I come get it. I'm heading up to Wichita Falls now to do some shopping, and I'll see him as I go through."

"Good," Butch replied. "Just make sure you never take it to where they are unless we get in a jam. I'd like to have something unknown if we need to have a race. While you're up there, get as many new phones as you can. I'm down to my last two, and we'll need the last one to set up the swap."

"I'll take care of it," Kevin acknowledged. "I've got two more for my personal use when I think it's appropriate. I'll get another twenty or so for us. Anything else?"

"Not that I can think of," Butch answered. "By the way, how are the sleeping arrangements going?"

"At least two of us are happy," he replied. "I just hope we don't need the vet to come up here anytime soon, if you know what I mean."

Butch laughed and said, "I surely do, I surely do. That's one of the last things we need, but Mother Nature is a cruel bitch, and she'll bust your balls when you least need it."

"OK, buddy," Kevin told him. "I'll run with it for now. If there's any major FUBAR, I'll find you somehow. Let me know how the sample turns out. That could prove to be very interesting."

"Sure thing," Butch said. "Thanks, old friend. I'll try to make it up to you someday. Until then, just thanks."

Kevin continued west on Highway 82 until he reached Henrietta and drove to his cousin's house. After knocking on the door and getting no answer, he walked around to the side and saw the car he was there to buy sitting beside the garage. After a quick inspection, he decided that it would do for now. It had been years since he had driven a car, and it would seem so small compared to his usual truck.

While there, he broke the used phone and soaked it with the hose connected to the house. Taking the wet pieces, he dropped them into the garbage can that sat just outside the back door. Returning to his truck, he headed back toward Wichita Falls and tried to decide where to do his shopping. As much as he hated shopping malls, he knew that it would be the fastest way to get as many items as possible.

Most of the items on the list were things to decorate or furnish the house, and he tried to restrict his purchases to those things he knew were necessary. Occasionally, he would find one of Leslie's requests and get it just to keep her happy. He wondered how many husbands did exactly the same thing—buy things that weren't needed, but just to keep the wife from whining.

The drive over had only taken about forty-five minutes, including the stop by his cousin's. Shopping had taken another hour, and he still needed to make at least ten stops to buy the phones. He figured it would be close to four o'clock when he got back to Henrietta and hoped someone would be home by then.

After going into every gas station and convenience store as he drove east, he finally had everything he would need for the next few weeks if all went well. As he pulled into his cousin's house, he saw his other car sitting in the driveway. Stopping in the street, he got out and went to the door. As soon as it was answered, he went inside and made the arrangements he had discussed with Butch.

Less than thirty minutes later, he was headed back toward Ringgold and the winding road that led to their house. As he drove through the densely wooded area, he knew that this place would be his second home for a long time. The thought of Gene's attempts to mimic him as they worked brought a smile to his face. The more he thought about it, the more Gene and Leslie seemed to be part of his family. As he pulled up in front of the house, Gene came bounding down the front steps as if he hadn't seen him in months.

"Whoa, boy," Kevin said as he stepped out of the truck. "There's no big rush. But since you're here, you can carry all this crap into the house. I need to have a few minutes alone with Leslie, so you just busy yourself with this."

"Can she make the call?" Gene asked anxiously.

"Yes, if she follows my instructions," Kevin replied. "But there's going to be hell to pay if she screws up. And you'll catch the majority of it. So be ready."

Kevin left Gene gathering the numerous sacks as he started bringing them into the house. Stepping inside, he told Leslie to sit on the sofa while he explained a few things to her. As he told her that she would be allowed one short call to anyone she wished, tears began to run down her cheeks.

"Now," he told her, "I'd prefer that you call someone that's not your immediate family. If they are monitoring anybody's phones, it would probably be one of them. If you know someone that they know and trust, I think you should call them and let them tell your family."

"Can't I call my mother?" Leslie pleaded. "I know she'd keep it quiet, and she's the one that'll be the most worried."

"I understand," Kevin said, shaking his head. "She's also the one most likely to have her phone monitored. Pick someone else. Like I just said, make it a mutual friend. That's the rule, otherwise, no call."

Leslie sat pouting for a couple of minutes and finally said, "All right, I'll call my mother's best friend. What can I tell her?"

"Just tell her that you're fine, maybe you can tell her that you've moved and are living with someone you really like but don't want to make any real big decisions right now," Kevin directed. "Make it sound like you may plan on making it permanent, but you want to be left alone for a little while so you can make up your mind. Tell her that you'll call later and let them know what you've decided to do. Also, tell her not to use the phone to tell your mother, make it in person."

"OK," Leslie sighed. "Let me have the phone."

Kevin took it out of his pocket and told her, "No, you tell me the number and I'll dial it. I'll also talk to whoever answers it and make sure you're doing what we agreed. Otherwise, I'll hang up, and there will be no more calls. Do you understand? I'm dead serious about this. I may be making a mistake as it is, but I'm trying my best to do everything I can for you guys. Don't screw this up for all of our sakes."

Leslie paused for a few seconds and then told him the number. As he dialed it, he watched her eyes. "What's her name?" he asked as it was ringing.

"Annie Martinez," she answered quietly.

As soon as the phone was answered, Kevin asked, "Hello. Is this Ms. Annie Martinez?"

Hearing her say she was, he said, "Hold on a moment, please," and handed the phone to Leslie. He sat quietly while he listened to the conversation and was certain that she was following his instructions. After a couple of minutes, he motioned for her to hang up. When she didn't immediately start to end the conversation, he reached out as if to take the phone, and she quickly began to tell Annie that she had to go but would call again soon.

After her final goodbye, he took the phone and said, "That was good, but next time, make sure you don't keep talking after I tell you to hang up. Please don't press me on this."

He took the phone outside and stomped on it. After carrying the pieces back inside and soaking them in the sink, he threw them into the trash beneath the sink. Gene was just bringing in the last load when he started toward the door.

"I'm heading home for now," he said. "You guys have enough groceries to last at least a week, and I'll be back as soon as I can. Gene, you keep her happy, and maybe next time we can run up to the Red River and do a little fishing."

Gene followed him out the door and stood watching until Kevin's truck disappeared in the woods. Leslie stepped out as he was watching and reached down to take his hand. "It'll be all right," he said as they watched the dust settle behind the departing truck. "I'll take care of you now."

TM

Chapter 45

The following morning, Rick was the first to arrive back at the operations center. After a quick check of every screen to see where Butch's vehicles were and determining that there was nothing obvious on them that would be of any benefit, he went into the cafeteria and started a pot of coffee. He couldn't help but think things were not going well.

Karyn walked in as he was sitting at one of the tables waiting for the coffee to finish brewing. "Good morning," she said as she eyed the coffeemaker. "Regular or your cowboy variety?"

"Regular," he answered tiredly. "I just can't seem to get into the mood to put out the effort this morning."

"I know what you mean," she said as she took a chair opposite him at the table. "It seems that we almost have him in our grasp, and then he's gone the minute we get to where he was."

"I just don't know what more we can do," he admitted. "We've got the publicity running as much as possible, law enforcement agencies looking, and we've bugged every house, car, phone or anything else that we suspect of being worthwhile. And still, we can't put our hands on him."

As he was finishing his sentence, Jerry sat down beside him and said, "It's going to get worse. We're about to lose our satellite for a few days."

"What?" Rick exclaimed. "We can't lose it just when we get it positioned to provide the support we need."

"I agree," Jerry replied. "But unless either General Modelle or General Nelson can pull some strings, it's being repositioned up in New York to use the infrared system in looking for survivors or victims in the World Trade Center rubble."

"That just about kills our best shot at finding him," Karyn remarked. "Now, unless he shows his face and is recognized, we would need to search thousands of acres on foot. And we don't have the personnel for that."

"Let's wait and see what General Nelson has to say before we get too upset," Rick told them. "One of them may have enough pull in Washington to keep it here for a few more days."

Rick stood and pulled the coffeepot out and began to fill his cup. "Anybody else ready?"

Both Jerry and Karyn nodded and got up to hold their cups for him to fill them. As soon as they were filled, everyone left and headed into the operations center. Karyn stayed for just a few minutes and then told them she needed to get back to the communications room to see what the teams had brought in overnight.

Moments later, Mike came in with a cup of steaming coffee in his hand. "Thanks to whoever made this," he said as he walked to stand beside them, watching the screens. "Anything new?"

"I'm afraid so," Rick answered. "Major Fleenor just informed me that we are going to lose our satellite for a few days."

Mike's cup paused in midair, and he asked, "On whose orders?"

"I don't know for sure, sir," Jerry answered. "I just got the word from the technicians this morning. They're supposed to reposition it sometime today."

"I'll look into it," Mike said. "Until they do move it, let's make sure we take every advantage of it. How's the computer search going for a match with either Gene or Leslie?"

"They finished the entire database up to the present time early this morning," Jerry told him. "Even the pictures of Leslie being taken from her house didn't register with enough common points to confirm that it was actually her. There have been absolutely no matches of either one of them."

"Have there been any close matches?" Rick asked.

"None," Jerry answered. "They set the criteria low enough to make a less than 50 percent matchup, and still no subject was identified."

"What about the people buying cell phones?" Mike asked.

"We have some fairly good face shots, but we're limited to running them against public records and using that information to determine who might be the man we've named Mr. Phuc," Jerry said. "So far, there have been no matches to his general height, weight, and the limited facial points of recognition. Without some better photos of him, it would be useless to try to profile him in the computer and run the program."

"It looks like we're stuck," Mike told them. "I better get General Modelle and have a little discussion on what our options are at this point."

Mike stood staring at the screens for a few more minutes and then shook his head in disappointment. As he left the room, Jerry went back to his desk and turned on his computer to see if there was any news from the satellite monitoring technicians.

Rick continued to watch the screens and saw someone come from the trailer at the stables and walk toward the barn. The display of Butch's house showed the truck and Corvette parked where they had been left last night when they returned from Red's. There was no activity at Leslie's house in Bowie, nor was there anything happening at Stacy's house in Arlington. The view of the trailer they had finally discovered was still obscured by the shadows from the trees, but there appeared to be no one around it moving.

"Crap," he said to no one in particular. "This thing isn't doing us much good right now anyway." He turned and abruptly left the room.

Mike sat behind his desk and looked at all the mementos of his career hanging on the walls around his office. Finally he picked up his phone and dialed General Modelle's number. As soon as it was answered, he asked the general to please come to his office.

Kathy walked in as he was hanging up and asked if there was anything she could do. After he asked her to please make a fresh pot of coffee and have Major Romine get some breakfast burritos, she nodded and left.

A few minutes later, General Paul Modelle walked in and asked, "What's happening, Mike?"

"It looks like we're losing our satellite this morning, sir," Mike said. "I'm not sure if you can do anything about it, but I'd appreciate it if you could try."

Paul took a seat across the desk and told him, "I'm sorry, Mike. I heard about it late last night from Washington. This has more to do with politics than real assistance, but the president has to be seen using every resource at his disposal. It should be for only a couple of days."

"I guess it would be fruitless to try then," Mike said.

"Yes, it would," Paul answered. "About the only thing that would prevent them from repositioning it right now would be if we were actively tracking Gene. From the reports I've had to send, Washington is beginning to question if it's worth the use of this resource given the limited success you've had with it."

"I understand," Mike replied. "I sometimes wonder myself if all this technical crap is any better than a good set of eyeballs on the ground."

"Speaking of that, what have you heard from the man you sent to gain Mr. North's confidence?"

"He's not due to report to Colonel Lynch until later this morning," Mike answered. "I doubt if there was anything substantial learned since we've directed him to be extremely cautious. It will probably take weeks or even months before he feels confident to broach the subject. As of right now, he's our best bet if Mr. North really does know where Gene is located."

Kathy knocked and came back into the office with a tray of cups and a thermos of coffee. As she sat it on the desk, she informed them that Major Romine would be back in a few minutes with their burritos. Hearing their thanks, she left and closed the door.

Moments later, Mike's intercom buzzed; and after answering it, Kathy informed them that Karyn was asking if she could come in for a minute. He told her to send Colonel Lynch in and sat back waiting to see what she wanted.

"Good morning, General Modelle, General Nelson," she said as she walked in. "I've just spoken to Mr. Bob Wilson, the gentleman we sent to meet Mr. North at Red's last night."

"Did he have anything interesting to say?" Paul asked.

"Sort of," Karyn answered. "He said he didn't want to push it so soon, but thinks he can arrange to be around Butch fairly often without it being suspicious. They discussed roping up by Decatur, and

Bob thinks he can get to know Butch by being there and occasionally meeting him at Red's."

"That sounds like he's following the script fairly closely," Mike commented. "We knew this approach would take a lot of time, but we're running out of options. The only other thing I can think of is to bring Mr. North back in for another chat."

"I don't think that's the best option yet," Paul told him. "Let's wait and see what Mr. Wilson can do. Unless we get lucky and somebody spots either Gene or Leslie, we're stuck playing a waiting game."

"What else do you have?" Mike asked Karyn.

"I just received the report from the inspection of the camper," she answered.

"What did they find?" Paul asked.

"There were a couple of Styrofoam cups, empty bags that had potato chips, some empty Coke cans, but nothing that would definitely tie it to Gene or Leslie," she answered. "As a matter of fact, it looks like it was being used as a hunting cabin. Although there was only one rifle, as we reviewed some of the tapes it would appear as if there were two or more people there at one time or another."

"I don't guess there was enough good quality to make any identification," Mike said.

"No, sir," Karyn told them. "It could have been a man with his son, daughter, or some other young couple. There's no way of telling from the images we were able to get."

"Looks like another dead end," Mike said. "Anything else?"

"No, sir, "she replied. "If you need me, I'll be back in my office."

She left as Kathy informed them that Major Romine had arrived. Asking her to send him in, Mike looked at Paul and shook his head. "This may be a longer game than we initially anticipated," he said.

"As long as there's no information about Gene in the media, we can safely assume that our secret is still safe," Paul told him. "If he does ever surface and the public hears about it, we need to start working on a cover story."

"Certainly," Mike said. "I'll have Rick, Karyn, Jerry, and Amy get together today and start building a comprehensive program to supply a feasible story to the public."

"Good," Paul said as he selected one of the burritos from the bag Cory Romine had brought in. "For now, we wait."

TM

Chapter 46

        The next morning, Butch woke early and started a pot of coffee while the girls slept. As he waited for it to finish brewing, he watched the national news channels to see what was happening with the search for the missing terrorist. Although it was still the same information, he noticed that it was no longer running as frequently as before.

When the coffee was finally ready, he poured a cup and headed out the door. As he drove out of his driveway and turned the corner, he looked to see if any unusual vehicles were at Tater Junction this time. There were none, and he began to wonder if they were still watching him as closely as he knew they had for the last few days.

It was still too early for Steve to be down feeding the horses, so Butch went into the office and looked through the mail from the last couple of days. Nothing new, same junk mail that always fills the mailbox and a few miscellaneous bills. After making out the checks and putting the stamps on, he was just getting ready to leave when the phone rang.

"Equestrian Center, this is Butch," he answered, wondering who would be calling this early.

The caller was looking for someone to help with a benefit for handicapped children, and they had been given his name by a former boarder of his named Tammy Terbush. He remembered her as extremely cute and having a wonderful sense of humor. As he talked with the caller, he said he would be glad to assist in any way he could. Especially if it meant a chance to see Tammy again.

The initial planning committee was scheduled to meet that night, and he told them he would definitely be there. As he hung up, he thought back to the last time he had seen Tammy and wondered why he had never asked her out. But he had made it a strict rule to never date any of his boarders although there had been a few that made him wish he could. That still didn't explain why he hadn't pursued that pretty little Tammy after she moved her horse to a strictly English riding facility.

But tonight he just may finally ask her to go out. It had been too long since he had danced with anybody that held his romantic interest. Of course it had been too long since he had met a woman that didn't weigh almost as much as he did, and that was absolutely against his rules.

He checked his schedule for the rest of the week, and there was nothing pressing. He gathered up the bills, took the note with the phone number of the caller, and started for the door. Just as he was about to turn off the light, Steve came in through the double doors at the end. Butch stepped back into the office and waited for him to come down the aisle.

"Good morning," Steve said as he walked in. "Did you make coffee, or is that from your house?"

"My house," Butch replied. "I hadn't planned on being here too long and didn't want to start a pot here this early. What do you have planned for today?"

"Not much," Steve answered. "After I feed this morning, I need to pull the harrow in the arena and both outdoor tracks. Maybe some cleaning around a couple of the stalls. Why, do you need anything?"

"No," Butch said. "But I probably won't be back until tomorrow. I'm going to take the kids into Fort Worth for lunch, maybe a little shopping, and then tonight I'm going to South Lake to help with a children's benefit."

"Sounds like fun," Steve replied. "I thought you did all of your benefits at your arena."

"This one isn't mine," Butch said. "This is another group, and I was recommended by a former boarder. She's actually one of the reasons I'm going there tonight."

"Oh?" Steve said as he raised an eyebrow. "She must be something special for you to be interested."

"Oh yeah," he replied, laughing. "I think she could be the next mother for my poor little orphaned children. Bless their little hearts."

"Well, have fun. I'll call if anything comes up," Steve told him. "I know the only reason you look for women is because you're worried about those grown kids of yours."

"Exactly," Butch said as he pulled a file from the filing cabinet. "I almost forgot. I've got her number from her old contract. I think I'll call her later and see if we can do a little boot-scooting after the meeting."

"Taking the girls?" Steve asked.

"Not a chance," he replied. "You never know, this might be a very late night, and I'll let them stay home and rest. Besides, they don't need to watch their own father trying to seduce the ladies. That's just not right, not right at all."

"Good luck," Steve said as Butch started for the door. "Call if you need help."

Butch just waved and walked back to his truck. As soon as he was back home, he got another cup of coffee and sat in his recliner. He pulled the piece of paper with Tammy's number on it and reached for the phone. As soon as she answered, he remembered her voice and smiled as he told her who he was.

As soon as the discussion regarding the benefit was concluded, he asked her what she had planned for after the meeting. As he heard that she had no plans, he told her that since it would probably be over by seven o'clock, they should go do a little dancing. As she quickly agreed, Butch silently congratulated himself and said he would see her there later. As he was hanging up, Mischelle walked sleepily into the room and sat on the couch.

"Who was that?" she asked.

"Just someone you don't know," he replied.

"Did I hear you say that you're going dancing tonight?"

"Yes, you did. And no, you're not going," he told her. "But I want to go down to the Stockyards in Fort Worth this morning after we have breakfast. So go get your sister out of bed, and let's try to make it down there by noon."

"Yeah!" Mischelle exclaimed as she jumped up and ran back to the bedroom. She leaped on the bed and straddled Jeannie, yelling, "Get up, you poopy butt. We're going to the Stockyards with Daddy after breakfast. And I know a secret!"

"Get off me," Jeannie complained as she tried to roll over. "What's the secret?"

"I'm not telling," Mischelle replied. "Maybe, if you're really, really nice to me. But I'm not saying a word until we get to Fort Worth. Let's go!"

Butch took both girls to Tater Junction, and while they were eating, Mischelle announced, "Daddy's got a girlfriend. And he's going on a date tonight."

"Is that your big secret?" Jeannie asked.

"Yep," Mischelle told her. "I'll bet she's got a tiny hinny and long dark hair."

"That's the only kind he dates, dodo," Jeannie said. "That's not really much of a secret."

"That's enough discussing my private life, girls," Butch reminded them. "I don't pick your boyfriends, and you don't pick who I see. Let's just finish and go get cleaned up."

Throughout the rest of breakfast, Mischelle and Jeannie kept sticking their tongues out and making faces. Butch quietly sat eating and shaking his head. They had finally finished when the waitress came by with the bill, saying, "They're just like you, Butch. Not only do they look like you, they act like you too."

Butch stood up and took his bill. "You've never seen me stick my tongue out while I was eating or open my mouth and show someone my chewed food. I don't know who gave these two their upbringing."

"We learned it from you," Jeannie said as they started for the door.

After paying, they went back home and got ready to go down to Fort Worth and visit the Stockyards. When they arrived, they wandered up and down the brick streets where the cattle were brought to be sold back in the 1800s. They went in and out of the various stores, and after they had stopped for a beer at the famous White Elephant Saloon, Butch told them that they had to go home so he could get a shower and clean clothes. As they were going back to the truck, the girls kept making kissing noises behind his back as they walked.

As soon as they arrived at the house, Butch made a quick call to the stables and made sure everything was all right. Following a shower and donning freshly starched jeans and a white shirt, he told them that he wouldn't be back until late and they could use the Corvette if they wanted to go anywhere.

He left them watching television and drove east on Highway 114 until he arrived in Southlake. Once there, he followed the directions he had gotten to the stables where the meeting was going to be held. He spotted Tammy as soon as he entered and walked up, saying, "Hello, pretty lady, have you ever wanted to go dancing with a real cowboy?"

"Hello, Butch," she answered. "Not until now, we still on for tonight?"

"I wouldn't miss it for the world," he told her. "I just love walking onto the dance floor with the prettiest lady in the room. Makes an old man feel special, you know."

"Let's just hope this doesn't take too long," she whispered as the chairman of the benefit started talking. "I've wanted to go dancing with you for a long time now. It's about time you finally asked me."

Butch looked at her with shock on his face. "Really?" he asked. "Why didn't you say so?"

"Dummy," she replied. "I gave you every hint known to man short of just asking. Maybe you should open your eyes and learn when a woman is interested."

Butch stood dumbfounded and just smiled. "Well, I guess it all works out in the end."

They listened to the plan for the benefit and what each of them was being asked to do. As each person was appointed to various committees and a time for each to meet, Butch's mind wandered as he tried to figure out just when he had missed Tammy's signals. Finally shaking his head, he listened to each speaker and made a mental note as to what he would be required to do. When the meeting adjourned, they started back to their cars together.

"Do you want to follow me to my house?" Tammy asked. "We can leave your truck there and take my car."

"Why don't we take my truck and leave your car?" Butch asked. "If I'm taking a pretty lady dancing, I don't intend for her to have to do anything except put up with me. Is that all right?"

"Sure," Tammy said as Butch opened her car door. "You just might be made into a gentleman yet. Follow me, it's only a couple of miles."

Butch grinned as he shut her door and walked to his truck, thinking that this was going to be one fun night. He had almost forgotten how cute she was and how good she looked from behind in her jeans.

As soon as they arrived at her house, she parked her car and walked back to his truck. He got out and came around to open her door. Once she had climbed in, he smiled and shut the door. As they drove to a small place called Cowboy Country, she would repeatedly reach over and touch his arm while they talked about the benefit.

Once inside, Butch asked her what she wanted to drink and went to the bar for a couple of Budweisers. For over two hours, they danced and talked about what had happened since they had last seen each other. Finally, Butch looked at his watch and told her that it was getting late and that his kids were home alone.

"Aren't they old enough to make it one night without their father?" she asked. "I kind of thought that maybe we would go back to my house and finish our conversation."

"Just what conversation are you referring to?" asked Butch as he rose and slid her chair out for her.

"About how you need to learn to read a woman's signals," she laughed as they walked to the door. "Like I said, I hope your kids can spend one night alone because you're so dumb, this might just take me all night."

Chapter 47

          Kevin woke the next morning in his own bed. The sun was barely peeking over the tree line in the east as he crawled from his bed and stumbled into the kitchen. As the coffee was brewing, he poured a glass of orange juice and walked outside to watch the sunrise. His old dog, Scout, was lying on the front porch and raised his head for the welcoming scratch. Kevin obliged him and sat in the wicker chair watching the sun start its slow climb into the heavens.

    Although the last couple of days had been tiresome, he had really enjoyed them. After returning from the kitchen with his cup brimming, he debated going back up to visit Gene and Leslie. Finally deciding that they should be left alone for a few days to resolve any problems they were sure to encounter, he went back to get one of his prepaid cell phones.

    As soon as Butch answered, he told him about the car, and they discussed where to drop the new cell phones. The issue of money came up, but Kevin insisted on sharing in the expense and they could settle any outstanding debts when they had a chance. There was never any questioning of what was bought or of its cost. Both men trusted the other to do the right thing.

    Just as the conversation was coming to an end, Kevin heard a female voice in the background. "That one of your precious children up this early?" he asked.

"Why do you ask, Kemo Sabe?" Butch asked.

"Because I know they normally don't get up this early unless you make them," he answered. "And that doesn't sound like either of them."

"It's not," Butch said.

"I'll bet that you aren't at home right now either," Kevin replied. "Don't tell me that you've snuck out for the night."

"No," Butch told him, "I didn't sneak anywhere, if it's any of your snoopy business."

"Come on," Kevin complained. "Tell a lonely old rancher tales of your exploits. And don't forget the juicy stuff either."

"Not a chance, Fat Boy," Butch laughed. "All I'll say is that this one may make me rethink my long-standing rules on interviewing for a future mother for my kids."

"You mean where the first interview is just spending the night and being gone when the sun comes up?" Kevin joked. "And phase 2 is that she makes breakfast, cleans up, and then goes home? And the final phase, number 3, is that she does the first two and then cleans the entire house before she leaves? You surely aren't changing those rules are you?"

"Well," Butch admitted laughing, "those weren't really rules, just guidelines. And anyway, I do have waiver authority."

"Go on," Kevin begged. "Tell me about this lady that actually got the famous Butch North to spend the night."

"To start with, I don't think I'm too famous," Butch retorted. "I'm just extremely picky. It's not that I don't like playing house, it's just that there are so few that I would want to play with. And this one, I've known her for several years and never really considered it because she had a horse at my place."

"That was a stupid rule to start with," Kevin said. "I remember one woman that was there a couple of years ago, I think her name was Toni or Tanya, something like that. Anyway, she was a tiny little thing with long dark hair. I always wondered why you never asked her out."

"Rule 1, don't date the customers," Butch told him. "And her name was Tammy."

"That's right," Kevin agreed. "You and your stupid rules, whatever happened to her?"

"Hang on a second," Butch told him as he handed the phone to Tammy.

"Hello?" Tammy said.

"Don't tell me," Kevin laughed. "You must be Tammy."

"Yes," she said. "Who are you?"

"I'm just an old friend of your buddy who's probably grinning like a shit-eating possum right now," Kevin answered. "Put that jerk back on the phone, please."

"I guess that answered your question," Butch said as he took the phone back. "Now, if you're through digging into my personal affairs, I'll say goodbye and see if I can talk this pretty lady into letting me take her to breakfast."

"You are one sly dog," Kevin laughed. "Now, you've lost at least two years with that woman, for what? Some stupid rule? What a dumb-shit!"

"Whatever," Butch said. "If it's worth waiting for, then wait. And you're one of the last people in the world I need love advice from. I've seen some of your sweeties, and although they're good-looking, they all seem to be kin to the Antichrist."

"I'll admit that some of my choices have been rather strange," Kevin admitted. "Especially the one you guys kept calling 'the skinny bitch'."

"I remember her too," Butch replied. "And not too fondly. I always wondered when you'd find the horns on that lady's head, she was evil incarnate."

"Aren't they all?" Kevin asked. "Oh, except your current love, of course. Well, I guess we've covered about everything this morning. I'll let you two go gaze into each other's eyes as you have your eggs. Just don't choke on them before we get this project finished."

"No problem," Butch told him. "I do know CPR and that world-famous hinny-lick maneuver. You take care, and I'll talk to you in a few days."

"You too, buddy," Kevin said as he hung up. He sat there quietly with the phone in his lap for a few minutes and then got up and told Scout, "You may be too old to chase rabbits anymore, old friend, but our boy, Butch, seems to have found a magic elixir. Maybe I'll give him a year's supply of Viagra for Christmas this year. Better throw in a complimentary visit to the cardiologist too."

Kevin took his cup into the kitchen and refilled it. He planned on taking it easy today and doing some odd chores around his place. There were several places where he need to do a little welding on the fences and nearly all of the equipment needed to be greased. The housecleaning would have to wait for a few more days until the lady that did it would be here, but he could at least pick up a few things and do some laundry.

While Kevin was busy back down in Vashti, Gene and Leslie were sitting around the table having a cup of coffee and talking about their former lives. The more she learned about him, the closer she felt. She could not imagine what it would be like to have lived twenty-plus years in a laboratory and to never know what it was like to have friends or relatives.

She vowed to try to make up for all those years and show him how important it was to have someone to share everything. As she held his hands, she knew that he was the type of man she had always been looking for. The mystery of his past and his possible origin meant nothing to her. Here was a kind and gentle man who had shown extraordinary intelligence and a keen sense of humor. Yes, this was just what she had always wanted in her life.

Gene was too happy right now to care what the rest of the world was doing. Finally, he had found someone that felt about him as Vicki had, and he silently thanked her for showing him why a man and a woman would want to live together. Just holding her hand made him feel better than he ever had in his life. And the sex, that was something that he could never have understood until he experienced it. As far as he was concerned, if they spent the rest of their lives out here, it would be all right.

Now that he knew what the rest of the world was like, he would do anything Butch or Kevin asked of him to remain free. Suddenly he knew that he had found his place in life. Two of the best men you could ever meet and the sweetest woman in the world. There was nothing that he wouldn't do to protect these three people who had done more for him in less than a week than those back at the lab had done in twenty years. And he would never let either of them down.

TM

Chapter 48

For the rest of September, General Modelle and the staff of the facility continued monitoring Butch. Mischelle and Jeannie finally left when air traffic was allowed to resume, and they found that there was very little activity around Butch's house. The exception was when Tammy would occasionally come out for the weekend. It was during these visits that General Nelson finally told Karyn to disable the listening devices they had placed within the house.

"We're looking for his involvement with Gene's disappearance," he announced during Tammy's first visit after the girls had left. "What we're listening to when those two are together has zero to do with that. We've already determined that Ms. Terbush has no knowledge of him, and whatever Butch knows, he isn't sharing with her. So I don't want to listen to their pillow talk or monitor their private affairs any longer."

Bob Wilson continued to go to Red's almost every night until he learned that Butch usually came out on Wednesday's for karaoke or on weekends when Tammy was visiting. He did eventually meet him at the National Ropers Supply arena south of Decatur a few times.

Although they shared a few beers and roped together several times, Bob heard nothing that remotely pertained to Gene. As they spent more time together and he got to know both Butch and Tammy, he reported that either Butch knew nothing or wasn't about to talk.

General Modelle and General Nelson debated again and again whether or not to bring Butch back in again. Colonel Ericson suggested going out to visit him and appeal to his patriotism and sense of duty. Any approach would reinforce Butch's suspicions, he argued. But trying to bring him onboard without letting him know why the military needed to find Gene seemed the best approach.

Major Fleenor continued to worry about what might eventually happen to Butch if Gene wasn't found before long. He knew that pressure would continue to mount and that the fate of one person meant nothing to those that were responsible for this program. He had developed an admiration for Butch and whoever Mr. Phuc actually was.

As fewer and fewer things occurred that could possibly tie Butch to Gene, Jerry began to believe that no matter what had happened during the first few days after Gene was spotted in Boyd, Butch was no longer involved. Granted, there were some unusual things that seemed suspicious, such as unexplained conversations on unknown phones. But that could very well have been Butch being involved with someone's wife and trying to remain secretive. It just didn't seem right to continue to violate that man's life.

Jerry even began to watch Butch's behavior and thought about trying to contact him without the rest of the facility's people knowing. Just how he could manage this with all the systems in place to cover every facet of Butch's activities, he didn't know. But one thing he was sure of, if it ever got to the point that Butch was actually in danger of radical actions by those that had the most to lose, he would somehow get word to Butch.

He knew that if he were ever caught trying to help him, his career and possibly his life were over. If the time ever came that he would have to make that decision, he needed to be absolutely certain that he had a plan that would protect himself.

On the weekends that Tammy didn't visit Butch, he would normally spend one of the nights with her; and they would go out to eat, go to movies, dancing, or just stay home. Butch never said anything about his involvement to her. It wasn't that she couldn't be trusted, he just didn't want to place her in a position that might get her involved. He hated not being completely honest with her, but he didn't think she would really blame him if it ever came out.

After Butch finally received the results of the DNA tests from Lewisville, he knew that there was a portion of Gene's genetic makeup that didn't fit anything found in the rest of the population. The lab's report listed Unknown markers and described them as possible contaminates. Butch was absolutely positive that there had been nothing to contaminate the samples, but was satisfied to let the lab think otherwise. It provided the explanation that he would have had to make if the lab had questioned the origin of the samples.

It was early in October that Kevin contacted Butch and requested a meeting to discuss a potential problem. The issue at hand was that Leslie had missed her period. Butch had known the chances that they were taking with Leslie and Gene living together and being left alone with only each other for companionship.

"I thought she was taking care of that," Butch said when they finally met at the Decatur Wal-Mart. "What the hell happened?"

"She quit taking her pills, I guess," Kevin answered. "Besides, how were we supposed to get her prescription filled without letting people know where she was?"

"We could have come up with something," Butch argued. "But I guess it may be too late now. How does she feel about this possibility?"

"She's happy," Kevin replied. "She admitted that she wanted to have his child, and you know that he's just ecstatic about it. I don't know which would be worse right now, her being pregnant or it being a false alarm."

"I hope it's a false alarm," Butch told him. "But we need to start planning on how to manage this if she is pregnant. What about doctors or complications?"

"Well, there is an old doctor down in Ringgold that's been there for over forty years," Kevin answered. "He's one of the old-school fellows, still running a small clinic that takes care of the few locals that grew up around here. I had to go there once several years ago when I almost cut a finger off while helping to clear the land where they're living."

"Do you think we need to get her in there now, or should we wait a couple of months?" Butch asked. "I really don't want to get any more people involved any sooner than we have to."

"I'm getting a couple of those home pregnancy tests to take back," Kevin said. "I guess we have to wait and let Leslie decide what she should do. Have you thought about finding someone like the old midwife thing they used to do?"

"I haven't had time to think about any of this," Butch admitted. "I'll have to take the time now I guess. For now, let's see what the tests show. Maybe we're getting ahead of ourselves."

"Even if we are a little premature, we better get ready," Kevin responded. "If not this time, sooner or later we could have to face the possibilities. Especially since both of them seem to want this."

"Try to explain the consequences," Butch said. "Not just the problems we would face with the pregnancy, but what type of child would be the result of so many unknowns given his genetics?"

"I know," Kevin told him. "I'll do what I can, but I still think if they're determined to do this, we better figure out how to handle it."

"You're right," Butch agreed. "I may have an idea, but I'll need to take a small vacation down South to see if I can work out the details. And it will take a couple of months to get it done."

"We seem to have some time," Kevin acknowledged. "But I'd bet it's no more than eight or nine months. Who would know the gestation period for something like this? I sure don't. I can tell you what it is for pigs, cows, horses, and a few others. But this is a new one for me."

"I think this would be a new one for anybody," Butch said. "We'll be writing a new chapter in the history of man if those two produce a child. Until then, I've got to get home and get ready for Tammy's visit."

"How's that going?" Kevin asked with a grin. "Don't tell me you're actually serious about her."

"It's going just fine," Butch answered. "She has her own life outside of me, and she doesn't try to run mine. We just have a good time together and are going to enjoy it as it is for now. I'm certainly in no rush for any commitments, and neither is she. Neither of us has fond memories of our previous marriages and wants to go through that again."

"I just never thought I'd hear you even contemplate it," Kevin told him.

"I didn't say I was contemplating anything," Butch reminded him. "All I'm contemplating is having fun and making sure she enjoys it as much as I do."

"It just looks to me that she's already passed phase 3 of your interview," Kevin remarked. "Doesn't that mean she's potentially the new mother for your kids?"

"She's potentially someone that I enjoy being around," Butch said. "And you're potentially getting into part of my business that you don't need to be. Now, you just get your fat ass back up there, and let's see what new problems we're going to face. Call me in a week or so. I'll work on the south solution in the meantime."

Gene and Leslie had spent their time together much as any newly married couple would have. Small chores around the house kept her busy most of the time, and she would go with him as he wandered around the woods and marveled at the things she had grown accustomed to years ago. Gene enjoyed just sitting on the front porch and watching the wildlife that passed by in the mornings and evenings.

His former life had been sterile, and the things he was seeing and hearing now had been from either on books or on the lessons he had received from Vicki. Now he was experiencing real life. Even getting dirty or an occasional scratch was a new to him. Everyday life held new meaning, and the joy of being around Leslie still amazed him.

Leslie's announcement about her possible pregnancy made him feel even more hopeful for their future. He was concerned about the possible problems and knew that Butch and Kevin would be upset. But this was one of the things that Vicki had spoken of, the desire to have a family and care for each other. The more they talked about it, the more both of them wanted a child.

Leslie knew that things would change if she was pregnant. She wanted to let her family know how her life was going, and this was something she desperately wanted to share with her mother. Kevin had not let her make any additional calls, but she had to get him to let her tell her mother. She even thought they might figure out a way for her mother to come help. She'd have to talk to him as soon as he came back.

Chapter 49

On through October, November, and December, the hunt for Gene continued. Satellite coverage was replaced and removed several times as those in Washington needed the attributes of this special version of the system. It became increasingly more difficult for General Modelle to justify its use due to the lack of progress or worthwhile images. As Christmas neared, there were still no further sightings of Gene or Leslie. Monitoring of her home showed that her mother would routinely stop by and spend a couple of hours each week, but no other activity.

The activity they saw surrounding Stacey's house in Arlington was equally devoid of any worthy information. Her activities were consistent with a normal workday life, and her phones showed only occasional calls to or from Leslie's family with no mention of where Leslie was living. The team finally decided to drop all coverage of her and shift their dwindling resources to the Boyd and Bowie areas.

Butch continued his increasing relationship with Tammy, and Colonel Ericson sent a special team to follow them when they took a trip down to San Antonio. The weekend there was spent visiting the River Walk, dinner with old friends from the air force, and an overnight trip to Del Rio and Ciudad Acuna. Butch and Tammy visited several local shops after they crossed into Mexico and, late in the afternoon, went into a restaurant named Ma Crosby's.

While having dinner there, it was obvious to the team observing them that there were several people living in the area that Butch had known while stationed at Laughlin AFB. Several of them would stop by their table and sit for a few minutes talking and discussing their lives since Butch had left to join American Airlines. It was difficult to determine how many of the visitors were former military or local civilians that had lived in the Del Rio area.

It was during one of the quick visits that Butch handed an unidentified man one of his business cards. It was not noted as being extraordinary since he had given cards to several people during the previous months. The team did not take any pictures of any of the numerous people Butch and Tammy talked to either in Mexico, Del Rio, or San Antonio except the family they had spent the most time with. There appeared to be no connection with any of these people other than their mutual association during Butch's military time in the area.

The thing the team missed was the writing on the back of the card Butch had given to the man. There Butch had written a number and specified that it was to be called on a certain day and from a public phone. Following dinner, Butch and Tammy drove back across the Rio Grande and spent the night in a motel in Del Rio that had been arranged by their friends in San Antonio. When the team checked the motel records the next morning after Butch and Tammy had headed east on Highway 90 toward San Antonio, they discovered that his room had received one call from Wright's Steak House in Del Rio. It had lasted only about five minutes and was quickly dismissed as one of his former acquaintances contacting him.

They followed Butch as he drove into San Antonio and turned north on I-35. The five-hour drive back to Fort Worth was uninterrupted except for two stops for fuel and lunch at a What-a-Burger in Waco. Butch did receive a couple of calls on his cell phone during the drive as did Tammy. Both of their phones were now being monitored, but their conversations were with friends or family and again had no bearing on Gene or Leslie.

It had been months now since Butch had shown any activity that would raise any suspicions, and now those few things were being seen as possibly having no real connection with Gene. In particular, Major Fleenor was becoming disillusioned with the continuing monitoring of Mr. North. As Christmas came and went and no evidence that

Butch was doing anything remotely connected with their search, he began to envision ways to contact him.

Jerry knew that it would certainly be risky, and his only hope of avoiding being caught would be due to his knowledge of the systems in place to watch Butch. It would definitely have to be when there was no satellite coverage and in a public place. He would also need to disguise himself to avoid being recognized by one of their teams that may have seen him at the facility or of being photographed.

Butch had fewer and fewer contacts with Kevin over the last few months except to learn that Leslie was definitely pregnant and that Kevin had taken her to the doctor in Ringgold and she and the fetus appeared to be healthy and normal. Her next checkup would be a couple of months from now, and Kevin would take care of any of the bills.

Even Kevin had begun to visit Gene and Leslie less and less. He had finally taken the car from his cousin in Henrietta and left it at their place with strict instructions not to try to drive it. He would always take the keys when he left, but there was little concern now that Leslie would try to leave. She appeared to be content with living with Gene and was looking forward to having her child.

Kevin had their requests for each other's Christmas presents and had gotten them along with some from him and Butch. They had found a small pine tree growing just north of the house, and Kevin had let Gene chop it down and carry it to the house. Leslie had decorated it with things Kevin had brought, and once the gifts were laid beneath it, Gene looked at it and told them this would be his first Christmas with a real family. As the tears ran down his cheeks, Leslie held him close and told him that it might be the first, but certainly not the last. Even Kevin had to wipe his eyes several times as he watched and eventually went to place his arms around both of them.

Neither of Butch's kids could make it down for the Christmas season, and he spent it with Tammy attending parties at their friend's houses. Christmas morning found them at his house, and after opening their presents, she told him that she needed to return home after breakfast. They had been together since Friday afternoon. Five full days and four nights together was about as long as they had ever spent, and both of them were ready for a break. As Butch made scrambled eggs and hash browns, Tammy picked up all the torn gift wrapping and tried to straighten up their mess.

Christmas morning back at the facility was somber as only a couple of people were there monitoring the few images they were getting from the satellite and the monitors within Butch's house. Jerry was alone in the operations center when Butch told Tammy that he was going to Decatur that afternoon to pick up a couple of items from David's Western Wear.

Colonel Ericson was due to take over at noon, and they were scheduled to lose the satellite at ten o'clock. Jerry knew that there was only one of the original team members left in the Decatur area and that his role had been reduced to following Butch when he was driving out of the local area or when satellite monitoring was lost. Unless that agent had been notified that they were scheduled to lose the satellite that morning, he would probably be still in his motel in Fort Worth.

Jerry had already bought a knee-length coat that was large enough for him to appear at least fifty pounds heavier if he put a pillow under an extra large sweatshirt he had purchased. If he was wearing the old black cowboy hat and sunglasses, he would pass for any of the rock truck drivers that resided in the local area. Additionally he had bought two prepaid cell phones from separate stores over the last few weeks and had written a letter describing what he wanted to tell Butch.

One of the phones was placed in a large envelope with the letter, and he would attempt to pass them to Butch sometime this afternoon. He had already made arrangements to drop his car off at one of the local dealers for minor maintenance and had the keys to the rental car he would use while his was in the shop. His plan was to switch cars as soon as he left the base and to put on his disguise once he was north of Fort Worth.

Once he was ready, he drove to Rhome and parked in the Giant Burger lot where he could watch Highway 114 and follow Butch up to Decatur. He purposely did not contact the agent that was supposed to follow Butch, but planned on calling Colonel Ericson when he saw Butch turn north onto Highway 287. He would say he was calling to make sure the agent was notified and to be where he was supposed to go after Tammy left. But he knew it would be impossible for anyone to get to David's before he could pass his envelope and return to his house back in Fort Worth.

It was almost two o'clock when he saw Tammy's car driving east on 114 as she headed home. Just a couple of minutes later, he saw Butch's truck stop at the sign less than a hundred feet from where he sat. After watching him for almost four months, Jerry was still shocked to be this close to the man they had expended so much effort to monitor his every move.

As Butch joined Highway 287 north, Jerry slid in behind him after a couple of pickups had passed. He had seen this area so many times in the past and had watched Butch drive back and forth that he knew exactly where he would be going. His only goal now was to enter David's quickly behind Butch and pass the envelope as soon as he could. He had rehearsed his introduction repeatedly and was ready to make the initial contact.

As expected, Butch exited 287 and turned left at the light onto Highway 51 south and past Wal-Mart. It was exactly as he had been watching and felt as if he had made this trip numerous times. Even the equipment sitting in front of Tractor Supply was familiar. Traffic was light as he followed Butch into the parking spaces in front of David's. He waited until Butch had opened the door and walked in before he got out of the car and followed him.

Inside, he got his first view of the interior and saw hundreds of pairs of boots, racks of jeans, a wide variety of hats, and other Western attire. He spotted Butch walking to the shelves where Wranglers were stacked by size. He went directly to his right side and slid the envelope on top of the 32 X 36 jeans Butch was getting. As he placed it on the top of the stack, he quietly said, "Don't look at me, just take this and follow the instructions. Use the phone inside and call me when you get back home and are in the barn. Do not call from your truck or your house."

He turned to his right and walked swiftly out of the store without Butch ever seeing his face. He quickly started his car and pulled back on the road to hurry home to Fort Worth. The entire exchange had taken only a couple of seconds, but his heart was still racing and his hands shaking as he realized that what he had done could well be classified as treason. Now that it was done, he wondered if he had just made the biggest mistake of his life.

Chapter 50

As soon as Butch got home, he walked down to the barn and waited for the horses to follow him. After putting a scoop in each feeder, he checked their feet to see if they needed trimming and did a quick check to see if there were any scrapes of cuts that needed attention. Giving them a final pat on the side of their necks, he shut the doors leading from the stalls into the barn and pulled the envelope from inside his shirt.

The phone was answered, "Are you away from your house and cars?"

"Yes," Butch answered.

"No names, no mention of how you got this phone or what you ever hear, understood?"

"Yes."

"You are aware that you're being watched, your phones tapped, your house and vehicles bugged?"

"I assumed so," Butch told him.

"We will never meet again, but I will call this phone with further instructions tomorrow evening at six o'clock. Hide it somewhere in the barn and tell no one you've got it."

"I'll be here," Butch said waiting.

"Bob Wilson is one of us, be careful," were the final words before the caller hung up.

Butch pushed the End Call button on his phone and stood staring at it for a couple of minutes. At this point, he didn't know if this was a ploy to get him to unwittingly divulge something or if there was truly someone within the organization that was trying to help him. Either way, he would be down in the barn at six o'clock tomorrow evening. Between now and then, he would think of how he could protect his information yet get confirmation from the caller as to his intent.

Jerry was still shaking when he hung up. He sat quietly waiting for the front door to burst open and troopers to storm in and take the phone from his hand. Never in his fourteen years of service in the air force had he ever even contemplated disobeying an order, and this was way past mere disobedience. Now that he had taken the first step, there would be no turning back. He took his phone and walked into the kitchen. Taking an empty Crown Royal bag, he placed the phone inside and removed the bottom drawer from beneath the counter and placed it on the floor where it would be hidden even if someone pulled the drawer out to look inside.

He walked over to the cabinet where he kept several different bottles of whiskey and other alcoholic beverages and took a bottle of Jack Daniels from the shelf. He went back into the kitchen, placed several ice cubes in a glass, and poured two inches of the golden brown liquid over them. As he carried the drink into his living room, he turned the television on and sat in his leather recliner.

Sitting with the untouched drink in his hand, he was oblivious to the show on the screen. The voices coming from the speaker were unintelligible, and he felt as if he were weightless and floating within a grey cloud. Nothing seemed real at this point. "Holy shit!" he exclaimed to no one. "I can't believe what I've just done."

Finally relaxing a little, he raised the glass to his lips and drank half of it without stopping. As the liquid burned its way down his throat, he realized that he was more tired than he had ever been in his life. He slowly got up and walked into the bathroom. Letting the tub fill with hot water, he sat the drink on the side while undressing. After slipping deep into the near-scalding water, he leaned back and took another sip of his drink. He remained there until the water had cooled below his body temperature and his glass was empty.

Butch had taken his phone and put it into a coffee can. After placing the lid on the can, he opened one of the plastic barrels that held the horse's feed and buried it under several inches of the pellets. As he walked back to the house, he wondered who would have risked their career to warn him of things that he already suspected. If nothing else, maybe he could learn how much of his activities they knew.

As soon as he entered the house, he picked up the phone and called Tammy. He really wanted to talk to Kevin, but right now, he wanted to be heard discussing normal things. Although his mind was racing elsewhere, he listened politely and made small talk while he fixed a Jack and Coke. Sitting in his recliner, he occasionally mumbled answers or just responded when he felt she was waiting for one.

After she finally told him she would call when he was paying more attention, he realized that he barely remembered anything they had discussed. Apologizing to her, he said he'd call after dinner later tonight. Quickly draining his glass, he carried it into the kitchen and placed it in the sink. He walked through the dining room and back to his bath. As he undressed, he put all the clothes into the hamper and started the water running for a shower.

When he finished, he dressed in a starched white shirt, crisp jeans, and pulled on a pair of Tony Lama ostrich-skin boots. Grabbing his black felt hat, he climbed into his truck and headed south down FM 718 toward Newark. When he pulled up in front of Venice Pizza and Pasta, he climbed out and walked in, carrying an ice-filled cooler of Budweiser. The karaoke was already going as he took a table against the back wall where he could watch both the singer and the front door.

He waived to the DJ and opened a can of beer. The waitress stopped by and asked if he wanted a glass or if he was ready to order. Saying no to the glass, he ordered a large pizza with everything on it. As she was walking away, the DJ gave him a questioning look to ask if he wanted to sing tonight. He held his can up and nodded yes which was understood that he wanted to finish it before he started singing.

He had only taken a couple of drinks from the can when Bobby, one of the owners, walked over to his table. "All alone tonight?" Bobby asked.

"I'm afraid so," Butch answered. "You know I can only take just so much of a woman. A man has to have a little time alone every now and then."

"I know," Bobby replied. "I was wondering just how long you were going to keep this one. You never seem to stay with one too long, and you've been seeing this one longer than any of the others I've seen you with."

"This one's obviously better than the other ones," Butch told him. "Most of the others were like rest stops along the road. Necessary every now and then, but not a good place to stay for very long."

"Is that so?" said Janet as she walked up. "Don't you be telling my brother-in-law any of your less-than-romantic ideas. Jeffery and I are trying to find him a good woman, and you keep bringing different women in and tell him that you need to change them like used underwear."

"Oh, Janet," Butch protested. "You know if I could find a lady as pretty as you, I'd never stray. Just look how happy Jeffery is. All I tell Bobby is that if he can't find the perfect one, like you, then to move on and try again."

"You're so full of shit," Janet said, laughing. "I'll bet that Tammy has you wrapped around her little finger. I've seen the way you two are when you're here."

"I only bring her down so I can have someone cheer for me when I sing," Butch protested. "When she's not around, I have to pass out beers to get people to clap. Why do you think I bring a whole cooler in when I only drink one or two?"

"I've never seen you stop at two," she replied. "I've even been tempted to have either Bobby or Jeffery drive you home once or twice. But I'm afraid of where you'd make them take you, and I don't want to have to come get all of you out of jail somewhere."

She turned and left as the waitress was bringing his pizza. Butch smiled as he watched her go. Their family had only been in business here for a short time, and he enjoyed their company. Not only were they a good bunch of people, they made excellent food. He tried to bring everyone here for at least one meal to help build their business. The country had way too many barbeque or hamburger places, and it was nice to have some variety out here in the country.

He sang a couple of Moe Bandy songs while eating his pizza and stayed to have another beer after he had over half of it put in a to-go box. After picking up his cooler and pizza, he waved goodbye and went out to his truck. As he was leaving town, he saw a black Suburban parked by the convenience store on the north edge of town. As he passed it, he flashed his headlights and waved. Might as well let them know he's aware of their presence and be friendly. Who knows, that might even be the mysterious caller.

On his way home, his cell phone rang, and he heard Jeannie's voice as he answered it. They discussed their Christmas presents as he drove, and she told him about what she had done, who she had seen, and then asked how things were going with Tammy. He told her about their Christmas, their trip down to Del Rio, and the visit to Ciudad Acuna. She remembered Ma Crosby's from the time she went there when she had lived with him.

As Butch arrived at his house, he told her he wished they could have had some time together during the holidays, but with the stables and everything else, there just wasn't time. Promising to try to go see her in the summer, he hung up and went inside. As he made another Jack and Coke, he thought about all the things he wanted to ask his caller tomorrow evening.

With nothing but waiting left to do, he called Tammy, and they talked for a few minutes; and he promised to come in and spend the coming weekend with her at her house. After tentative agreement on whether or not to go to a movie, dinner, or to stay home, he said good night and went to bed. Throughout the night, dreams of spies and counterspies from the old *Mad* magazine kept chasing each other through his mind. The problem was trying to determine who the good spy was and who was bad.

Chapter 51

Early the next morning, Butch woke up and started the day with his usual pot of Folgers coffee. Taking one of the remaining phones and a glass of orange juice, he walked down to the barn and whistled for the horses. As they came loping across the pasture, he stood just inside the open stall doors and watched. They held their tails high and occasionally nipped at each other as they came through the gate that allowed him to separate the pastureland into different sections. That way he could let the horses and cattle graze in one area while another was left to grow. By rotating the pastures, they never overgrazed them, and there would be constant new growth.

As soon as he poured their pellets, they shoved their heads into the feeders and began eating. Butch pulled the phone from his shirt pocket and dialed. "Good morning, Fat Boy," he said when it was answered. "I sure hope that I didn't wake you. I know how you rotund folks like to lay in bed all day eating bonbons and drinking chocolate milk."

"You sure know how to start a fellow's day off right," Kevin responded. "What makes you think I want to talk to you this early? Did the poor little fellow have a bad night?"

"They're all bad when you sleep alone," Butch said. "But that's not as bad as waking up with some of those old hides I've seen you bed down."

"Look who's talking," Kevin replied. "I swear you'd pick the ugliest pig in the litter."

"I may pick them ugly," Butch laughed, "but I've found that the ugly ones have the best personalities. You keep going for the fancy ones, but even if you put lipstick on a pig, you still wake up with a pig."

"So true, so very true," Kevin acknowledged. "What's up?"

"We need to have a face-to-face," Butch said somberly. "I've had a very interesting call, and since what I do could impact you, I want you to know what I'm doing."

"No problem," Kevin replied. "When and where?"

"Usual big store north of me," Butch answered. "High noon, that'd be lunch time to you folks that tell time by the rumble in your gut."

"I'll be there," Kevin said. "I need to put a bag in your truck anyway, and if you have anything for me, I'll park somewhere that you'll pass when you walk back to it from the store."

"Good. We can discuss the mare's condition and see what we need to do when she foals," Butch told him as he prepared to hang up. "I'll see you there."

Butch walked back to the house and checked the local weather to see if there would be any forecasts that would impact the stables. This time of year, a sudden drop in temperature would mean all the self-watering systems would freeze and require using buckets in each stall. Then, there would be the inevitable breaks in the plumbing system as the plastic lines froze where they were exposed.

The rest of the morning, he spent cleaning house and doing a small load of laundry. Shortly after eleven o'clock, he left and drove by the stables to see how Steve was doing and check on the supply of hay and feed. Everything was running smoothly, and there were plenty of spare buckets for the water if necessary. Finding nothing that would cause any concerns, Butch headed for Decatur.

As he pulled into the parking lot at Wal-Mart, he watched the now-familiar black Suburban drive past and turn into the lot for Tractor Supply. Butch parked as far from it as possible to make it difficult for the driver to walk to his truck or see who parked beside him. He locked the truck and looked into the bed to make sure there was nothing under the toolbox that would interfere with Kevin's placing his sack there.

As he was walking toward the store, he saw Kevin driving toward him and knew that he had been parked somewhere waiting for his arrival. Now sure that Kevin would not be seen putting anything under his toolbox, he walked in and took a grocery cart. Pushing the cart to the cake and pastry section, he waited for Kevin to round the corner.

"I knew you'd want to stop here," Butch told him as Kevin came up beside him. "I thought I'd try to steer you over to the fruit section before you filled your cart with doughnuts."

"You're way too funny," Kevin replied. "I'm going to buy a few things for my adopted kids while we're here. Amazing what those two can eat, and that skinny little lady is starting to really put on some pounds. What's this about an interesting call?"

"I think I was called by someone from the other side," Butch said as they slowly pushed their carts down the aisles. "I was given a phone and instructions yesterday and took the call last night. The caller just told me that I was being watched, which we already suspected, and then said that someone I recently met is part of their team."

"What do you think?" Kevin asked as he selected various items and placed them into his cart.

"It's either a setup or someone's turning," Butch said. "I'm not sure at this point, but I'll talk to him tonight. Regardless of which side he's actually on, I don't plan on telling him anything about where Gene and Leslie are living. If he wants to provide anything that helps us, I'll certainly listen. But he could also be providing information that is meant to mislead us if we act on it."

"That's your problem," Kevin told him. "You just make your decision, and I'll live with it. You're the only one that can judge what they're up to. If you're wrong, that's a chance we have to take. It would be nice to have someone on the inside though. Just in case they find us like they did the little camper. That was a close call, a couple of more hours and we'd have been caught."

"I'll let you know what I think after I talk to him again," Butch said. "How's Leslie doing?"

"Fine," Kevin answered. "We went to the doctor I told you about, and he's still running his little clinic out there. I swear the man's in his eighties and still seeing patients. Granted, not many, but I think he just does it to keep busy now."

"That's good," Butch said. "I certainly don't want to have to take her to one of the larger hospitals. I know we couldn't get her in without giving away her identity, and I'm sure her name is on every watch list in the country. Who did you tell him she was anyway?"

"I just told him she was my niece and that she was going to be living with me for a year while her husband was overseas with the army," Kevin answered. "I told him her name was Terri Miller. I don't think he ever remembers it because he just calls her young lady."

"What about paperwork? Did you list your name or make up something?"

"I used O'Neal as my last name since there's a family up there that's been around for generations," Kevin answered. "I swear that old man just swore that he knew my grandmother and all my cousins. I even had him convinced that he delivered my daddy. I don't think we'll have any problems. He still keeps his records on paper, won't take a credit card, and prefers cash."

"Good," Butch said. "Let's just hope that we don't need anything too exotic. I doubt if he would have anything remotely modern if there are any complications."

"Probably not," Kevin told him. "He even reminds me of that doctor on the old *Gunsmoke* shows, what was his name?"

"Doc Adams," Butch answered. "He was played by Milburn Stone. That was a great series—James Arness, Amanda Blake, Ken Curtis, and Buck Taylor—a real classic cowboy show. Too bad they don't make them like that anymore. All the crap they have now—reality shows, court shows with trailer park trash airing their laundry—give me *Leave It to Beaver* or *Gunsmoke* and I'll watch it. The rest of it isn't worth the electricity it takes to run the television."

"You've outlived your usefulness old boy," Kevin joked. "You need to be put down before you become a real drag on society. I hope your poor kids don't ever have to take you in."

"Hell, Jeannie has already told me she plans on making me live in a cardboard box on her porch," Butch laughed. "I just hope Mischelle will be a little kinder to me. Maybe she'll at least pick a good retirement home with pretty young nurses."

"Don't count on it," Kevin said. "As mean as you've been to those sweet little things, you'll be lucky if you get a cardboard box. If I was them, I'd make you live under one of the bridges and pray for a flood."

"You're such an asshole," Butch told him. "I'm glad I didn't have a sorry piece of crap like you for a son. I'd be afraid to close my eyes at night, scared you'd try to sneak in and slit my throat."

"I wouldn't do that," Kevin joked. "I'd superglue your hands together so you couldn't hold a can of beer. Then make you beg for a straw so you could drink it. That would be suitable punishment for you."

"Maybe my kids aren't so bad after all," Butch said. "They've never threatened to take away my beer."

As they walked down the beverage aisle, Butch reached over to a case of Budweiser and slid a fresh stack of hundred-dollar bills into the handle opening. "Speaking of beer," he said, "I recommend this one. Why don't you take it, and I'll call you later with any news."

"Looks like good beer to me," Kevin said as he placed the case into his cart. "I'll certainly take it. Let me know if there's anything you need me to do."

"I'll call if I do," Butch said as he pushed his cart away. "Take care, old friend."

Butch finished his shopping and hurried back to his truck. As he loaded the bags into the backseat, he took the sack from beneath the toolbox and laid it on the console in front between the seats. As he drove out of the parking lot, he saw the black Suburban leaving Tractor Supply. Shaking his head, he wondered how long they were going to play this game.

As he came to the turnoff for Highway 114, he saw the Suburban continue south on 287 and head toward Fort Worth. As soon as he got to his house, he unloaded the groceries and made a quick lunch. As he watched the news, he called Tammy, and they decided to just stay at her house and watch a couple of movies when he got there. The best news he heard was that she would make dinner and had a brand-new bottle of Jack Daniels waiting for him.

The rest of the day slid swiftly by, and he made sure he was down in the barn ten minutes before the six o'clock call was to be made. As soon as he had retrieved the phone from the feed barrel, he put it into his pocket while he fed the horses that had followed him into the barn.

He had the phone in his hand waiting when it finally rang. "Hello," he answered.

"How was your trip to Decatur," the man asked. "Did you get all of your shopping done?"

"Yes," Butch replied. "But I'm sure you didn't call to ask how my shopping trip went. What can I do for you?"

"It's not what you can do for me, it's what I can do for you."

"And just what do you plan to do for me?" Butch asked. "And what makes you think I need any help?"

"You may not need it right now, but the time may come when you'll need my assistance. For now, I just want you to know that some of us don't believe that what is happening is the right thing to do."

"What's happening that you disagree with?" Butch asked.

"Invasive methods of listening to your conversations, monitoring your movements, things that are contrary to your basic rights as an American."

"I agree," Butch said. "The question is why they're doing this."

"I'm sure you've already made the connection. My problem is whether to believe that you're completely innocent or if you're trying to be subversive."

"I think I know why you folks are so interested in my activities, that's true," Butch told him. "Just what do you think you'll learn? Especially since I know your cars when I see them and can generally tell when some of your people are around."

"They want their person back. That's the only thing they're interested in."

"How do they expect me to give them something that I don't have?" Butch asked. "And even if I had him, why do they want him so badly? I'm not about to believe the story you've been telling."

"I can only tell you that until he is returned, you will be the central focal point of their investigation. It's your decision as to what to do after that."

"And exactly how do you plan on helping me?" Butch asked again.

"I'll alert you when I think you're in danger, that's all. I'm not going to ask questions when I don't think I want to know the answer. Let's just say that I don't agree with some things here and know the extent some of these people will resort to in order to get their man back."

"And how do you intend to do that if you can't contact me on an unsecure line?" Butch asked.

"You were in Korea. I'm sure you remember the code that was to be broadcast if you went too far north or just needed to be told to head south as quickly as possible, don't you?"

"Yes, I remember," Butch answered. "Jackrabbit."

"That's it. If you ever hear that on any phone you have, or if your friend Mr. Phuc hears it, you have very little time to disappear. And believe me, the danger here is as real as it was over there if you failed to react quickly."

"I'll be ready," Butch told him. "I'm sure you'll find a way to protect yourself, but if you need me, you know how to reach me."

"Yes, and don't expect to hear from me unless I think it is absolutely necessary. As soon as you hang up, I think you should destroy this phone. Probably the same way you've been doing all along."

"Does that mean that you've monitored those calls?" Butch asked surprised.

"No, but the speculation is that you've been using prepaid phones and codes. You've been very resourceful, and so far, you've kept one step ahead of us. It has been very interesting. Be very careful, and maybe someday in the future we'll get to meet. But for now, forget you ever heard from me unless I make that one call. Goodbye."

Butch stood staring at the dead phone and made up his mind. The trip he had made to Del Rio had been merely a chance to put in place a preliminary plan. Although it seemed that he had someone inside that would help protect him, he better make sure it would be ready if he got notified. At least he hoped they were there to help him.

Chapter 52

The next five months passed with no progress in finding Gene. With no information coming in that even hinted at his location, some of the staff began to wonder if he was even still alive. How was it possible for a person to disappear completely with no family or friends to assist them? Every single system of monitoring everyone they had targeted was proving worthless in providing a single clue.

Every phone call was reviewed time and time again. Each frame of the images had been scrutinized. The few sporadic reports of sightings had proven false, and even those had dwindled to almost nothing in the last couple of months.

Bob Wilson had spent several hours with Butch and finally told them that he didn't believe that the man had any knowledge of either Leslie or Gene. He emphasized that Mr. North had continued to express a lack of interest every time any mention had ever come up about his former stable hand. Several people had known that Gene was working there, including Gay Lynn, and conversations between Butch and her had touched on the night they were all there. Butch always denied knowing to where any of the people had disappeared.

Butch would often joke that Gene and Leslie had run away together and were living in Oklahoma where strangeness was normal.

Bob reported that unless there was some other reason for him to continuing the current plan, he was wasting time and resources. There appeared to be no reason to prolong this attempt that was proving worthless.

Even the monitoring of Tammy's phones had been devoid of any useful information. Her conversations with Butch were as normal as any dating couple. There was never a word related to Gene or Leslie other than when they discussed the events that had been brought up by other people.

There were no further hints of using phones other than the known cell or home phones. Finally, the calls that had seemed mysterious were deemed unrelated, possibly relating to an affair that Butch had been having with someone he didn't want anyone else to know. Speculation about this centered on it being one of the local wives he was seen to dance with at one of the local bars.

When the satellite coverage was finally terminated, the red truck had never been seen again. Reviews of the camper coverage showed other trucks arriving after they had already investigated that location. When Mikey Carmichael, the owner of the land, was finally contacted, he told them that he had bought the trailer to be used as a hunting cabin if he decided to lease it. The rifle that they had found was his and had been left there in case he stopped by and saw any of the feral hogs that had been running in that area.

General Modelle had been recalled to Washington late in April to report on their lack of progress and whether or not personnel changes would be necessary. He staunchly supported their efforts and finally convinced the members of MJ 12 that replacing the current staff would be detrimental to the overall mission of the facility. He argued that although Gene had disappeared, the facility's main purpose was the development of a hybrid with human and alien genetic features. In this, they had been successful and that they were close to having another specimen.

Kevin had found a small stray dog and presented it to Gene and Leslie for them to care for. He had begun taking Gene up to the Red River and teaching him to fish during his infrequent visits. They had built trout lines and routinely caught several nice-sized catfish which they would have for dinner that day. During these trips to the river, Kevin would let Gene drive the truck and tried to teach him everything a boy normally learns from his father.

Leslie and Gene had been calling him Uncle Kevin, and that would be his name when she made her visits to the doctor as Terri Miller. The doctor had expressed no concerns about her pregnancy, continually telling her things were normal and that a young lady such as her shouldn't worry. After determining that the baby should arrive no sooner than the middle of May and possibly early June, he told her that it wouldn't be necessary to come back unless complications arose.

One evening while Kevin and Gene were fishing up on the Red River, Leslie began feeling the expected pains. She had occasionally gone with them when they were fishing, but hadn't gone during the last month or so. She checked the clock hanging above the television to see if it was about the time they normally returned. As another spasm hit, she began to be concerned and wondered if they would make it back before something had to be done.

As the pains began to grow closer together, she frantically looked for the phone she knew Kevin kept to call Butch. The small bag he brought out when he was going to spend the night was sitting on the floor beside the bed in the spare bedroom. She searched through the few items still inside and found the keys to the car he had left parked in front of the house.

As she grabbed the keys, she finished her search and found no phone. Almost desperate now, she scribbled a quick note saying she was heading to the doctor in Ringgold. As another contraction hit, she put the note on the table and quickly headed for the car. Hoping that she would either see them arriving or maybe meet them on her drive out, she started the engine and backed out. Still not seeing them, she accelerated down the dirt road as she clutched her swollen stomach.

She had just turned onto Highway 81 and was speeding south when the lights of a Texas Highway Patrol car came on behind her. After a quick debate as to whether or not to stop, she pulled to the side of the road and rolled down her window.

The patrolman left the red and blue lights flashing as he strolled up to her door with a pad in one hand. As he bent down to look in, she exclaimed, "Help me! I've got to get to the doctor right now! I'm having a baby!"

Thomas took one look at her and said, "Get in with me. I'll make sure you get there as quickly as possible.

He helped her back to his car and pulled onto the road with the lights flashing brightly. As they sped south, Thomas called the doctor, almost surprised that it was the very same one his daughter used. Within minutes, they had pulled up to the clinic they called a hospital. As he was helping Leslie out, another car stopped beside them.

"Hello, Amber," he said. "Care to give me a hand with this lady? She seems to think she's ready to give birth."

"Sure, Thomas," Amber said as she briskly walked to the entrance. As she unlocked the doors, she told him, "Just take her straight into the examination room. The doctor should be here shortly."

Thomas helped Leslie into the room and left her sitting on the examination table as Amber started preparing for the doctor's arrival. Taking a final look at her, he started back toward his car. Thinking that there was something very familiar about that woman, he knew he had either seen her or a picture of her. He was standing in front of the doors thinking about it when the doctor's car arrived.

"Evening, Doc, sorry to have you brought back in from dinner, but I stopped a speeding car just north of town, and the lady inside needed to get here in a hurry. I'm surprised that she didn't have that baby in my car driving here."

"Got yourself a real emergency this time did you, Thomas?" said the doctor, who had known him since he was a little boy growing up there. "Must beat sitting up there waiting for drunks coming back from the casinos on the reservation."

"Yes, it sure does," answered Thomas as he held the doors open for the doctor.

"Amber here already?" the doctor asked as he walked into the waiting room. As he looked around, he asked, "Where's the patient?"

"Amber got here just after I did, and we took her into the examination room. If you don't need me anymore, I better get back on the road before some damned Okie tries to sneak over," Thomas said as the doctor continued on down the hall.

"No, guess that will be all. Thanks, Thomas. You be careful out there, and tell the little lady I said hi and to bring your daughter in next week for a checkup."

"Sure thing, Doc," he said as he turned and left the building.

Entering the examination room, he saw that his only nurse, Amber, had prepped the young lady lying on the table. As he walked up, he nodded at Amber and asked the young lady, now in a standard white patient gown, "Well, young lady. I hear you think you're ready to have a new baby. Is that so?"

As she let out a scream, she yelled, "Yes! My baby, it's coming! You gotta do something now!"

The doctor went to the end of the table, lifted the gown, and told Amber, "She's right. Get me a sterile sheet, and my delivery instruments. Hurry, this one is ready to greet the world."

As Amber returned with a white cloth over her arm and a tray of instruments, she heard the doctor say, "Here it comes!"

Rounding his right shoulder, Amber saw him put his hands between the woman's legs and accept the new life. The doctor looked down as it was born, and his eyes opened wide in amazement. "Holy shit!" he exclaimed as Amber got her first glimpse of the newborn. Looking down at the doctor's hands, she gasped, dropped the tray of instruments, and placed her hands over her mouth. "Oh my god," she whispered through her splayed fingers.

Thomas had barely left, heading back north when Kevin and Gene rounded the corner two blocks away. He just knew he had seen the lady before, and he would pull his watch sheets from his folder when he got back to the highway.

Kevin slid to a stop and told Gene to stay in the truck as he flung his door open and ran toward the entrance. As he entered the waiting room, he heard the exclamations from the examination room. He pushed the door open and stared at the doctor holding Leslie's baby, the nurse was still standing completely still with her hands on her face.

He took one look at the baby and Leslie as he said, "Doctor, are they both all right?"

The doctor looked up from the baby and answered, "I don't know, I think so, but I've never seen anything like this."

Kevin could tell that Leslie was breathing all right, and from his experience with his own wife and kids, he saw nothing that would cause concern over her. The baby appeared to be breathing, and he watched its tiny mouth open as it tried to cry. The sight of its enormous eyes and enlarged head was certainly surprising, but it seemed to be doing all right.

"Look, Doctor," Kevin told him. "Finish as quickly as you can. I need to get her and the baby to a specialist immediately. You aren't equipped to take care of this problem. Now, get them ready to travel. I'll be back in a minute, and we need to get them there as soon as possible."

He turned and hurried back to where Gene was anxiously waiting in the truck. "Leslie's all right," he said. "The baby seems to be doing fine, but we need to get them out of here."

He pulled one of the phones from under the seat and dialed. Butch was at the stables when it rang, and he immediately walked back into the barn to answer it.

"We have a problem," Kevin told him. "Leslie has just delivered her baby, and we need to get them away from there immediately."

"Are they all right?" Butch asked.

"So far," Kevin replied. "The baby is somewhat abnormal in appearance, but seems to be doing OK. Leslie looks all right, but the doctor and nurse are going to be a problem. I know this is going to cause a lot of unwanted interest."

"OK," Butch told him. "Make sure they can travel and get them back to their house. Get anything you need from the doctor, and when you get away, call me. I need to contact someone that will help us."

"I'll call as soon as we're back at the house," Kevin said as he hurried back toward the hospital.

"When you get them home, start packing," Butch said as he pulled a card from his billfold. "Keep this phone alive and expect a call within the hour."

Kevin walked into the room where the doctor had finished tying the umbilical cord and had wrapped the baby in a soft white blanket. Amber had taken care of Leslie and was waiting for further instructions from the doctor. "Can they travel?" he asked as he watched Leslie take her child and hold it to her breast.

"I assume so," the doctor replied. "But I strongly advise against it. She needs to rest and let us determine if there are any complications. We don't know what problems there may be with the child at this point, and we need to closely watch it."

"That's impossible," Kevin told him as he walked to Leslie's side. "Leslie, if you can get up, we need to get you and the baby to your specialist. Do you think you can make it?"

Leslie nodded, and Kevin helped her off the table. With the baby held securely in her arms, Kevin led her out of the room. "What is wrong with that baby?" the doctor finally asked. "And where are you taking them?"

"There's nothing wrong," Kevin answered as they walked out of the exit. "And you don't need to know where we're going."

Amber and the doctor stood dumbfounded as they got into the truck and started backing out. They saw Gene as he got out to help Leslie get inside with the baby. As the truck sped away, they looked at each other and slowly walked back into the waiting room.

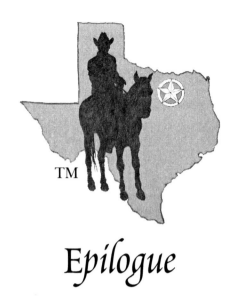

Epilogue

Thomas was sitting just north of Ringgold looking at the photographs he had been carrying for several months. The majority of them were fairly recent, and he quickly laid them aside. Finally, he found the one he was searching for. As he looked at the old high school picture of Leslie, he was certain that she was the same as the one he had left at the doctor's office.

Typed across the bottom of the picture was a number of the FBI office that was to be contacted if the person was spotted. Special instructions were also provided that specifically told him to make no attempt to apprehend, but to immediately call and kept only as close as necessary to watch the wanted person.

He took his phone from his case and dialed the number. As soon as it was answered, he quoted the identifying number from the wanted photo and waited for an answer. Within seconds, he was being asked where he had seen the subject and if he was still able to observe her.

As soon as he told them he had left her at the local health clinic, he was directed to drop any other duties and return to where she had been. He was to call them back as soon as he had returned and let them know if she was still there.

As he sped back down the road, notification was relayed to the operations center where Major Fleenor was the only person left for the day. As he answered the phone, he knew he had to get word to Butch that there would be a team dispatched. Jerry quickly took the message and replaced the phone. Without waiting, he dialed Colonel Ericson's home and told him that he was needed immediately and that he would call General Nelson.

After making that call, he went out of the room and took the elevator to the top floor where he told the guard that General Nelson and Colonel Ericson would soon arrive and to make sure they came to the operations center immediately. He then walked to his car and took a phone from under the seat. As it rang, he hoped Butch still had his with him and would answer quickly. When Butch finally answered, he said clearly, "Jackrabbit, jackrabbit, jackrabbit." He hung up and replaced the phone before returning to the entrance where the guard was waiting.

Butch hung up his phone and took the one he had used with Kevin from his pocket. As he dialed the number from the card now in his hand, he wondered if they would have time to get Gene and Leslie away from their home before the inevitable helicopters would arrive.

When the call was answered somewhere in Del Rio, he said, "Sancudo, my friend. I have a package coming to you, little mosquito. Take care of it, and I'll talk to you after it arrives. It should be there in three or four hours."

As soon as he heard that everything would be ready, he dialed Kevin on the same phone. As soon as it was answered, he told him to forget going back to the house and to head immediately for Abilene. If Leslie developed any problems, he was to take her to any emergency room and make sure the child remained out of sight.

As he was hanging up, he saw two helicopters speeding north across the sky. He knew exactly where they were headed and hoped that Kevin and his precious cargo would get far enough away before they arrived. There would be too many things left behind to keep them from knowing that it had been Gene and Leslie.

He also knew that Kevin's identification would soon be determined. The car that had been left beside the road would prove to be his, and the items he had left during his visits would verify his knowledge of Gene. Butch now knew that his old friend Kevin would shortly become the target of another intense search. Shaking his head, he said quietly into the fading light of the day, "I'm so sorry, old buddy. I've gotten you into this, and now I'll have to try to save you. I'm so sorry."